MIGUEL ANGEL ASTURIAS was born in Guatemala in 1899 and died in 1973. He received his law degree at the National University, Guatemala City, in 1933. After study at the Sorbonne in Paris, he entered politics in 1942 as a member of his country's congress. Four years later, when his early novel EL SEÑOR PRESIDENTE was published, he joined the diplomatic service as a cultural attaché in Mexico. Later he spent eight years in political exile in Argentina, before moving to France in 1961. In 1966 he returned to the diplomatic service as Guatemala's ambassador to France. His many awards include the Gold Medal, University of San Carlos; Prix Silla, Monsegue, Paris, 1931; Prix des Critiques, Paris, 1952; Prix Lenin, Moscow, 1966; and the Nobel Prize for literature, 1967. His books include LEGENDS OF GUATEMALA, MEN OF MAIZE, TOROTUMBO, and the Banana Republic trilogy: STRONG WIND, THE GREEN POPE, and THE EYES OF THE INTERRED.

MULATA

MIGUEL ANGEL ASTURIAS

Translated by
GREGORY RABASSA

 A BARD BOOK/PUBLISHED BY AVON BOOKS

For Clementine, my all

G. R.

Originally published in Spanish under the title *Mulata de Tal.*

AVON BOOKS
A division of
The Hearst Corporation
959 Eighth Avenue
New York, New York 10019

First Bard Printing, June, 1982

BARD TRADEMARK REG. U. S. PAT. OFF. AND IN
OTHER COUNTRIES, MARCA REGISTRADA, HECHO EN
U. S. A.

Printed in the U. S. A.

WFH 10 9 8 7 6 5 4 3 2 1

Contents

Part I

Part II

Part III

MULATA

I

The Fly Wizard Sells His Wife
to the Corn-Leaf Devil

Cheat! Tramp! Pig! Having fun among the simple people down from the hills and villages to have a good time at the fair, which was less of a fair than a lair of wild delights, now that they had done their duty at church and bought or sold their animals, there was time to gab with friends, and anybody picking a fight would get himself chopped up with a machete or stuck with a knife, and all around there were clusters of eyes glistening at the sight of such pretty, teaty, well-haunched women who were the product of an over-abundant rather than an aberrant nature.

Slicker! Licker! Tricker! Cheat! Son-of-sixty-thousand-whores! Married and, judging by his fly that fluttered like a tavern curtain, in search of one of those women who go around bearing and say they are maidens, or, in more respectable terms, go around pairing and say they are laden! That was how he wandered through the fair in San Martín Chile Verde, the same way that he had walked through the fair in San Andrés Milpas Altas, and the one in honor of the patron saint of San Antonio Palopó.

Lots of people and among them this fellow with his prodigious fly that would stay open a little when it was being closed and would stay closed a little when it was being opened, as if it had been put together with buttons made from dying-with-laughter bone and buttonholes of open-close Sesame . . . now it's open, now it's closed! . . .

The older women, without paying it much mind, thought it was carelessness or a trick, now it's open, now it's closed, some called him down for being abusive, others pardoned him for a fool, while the fellow kept his eyes off the angry looks of the men, who felt challenged by his going around making them look ridiculous, now it's open, now it's

11

closed!, he would smile at the twenty-year-old girls who sneaked looks at him, comical and comical as a woodcock, now it's open, now it's closed, or he would laugh in the faces of the warrior-women who coughed at him as they passed, as if to tell him: just remember that our mission here at the fair of San Martín Chile Verde is to take the starch out of the big-flied and the unflied!

All of this in the main square, where stores and bars were crowded in together and where, after all, anything was allowed; but that now it's open, now it's closed was out of place in the church.

In the church, in the church that was melting in the blinding sun like a huge piece of white marzipan as it held up the dome and the blue belfries, colors inherited from the shipwrecked days of thick milk and a stick of indigo, cousin of the stick of balsam that flayed the air with an oppressive smell, and ancient as the stucco saints in the frontal niches, hidden under the feast-day adornments of pacaya leaves, red-crested vegetable roosters, garlands of live-oak leaves, camomile necklaces, banners, lights, and little paper flags.

And when that fellow reached the church with his prodigious fly, he left behind the smell of fritters and cracklings, flies that stuck to the foreheads of people swallowing honey pancakes in the forenoon, the freshness that the smell of pineapples gives off, and the music from the fair that seemed to make the approaching noon even hotter.

Once inside the church, having climbed the seven steps hollowed out by the feet of standing men and women or by them kneeling, a candle in their hands, listening to the High Mass, the religious man in charge of selling prayer cards, candles, rosaries, votive offerings, and missals, an irritable little old man, came over and whispered in his ear: "Your maleness is open!"—an allusion which the fellow appreciated, quickly making the sign of the cross on his fly without closing it, knowing it was that way, unbuttoned, that he had to enter the church, rubbing his front against the crowd of women who were smelling like poppies from the heat of that time of day, the warm glow from the flames on the candles, the burning tallow, stearin, and wax, the crowd of parishioners, the chocolate-cinnamon-colored women who gave off a smell of greased hair, blacker than coal, of low-cut necks, of dripping armpits, smells that blended well with the aroma of the incense, the holy water, the floral decorations, the creosoted wood, the banana oil in which the gold powder of the altars was dissolved, and the heady fragrance of the mahogany of the confessionals, pews, rails, and kneeling-boards.

And so he left the fair in San Martín Chile Verde, riding a horse that seemed to emerge from his open fly, his eager little horse with a heavy mane and hoofs like the heels on a pair of old shoes. His good friend Timoteo Teo Timoteo really had a horse! It made one's chest tighten up to watch him go by, raising dust with his front feet, and if you just brought the spurs close to him, he would stop and stand on his hind legs, walking like a person with his fly completely open.

That was all that Celestino was thinking about, so obsessed as he was as he returned from the fair, where he would have liked to have gone on his friend Timoteo Teo Timoteo's horse so that he could have attracted more attention.

And the discussion started as usual when he reached Quiavicús, a village that crowned its hill like the cap on a tooth.

His friend Timoteo Teo Timoteo, with his fat food-booze belly, berated him for his improper behavior.

"A person from Quiavicús, like you, old friend, making a spectacle of yourself by not taking proper care of your fly! Button it up when you've finished taking a leak! And if you can't go to the fair and behave yourself properly, then don't go, for God's sake, don't go, because it just isn't fair for you to make a laughingstock out of our town!"

What Celestino was thinking while his friend Timoteo Teo Timoteo was talking was that his friend envied him, because no one ever looked at his friend, well groomed, fancy-talking, riding a stallion with halter and saddle, and his cashmere blanket.

"Such foolishness, Celestino my friend! What I would like to know is who ever gave me such bad advice as to become your close friend! Your poor wife even refused to go to San Martín Chile Verde with you after the things

13

you did at the fair in San Andrés Milpas Altas, where you went around the same way and where I must confess that if I hadn't dragged you away, no one would have believed that you were my good friend. The poor thing told me that she was in a cold sweat and kept nudging you in church to button up, and there you were opposite her with your fly half open. This time your wife—it may be gossip but you should know—said that she was not going to be mortified by you, and she didn't go, the proof is that she didn't go with you."

Celestino Yumí was listening to his friend Timoteo Teo Timoteo without answering, a silence that made his friend want to shake him and awaken in him that well-mannered person who was there, fearful that some witch doctor—and so many of them were around, some of them quite evil—might be canceling out his baptism.

"Why, Celestino Yumí, my old friend, why don't you do me the favor of unbuttoning your fly here in the village and going around that way if you want to? There aren't many people in Quiavicús and we already know each other front and rear because we take care of our most pressing needs right out in the open. Why wait for the big holidays, the crowds of people? No, my dear friend, I can't figure you out! Where everybody goes to show off the best he has . . . Did you see the agricultural exposition in San Martín? Did you see! They saw you! You go so they can see you with your cage half open! At that exposition Quiavicús exhibited an enormous potato, two huge ears of corn, everything the product of my care, my seeds, and my land, and what use was it, what use I have to ask myself since you spoiled everything with your antics, and everybody who looked at the sign over our booth that said 'Quiavicús' would start to laugh because Quiavicús was where the clown with the open fly was from."

And trying to convince him:

"Promise me something, Celestino, don't ever go without first promising your dear wife and me—" from behind some mats hung up to serve as a wall there was a rustle of petticoats and Celestino's wife appeared, teary, out of sorts— "promise that next year, if God keeps us alive and well,

14

that you will go to the fair in San Martín Chile Verde the way respectable people do."

Celestino Yumí promised him and it was simply a matter of promising, the same as throwing himself into the arms of Catalina Zabala, his wife, without knowing whether he was laughing or crying with pleasure.

"And now—" his old friend Timoteo Teo Timoteo raised his voice—"let's christen the promise with a glass of fine old wine. It's good—" he licked the cork—"because this wine is expensive but it turns into vinegar overnight."

And he poured the ruby-dark and oily liquid into three glasses that were as thick as a myopic's spectacles.

The Yumís headed for home before night fell. Celestino in front, Catalina behind. He, with his glowing hat thrown back around his neck, all the dampness of the evening filling his brows with the smell of balsam wood, light on his scaly bare feet, carrying his machete with his hand on his shoulder and holding the other one close to his face as he smoked. And she, her shawl slung over her right shoulder, petticoats and skirt tucked up into her sash so that they would not drag, long braids, and barefoot also as she raised the dust as she went along, walking half on tiptoe, scarcely letting her heels touch the ground.

"Now that you're back home," said Catalina Zabala, also known indiscriminately as Catarina or by the tender diminutive Niniloj, "you can't tell me that you didn't go to the fair except to pull your usual stunts. I had to get down on my knees and beg the neighbors not to drive us out. They were all set to come in here with their machetes and skin us alive, burn down our house, and so long Mr. Fly. That was what your enemy the Deputy Mayor said, and only because I begged on my knees and kissed more than one neighbor on his flea-bitten foot did they change their minds. They were sorry for me! Can you imagine, you have to imagine in that place where you imagine things, how awful it is for a wife to have everybody laughing at her and calling her good-for-nothing, because you seem to help everybody who doesn't like me by going around the way you do with nobody around to button you up. There are other people

15

who are even nastier and say that you made an offering to the patron saint so that he would give us the little ones we want. And there are plenty of people who say that you're impotent and that you're so impotent that you don't button yourself up the way a person should after he goes. Oh, but I got some advice from Señora Geludiana, the one who lives in Fuegueros, that next year, for the feast day, I ought to make you a pair of pants without a fly and if you buy a pair from the Chinaman the way you do every year, that I ought to take my needle and thread and sew them up ahead of time so that you won't have the chance to go sneaking around and pulling any of your tricks."

The unfriendly faces in the neighborhood, doors slammed in his face when he went over to say hello to people he knew, friends who would grit their teeth and walk away when they saw him coming, everything was against him in Quiavicús after the feast day of the patron saint of San Martín Chile Verde, where he had gone to fulfill a promise which only he knew to whom he had made it, even though this deep knowledge, without any thought, had remained motionless inside of his conscience, and another piece of knowledge that thought had shoved aside had bloomed in his mind with the explanation that he was doing it on his own, as a whim, so that everybody would notice him, poor, badly dressed no matter how many times he changed his clothes, without a good horse, no food, no girls.

Niniloj, his rib, was sleeping next to him on the floor, on a canvas mat, each one wrapped up in a colored wool blanket, colors and figures that would protect them from bad dreams. He felt around in the darkness that had become part of the earth that was sleeping too, he threw his poncho over her to entomb her in a better warmth, and noiselessly he slipped out through the reed door toward the clearing.

As he looked at the stars with the eyes of a good wood-cutter, he could see that soon it would be midnight.

And he went forward resolutely.

His feet were breaking up the chunks of soft earth along the road that led down to the wide river that passed by many towns, even though people in Quiavicús, the rich people in Quiavicús, had said that it was theirs and had tried to claim possession of it in that way a person tries to own a thing

16

by halting it for an instant with cement dikes or stone walls.

Before he reached the river, he turned down an ill-defined and hazy road that went under the low-hanging branches of a newly planted live-oak grove. Rich people do what they want to with trees, ingratitude of ingratitudes! They plant them and just when they start to grow tall they cut them down if the wood is bringing a good price, and for every tree chopped down another seedling, always with the foul intent of cutting them down over and over again.

No wind was blowing and without a wind who could tell whether or not his visitor would come. The shadows were not too deep, thanks to a half moon that was licking at the clouds and a herd of stars that was following it along in its peaceful turn.

A handful of frolicsome wind was moving the branches and the cold dew wet him the way an early-morning rain would. He swallowed his protests and left a flock of dirty words creeping about on his tongue, a man's words, obviously words that only men say, and which only men think of saying.

At once the wind began to toy with the highest leaves, eating leaves, it dropped the ones it ate, and finally it let itself slip down to the trunks, until it sat down on the ground and settled next to Celestino.

In the bluish shadows, in the midst of the silence which the distant river was translating into the crackling of liquid vertebrae, Celestino Yumí stuck out his tongue and saluted:

"O Lord, so close to me here and still far away, because my human condition would not be able to bear your sapphire presence, please do not let the riches and the treasures you have promised me be just dreams!"

Yumí never saw the one he spoke to. It was an invisible body formed by the wind, one which fell on top of him with the weight of a net full of corn leaves, just the leaves, just the *tazol*, and so much like the *tazol* that he called him that: Tazol.

"Very good!" Tazol whispered in his ear. "Very good, Celestino Yumí! You were able to achieve in San Andrés Milpas Altas, in San Antonio Palopó, and in San Martín Chile Verde what I could not have achieved. All those women . . . Not all of them, I mustn't exaggerate, most of

17

them in the churches in those three places, when they looked at your half-open fly, sinned mortally and as there were no priests in the confessionals, they received communion in sin. . . .

"During the procession in honor of the Virgin, I don't know whether you noticed it or not, but you played your idiot role so well that I don't know whether you noticed, the Angel of Praise made a mistake and said: 'I am the Angel of the Golden Fly!' and even though he corrected himself right away and said, 'I am the Angel of the Golden Ball!' everybody laughed and began to repeat: 'I am the Angel of the Golden Fly!' And that was the end of prayers in the procession, except for the old women who pray like toads."

And with gratification:

"Tazol also thanks you for something that you do not know and which you will go on doing without knowing, I command you to play the boob. Your fine old friend, Timoteo Teo Timoteo, as he consoles your wife, seems to become more fervent than is necessary. A man who begins by consoling a woman, everybody knows how it ends, cutting off the word after the first syllable and giving us the word ground. On the ground and with force. How happy I feel that that old worshipper is in the hands of Tazol, and that you, because of what I have been telling you, will finally give in and give me your wife—why do you love her if she is deceiving you?—in exchange for my making you rich."

Celestino Yumí was sweating turpentine like a pine tree. Down among his few beardless cuckolded hairs his turpentiny sweat ran across his chin, just as in the inlets along the coast, near Puerto de San José, near the Laguna del Quita-Sombrero, the heat of Tazol.

"Will you give me your wife?" he insisted.

Celestino did not know what to answer.

"I will not give her to you, Tazol," he heard himself saying, "because I love her and she is a big help to me, and if she cheated on me with my friend, you know very well that even though that can happen it didn't happen this time, and maybe we'll have a little boy. I'll believe that it's mine and I'll love him too."

18

"How loathsome, Celestino Yumí, your son, the son of a rich man!"

"What can I do! If it's already in her belly, how can I help but love it!"

"And what if there isn't any child?"

"That will change soon enough, Tazol."

"At least cut off their hands with your machete so that they won't be able to fondle each other again!"

Yumí was silent.

"A friend told me because I am your friend, and you ought to tell them, that he saw them when they deceived you, in the middle of the river, on a sand spit, next to that big stone you can see over there . . ." And the wind, at Tazol's bidding, lifted up the branches and Yumí could see the huge stone lit up by the moon amidst the waters of the river.

"And later on you'll tell them," Tazol added, " 'I went down to the river to swim and the stone called to me and it confirmed what my friend had told me.' They will deny it, but you will take them to the little island at machete-point and you will ask the big stone."

The trunks of the twisted trees, which do not grow but rather creep into the air, stretched out like great scaly serpents and Tazol disappeared, where no one knows, leaving Celestino Yumí with his sadness and his machete.

He did not hesitate. He was almost stuck in the mud. Pebbles rolling downhill behind him, dead leaves, lizards, feet, back, and elbows leaning on the damp, sandy, warm ground.

He reached the riverbank, he rolled up his pants legs, to wade where he was going, but it was too deep, and then he took off all his clothes down to the skin—they ought to see him like that if they wanted a scandal and not with just his fly open—and, as if the new moon had unbuttoned itself, he set out swimming to reach the little island and . . .

A beach of fine sand was all around him. A few plants, some of them bent over, ravished, crushed against the stony surface, as if someone had lain on top of them.

Celestino Yumí raised his fingers to his mouth to close his fleshy begonia-leaf lips, without having decided to say anything. He was tired of standing and he sat down to await the light of dawn, certain that the mystery would end with the appearance of the sun. A woman's deception is always a mystery.

Finally, his backside cold as a rifle butt, he dug himself into the damp sand, but now the stars were becoming more distant and he stood up, resolved with his eyes closed to do what he did not want to do, and out of the stone, he never knew from where, there came a very harsh voice, answering his question, that yes, it was true that his friend Timoteo Teo Timoteo and his wife, Catalina Zabala, had laid their two good joys there next to it.

"Twice!" Yumí said to himself. "Machete, why do I keep you sharp!" and up above, the mother of days was letting her rosy rose fall down onto the waters of the wide river, and it brought to mind what love can do if it is not halted by Tazol. His friend Timoteo Teo Timoteo drawn away from the love of his wife Juanita, and his Catarina drawn away from his love. Oh, how the loving little name of Niniloj that he had always used was painful to him now!

And even though his thoughts were running faster than his feet, he was able to reflect:

"And me playing the fool with my damned fly open at the fairs from the very first minute right up until the Mass for the dead and the ones who had died at the fair, just so I could make people sin in church and in the procession, with Tazol's promise that if I did it for two years running I would become rich, much richer than that goddamned Timoteo Teo Timoteo. And what a person won't do to get rich: steal, kill, assault, rob, everything that work will not produce, in order to get good land, good cattle, fine horses, fighting cocks, and the finest weapons, and who can you spend it on—a woman . . ."

Tazol cut off his advance. The well-known breath of cool air, the brush of water from the pearls of dew, and the way the wind seemed to uncouple itself from in between high trees.

"Where are you going?" Tazol asked him.

"The stone in the river has confirmed everything for me," Yumí answered as he wept, "and I want to cut off their heads while they're asleep!"

20

"No good! Terrible! There's a better way to get even with your wife! Give her to me. I'll make her work until she's so tired she drops. I'll only give her just what she needs to eat in order to survive, her three daily tortillas and her piece of dried meat, no coffee, hot water with the leaves off some tree. She'll wear down her nails working so hard, her hair will fall out, she'll lose her teeth, and her skin will shrivel up from overuse, like ashes, dull eyes, thick lips . . ."

"And my friend?"

"You can kill your friend."

"Me? Of course!" Yumí said in anger, raising his machete to cut the luminous air of the mother of days which was already turning his limbs to orange. "And thank you, Tazol, for having spared me the duty of doing away with Catalina! It would have been very hard for me to cut off her head while she was asleep, without opening her eyes, listening to my heart calling to her. Niniloj! Now all I have to do is cut off my friend's head."

"It's not a matter of killing him. First listen to Tazol. The vengeance he has prepared for your friend—"

"The son of a bitch!"

"—the way things will go, your money will be all free and clear and his will all be mortgaged, and not just any little village lump of money—real money."

"Tazol, I'm all ready to be the richest man in Quiavicús and everywhere around here . . ."

"But you already know the price."

"Well, a woman who cheats on her husband isn't good for much—what value does she have?—and you can have her!"

"Is the deal settled?" Tazol asked, because men's souls are so subject to change.

"Settled," Yumí decided, "but how do I give her to you?"

"Leave the authorities out of it. It's best for us to keep her love affair with that rich fellow very secret. Oh, don't worry, you'll be ten, twenty, a hundred times richer than he is!"

"Tell me what I have to do, Tazol, you know that I'm not very bright. Even though I'm a good worker when it comes to practical things, very good—I can do twenty jobs in one day—I wasn't born to understand things very well.

21

Words always escape me. Even though I listen to them I can't seem to understand . . ."

"And you've got more than your share of mental laziness. You just expose yourself to the light of day—"

"We poor people try not to think."

"Well, when you wake up rich, as you shall one of these days, everyone will swear that you understand everything— finances, politics, religion, eloquence, technical things, poetry —and they'll come to ask your advice . . ."

"Just because I'm rich, not because I know anything."

"Exactly."

"Fine, but just tell me now how I can turn my wife over to you, how can Niniloj disappear from my side without the authorities' becoming suspicious and without my rotting in some jail where they won't even bring me anything to eat."

"This is how you will do it. Listen carefully. Tomorrow, when you get home at nightfall after spending all day in the forest getting your wood together, you will complain of a headache and then of a stomach-ache, as if your head were going to burst and your insides explode. Complaints accompanied by plenty of groans, groans that will turn into cries, so that she will become alarmed over your affliction without knowing what to do and what not to do, whether some mint tea with chicken, whether a cloth soaked in rum, whether a singed rag, whether a poultice of hot ashes, and when she's most confused you will ask her please to call your good friend Timoteo, because you think that you're dying. She, who since you came back from San Martín Chile Verde has been looking for every chance, will think that it's wonderful that she can go get your old friend, have a few kisses on the way and, who knows, maybe roll around a little. You know of course that your friend's wife, Doña Juanita, is deaf."

"Then I will have to play death's door, twist around on my mat, chatter my teeth, bug out my eyes, and moan as much as I can."

"All from a pain, you can tell her in the few moments you feel relief, that besides hurting you more than you can bear and laying your insides bare, is all over your body."

"She'll run and call my old friend when I ask her to."

"Not because she sees you in pain, but to give her a chance to be alone with him."

"But wouldn't it be better, I think, even if I'm not so bright, for her to go first for the officer on duty, somebody in the police station, and tell him, 'My husband is dying!' "

"It's not a bad idea and it came to you out of the love you still have for her even after what happened in the river, when I get my hands on that devil she'll pay for every little thing."

"Yes, I do love her, Tazol, and there's no use denying it. I love her, like, I can't say how."

"And do you think that anybody can say how he loves or how he hates?"

"What I know is that with everything that's happened—oh, but my friend Timoteo Teo Timoteo went to the fair in San Martín Chile Verde . . ."

"He went, but he came back before you did, under the pretext that he couldn't stand the discredit your fly was bringing to Quiavicús."

"With everything that's happened I feel as if somebody had opened up a trench in my chest, and that they were going to bury me in myself, because that's how a part of me would be buried in me, rotting in me, turning into ashes and dust."

"When you see how rich you'll be, surrounded by women, then you tell me whether you love her and remember anything about that poor heifer. Love can still do good things even when everything is bad, and it was love that told you about that fine step of looking for a policeman at headquarters or somebody at the military post."

"I think—"

"We already have the authorities on our side, and with those reinforcements Catalina will run to wake up your friend going along the path that cuts through Don Agapito Monge's place—it's the only way to get from the square to where Don Teo Timoteo is. When she gets onto that path I'll raise a big windstorm and throw dust in their eyes, I'll blind the constable and the sentry, and I'll run off with your wife."

"That's good, that's good thinking, Tazol. The authorities won't blame me—she was coming along with them when the wind took her away—and they'll all be kind to me, and my old friend will weep with me . . ."

"Try to weep."

"But I'm already weeping, with all my heart, because she's my wife, the only thing I have and I'm going to give her to you, Tazol, just because she was unfaithful to me and because I want to be rich."

"Very rich! Just think of the land you're going to buy, the crops you will grow, the banks that will be taking care of all your millions."

"Banks?"

"Yes, because you won't be able to store up all those corn leaves, a thousand times more valuable than the ears of corn that you'll be storing up in your cribs."

"Full of Tazol, full of corn leaves . . ."

"Yes, Celestino Yumí, that is who I am: Tazol is dry corn leaves, and dry corn leaves you shall bring home, all that you can, and all those corn leaves, all that Tazol, will turn into bills of a hundred, five hundred, and a thousand pesos."

"I get dizzy thinking about so much money. I'm like the hawk at the moment he sees his possible victim down below on the ground, he suspends himself, without moving his wings, neither advancing nor going back, and then he spirals down onto his victim."

"What are you talking about?"

"How I feel like a hawk hovering over the house of my friend Timoteo Teo Timoteo. He doesn't keep his money in the bank the way you advise me to, so that if I set fire to his house I'll leave him mumbling to himself on the corner."

"Well thought out, Yumí, but not yet. Listen to the advice of Tazol, who is your true friend. You will set fire to Don Timo's house when you are rich because then there will be no judge, policeman, or magistrate capable of imagining, much less accusing you, of having done it, even though they saw you with the torch in your hand, because later on they will come to your house to borrow money, which you will be very generous with. Because, Yumí, I want to think of you not as a poor rich man, a rich man who before he spends a cent thinks like a poor man, but as a rich man, a rich man who spends his money without thinking about

24

how much he is spending. And how easy, how very easy it will be to build up your reserves by just bringing more corn leaves home."

"Before we separate—" Yumí fluttered his eyelids in an effort to hold back his tears—"don't be harsh on Niniloj, because that will make my richness bitter."

"Don't give it a thought! Rich people don't think about people who suffer!"

"But, Tazol, my friend, don't be too hard on her! I beg you by the joints on my fingers! By the nine joints on the fingers of each of my hands I beg you!"

An Agreement to Trade Is Never Unmade

Yumí returned home with two bundles of wood, just as eagerly as he had left, and as soon as he was in the house and saw that Niniloj was watching him unload, he burst out into terrible moans, opening and closing his mouth as if he could not get his breath at the same time as if he wanted to belch a dry belch which refused to come out, which only grew greater with the efforts he was making to get rid of it, the headache which was knifing through his temples, all of it feigned, but feigned so well that in the end he could almost feel the pain, the nausea, the drooling, the cramps, and his brains' losing touch with everything including the bones of his cranium.

Niniloj, skilled as few others in ways to cure indigestion, ran to get some oil from the votive lamp to grease him with, but she had barely laid her dark fingers on her husband's stomach when Yumí tightened it and roared as if she had touched him with fire.

"Go-o, woman . . . connnstable . . ." he said brokenly and, after a moan, "go get the constable or a soldier, or both of them, and on the way back stop and tell—" he was

25

losing his voice—"tell my fr-fr-friend Teo that I'm dying! There's no priest in the village, how will I be able to confess! Everything in the house," he spoke quickly, as if feeling better, "everything in the house is yours, but run and get the constable, a soldier, and my friend!"

Catocha put on her street skirt and snatched her shawl from the mat so that she could run off in the dark in search of the constable, a soldier, and his friend. He must have been seriously ill to ask for so many people.

The constable was asleep. Catocha shook him. He was sleeping with his hat over his face and when he felt himself being shaken he got up, slowly raising the lids of his eyes. Two eyes that were corrupt with sleep. The first thing he did was instinctively to grasp his machete and, without answering, after stretching, he set off, stepping lightly behind Catocha.

The officer on duty, his cigar extinguished in his mouth, his eyes glassy from alcohol and lack of sleep, ordered a corporal to attend the victim, and along with the corporal and the constable she went over to wake up the friend. Doña Juanita, deaf as a post, did not hear very well what it was all about and Don Timoteo, talking to the constable and the corporal, commented that God had punished Yumí for something everybody knew about.

"What does everybody know about?" inquired the corporal, his face as round as a pie and with beady little eyes.

"That business about his fly. He was going around making a fool of himself at the fair in San Martín Chile Verde. And God does not punish with a stick, but as you people can see. And just how did this happen to my old friend?"

"Very suddenly. He got sick when he came back with the wood."

"But there's one thing, my dear lady, if my old friend doesn't pull through, we all have to die someday, you must sew up his fly, it doesn't do any good just to button it, so that he won't be kept out of heaven because his fly is open, and if he's unlucky enough, God forgive him, to go to hell, so that they won't burn up his cage and its inhabitant down there."

His friend Catalina was not listening. She was in no mood

26

for jokes. Overcautious old man, why didn't he walk faster?

"My poor friend Celestino, his illness caught him off guard. That's why I go to the capital once a year and get myself examined by the best doctors."

"Oh, Don Teo," Catocha complained, "when you're poor you can rot before you get to see a doctor. All we poor people have left are the healers, they take care of us, and there are times when they know more than real doctors."

"But it's not the same thing, my dear. How can you compare them? A doctor is a doctor!"

"What I mean is that when the sick person is well-heeled like you, then they're all great doctors, but if the one they're looking at is poor, they're not doctors or anything. They make a face and go away—running more than walking. That's what I've heard. Felicita Balcárcel said that, because no one has ever seen a doctor in these parts. An intern came during the smallpox epidemic. But he was green, very green, and instead of curing, you know, friend Teo, how he ended up, well, nothing more or less than going to bed with a smallpox victim, a young girl named Carmen Opil, they said he had fallen in love with her. They roused him up when they went to take the Opil girl out of her house, and when he realized he had been sleeping in the arms of a dead woman, scabby, soaked in pus and blood, he bought a gallon of cheap liquor, and poured part of it over himself because of the plague, because it was contagious, and part of it he drank in order to forget. What happened was that, drunk, afraid of catching smallpox, he went wild with the alcohol and ran to find some water, but instead of going to the big river he went to the river of ashes, and while he was bathing, scrubbing himself with strong soap and sand, from some rocks that stuck out there they shouted warnings to him because the sewage from the San Lázaro Asylum where the lepers were flowed into that river. Another gallon of cheap liquor, another alcohol bath inside and out. But he didn't stop. Completely drunk, he ran all the way to the capital without any shoes on, his hair all wild, his eyes popping out, a madman ready for the asylum."

While Cata was talking, they entered Agapito Monge's path, where on the right could be seen a bright green

27

palisade fence, a rather tall tree, a squat telegraph pole, just like a cross with wire, and on the left scattered boulders and reddish pine trees.

The four of them—corporal, constable, friend, and Catocha—were pleasantly surprised by a playful breeze that suddenly was turning into an unpleasant wind and before they knew it into a hurricane, with thunder and lightning and balls of fire. Everything rose, pulled up by the force of the wind, large trees, thick clouds of dust, the telegraph pole, after dancing furiously among the wires, stones, pieces of limestone, clods of dirt all turned into powder. And in the midst of the furious windstorm, they, the friend, the constable, the corporal, and Catocha, hanging onto the twisted and firmly rooted guava trees.

When the immenseness of the hurricane stopped howling, friend, constable, and corporal opened the eyes they had kept tightly closed because the dust was blinding them, and what was the surprise of the three not to find Yumí's wife, who had been with them. They searched vigorously for her all around, hoarse from shouting her name, "Catalinaaa! Catalinaaa!" with greater and greater urgency.

The constable, agile as a deer, jumped down the bank, fearful that the hurricane had thrown the lady, who had been in the lead showing them the way to her place, into the middle of the river; she would have been badly bruised and she would have been carried away like a basket of clothes by the waters all roiled up with cataclysmic green mud.

But there was nothing in the river and shortly afterward, under the eyes of those who had followed the search from up on the rocks, he climbed up, disheartened—everything they did to find her was useless—without daring to say, even though they were thinking it; "That's how people disappear."

In spite of all the sadness with which they reached Celestino Yumí's place, they still had not lost the hope that she had taken refuge there, although just by hearing the sick man calling her they could understand how monstrous was the tragedy of that poor man, who at death's door would have to hear from their lips the news that his wife, his Catocha, his Niniloj, had disappeared, dragged off by the hurricane with its obsidian claws and wail of an owl.

They decided not to give him the news until they found her, even if it was her corpse, broken against a tree or some crag or simply with her skull broken open like a jar on the ground.

But she could not be found. They shouted. The people of Quiavicús came out, patrols with lighted torches all through that night that was endless for those who were waiting for dawn, certain, quite certain that with the light of day, dead or alive, they would find her.

But the sun lighted things up completely, noontime came and went, and toward evening the searchers returned to Quiavicús, dragging their souls, without even the slightest sign of her whereabouts: a piece of cloth, a handkerchief, a ribbon, a shock of hair, a trinket . . .

The whole village was looking for her, from the tree-chopper, whose face was becoming log-colored, to the sexton of the church which was always closed due to the lack of a priest, going down through the well-to-do people who went out with their shotguns and their dogs, as if they were going hunting, and the country people, who did not give up, who would not accept the disappearance of a woman from the face of the earth, snatched away by the air, even though there was the testimony of a soldier, a municipal official, and an important citizen, and they beat the bushes divided into groups, some of whom climbed the prickly eucalyptus trees in order to get a better view of the countrywide, as they said for countryside, others went deep in the brush, and still others tracked through the caves along the river which had sandy gums, huge stone teeth, and the liquid tongue of a fleeing mirror.

Without discussing the matter further, it was decided that Teo Timoteo should undertake giving Yumí, mortally ill as he feigned being, the fatal news of the disappearance of Catalina Zabala, his sainted and good wife, just as soon as he recovered.

"It's all a punishment," his friend adduced, without his friend's hearing him as the latter was rolling desperately around under his covers, "the punishment of heaven for your having had the audacity to go to High Mass in San Martín Chile Verde with your fly open!"

"The fact is that this fellow—" the constable stroked his machete to give himself more authority—"was always one of the worst . . . but, I wonder, why didn't God punish him?"

"And what shall we do?" put in Doña Juanita, ready to put her hand behind the flap of her ear and following with flashing eyes the movement of her husband's lips for the answer.

"Let's call the faith-healer."

"The gravedigger?" the deaf woman asked.

"The healer!" Don Teo shouted almost in her ear; she shook when she managed to hear and put on a pleasant expression.

The sick man began to swallow his moans and was falling asleep, with his eyes closed and his body stretched out motionless, but more wide awake than an alarm clock, anxious to hear what they were talking about, the things they were saying about his poor wife, dragged off by the wind. Oh, who can tell where Tazol is keeping her! He curled up like a worm before the frightful thought that he would never see her again, whether alive or dead, awake or asleep.

He was about to get up and shout that he had nothing left and confess to his friends that he had traded his wife to Tazol out of an ambition for money so he would become the richest man in Quiavicús. But he did not have the courage and what would it solve since the agreement was made and the item delivered.

"He's feeling better, but he's crying," Don Teo murmured. "No doubt his heart has a premonition of the sad news I must pass on to him when he gets better."

"We're leaving now," the constable and the corporal said.

"I'll tell Yumí that you were with me." Don Teo Timoteo held them back. "It's all very compromising. Me alone with my friend's wife. What would Celestino think except that the devil had snatched her from my arms?"

"Yes, of course," the constable answered, "but at the police station we'll draw up a document stating everything that happened in all of its details. Besides, the Mayor's sure to ask for help from nearby authorities, with the idea of continuing the search for her not only here in the jurisdiction of Quiavicús, but in neighboring jurisdictions and even farther away if necessary, because she has to turn up somewhere. The hurricane dragged her away, it dragged her away and it would have dragged us away if we hadn't held onto the guava trees; what we have to find out is where it dropped her."

"Everything you say seems most opportune to me and with sound authority," Don Teo said in support, and the soldier, a corporal with ambitions to be a sergeant, nodded his head affirmatively, not saying anything because he was not well versed in such things.

"Goodbye, ma'am," added the constable, referring to Doña Juanita, who was holding her husband's arm. "Don Timoteo Teo Timoteo knows how I like to hear him talk, because even though he wasn't always well-heeled he talks like a rich man."

"That's not the way it is at all. My family always had position and I inherited what I have from three childless uncles and an aunt who had left the main part of her estate to the parish priest of Santa Lucía Cotzumalguapa, with the understanding that if the good father died first, it would all be mine, and he died before yours truly. Poor sainted man, he burst from eating too much pork! He was out of his head for pig meat. And night and day I used to send him cracklings, pickled loins, pigs' feet, sausages, blood puddings, until he had a stroke from eating so much pig meat and died a saintly death."

The constable, followed by the corporal, went across some stony ground that was cold from the night dew, wetting their sandals, while Don Timo went over to the bed and put his hand on his friend's forehead, not daring to wake him up completely.

Suddenly Yumí began shouting for his wife.

"Niniloj! Niniloj!" he shouted and wept.

His friend did not know what to do. Finally, in order to bring out the truth once and for all, he bit his tongue and said, "Easy, dear friend. Your wife will be here soon. She only went to get the healer."

But Yumí's calls to her became more and more pressing, and Don Teo decided to go all the way, taking advantage of the fact that the other man had his eyes closed and that

31

the hinges of his wailing were spread out across his cheeks, opening the door to the immense grief awaiting him and which he might have been sensing as he forgot the physical suffering that up until a moment ago was making him complain.

"Well, you see, friend . . . Can you hear me?"

Yumí, knowing what he was going to say, accepted with a movement of his head.

Despite the fact that he knew everything his friend was going to tell him, hearing it seemed frightful to him; hearing as reality and not as a nightmare that one can awaken from what the man had on his bitter and trembling lips.

"Well, now, old friend, your wife won't be coming right back." ("Why," thought Yumí, "doesn't he tell me that she'll never be coming back?") "She didn't run away, she was run away." He used that sort of joke to lessen the impact of his words. "Yes, she was run away. We were coming along with the constable, Atanasio Surún, and with the first corporal, Cirilo Pachaca, whom you had sent for, according to what she told us, since you wanted to talk to us because you thought you were dying, when we got to the palisade near Agapito Monge's, a windstorm came upon us, a completely unexpected wind, a hurricane that uprooted trees, lifted animals up bodily, sheep and calves, and your wife along with them. We didn't see her go because the dust had blinded us, but when we came to, when we said 'What's going on?', your poor wife had already flown off, there wasn't a trace of her. What happened? We don't know and maybe we never will. One has to be prepared for everything, my dear Celestino Yumí. I ran to see whether she had reached here on the wings of the wind, she was so upset over you that God might have done her that mercy, pick her up bodily and bring her to the side of her dear husband; the constable, Atanasio Surún, with no thought of the danger, threw himself down the precipice, fearful that she might have plunged into the river and would drown when she lost consciousness and be dragged along by the current. The first corporal, Cirilo Pachaca, remained there at the same spot on Agapito Monge's path to see if the wind that had carried her off would bring her back, which can happen and has happened. But it was all useless, and the only thing we

32

can ask God and the Virgin for is that even if she is wounded or battered—let's hope she isn't, of course—we will find her alive. And today, and tomorrow, and the day after tomorrow, until we come across her, she will be searched for in the mountains and valleys by every able-bodied man in Quiavicús."

The deaf woman, not hearing what her husband was saying, since he was speaking so softly to his friend, contented herself with an occasional sigh.

"What a terrible thing, Celestino Yumí! What a terrible thing! We finally learn that there is a punishment worse than death for our faults, disappearing so that no one will ever find our resting place, and as far as I'm concerned, for I'm a believer, all of this evil has come to you, like a thunderbolt, because you acted like an exhibitionist at Mass!"

When Yumí heard that his wife had really disappeared, he forgot that he was playing sick, he forgot his stomach-ache and the illness that was coursing through his body, the illness that was strangling him, which Don Timoteo Teo found quite reasonable, because what were those pains compared to the blow, the clout on the head that Niniloj's disappearance was.

And he too went out searching for her, among those who were searching for her and would keep on searching for her for many days afterward, a tragedy in which the slavering of gossip was not absent. Some people thought that, taking advantage of the hurricane, Celestina Zabala, who was sick and tired of her husband's boasting, had fled to the capital, and who could find her there in the imencity?

Yumí came and went from his house, crazy, going from one side to the other. He was the only one who was searching for her now. He was the only one who called to her: "Niniloj! Niniloj!"

Only now that he had lost her did he realize what his wife, Celestina Zabala, was. Her strength for work, her companionship in poverty, in their lack of means—they were terribly, so terribly miserable, and she never complained when there was nothing to eat, squatting next to the fire to warm her empty stomach, or imagining rich things when the only thing they had on the fire was what

33

their friend Timoteo had given them. And her sharp needle for mending. Mending after mending, stitch upon stitch. And from those patches, as Celestino touched his clothes, he could feel emerge . . . How small she had been in his life, because she was so good.

And not simply adjusted to her fate alongside a man who had no land, no plots, no garden, who lived by cutting wood and selling it in Quiavicús, who made deliveries to a few houses, but jolly and song-loving, as if she were exceedingly happy, because her happiness, to tell the truth, consisted in seeing all of his good side and none of his bad side.

And except for some complaints about not having a child she never spoke about what they lacked, because what did belong to them was the piece of land around their house, because it was land that did not belong to anyone, the village maybe, and they owned a change of clothing, two pants and two jackets and two shirts and a pair of boots, a daily change for her, and for Sundays a black skirt that she also used for feast days and funerals.

"My friend Celestino is already exaggerating his grief," Don Timoteo Teo Timoteo volunteered sententiously in the Mayor's office. They had sent for him to sign the deposition in the office. The corresponding deposition. For the Mayor all things had a first name and a family name, and the first name of the deposition was Corresponding.

And in everybody's eyes, Yumí was not acting like a good Christian, he was not resigned to his loss, and the fact was, alas, in no one's eyes more than his own, since joined to that overwhelming pain of the broken stem of something that had been uprooted there was remorse, which persecuted him like the tip of a sword stuck into his ear, a tip of cold flame that dripped words of blood, and because he could not share with anyone, no one at all, the reason for his despair, his upset, his moments of madness or the feeling that he was going mad. He had traded his wife so that he could have land and wealth. And he alone knew it, he and Tazol, and that was why they ended up considering him a mental case who lived off public charity and went shouting through the streets and woods and along the river: "Niniloj! . . . Catalina! . . . Niniloj! . . . Catalina! . . ."

34

Someone told how he had seen Yumí with a noose in his hand contemplating trees from top to bottom, as if calculating their height. The best thing for him to do would be to hang himself, everybody commented. In his unhinged conscience there was growing, just like the whirlwind that had carried off his wife, the remorse over the fact that it had been he who had traded her, he who had sold her, just like an animal, how awful! just like a heifer, and worse yet, because he had given her to an unknown being, an occult force, an omnipresent invisible being.

"Your friend is going to hang himself to the guerguero tree, and he's going around practicing," the neighbors told Don Teo, and the latter ran to his house where he finally found him with his head all white, not because he had turned gray but because he was sleeping among the ashes that had been piled up.

Without saying a word Don Teo left the house; he was on the point of going back and giving him a few kicks, but he looked so pitiful that he decided to keep quiet.

What insolence! He made a muttered accusation, a man like that making love to Catalina.

"It's better for him to hang himself," his friend told the neighbors, but they told him exactly how he was practicing; there was no danger.

He was hanging himself by one foot.

"By one foot?" Don Teo frowned.

"Yes, by one foot. He hangs himself by one foot. And the other day, when someone saw him hanging like that, he went over and asked him: 'Yumí, what are you doing that for?' and he answered, his head hanging down almost to the ground: 'Because I want to hang myself!' . . . 'Oh, Yumí,' the other one said to him, 'if you want to hang yourself I think it's just the opposite, you have to put the noose around your neck!' And Yumí replied, still head down, hanging by his foot: 'I already tried it with the noose around my neck, but I didn't like it, I felt that I couldn't get any air, that I was strangling!' "

Don Teo and the one who was telling the story they both took to be true laughed together.

Another day, a Sunday, after Mass—they had managed to get a priest from a neighboring village to come and

35

celebrate in Quiavicús—someone came over to Don Timoteo and confided in him that the spiritualists (they both crossed themselves at the same time) were certain that the Zabala woman had been carried off by an evil spirit.

"That's just one big lie," Don Teo Timoteo snorted.

"Jesus saves!" the neighbor who had mentioned the spiritualists hastened to say. "God be with us."

"God save us. That's why I wear this kerchief around my neck because colds always reach me through the back of the neck."

"And Yumí through his feet!"

"Ha, ha, ha," laughed Don Teo, "a cold can't hang anybody!"

"But it can fuck you up, if you'll excuse the expression!"

"Well, as I was saying, that business about the Zabala woman's being carried away by an evil spirit is a big lie. The constable and the first corporal—who are over there as large as life, you can go ask them—and I were going along with her and it was the hurricane that carried her off and threw her no one knows where."

"Thank God we heard Mass! I'm going now, Don Timo, and when you see your friend Celestino, tell him that even if he can't get any air and feels as if he's strangling, he should put the noose around his neck."

"How could I say a thing like that? That's all we need!"

"Now you really are going to hang yourself, Celestino Yumí . . ." a big ugly bird hummed to him, it was so old, with a naked neck and hairy legs, long claws, covered more with dry manure than feathers, that it made one sick to look at it.

Yumí, trembling, either from the chill of the dawn or from fear, recognized the voice of Tazol and did not answer him, feeling around up in a tamarind tree for the strongest branch to hang himself from, this time by the neck, kissing the noose that would free him from the remorse of having traded his wife for riches. Poor thing! Was she living the way she had lived on earth? Was she in hell? Who knew what pain, what suffering she was going through, only because he wanted to be rich!

He sat on the thickest branch and tied the rope on with a slip knot. Sitting on the branch, he swung his legs in empty space. What an urge! With the noose in his hands, stretched out on the branch, he was fingering it before slipping it around his neck. But as if his head and his body had suddenly turned to hard bone, he became rigid.

"Now you really are going to hang yourself!" the bird repeated, "and if that's how it's to be, it will happen all of a sudden!"

Yumí, with two sea shells in the place of ears, where his throbbing heart was buzzing, recognized Tazol's voice once more in the tones of that old bird and did not answer. His answer was all ready: the noose around his neck, the slip knot, and . . .

He was about to leap when the ugly bird pecked at the rope—old as he was, he got the strength from somewhere —and it was so quick that in a few seconds he had the rope unraveled. The other one got back his breath, which, even before he fell into space, had been cut off in his throat. Handfuls of fighting scorpions rained down upon him.

"But, Tazol," he said, "why do you do this to me? Why, Tazol? I gave you my wife, cursed be the hour, and you didn't give me anything. Loneliness at home, everywhere, that was all. And what little we had the neighbors carried off, because they must have said to themselves, what do they need it for if they're not around. I was around, but I really wasn't. Since she got lost through my fault, I haven't been anywhere. Where am I? I don't know, I don't know.

"Where were you, Tazol, false enemy, while I was searching for my wife, no longer on earth but in my dreams?

"Niniloj! I would call strongly and quietly before flopping on my mat, more tired than sleepy, hoping that at least she would visit me in my dreams.

"But it was all useless. She wasn't even left in my dreams! Not even in my dreams was she left, Niniloj!

"You carried her off, without leaving a trace, plucked up off the ground by the hurricane, and since that time, even out of fatigue, I haven't closed my little puffy eyelids. Not since then. Or have my feet, the eyelids of a person who walks along, left any shadow on the ground, a long time. I haven't stopped anywhere. And if I hang myself, I know that I'll keep on looking for her, even though I know that

37

it's useless to cover the whole earth, because you, Tazol, posing as my protector and friend, have carried her off.

"My last attempt to find her was on that high mountain that is also disappearing, a white mountain that dissolves, with a sound of effervescence when the wind touches it.

"Every moment, every day, there is less mountain, and also every moment, every day, there is less Niniloj, less Catocha, less Catarina Zabala. The poor mountain is only shoulders now. You cut off its head. And my wife is only shoulders too perhaps, because for me she is the mountain, the whole mountain, dissolving hour after hour, which you, Tazol, carry off in clouds of dust and scatter between earth and sky.

"Nine days I went around and nine days I spent on top of that white mountain of effervescent hot earth, sometimes standing upright calling her, asking the mountain if it were not Catarina Zabala, if it were not my Niniloj, it, the mountain, and sometimes on my hands and knees, in moments in which whole stretches of white mountain, just like clouds, would tumble down, and I did not come across her or have any answer as to whether the mountain were she, although one night when the white ground covered me, I was like a snowman, with my eyes open, without sleeping, I said to myself: 'No, Niniloj cannot be the mountain, but she is the one who is helping Tazol carry it off, little by little, and with shears of stars she must be turning it into that powder finer than the pollen that floats away like smoke.'

"The people who live near the mountain can testify to it. I swear it, Tazol, I swear it by this holy cross I make with my fingers. I wandered around a few nights hoping that the very fine dust being raised by the soft blowing of the wind would fall on me, because I was sure that Niniloj was the one who was sifting it off on top of me, and so I became a kind of ghost, so certain was I of becoming a ghost that when I would return to Quiavicús sometimes to find out if she had come home, people would close their doors and windows when I passed, and I could hear their voices: 'There he goes . . . there goes the ghost of the white mountain!'

"And the last words I heard from my friend Timoteo

Teo Timoteo were these: 'If, as you see, friend Celestino, the wind is carrying off the white mountain, why couldn't it carry her off, why couldn't it carry off your wife, and she dissolved for me just the way the mountain does, without even having time to attract a flock of vultures, because we didn't even have that sign, for if a great black crown of birds had formed in the sky, we would have known where to find the body of your sainted wife. And you,' he added in the friendly, affectionate tone of a rich relative, 'look like a beetle, you're so thin; eat, even if only to have enough strength to keep on searching for her, because that's how it is, as long as you don't find her, as long as you know nothing about her, you'll keep on searching for her until the end of your days. If you don't eat something, my friend, you'll die.'

" 'That's what I want to do,' I should have answered my friend, but I said to myself, why say anything if no one can understand your grief, because you can't tell the truth to anyone, only to Tazol, but what more does Tazol want from me, since he already has the one who helps him sift the white mountain, although sometimes, wise as you are, you have been careless, and I have felt her spirit, like an animal of the woods, prowling around my place, and I have heard her, with my eyes closed—once I opened them and the noises went away—I have heard her get the fire ready, blow on the coals, make tortillas, I have heard her when she put the pot of corn on the fire, the water and the kernels bubbling, and then, lifting the pot off the fire and going out to throw away the cooking water, to the morning star, the cooking-water star, whose blue firelight . . .

"Oh, my God, I should take my jump!"

But then he remembered that the ugly bird had pecked at the rope and that instead of hanging himself all he would do when he fell would be to land with a tremendous thump.

"Take a good look from that branch at what's waiting for you down below!" croaked the ugly, featherless bird, its eyes eaten by lice.

He lowered his eyes and could not believe what he saw. The tree had grown very tall, very tall, and it did not even seem to be on the ground. In what cloud had it been planted? Well, from that height he could see the whole

39

world and by just glancing down, at his feet, his eyes encompassed fields sown with corn, sugar cane, cacao, tobacco, cotton, fruits, a great river and its bridges, a two-story house surrounded by outbuildings, pastures full of cattle, herds of horses, others in stables, milk cows, magnificent bulls, thoroughbred dogs, barnyard fowl of every description, some local, some he had never seen before.

He took the noose off his neck the way one takes off a useless collar. His eyes were not up to seeing so much at his feet.

"And all of this, Celestino Yumí, is yours!" the ugly bird announced to him, and at that moment he thought it was a sublime bird, a beautiful messenger of the gods.

"Mine?" asked Yumí. He could not believe it.

"Yes, yours, Yumí."

"Then my friend has really been screwed!"

More than knowing that all of that world of countless riches belonged to him, he was happy at being able to present himself as a rich man in the house of his friend Timoteo Teo Timoteo. He would turn yellow with envy and jaundice, and that would make his bile flow into his blood when he found out that Yumí was richer than he was.

His heart, which had been growing smaller with sorrow, was becoming inflated with pleasure, and what he was looking at . . . if it were not a dream . . . if his eyes were not lying to him, among the people who were going about in the midst of that property of his, among the fields, the buildings, the corrals, the stands of fine wood, he thought he recognized Catalina Zabala, very small, very tiny, perhaps he was looking at her from very high up. Barely recognizable in her miniature size, like a little cloth or clay shepherdess, the shepherdesses they have in a Christmas crèche. That was it—finding the Zabala woman gave him a sense of rebirth. He had been reborn twice in those few minutes. When the ugly bird had pecked at the rope when he already had the noose around his neck, really ready to hang himself that time, and now that he had found his dear wife, his Niniloj.

The ugly bird flew down with him out of the tamarind tree. The trunk of that most beautiful umbrella of God had grown so much, green, leafy, perfumed with red flowers and fruit in goitered pods, fruit that seemed to have been old at birth, and it seemed that they spent a whole week descending and would have fallen from fatigue if they had not managed to make hammocks out of the strands and slept in them at night, accompanied by the hairless stars, hard skulls of dead goddesses, or to sit on the stumps of arms that lightning had cut off the huge many-storied tree, along whose trunk they kept on descending. Finally they set foot on the ground, the way one comes to Sunday after six days of heavy work.

Tazol was waiting for him. Since he had snatched Catarina away, which was no kidnapping, because he had agreed to turn her over in exchange for becoming rich, he had not met him again.

And he complained as soon as he saw him.

"Why were you silent, Tazol? I didn't ask you to give her back to me—an agreement to trade is never unmade—but I did want you to tell me where she was, whether she was alive or dead, whether she was happy, whether you were punishing her cruelly as you had proposed, how ungrateful I was . . ."

Tazol took on partial shape. He was like an enveloping wind, a wind revolving about an axis, just like a flogging snake surrounded by fiery flying fish.

Yumí threw himself to the ground—it was not enough to kneel—wanting to grasp within his arms everything that he had seen from up on high and which he now found reduced to the surface of a concave mirror, but instead of fields his elbows struck sharp stones, thorns instead of flowers, shadows of the tamarind tree instead of horses and cattle. In one word, nothing.

The ugly bird pecked at him, and he, disappointed, deceived, furious, was on the point of giving him a kick.

The embodied Tazol, a wind with a young face, his mouth afflicted with moles along the wrinkles of his smile, was handing him a large cardboard box, the kind that toys come in. Yumí, if he had had the strength to lift it, would have thrown it in Tazol's face. A box of toys instead of the riches he had been promised, after he had given him his wife, was the cruelest of jokes. Inside he could see a Christmas crèche with everything that he had seen from up above

41

reduced to a miniature world. But now no longer in the concave mirror of the first vision, but in real and palpable form. Every one of those tiny objects could be touched. The ponies, the cows, the bulls, the calves, all of clay, the wire trees with paper leaves, the cardboard bridges, the match-stick fences, the chicken-feather chickens, the same for the roosters, the rivers of fire glass, the mirror lakes, the canvas mountains. And that shepherdess with black braids, lemon-colored skin, and feet like Catarina's who could be no one else but she. He had found her at last, he was touching her, reduced to an inanimate thing, and his emotion was such that he felt that his heart would tear open his breast.

After his fit of temper why was Tazol making fun of him like that? He made a move to steal the shepherdess Catarina from the crèche.

"Stop right there!" croaked the ungainly bird at the same time as he gave him a tremendous peck. "If you touch her she'll fall apart in your hand. Before you take her you have to be rich."

And after the cloth-ripping voice of the bird there came the clear voice of Tazol:

"Yumí, my friend, these are your riches, but . . ." And he was silent for a long time, as if thinking, but what he was doing was enjoying the lines on the face of that man who had grown old with grief, for he liked to feed on human suffering, pride ground to dust on the face of a man, a fragile creature, like an egg shell; made of corn, he, Tazol, was the waste product of that beautiful creature formed out of the flesh of the ears, and it was from this fact that his enmity had been born, in being Tazol, the useless leaf, no longer useful when dry or used to feed oxen with, while man was the pulsating meal of the kernels, the laugh of the kernels when they were teeth, or their weeping when they were tears.

"Yumí, my friend," he repeated, "these are your riches, but what would they think in Quiavicús, the ones who know you as a poor miserable man, if overnight you became an all-powerful rich man? The least they would say is that you had exchanged your wife with the Devil for so much wealth. And that won't do, not because they might do

42

something to you, no, money is the best shield: against God, money; against the law, money; money for meat; money for glory; money for everything, for everything, money. But weigh well what I tell you; it is better to hide the apparent than the real. I want you to hide the apparent, and therefore this box, with all your riches, you will hide in some cave along the river known only to you, so that it will be given to you little by little as the fruit of your good luck and your work."

Yumí understood by guessing—why explain it, since with Tazol one grasped things by guessing—but that business of having to work did not please him very much. A rich man means an idler. An idler for whom other people work.

Tazol guessed his thought.

"And that will be you. I am the one who will work to make you rich."

"But I gave you my wife."

"I am giving her back to you. She's in the box of toys."

"And how do I start?"

"Wealth, Yumí, is like a slip knot."

"Are you trying to tell me that my riches will hang me?"

"That depends on you. For the miser, wealth is the worst of hangings, the same for the spendthrift, the generous man . . . But what I wanted to know is that the slip knot of everything you will possess, and which you already possess in miniature, is on my arm, stronger than the branch of the tamarind tree you had chosen to hang yourself on and die, and when I give you wealth, like a rope, putting it around your neck like the most valuable decoration a human being can desire, the noose of the millionaire, it will all depend on you whether you hang yourself as a miser or as a spendthrift, by hoarding or by wasting."

The ugly bird woke up sleepily, opened a yellow moonlike eye, and spoke slowly after coughing several times:

"You will say to your friend Timoteo Teo Timoteo, to the wife of the Mayor, to the best newspaper in town, to the druggist and to the barber that you had a very strange but meaningful dream. That you heard someone calling you, and the voice that was calling you was the voice of your dear wife, your castoff Niniloj."

43

"Castoff?"

"Of course castoff! You swapped her for wealth. But that's all over, and listen to me, damn it, or I won't give you any more advice. Tell those people, and anybody who wants to listen to you, that your dear wife—she's still that as far as they're concerned—was calling to you from one of the deepest caves in the white mountain which is being worn away by the wind. Without your asking their advice, they will decide that you should go look for her, since in your dream you have even seen the place where she is, and from where she was calling you, unlikely that she is alive, but perhaps what she wants is for you to give her Christian burial."

Yumí leaned back against the trunk of the tamarind tree, not because he was tired but because his legs were trembling.

"Those who advise you to go," continued the ugly bird, after closing his moonlike eye and opening the other one, sunlike, with the whiteness of salt, "you should ask them to go along with you. It would be better if many of them went along with you, and better still if your friend goes, and the constable, Atanasio Surún, and the first corporal, the one whose last name is Pachaca and I think is called Cirilo. They were the ones who went with the woman who is not dead, only missing, on the night of the windstorm."

"My friend will go."

Tazol, who had appeared bodily, put his hand on Yumí's shoulder, interrupting the ugly bird: "Take along the noose you were going to hang yourself with, and a few other nooses."

"If you're going to tell me to hang my friend and my other neighbors I'm willing to do it as long as I have some guarantee."

"No hangings. On the contrary, they have to live so they can see you rich. You will bring the ropes for other uses. In sight of everyone you will tie the noose around your waist, very tight—be careful that you don't do a bad job out of nervousness or haste—and, once tied, you will jump into the cave I am making on the hill with one of my blasts of dry wind while I talk to you here."

"And how will I recognize the place?"

"Very simple, where some engineers had been a while ago with their tripods. You'll see the marks there. Jump down into it and I'll be waiting for you down below."

"Won't they see you?"

"They'll see the wind. And after an hour, when everyone will start to say, 'Poor Celestino Yumí, another one who never came back from the blinding white hole, where the sun penetrates as if through the mist,' you will come up with a huge leather pouch full of gold coins. No one will be able to doubt then what they will have seen with their own eyes, the origin of your wealth. Everybody will recount when they get back to Quiavicús how you didn't find the Zabala woman, but you had the good luck to come across a huge leather pouch full of gold coins. And there will be no small number of them who, through ambition or as victims of the delirium of finding treasures, will drop down that very night with lanterns and pine-handled axes to the bottom of the cave; with no need for any hangings, they will remain with me, thanks to your efforts, and what better tribute, since I will use those bodies to ferment liquors that I will sell later at high prices to those who feed on human flesh."

"Do cannibals still exist?"

"They never stopped existing. They don't eat the corpse materially, but they stuff themselves on human flesh, people who exploit the working man, ranchers, coffee growers, plantation owners, those in whom the Christian and the wild beast are all woven up together."

"I'm only afraid of one thing. If my friend Timoteo, who will envy me, is among those whose ambition makes them go down after me to look for more bags of gold, what good will it be for me to be rich?"

"He won't be among them—that's why he has money. Three of his peons will be among them."

Early in the morning Yumí ran to tell his friend about his pretense, his dream, and he went to the Town Hall, and he told Atanasio Surún, and he went looking around the Post until he found the first corporal, Cirilo Pachaca, and in the town he told everyone who wanted to listen, and all of them decided unanimously that often what is seen in dreams results in reality, and that Yumí should take the risk, lower himself down, if he recognized the cave from where his wife was calling him, in the dissolving mountain, until he came across her, dead or alive. And a corpse in a case like that was most important since then he would no longer keep on searching for her, shouting for her in the night, keeping the whole population awake while they always worried for his life, never knowing where he was wandering, almost always on the white mountain or along the big river or through the deepest canyons.

The weather was favorable, they all could see. If it started to rain it would no longer be possible. And Don Teo was thinking along these lines. There was no flock of buzzards where the body was, because she had fallen into the middle of that asphyxiating, foggy world of brutal pulverization that was the white mountain. That was what had saved her from the beaks of the birds of prey. It was better that way, since Celestino Yumí would not have to recover her remains all pecked up. No bird, big or little, ever flew over that mysterious mountain.

Everybody—the friend, the constable, the first corporal in the lead—marched along with him, the sexton followed with several parishioners, the druggist, the barber, since, as the latter said, "we don't want them to come back and tell us about it, we want to see with our own eyes, and that's why we have our feet and our good legs, and here we are. Some women, acquaintances of the Zabala woman, got together to bring sheets to cover the body with, wondering whether Catocha would be worm-eaten or whether she would still be showing her feminine perfections.

Everything happened as Tazol had predicted.

Yumí, when he pulled on the string of ropes that he had used to go down with as a signal for them to pull him up, returned with a leather pouch full of gold coins. He gave some away, to his friend, to the constable, to the corporal, to others who had helped him, and everybody, after biting them, avowed that they were solid gold, old-fashioned coins, the kind not seen any more except rarely.

Overnight he had become rich in everybody's eyes. He bought good land in Quiavicús and other places which brought him a hundred in return for every thousand he had put in, without fertilizing, mysteriously, as always happens

46

when a person is lucky. Fine crops of corn and beans, cane fields that produced stalks of a thickness rarely seen, coffee trees heavy with berries, and on the coast cattle, and in other places cotton fields, in addition to the domestic fowl, from hens to pheasants, that were multiplying rapidly.

"When God gives," his friend sighed, "he gives whole hog!"

The Fly Wizard Meets That Certain Mulata

The richest men in the region, Timoteo Teo Timoteo and even richer than he perhaps, Celestino Yumí, arrived at the fair in San Martín Chile Verde riding horses that gave pleasure to the onlookers, people on foot who were proud as they watched them pass looking like a pair of posters.

They did their religious duties, early Mass where Don Teo received Communion, his spurs jingling as he went up to the altar rail, Yumí finding some pretext not to receive, because the fact was that from the time he lost his wife he had become a blasphemer, an unbeliever, and without fear of God or High Mass, a Mass sung by three fat priests, so that everybody looked at them more than at the priests because they were the richest men around, and their clothes were something to be seen, and each one carried a roll of bills in his pocket, each one took out a big bill to toss into the collection basket for charity that two altar boys were passing around, while a monk was preaching, announcing to all the mortals therein gathered that impious science was in retreat—those good people listened without knowing what science was or impious or in retreat—and that a proof of the uselessness of science was that it could not explain why every year, year after year, on a fixed date, a certain saint in Italy bleeds. "Go there," he shouted at them, "and you will see for yourselves!" But who could go, since by putting a few pesos together and pawning some little thing, they had only been able to make it to the feast day of San Martín, and the only trip they had marked out was the one to heaven, if God and the Most Holy Virgin and Saint Michael the Archangel would help them.

After High Mass, after breakfast, a banquet of chocolate and bread with egg in it, the friends went over to the fair-grounds to sell the cattle they had brought along. The cow-hands invited them to have some jerked beef and coffee, and to please them they accepted the offer, a light meal washed down with a few swigs of rum, just enough to spark up Yumí and for him to drag Don Teo off to where things were going on, looking for some good females, and this time he would have good reason to open up his fly, not like the time when he was going around that way like a fool because of the demands of the one who had given him so many riches in exchange for his wife.

She was half sitting, with one buttock on the back of a bench, her feet on the seat—Yumí found a Mulata.

The deep black eyes of the girl prevented him from going on his way. He stopped and looked at her with the insolent security of a rich man who knows that the woman who can resist him does not exist, much less that one there, a paragon of misfortune, dressed in a yellow outfit that was in its dotage from age and use, her coltish body looking for someone to tame her.

Celestino, more tipsy than was good for him, with the drinks the cowhands had offered him so early inside of him —they had been repeated several times—held out his hand to her, but she just stayed there without budging, looking at him, looking him over with the extinguished coals that were her eyes, just as if there were heat in them, up and down, and after a sudden fit of laughter, like a dog with white teeth that look like marble kernels set into living gums, she turned her back on him and ran away, but not before she shouted back at him, "How come you don't have your fly half in bloom!" and, flirting from a distance, without stopping her laughter, she added, "I know you, you gnat!"

Yumí squatted down on his legs—they were not obeying him very well now—and, tipping his hat forward, he hauled out one of his pistols and shouted at her, "If you don't stop I'll plug you."

The Mulata's smile froze—her teeth were no longer kernels but hailstones—and she tried to shorten the distance; it would be harder for him to kill her from close by. She came up to where Yumí was, ready to shoot, and she said to him at the same time as she shook him by the arms, "You wouldn't be such a fool!"

Celestino, content to have her nearby, immediately put his fingers behind the back of her neck like a comb, in her hair, a caress she answered with a gesture of annoyance.

"How much do you want?"

"What you've got in your wallet!"

He pulled himself toward her body with his right arm, feeling around her behind, while his left hand went for his wallet.

But the Mulata, after giving in for a minute, pushed him away from her.

"First the wallet!" she repeated imperiously, rubbing against him with everything there was in her of a flexible root, a root that had been buried for centuries under ebony wood, and was now dressed up in flesh, just as ready to be a snake as to be a woman.

Yumí, with an urge to carry her off on horseback, up in front of him like a trophy, and make her his in some forest, handed his wallet over to her, took out of his pockets the rolls of fifty- and one-hundred-peso bills that he was carrying and gave them to her. And all of that invaluable booty she put between the tantalizing breasts that Yumí could not get his hands on, because as soon as he touched them she would twist away and slip out of his grasp, without completely getting away, since she would leave him another part of her body, near her legs, or she would even pass her mouth across his face without kissing him, breathing hot upon his nose, his eyes, his ears, and his mouth.

"You're coming with me, Mulata!"

"Are you single?"

"Single and rich, very rich."

"Only as long as you marry me."

"Of course."

"Let's go to the Town Hall then."

"Is it open?" Yumí resisted.

"All during the fair, just for this purpose, so that from every fertilization, from so many bellies left behind, the children will at least come out knowing who their father was. A concern of the Mayor who just came here, every new broom sweeps clean, but nobody pays any attention to him."

"But getting married so fast like this . . ." Yumí resisted; he had prescribed her *in peto* for some rolling around and nothing else. "And we don't have any papers. They call for them, birth certificates at least."

"Papers? We don't have any papers? What about these?" And she took a few green bills out of his wallet. "Are they beans or something? Of course, if you don't want to, just leave me, here's your money back." And when she said that, as she took out the wallet and the rolls of bills from her breasts, she showed her firm, elastic breasts on which Celestino fell, almost tearing the neck of her dress, kissing them, lips, tongue, the edge of his teeth, which could not dent the honeyed firmness of those precious things.

"Let's get married, what the fuck!" he challenged with his mouth still in the neck of her dress, his eyes intent on looking at, rather than imagining, the granulated tips of her nipples, dark pink in color like a wet begonia. "But if I'm going to get married—a person who does a lot of thinking about it doesn't get to do it, it's best right away—I want to tell my friend Timoteo Teo Timoteo. Let's go tell him. He'll come with us and be our witness, and what better witness that we're married can I have when I arrive in Quiavicús with you than my old friend?" And he remained thoughtful, lucid, fresh, with the surprise of the marriage his drunkenness had left him, thinking that his dear old friend really was his witness in everything, because without his knowing it, as planned by Tazol, he had served as the "I saw it" when the hurricane had carried off Niniloj, how far away, how lost she was!, and later on when he had gone down into the white cave in the mountain that was disappearing in clouds of dust, another great chunk had already disappeared, and come up with the leather pouch full of gold coins.

Don Timo, who was also going around fairly tipsy, dancing in the Chinaman's canteen with a barefoot girl who stank of hair and was salty with sweat and menstruation because like an old tom cat he liked tender mice, when he heard the news of his friend's hitching up with the Mulata, jumped for joy, forgot his partner, made them hug each other in front of him, and was about to try to give them his blessing.

"Wonderful, old friend, and if the burden gets too heavy along the way, drop it and I'll pick it up and carry it!"

"I'm not about to drop her to please you, old friend, and I'm chuckling over the fact that you've got some of the blame for my getting mixed up in this."

"That's all I needed!"

"You don't understand. Who was Niniloj with when she disappeared? It's your fault that I'm a widower, because if you'd had a grip on her . . ."

"God save me, may he turn me to stone, the cure would have been worse than the illness! If the windstorm hadn't carried her off, you still would have lost her forever, friend Yumí, and you would have lost this good friend of yours who loves you in spite of everything, because they would have found us turned into two stones."

And while they were talking they had not noticed where they were going. They were already in front of the Town Hall, which was carpeted with pine boughs and had over the door an arch of sugar cane, flowers, and flags.

Flies, teaty women selling corn drinks in jars which they uncovered while they ladled the sweet or bitter corn liquid into round cups, a few drunks in the jail, hanging onto the barred door, disheveled, their clothes torn and some bruises and scratches on their faces.

"And why don't you be a witness?" the Mulata proposed, and all of her hot breath wrapped up Don Teo's face, and before he could answer yes, with great pleasure, he had to run his tongue along his lips.

"Naturally," Yumí accepted, finding that the idea was wonderful because then they would be friends twice over, and he said so, and the other one replied, explaining to the Mulata while they were waiting for the Mayor: "We're

51

close friends because Celestino baptized Compungido for me."

"Compungido?" the Mulata laughed, and who could make anything of it, think it was an insult, when all he had to do was look at her magnificent teeth while she laughed.

"It's the name of my first-born. He was born on the day that the Bristol Almanac said something about repentance and compunction. But his name was too long. We call him Ungido. And I'll carry your first child to the font . . ."

"To the drinking fountain, because I don't want my child to be a Christian."

"Woman," Yumí put in, "my friend is a good Catholic."

"We'll put his name in the Civil Registry and that will be enough, with the name of Antichrist, and that's all— ha-ha-ha—old friends, it makes me laugh . . . sons of . . . from where? Because I'm barren!"

"The specialty of my dear Celestino Yumí, because his dear wife, all things considered and good as she was . . ."

"Don't you throw dirt on her, Don Timo!"

Celestino protested, and held back between his lips "you useless old man!" How could he think of comparing Niniloj, who was a fawn, to the Mulata, the mistress of a rich man! He only forgave him because he was a little drunk.

And on horseback, sitting up front in Yumí's lap with the license from the Town Hall and the money tucked in her breasts that were as firm as the tips of a set of tongs, the Mulata left San Martín Chile Verde, changed into the wife of one of the capitalists of the region. The old friend went along with them, shouting and spraying the sky with shots from his revolver. For lack of festive rockets, simple bullets.

An interminable neigh from the horse Celestino was riding, an ash-colored stallion with white spots and who no doubt had smelled some mare in the vicinity, made Don Timo exclaim: "The one who should be neighing is my old friend, the lucky dog—what a female he's got!"

"He is the one who's neighing, didn't you notice?" the Mulata answered, rubbing her round parts on the saddle between Yumí's legs and against his manly chest, where his heart was beating rapidly.

52

On arriving in Quiavicús, he brought the Mulata, his second legal wife, into his big house, a sumptuous and until then an empty residence, a lonely one; but it was not what we might call a successful debut. Besides the discomfort of bodies that do not know each other—the man must adjust to the body of the woman and the woman must adjust to the body of the man—the Mulata's whim of receiving him from behind embittered him. The back says so little when on the other side there are eyes, mouth, lips, face, all that is beautiful and ugly in a person.

His begging was useless, his threats were useless, useless too were his tempting offers of jewels, perfumes, silks, trips, whatever she wanted. The Mulata never consented to turn over and face him.

It was not a honeymoon, it was a back-moon, and as soon as he made that reference she broke into tears. That was what she was in effect. The back of the moon, and that was why she could not show her face in love. Never, she would repeat as she wept in bed, never will you see the face of the moon, Yumí, always the back!

Celestino, without completely grasping the meaning of her rather enigmatic words, was moved, considering her frustration as similar to that of the moon with the sun, and he became resigned to his fate, bothered by the fact that he had dreamed and still dreamed about an heir to his substantial fortune, he no longer knew just how much he possessed in land, cattle, crops, stocks, and money in the bank.

"Richer every day, my dear old Celestino," old Timoteo Teo Timoteo would repeat to him when they met, covering up the rancor in his eyes, barely hiding his great envy, his mouth tight as he showed a bitter smile.

He could not forgive him for his superb crops and the abundance in which Yumí lived with the Mulata, wasting his money on banquets, picnics with close friends, laying out gardens, buying statues for the park around his house, fountains and artificial grottoes, where the echo would multiply whatever was said in one of its corners many times over, and softer every time.

Yumí, with the pretext of going to buy some better breeding animals, bulls, stallions, mares, thoroughbred milk cows, would leave Quiavicús accompanied by his best riders, whom he would leave in some neighboring village to eat and drink at the expense of their boss.

When he felt alone, deep in the woods, after they had left Quiavicús far behind, he would return at a gallop along a byway, and when he reached the river where he had hidden the box of toys that Tazol had given him, he would set out toward the cave, and he would take something else from the many things there were in that miniature world.

But this time an unpleasant surprise, he noticed that his ambition had been so great that the box was empty. He had taken out everything, and now they were the houses on his property, the buildings, the corrals, the henhouses, the horse pastures, the bridges, the flocks, the armies of turkeys, the loaded fruit trees, the salt licks, the flour mills, the wagons, the oxen, the teams of horses, and the little church which, in spite of the protests from the Mulata, he had brought back from one of his trips and the next day it was standing there, without benefit of any supply of materials or of masons, a miracle that made sense to everyone, because that man, even though he was rich, was a man of great charity toward the poor.

This time in the box, in the whole box, there was only left a tiny shepherdess: Catalina Zabala, his Niniloj, as he still called her. What was he to do? Should he leave her? Should he take her with him?

The Mulata was terrible. When she was in a bad mood she would throw herself at him, just because he was he, trying to scratch out his eyes. And at night, stretched out at his side, she would weep and bite him so hard that many times her great mouth of a proud beast was smeared with blood, blood that it savored and swallowed, while she scratched him over and over as she touched him, and her white eyes would show no pupils, her breasts would be teary with sweat. And all of this quite often night after night, unable to sleep, always fearful that the beast would wake up and grab him unexpectedly, explosions of fury that coincided with the phases of the moon. She was not a woman, she was a wild animal. She was a sea. A sea of waves that had claws, beside which he slept in apprehension when he managed to fall asleep between blinks, a little sleep without her waking up—she was always insomniac and turbulent—to complain and cry sometimes like a coffee-colored doll, whispering in his ear: "I'm your pet! I'm your pet!" or become enraged and attack him as if he were her worst enemy. A hundred dogs, a hundred tigers would come out of her mouth in search of the morsel that would satisfy not her appetite but her raging need to destroy.

And during the day there was battle sometimes. For any reason at all plates, cups, glasses would start to fly—whole dinner services destroyed on the floor, on the furniture, the shelves, services that she herself would replace with others more easily breakable.

Yumí kept his cribs full of dry corn leaves, *tazol* instead of ears, knowing that only in that way, transforming into bank notes those remains of the sacred plant, would he be able to confront the expenses and the demands of the Mulata.

"What shall I do?" he repeated, thoughtfully as he faced the empty box. "Shall I take the shepherdess or leave her here?"

He decided to leave her. He galloped back along the by-way, through groves of pines, old cypresses, live oaks; he picked up his men in the village where he had left them, and he returned to Quiavicús.

What did he return to? To a most unpleasant surprise. One of his peons, before cutting the dry stalks, had set fire to the dried-out cornfield in order to get ahead with the clearing, and the cribs were empty, not of corn but of corn leaves. He sent for the man and flogged him with such fury that he broke some of the lashes on the whip. It was terrible. He had never done anything like that. It was something unheard of.

"And now," he said after whipping him, "take care what you fill my cribs with, and make sure that it's not corn."

That poor unfortunate spent the night scraping the earth, after gathering together the most voracious locusts, in search of the few dried corn leaves that had not been burned in his clearing operation, and since the harvest was so slight, he went over to the hulling machines, many-toothed instruments that glowed blue in the light of dawn, and he gathered up the empty ears to fill the cribs with that rubbish which made him cough continuously with its dry powder, its dead scales, aided by an army of red ants, ants that brought whiteness because wherever they went they left the land looking like a shaved knee.

It happened. What happened? Everything happened. Nothing happened. But that light . . .

Fire! Fire!

A fire without flames or smoke, with a fixed glow, stabilized outside of time, in the world of a true dream, of real, touchable, truly real things, and yet a dream, dream, dream . . .

Celestino ran to see what was going on. And half asleep, scratching himself, scratching himself, trying to get rid of the scales of sleep and find, at last he found it!, his human presence as boss in front of his foreman and peons who were hurrying to put out the fire with buckets of water, that ruddy glow which was coming from the cribs full of ears, phosphorescent, hydrogenated, flaming up in the swampy greenness of the dawn.

Yumí ran, followed by the Mulata, who had jumped out of bed just the way she had been sleeping, naked, and naked she went after him to face the flames whose light was reaching out to lick at the country house where they were spending the corn-harvest season.

Yumí was like a madman. Instead of bills he found the cribs full of gold pieces. Every ear was gold. Ears where instead of kernels of corn there were kernels of gold, burning with the unmoving flame of a firefly. They were not ears of corn but ears of fireflies.

Celestino, feeling the mirrors of thanks that were pouring from his weeping eyes—how could he not thank Tazol for all of his beauties?—touched himself several times, pinched himself several times, bit his lips. He wanted to know if he was awake and he was awake, if he was in possession of his five senses and he was in possession of his five senses.

In the bluish mirror of the air the hands of the peons, of the foreman, of the young men, disdainful of the golden metal, pursued the naked Mulata, like an apparition cut from living stone. They did not breathe. They did not blink. Her scissor legs cut them into pieces. They were pieces of men pursuing her, while she, electric, atmospheric, was dancing like a will-of-the-wisp. But it was made of flesh. Flesh of black mother-of-pearl, covered with a light volcanic fuzz. She was dancing with her neck encircled by a necklace of small golden bananas, from which a plantain hung that beat at her breasts while she danced. That was how the peons were looking at her. The foreman. The young men. Around her waist and her forearms, golden bananas and purple bananas, moving in time to her hips, her buttocks, her feet, her ankles, while she danced on top of golden coals that did not interest the men in their amazement, did not interest them, ready to attack, attack her brutally. It was madness when the most daring of them pointed at her sex, her double sex, without love, with hatred, and the bestial and moonlike Mulata turned her back to await the penetrating, virile, compulsive attack from the side opposite the face, through lead-red and tightest ring of Saturn.

The peons drew back roaring: "Gold is better! Gold is better!" And they would have carried off everything if Yumí—while the Mulata, followed by those blinded males, was losing herself in a Milky Way of breeding stallions who rolled, who bit each other, who kicked, ejaculating by themselves, vertebrates like waves of the sea, bodies falling into the emptiness—if Yumí had not set a fire to save his riches, but this time real fire, flames, smoke, and coals that were devouring the cribs.

Earth! Earth! To put out this new fire, and they put it out, but they buried the gold.

When the Mulata felt the body of her husband fall beside her in bed, weighted down by fatigue, she grabbed him by the hair and laughing hoarsely and wrathfully beat him against the pillow until she grew tired. A viper that has hypnotized its victim and demands that it not be defenseless, demanding, obliging it to participate in its own death like an invited guest.

Two, three, many times Yumí went to the house of his friend Timoteo Teo Timoteo, resolved to tell him that if indeed he was very rich—neither he nor anyone else knew how high his riches had piled up—he was very unfortunate.

But the one in second place in the world of business, money, exhibits that were awarded prizes at agricultural expositions, the transformation of Quiavicús from a village into a beautiful city, would receive him with inexplicable and fun-making little smiles, and he would not dare tell him what was going on.

The Mulata, after that dawn of golden fires, would get intoxicated night after night, exposing herself to an inner flame which would make her mad as she breathed it in. She sang, laughed, danced, she would have herself chased by archers who were so good that they would shoot their arrows at her and aim for just the slightest scratch, a feeling of multiple wounds in which she would twist around, a skein of honey that went beyond the nectars of humming birds, sugar cane, or maguey, the drunkenness of gesticulating smoke, until she would fall out of time into a vague and gnawing eternity, her immensely wide pupils were two moons of tar, two solitary coagulants in the midst of absolute terror, fear, fright, doubt, a weeping in shouts, the weeping of someone without an owner, without a handle, and right there, the suicidal furor, the wish to do away with her present image in exchange for a future image, beating her face against the impassable, and right there, the howl, that most anguished howl as she found herself once more with her lunar, vertebrate, pierced-through, passive, climacteric self, and right there, as she doubled up with the simian sadness of a monkey who sharpened his nails with his teeth as she heard the news, the terrible news: Yumí, her husband, had a skeleton of gold.

She would cut off one of his arms, then the other one, then a leg, then the other one, and she would put him in a bin, thorax and head of white gold, waiting for his death so she could skin him, throw away what would rot, and extract intact the rest of the treasure.

Vague stories about the man with the skeleton and cornfields of gold attracted adventurers, treasure hunters, and Gypsies to Quiavicús, and, following in their footsteps, merchants in search of compensation—merchants always seem to be retrieving something—angry women of ill fame, female pimps who sold liquor and tobacco, and policemen who carried off noisy drunks and violators of municipal ordinances which were enacted on the way to jail.

Celestino Yumí said to himself: now is my chance. Quiavicús full of strange people. He could go for the little clay shepherdess, for Catarina Zabala, his wife in the eyes of God, hide her among the strangers and even pass her off as an acquaintance, while he got rid of the Mulata.

The Fly Wizard, His Dwarf Wife, and the Aforesaid Mulata

With the long strides of his best horse he flew along, accompanied by his riders, to the village where he always left them. And from there he went back, retracing the road to the caves along the big river that passed by Quiavicús. But torrents of diabolic and shining water had come down from out of the mountains and everything was a mud flat, thickets, the loneliness of flooded lands.

What could he do?

No trace of the road. Overwhelmed, he did not notice that the horse kept on going along, reins loose, step by step.

He's going where he feels like, he said to himself, and he thought of reining him in. How could he go back to Quiavicús without his treasure?

Hold him back or let him go along like that?

The horse was moving faster than his thoughts and from the distant murmur of the water he soon noticed that they were nearing the river. He could feel his heart beating even in the points of his spurs, and he dismounted in front of the cave and kissed the horse, and murmured to him: This is the last trip and I haven't come for riches but for my greatest treasure, Niniloj, and, thinking about her, he became ashamed and wept, having traded her as he had done for goods which, more than goods, had been a gathering of curses.

Having said that, he went inside and lifted his wife out of the crèche. She was a little clay shepherdess who moved at once, moved her feet, her arms, her head, and her lips to speak and it was the voice of the one who had disappeared, the one carried off by the hurricane, and she moved her eyes and they were Catalina Zabala's pretty eyes, and she moved her hands, and all of her was moving, walking, and with a leap and with Yumí's help, she came up out of the crèche.

But—oh, woe!—she was a little dwarf.

She was a dwarf with bow legs, large knees, very long and muscular arms, her big head set on narrow shoulders, and her chest inflated sómewhat toward the front.

Should he take her with him?

How could he take her!

And still he could not leave her after he had brought her back to life.

She, meanwhile, removed from the conflict brought on by her disenchantment, was talking as if nothing had happened since she had left him prostrate in their house, sick, dying (everything he had feigned) and how quickly the constable, the corporal, and the friend had come with her.

Yumí, his eyes drenched with tears, intimated that he was crying with pleasure at having found her, but his store of tears was dropping down one after the other as he looked down at that travesty of a woman, whom he told in his stupor that he was the richest man in Quiavicús, that he had a beautiful mansion, and that he had remarried.

"It doesn't matter," she answered, resigning herself to her fate, and the Zabala woman seemed to be speaking from the ground, little dwarf that she was, "take me with you, which is what I want most, and since you tell me that there are a lot of people in Quiavicús, we'll pretend that I came with one of those Gypsy tribes and they abandoned me and you will tell your wife to adopt me as your child."

Everybody who was taking gold out of the cribs was amused by the small steps and gestures and the movement of the long arms of the dwarf who said her name was Juana Puj. But the gold began to peter out and news was going around about gold deposits in the effervescent mountain, the white mountain that the wind was carrying away, and everybody went there, followed by the little dwarf, who had been seized by an old mustached pirate with a clump of black moles by his right eye.

Yumí did not know what to do. He was left once more without his real wife.

"Go offer that bad man this jewel," said the Mulata and she took off one of her rings, "in exchange for the dwarf girl. I need someone to amuse me and dwarfs are evil, but they're funny."

Celestino could not believe his ears, but the Mulata repeated the command and he did not stop until he had reached the pirate. An emerald ring? Take her, she's yours, I give her to you.

And Yumí, sad in that heart of his which was already paining with so much feeling, gave his hand to his little wife, who lifted up her beautiful eyes tiny as flea bites from her small size and looked at him thankfully.

"Here she is." Yumí returned home with the little dwarf and trembled as he turned her over to the Mulata. "She really does make you laugh, she's funny."

"The first thing I'm going to do is dress her up like a doll," she said. "Blue on Monday, yellow on Tuesday, green on Wednesday, red on Thursday, white on Friday, pink on Saturday, and all colors on Sunday. What do you think?"

"Fine." Yumí opened his lips, barely able to talk, distraught at seeing his little wife converted into a toy for the Mulata, all because of his fault, because he had got mixed up in a deal with that devilish Tazol.

"But not just her dress. Shoes and everything will be the color that matches each day, just like the bows in her long hair. And I'll make up her mouth and eyes. What's your name?" the Mulata turned to ask the little dwarf who at that moment was smiling up at Yumí.

"Juana Puj."

"No more of that ugly name! How terrible! From now on . . . let me think . . . your name will be Lilli Puti, for Lilliputian. And now I'm going to give you a bubble bath—you'll like the nice feeling of the bubbles, a lot of people don't know how they feel—and I'll perfume you with aromas that will make our friends the perfume makers happy."

61

Yumí bit his lip. Living together, not being able to talk to her, his real wife, changed into a toy, a diversion, a doll in the hands of his other wife. Hearing his Niniloj being called Lilli Puti ...

But if he was suffering in his self-esteem, greater yet was the redoubled affliction of his fears. Fear that the Mulata, a vandal by nature, and with no law except her own whim, would tire of the little dwarf and her clothes and would smash her somewhere, beat her, or punish her, as she did.

After a few weeks of changing her little dresses, giving her bubble baths, perfuming her, combing her hair with aromatic oils, she locked her up in a closet and there the unfortunate living doll would have ended her days if she had not stuck her nose close to some holes that had been opened by huge moths, gigantic moths that had perforated the wood with the rapidity of a drop of fire.

Yumí, who had called the moths to the aid of his miserable wife, tried to complain, but the Mulata, jaundiced right up to her paste-colored corneas, raised his hair with her threats: "Be careful with me, golden skeleton, because I can start the amputations any time now, and as for that dwarf, take her if she's good for anything, she can help in the kitchen or in the laundry, I'm sick of her and I don't want to see her again!"

And she added in a more pleasant voice: "I'm going to buy a bear. They're more fun than dwarfs. Some circus people who are around offered me one, and maybe I can train it and it will be able to help me quarter the golden skeleton."

Yumí pretended not to understand, but he knew that the Mulata, ignorant, ambitious, and perverse, would prefer his golden bone structure over any other kind of wealth.

Heavy-hearted, he took the dwarf out of the closet and handed her over to the cook, an old woman with a corrosive look who, as soon as the master had left, picked up a piece of firewood and threatened to throw her into the fire if she did not behave, because dwarfs, may the evil eye fall on them, are the devil's spiders. Lilli Puti, your name is Juana Puti!

The woman who ground corn, kneeling by a three-legged

stone, took pity on the midget and told her not to be afraid of the cook because she was a drunkard who was drunk most of the time, and that her way of cooking was to offer prayers to certain wizards so that the meal would cook all by itself and just the way her employers wanted it. The one who does the cooking, as I have learned from dreams, from what the other servants say, and from the way the cat raises its back when footsteps and the noise of pots and blowing on the fire is heard around here, without anyone's seeing a living soul, is the former cook. She spent her whole life here and they found her dead one morning. But she didn't stop serving just because of that. She stayed on without pay, like all the souls of the other world who help us, who give us a hand working for the bosses. I too, at my millstone, have a soul who helps me, the soul of my mother, who was also a corn-grinder.

"But a dwarf," the corn-grinder went on, "what soul can she have to defend and help her, because now, according to what the bosses say, no more silk dresses, no more little velvet shoes, you will have to work: clean the henhouses, the bird cages, feed the monkeys, and play with the mistress's bear that used to play with a dwarf in the circus."

A washerwoman, the one who washed in the afternoon, reeking of water, with more dreams than actual hair, would amuse herself by putting the dwarf up on her back or her shoulders while she washed. She would play piggy-back and amidst her humming and the wheezing from the breath that would escape from her lips sometimes, she would tell her that she did her job happily and without getting tired because of the soul of an aunt who had also been a washerwoman and who helped her with her work.

"They all have a soul to help them," the little dwarf complained sadly in the ear of that good woman, bouncing along on her back while she washed. "Everybody has a soul to help her except me."

"There must be some other Puti," the washerwoman answered her, her wheeze eating out her lungs, dead tired at the end of the afternoon, her hair hanging over her forehead, freezing from the water, reeking with the smell of pig grease.

"Another dwarf? But I was the only dwarf in my family," said the one who was none other than Catalina Zabala, even though at night she would weep when she woke up and heard from some place in that same house a voice that used to call her Niniloj, near the one that had named her Lilli Puti, even though among the servants she had become Juana Puj again.

A horse spider, something between a toad and a spider, between a spider and a newborn child, wrapped up in sleeping hair, driveling, hairy, climbed the roof which kept the sun off the washbasins.

Lilli Puti drew back, as if that horrible creature was going to drop on her, and she gave a little cry.

"Don't be frightened, little dwarf," the washerwoman said. "I have an idea that that's the soul that looks after you!"

The dwarf closed her little eyes so as not to see that from inside the spider's sharp-kneed legs his glassy eyes encased in small bloody cartridges were peeping out, two infinite drops of light in a body of darkness.

"Aha!" the other one said, with a serious laugh, fearful of having found the truth, of having found the soul that favored the dwarf. "Aha, you hadn't told me, but what better defender, what better guardian to have than a horse spider!"

Juana Puti, as she was known among the servants, those who did not like her, slipped on the mud of the wash stand, bent over from so much washing, and started to run, while the spider spun around rapidly, disengaged himself from the roof, and chased her for a good piece.

And like spiders and mice, dwarfs prowl through houses at night, and the little dwarf girl, the transformation via a clay shepherdess of Catalina Zabala, being nothing less than a curious woman interested in knowing what was going on in a certain bedroom, as soon as the help was asleep, would come out of her den, spending the night among cats, dogs, pigeons, and rabbits, and would slip along through pipes and drains, slipping here, holding on there, so as not to make any noise as she stepped through a broken skylight that would give her entry, until she came to the parlor leading to the master bedroom.

She knew the house like the back of her hand from when she had gone around dressed up like a doll and she went so lightly that she barely paid any attention to the striking clock with the pendulum-clapper, every minute a resonance and every hour the mournful bells that made big-eared little devils like her raise their hands, hands with very long fingers, on which they would tearfully rest their shiny faces, with hard horns and beards and smoke-carved brows.

Why did the Mulata call that moving hulk the Clock of Babylon? Did the time counted out by that monstrous clock serve her as an aphrodisiac?

Every minute a resonance, as if every minute were really the end of everything.

"It's the end of the world!" the Mulata would shout. "Why not take advantage of every free minute that passes by with lovemaking!"

The bells would puff up their sleeping metals in a sonorous splendor which would leave an inalienable emptiness behind in the atmosphere, a sort of deafness in a cavity without acoustics.

Could that be time? Could time exist? Would it not turn out to be the emptiness felt when the bells in the Clock of Babylon stopped ringing?

The Mulata rode horseback in the morning and in the afternoon she played with the bear. The beast would stand on his hind legs and dance to the rhythm of flutes played by blind people, blind people from the vicinity, while, naked, she would jump around the bear holding a tambourine with golden jingles.

And those absences, whether she was racing across the fields or dancing in the gardens with the bear, would be used by the dwarf to speak with her husband, whom she was seeing less and less of for fear that they would be discovered.

Celestino Yumí, the all-powerful, the richest man in Quiavicús, would lock himself in his room to get away from the people following him, the ones that the Mulata had put on him, afraid that he would drop dead and that someone else would get his golden skeleton, and he would call on Tazol, but there would be no answer.

"Take away your riches! Take them away! Take them

away so that the Mulata will disappear from before my eyes and I will go back to being what I was, a poor woodcutter on my own place, with my dear wife back to her normal size!"

Squander his fortune? A useless effort. The more he spent, the more he had. Get rid of the Mulata? How? Hadn't he given her oil of *chiltepe* root, a deadly poison, and she hadn't even had a stomach-ache? And hadn't he pretended that he was cleaning a shotgun and given her a blast of birdshot full in the chest and she had barely stirred?

"Celestino," the dwarf told him, "this wife of yours, just so you should know, does not have the *prefections* of a woman, but neither does she have the *prefections* of a man. You have to know that I goed to spy on her, while she was taking a bath, and she isn't a woman, because she isn't a woman, I guarantee you, if I know my prefections, but she isn't a real man either, because she doesn't have your prefections, which I also know."

And having said that she rubbed up against Yumí.

"You mean to tell me that she's a . . ." Celestino swallowed the word.

"I don't know what she is, but she isn't a man and she isn't a woman either. She doesn't have enough inky-dinky for a man and she has too much dinky-inky for a woman. Since you've never seen her from the front . . ."

"Who says so?"

"I do. These eyes, Celestino. We dwarfs see everything. And how ashamed you be—your face and ears are all red!"

"It's true. She only gives me her backside."

"That's it. There's your explanation!"

"Never her face."

"I'm not telling you anything new, then."

"She explains to me that the moon also does it that way with the sun, that because of that the moon always has her back turned, we never see her face, because if she were to turn around the sun would take her from the front and they would breed monsters."

"That may be so. But the moon, from back or front, we know is a woman, and this Mulata of yours . . ."

"Don't call her mine, Niniloj, don't call her mine! Don't offend me for no reason! She's not mine, she was forced on me by the desire for a woman and the liquor I had in my head and the damned money I was carrying in my wallet, which was what she loved up to!"

And after a long silence, during which she played as if she were playing a piano, running her little fingers over the knuckles of her husband's fist, the latter murmured, "And what can we do then if she's neither a woman nor a man! What a son—or daughter of a bitch! What can I call her? Even there something that's not a man or a woman gets everything mixed up because a person doesn't know whether it's masculine or feminine."

"You went to school and you know all about those fancy things of masculine or feminine. And the more I think about it, the more I say to myself: What good did it do you to go to school if you ended up as a woodchopper? None. They taught you how to read and everything else you learned and then there wasn't anybody to help you any more. Just the opposite, you telled me that when you went looking for work as a farmhand and if the bosses heard tell that you knew how to read, they would send you away and not give you any work."

"Well, if I can still remember, there's a gender that's neither rooster nor hen, the neuter gender . . ."

The thump of the footsteps of a large animal announced the proximity of the bear. The Mulata was following him with a basket full of apples, oranges, mangoes, medlars. The dwarf disappeared in a flash, not before she promised Yumí that she would do the possible and the impossible to get him away from the Mulata.

"Poor thing," Celestino remained pondering, "what can such a defenseless thing do against a woman who is all-powerful because of her limitless cruelty!"

And when she (or he) came close, Yumí thought: not a man and not a woman, what can she be?

The day gave no indication of the storm that would come that night. At dusk the Mulata began to smoke her maddening smoke. She was smoking and sipping drinks of an amber liquor which she later changed for a sweeter one, pale violet in color.

Smoke and drink were turning her into a fury, Yumí was trembling. His flesh was trembling, as if that trembling were the preview of the blows, the lashings, the loving pinches that she would doubtless bestow on him. But it was not to be with him. There was someone else stronger and she woke up the sleeping bear with her whip and began to punish him furiously. The unfortunate animal threw himself back, blinking, pawing, and little by little he rose up on his hind legs, and with his feltlike front paws he tried to contain the rain of lashes that was beating on his face. Finally he sprang. It was horrible. He jumped as though he had no weight, the way a house leaves the ground during an earthquake, tossed into the air all of a sudden, and he flung himself at the Mulata. She, with her beast's teeth bared and her eyes closed, kept on beating blindly, curled up to defend her face against the wild animal who was tearing at it.

Yumí watched the battle between the Mulata and the beast without knowing what to do, his nostrils fluttering from anguish, his heart in a fist, wanting the bear to get it over with. Intervene, defend her . . .

The dwarf jumped out of the Clock of Babylon just as the bear was about to finish off the Mulata, one of his paws sunk into the neck of the person who was twisting with pain, pleasure, it was hard to tell, and she jumped on top of the white beast and said something in his ear.

Something like "Bear, do you want some sugar?"

A bear is always a child. The sound of "sugar" disarmed him and he turned like a child to stick up his snout so that the dwarf could slip a lump of sugar in between his teeth and onto his tongue.

Yumí ran to pick up the Mulata. He carried her to her bed. When she sensed him near her she grabbed him by the hair and made him stay there with her. She was complaining, but they were laments of pain and pleasure, of suffering and delight, of wounds which awoke in her the desire to be possessed (m. or f.). Yumí tried to get away from the Mulata's bloody hand—drops of thick blood sprinkled his face—but he could not manage and even less when along with caresses, laughter, and tears she broke

68

into complaints about her fate as a stray dog, a dog who had no owner.

The surprise of the servants, of the chickens, the cats, the ducks, the turkeys, the rabbits, the pigeons, the dogs, the cats in the courtyard where all of that Noah's Ark was sleeping was great when the dwarf slipped off toward her den with the bear, who before lying down gave a few turns, trampling on those of the small animals who did not flee in time, and on even more of them when he set his big behind down to stretch out with the sugar in his teeth, tired, vexed, with the breast of a sad beast.

The Mulata rewarded Lilli Puti for having saved her life. She made her come back from among the servants and once more dressed her up in a different color each day and in all colors on Sunday, bathed her in perfumed soap bubbles and played with her like a doll.

One night the Mulata, while she was inhaling that smoke that smelled like lavender and made her like a sleepwalker, asked Lilli Puti to pierce her arms with a large hat pin.

The dwarf barely pricked her, afraid that she would make her furious, but the other one, it seemed, asked her to bury the point of the pin deeper into her flesh. And then deeper, and then deeper . . .

"I want to feel," the Mulata shouted. "I want to feel!"

Blood gushed out of the pricks, and she did not feel anything, demanding that the dwarf, whom she pinched a little, pierce her stronger and deeper.

"Someday you'll come with me," Lilli Puti said in her ear, "to a cave that only we dwarfs know about, and there they really know how to pierce and make people feel indescribable things."

"Where?" asked the Mulata, not giving it any importance, her dark eyes fixed upon another idea.

"Where the moon goes to sleep during the day and where, while she irons her clothes which have already been washed by the dew, she is naked and you can see everything she has of a woman about her mixed up with her goatish virility."

The Mulata brought back her distant eyes, forgot about

69

the pricks—her arms and legs were bleeding—asking the dwarf, so that she could hear better, to pass the pin through her ear lobe, from one side to the other, because hearing without feeling was not hearing.

The other one did it and while she was perforating the lobe of gilded ebony the Mulata asked her: "And how do you get to that cave?"

"How do you get there, you say? Well, it's just a matter of getting there, if you go with me so you won't get lost and so they'll let you in. It's a cave in a mirror."

"A cave in a mirror . . . You must mean underwater." And without waiting for the other one to reply, she added: "Let's go, but pierce the lobe of my other ear with this other pin, look, it has a head of precious stones."

And then she proposed to her: "Don't you want to try some of my smoke?"

"No, ma'am, because as soon as I try it I begin to laugh and laugh and laugh, until I cry from laughing, without stopping my laughing because of that, I go on laughing, on and on until I can feel my teeth getting loose."

"And would today be a good day to go to the cave?" the Mulata inquired, her ear lobes bleeding, just as if she had ruby earrings on, and her arms and legs were also bathed in blood.

"I think so," replied the dwarf, "and we can get there along the path your smoke is making."

"But what will the moon say about me when she sees me with these ears pierced by pins, my hands and legs also pierced. She'll think I'm some kind of insect."

"She'll think that you be sacred. And she won't see you, because her face is turned opposite the sun. We dwarfs hang on her back and climb up to her shoulders and her neck, but we can't climb down on the side of her breasts or look at her from the front. And those who have tried it have been thrown out into space."

"And why is the moon only seen from behind?" whispered the Mulata sleepily, drawing in a great mouthful of smoke from her cigarette.

"Because with her back to the sun, he can't make babies with her. God save us from that, if she turned around

70

and was ready to lie down with the sun from the front and have babies, well, they would be monsters!"

"Dwarf, you speak as if you were a big person!" She got up laboriously. "Take me to that mirror cave, but help me walk, I'm as heavy as a stone."

And she began to laugh, until it seemed as if the dwarf would be chewed up between those teeth that were being moved by that interminable laughter and hung as if they were loose in the air, as if all the air were laughing along with her.

Lilli Puti served as her cane. And there they went. The Mulata dressed in an interminable laugh, the pins stuck in her ears, her hands, her arms, her legs, wounds from which a red laugh also felt like bursting out, laughter made from drops of blood.

"Well, this is the cave," the dwarf announced at the entrance to a cavern, "but we're not going to go in without first gathering up the feathers of the Grumpy, the bird who lives off bad moods, so upset that he tears out his feathers as they grow and that's why he always goes around plucked."

Among the rocks as the high clearness of the night was wetting them with a very tenuous light, they found some black feathers that had a few white strands along the edges.

Lilli Puti picked them up right away and told the Mulata, who was no longer laughing but silent, funereal, hanging her head, just like someone who had been accused: "Now I'm going to put a feather from the Grumpy Bird in your hair—your hair is very beautiful, it shines like black water—and let's go inside the cave where since there is no moon today she is sleeping with a white back, not white, golden, like lemon-colored clay, the color of your back."

They went in.

"We've come here to see you," mumbled the dwarf, while the vision of the curled-up satellite excited the Mulata, with all the smoke that was still wandering around through her head, through all the paths in her brain, until it made her think that the round piece of sky there could be whipped like the bear, and she took off the feather from the Grumpy

71

Bird, and with the feather she began to whip the moon, then she drew out the pins and stuck them into her, and dug in her nails which became filled with melted ice. The moon did not wake up. The dwarf, having sensed what would happen—people who inhaled that smoke fought with the moon whenever they had her within their reach—ran out of the cave and with the help of Celestino, her husband, covered the entrance with stones and more stones and then with earth and more earth, and then with trees and more trees, until they made it look like a vegetable cheek on the hill, where before it had been sunken in.

"I'm going to get my weapons ready, in case she gets out and tries to kill us," Yumí volunteered.

"She'll never get out," the dwarf affirmed. "Between the smoke and the moon, who could get out? Roll up your pants because we have a long way to go, we have a lot of walking to do."

"Shall I carry you?" Yumí proposed to Catalina as he looked at her, the size of a small child.

"Don't ever insult me like that again, a terrible insult, Celestino, because all you do is remind me that I'm a dwarf, and that hurts me very much because it's your fault that I'm a dwarf."

Yumí was quiet and went ahead in shame, followed by that tiny person, and he heard her say: "She'll never come out again and we're going to enjoy your wealth in peace. I want you to buy me a pony. I'm going to have a little house built for me, just my size, with furniture and everything just for me."

"But I won't fit in it."

"You can crawl inside."

"And what can I do inside? And how can I have you?"

"Didn't you ever rape little girls?"

"No, never. What a question to ask! Lord, what a question!"

"Well, that's how it will be with me. But here we are just like the Mulata who never talked about anything else."

"And what else could she talk about, wretch that she was?"

"Well, she's going to die in there from smoke and moon."

"Did she have enough of the plant?"

"Three bags full."

"Then, Niniloj, she'll die in there."

"And she's going to die like all addicts, alone and in the dark. In a few hours the moon will have to go out again to sail along like a little ship."

"Alone with her smoke inhabited with laughter, facing strange nightmare visions reflected in mirrors where it's just as easy to see a giant as a dwarf."

"Lilli . . . putian like me?" she said sarcastically.

Yumí comforted his wife, telling her that he loved her just the same, that he did not see her as a dwarf, but just exactly the way he had seen her the first time he had met her. He explained that we only see people one time, the first time we see them. After that we no longer see them or look at them any more. They become invisible for us. Oh, if he could only make himself understood.

"You're consoling me, Yumí, but because I'm a woman I'm ambitious, and more than your words—why should I hide it?—your riches console me. Why should I care if I'm the way I am, a dwarf, as long as I have the whole world at my feet?"

When they reached home, they sat down to a table set for dinner, and they had to put some cushions up so that the new, the real wife of Yumí could make her head reach the level of the plates.

The servants of the house could not get over their surprise. Just like a fairy tale. The cook swore and swore again that she had never called her Juana Putí. Her *nahual*, her guardian spirit, is a spider the size of a chick, the washerwoman explained.

The dwarf grew restless. On the silverware, on the blades of the knives, on the curve of the spoons, a strange magnetic light was shining. The moon was coming out. The new moon. The little boat. It was a golden fingernail spread around a shadow.

"Do you see her, Yumí?" his wife asked, pushing away the spoonful of soup that she had raised up to her little mouth.

Celestino gave in before the evidence.

The Mulata. The back of the Mulata. That was the shadow that the moon was carrying.

"Yes, yes," he affirmed, "it's her back, the only part I ever had of her when man and woman share their best knowledge."

"There's no more need to worry that she'll come back, Celestino Yumí. Put away your weapons and tell the guards they can rest."

"I'm afraid that when the moon goes back to sleep, after the full moon and the waning moon, then the Mulata will escape from the cave. She's a terrible creature."

"When the moon lies down to sleep, the pitch-darkness will blind her and she wouldn't find her way back even if she managed to escape from the cave. Besides, I intend to leave her a stronger plant that I know where to find."

"Very good. Tomorrow, while you're looking for the plant and bringing it to her, I'll attend to my affairs. They're so out of hand that I'm afraid they'll pull some other worthless stunt on me: burning the cornfields after the corn is harvested."

The dwarf, with a sack over her shoulder, set out the following day for the cave, and with the help of the Grumpy Bird exchanged the plant in the bags she had left for the Mulata for a stronger and more delicious plant.

And Yumí filled his cribs with corn leaves, hopeful of increasing his capital to the maximum, so that he could flee with his real wife in case the Mulata escaped from the cave and he could take them all along with him; but what was his disappointment to find that they were no longer changed into bank notes, those leaves of dry *tazol*.

He understood. His protector would no longer help him because he had imprisoned the Mulata, and he had to be content with what he had, always happy that his old friend Timoteo Teo Timoteo was being consumed by envy, almost speechless, at knowing that he was rich, and his friend would pout when he saw him pass, as if he had a pain in his stomach.

"Have you got me in your insides, you pout so much when you see me," Celestino asked his friend one day.

"No, old friend, I've already passed you." And he laughed. "I've already passed you out of my insides!"

"You really got the better of me on that one! So you can

74

go ahead and laugh and still think I'm the same fool I was before, because when I asked something foolish like that, you came back with a good answer!"

The visit to his friend did not end well, however. Don Timoteo Teo Timoteo threw many things up to him:

"Very strange, friend Celestino, everything that happened to you since that festival in San Martín Chile Verde, do you remember, when you went around with your fly half open and half closed. Yes, ever since then so many abnormal things have happened, without any explanation. The disappearance of your wife, God keep her, because I think the hurricane carried her out to sea, but even that, old friend, doesn't it seem strange to you, that disappearance of your wife, dragged off by a windstorm? And excuse me if I seem to be counting your ribs, but there are accounts that have to be drawn up. Then, looking for your wife, that dream in which you heard her say that she had fallen into the white mountain, that mountain that the wind is carrying off and now is nothing but a dwarf mountain . . ."

When he heard that, Yumí shook all over, without his friend's noticing it as he went on talking.

"Instead of finding her you found a large bag of gold coins, and you became rich even beyond your find, because it might have fooled other people, my friend, but not me, not me, because I'm rich too and I know what things produce. How you became a millionaire with just that bag of doubloons! And then we went to the fair and you ran into the Mulata, and you married her in a civil ceremony—when has something like that ever been seen, your being a Christian?—and then the two of you spending in grand style . . ."

"Land produces when it's helped along with good fertilizer." Yumí attempted to interrupt to stop that litany of reproaches from his old friend.

"Land really produces when it's being fertilized by magic, friend, and only then can it produce so much that a person can spend without limit."

"And . . ."

"And nothing, old friend, because everything about you is very mysterious. Now you say that the Mulata took a

75

trip to Europeland and that she left you a bear and a dwarf girl at home. Yes, yes, Celestino, it all makes a body want to cross himself."

Celestino gave a little forced laugh at what was so obvious. The strangeness of his life and everything that had happened since his pact with Tazol.

He had traded his wife for wealth, even though it now seemed that he had begun to undo the pact.

The dwarf, mistress of the house, stopped the pendulum on the Clock of Babylon, whose tick-tock reminded her of her nights of waiting, hoping for the Mulata to go to bed so she could spy on how she lay with her husband.

The bear had been on her side from the beginning. The beast did not find that diminutive being strange. In the circus he had been friends with pygmies like her.

And every new moon the dwarf took care to carry fresh plants to the Mulata. Sometimes she heard the laughter of the happy mad-woman. Grass for the Mulata and golden grains of corn for the Grumpy Bird who had been converted into the guardian of that cave walled up like the cheek of a mountain. Only a pygmy could have slipped in where she did, just like a horse spider, completely without shape in his movements. Inside she would climb from rock to rock without the Mulata's noticing. Marijuana smoke, the laugh of a happy woman, and the eternal speechlessness of the moon filled the cavity, and when the satellite, so beautiful, went out with her back turned, the Mulata had fun watching the face of the sun, hoping that some time the moon would go out frontward, so that he could possess her as is ordained.

One time the Grumpy Bird did not want to let her by. The few holes where the dwarf had gained access to the cavern were walled up. She put her grownup's ear, a huge ear for her size, to the rocks, anxious to hear what was no longer echoing inside, the happy laugh of a madwoman, and she climbed up to whatever airhole she could find to test the air that came out from inside and she could tell from sniffing that it no longer smelled of marijuana smoke but of the fresh smell of the earth.

She became alarmed and in the absence of her husband, who was going about his properties on the coast branding cattle, she went up to the bear and standing on a ladder she poured out her anguish into the ear of that white personage, complaining to him of the disappearance of the Mulata who had escaped from the cave, where she had had her imprisoned with the enchantment of the smoke that made one drunk and the moon that bewitched.

Moving his head from side to side like a mechanical toy, the bear considered the gravity of the news. For the little dwarf, for him, for everybody. From one moment to the next she would show up at home, after having eaten the Grumpy Bird.

"When I was there nothing had happened to Grumpy," the dwarf explained.

But the bear, uncurling a snort, thought that the Mulata would end up coming out and swallowing the featherless bird, feet, beak, and all, increasing her annoyance by it.

The dwarf, aided by the bear, closed up the doors and windows with stones and mud. And in a dark hallway, ready to give battle, the bear with his teeth and claws, and she with the pendulum from the Clock of Babylon—she could barely lift it—they waited for the imminent appearance of the Mulata. The idea was to blind her so that she, in darkness then, would ask for smoke, thinking that she was still in the cave.

The little dwarf laughed. "We'll give her some straw from an old broom and we'll really laugh so that she will know that there's such a thing as a real laugh."

Celestino got down from his horse, startled to find the house all closed up. But quickly, without anyone's telling him, he sensed the drama of the Mulata's escape from the cave.

He left his horse—the atmosphere was like a mirror—and ran shouting toward the doors.

"What's going on, Catalina?" And without waiting for an answer, he added: "Has she come back?" All the muscles of his face paralyzed to such a point that afterward it was hard for him to get rid of that mask of fear and terror.

Catalina got down from the haunches of the bear, just like a flea, and sought refuge in the arms of her husband. Yumí lifted her from the ground and pressed her to his face like a young child.

"What's the matter, old girl, what's the matter? Why is the house all closed up, why were you running away with the bear?"

"Oh, my husband! The Mulata got out of the cave, she ate the Grumpy Bird and we're afraid that she'll be back here at her own place any minute now."

"You were wise in closing up the house, but let's not stay here. We have to run away into the woods. The only thing left here are the trees. Can't you see? The servants are running away too."

The bear, after a snort and sniffing on the ground, ran away with leaps and bounds.

"What's going on?" Niniloj asked, clinging to the neck of her husband just like a small child.

Celestino Yumí did not know what to answer. He had lost his speech. He was looking for his tongue. Not only had the servants fled but also the field hands, and they were fleeing with everything they could save from their houses: their tools, their clothes, their chests, their mats, their hammocks. And then, after the peons, in a river of movement, the animals fled, and behind them all the Clock of Babylon, from which there had emerged tick-tock, tick-tock, tick-tock feet, the feet of time are the quickest for flight. And behind it there fled deer, wild pigs, monkeys, coatis, jaguars, wild cats, tapirs . . .

Yumí, with the dwarf on his shoulder, hid his face from the dampness that burned as it came, as if it were rather a snuffed-out glowing of the sun. Then the burning of the air became unbearable. It was the Mulata coming back. There was no doubt about it. The moon was in its splendor, lighting up the fields, the river, the peaks, the few clouds that were fleeing across the sky. And in contrast to that blue peace which was coming from on high, to that golden peace raining down from the moon, under Celestino's feet the earth shook with a long stretch, as if it were waking up.

Trees, hills, valleys, everything on the unstable surface of land that was being converted into the waters of a wrathful sea, everything that could not be sustained was pouring down in apocalyptic masses, the pillars of the house like the legs of a drunkard, the roofs were on the ground with a thump and the walls had cracks that were opening and closing, falling into pieces, while the cornices wavered just as if the earthquake had become a serpent and was running along over them.

Dust and silence. Moon, dust, and silence. Moon, dust, heat, and silence. The breath of oven fire, the red satiety of fires which stained the horizon garnet. The heat was increasing. The leaves began to be singed. The immobility of the trees was tragic, their impossibility of escape and fleeing from the flames. The Mulata was coming back. There was no doubt about it. The Mulata was coming back. Where could they take refuge? Danger was all around them. Catarina, on Celestino's shoulder, was looking at everything with the eyes of a monkey without salvation. Yumí knelt so as not to fall when the oscillating movement of the earth turned it into the bucking of a horse being broken. The earth was trembling, with dull, unending echoes. A torrent of hot rain. The last howl of a dog. A fissure that was opening and closing. Another one that stayed open. The earth was swallowing up the trees. Nothing, a clump of woods with age-old trunks and branches would disappear suddenly in an opening and closing of the earth. And nothing, the dust. Fissures, rumbling. Rumblings from the immense stones of the river as they rolled along like grains of sand. The Mulata was coming back. There was no doubt about it. The back of the full moon was turning everything gold. Everything was beginning and ending with every shake of the earth, with every tremor. Until dawn. Soft rain. A sunrise, without the trill of birds, in the desolate silence of death, without the bleating of sheep, without the crow of roosters, without the barking of dogs, without the lowing of cows.

It would have been better if it had not dawned. Where was the green of his fields? Where were his potato patches that reached to the horizon? Where were the corrals, the orchards, and the little cornfield with dwarf plants just like Catarina, and down below the extension of cane fields, and up above the coffee groves and rice paddies, everything that a glowing shadow was covering little by little, like the huge shell of a half-liquid tortoise.

A hundred sobs came from his chest. The peons came

to tell him that the hot lava had buried everything, without leaving anything alive, a boiling wound which when it cooled was hard as rock.

The Zabala woman, who was sleeping half in a faint, dead with fatigue, awoke with her husband's sobs.

"Did the Mulata come back?" she managed to say when she came back to reality.

"You can bet she came back! Damned Mulata, I never did know what her name was!"

"What about the bear?"

"Well, he's right here too," Celestino answered heavily; those questions in the face of the great tragedy showed that dwarfs also have little brains. Asking about the Mulata and the bear when they were completely ruined, with nothing except what they were wearing.

The sun was driving forward in search of green in what was now lava and ash, desolation, the quiet of a black steppe, cracked where the earth had reached the height of a hill or had dipped into rather deep gullies.

Ash and lava. Old friend Timoteo Teo Timoteo had died under the weight of the wall when Quiavicús fell down, a city that had been wiped out. The river changed its course, coming closer to what had been the village. Sand beaches in the shape of a half moon, without the enormous stones that had rolled away like feathers with the push of the earth that was sinking like a hammock or bucking like a horse, up and down, down and up. The path of the lava was hardening everything.

"You would have been better off living with the Mulata, you would have kept your riches," the Zabala woman pronounced out of her smallness, but in her voice one could feel the falseness of her words. Nothing made her as happy as having triumphed over the Mulata, even though the Devil had carried everything off.

Celestino forbade her to speak like that.

"The Devil didn't carry off anything. We lost everything in sight of our own eyes because of that volcano that is growing up where our house used to be, and by the quantities of lava that it threw out."

"Well," the dwarf argued, "I won't say that the Devil carried it off, but I will say that the Mulata did."

"It's the same thing," Celestino was on the point of answering, but he repented in time; that dwarf was already making him talk more than he should.

"And now," the dwarf reflected in her insides, which were the insides of a grown woman and not those of that smallness, "until God wishes us to have a house again, we won't die, we'll hope, first that the volcano will stop growing—it's so high already—so we can know where to build our place and live with the bear."

"Why with the bear? We can sell him."

"Absolutely not. The bear saved me from death when we shut up the house with stones and mud and it began to tremble and part of the roof fell in just before you came back."

"I'm not ashamed at having been away, of having left you all alone, even though you were in trouble. Thanks to that little trip I managed to sell some cattle and bring back some money."

He sank his hand into his pocket and immediately frowned. Instead of bank notes he felt something like dry corn leaves.

He took it out, without saying anything to his wife. Blasted corn leaves instead of money.

"Did you throw away what you brought back?" she asked, drawing him out of his difficulties without knowing it, because she made him give a quick explanation of what was unexplainable within the logic of things, just as he had been told by his friend Timoteo, dead in the earthquake.

"Yes, I dropped it somewhere. Riding so hard to save us. It must have been when I took out my handkerchief."

"But there's a sound of bank notes in your pocket."

"They're corn leaves."

"And why are you carrying them?"

"In case I had to do my duty."

"You threw away the money and you kept the leaves to do your duty with! When God takes away, he really takes away."

"But he'll give it back," Yumí exclaimed, thinking that he could make peace with Tazol, "and in the meantime we have our road ahead."

"That's what we have left."

81

"The road and the bear."

"The road and the bear and me."

"Why did you say that?"

"Because we're going to earn our bread with the bear and with me. You used to be able to play the harmonica."

"You don't forget things like that, but why should I play it?"

"You will play and the bear and I will dance in the main squares, at fairs, and that's how we'll earn our bread."

"That's how it will be, while we earn enough for me to buy my ax and go back to the forest to cut wood."

"Yes," the bear answered the dwarf, with his head, so happy that he finally left it hanging down, as if he were looking for something on the ground, her, no doubt.

"And do you know, Celestino, how you will announce the show? Like this: 'Ladies and gentlemen, young people and old, children and parents, you are about to see the dance of the Clock of Babylon.' "

The bear, as if he had understood, began to move his head from one side to the other, like a pendulum, and the little dwarf began to run from one side to the other, in time to the bear's head, repeating gracefully: tick-tock, tick-tock, tick-tock . . .

They went along roads and through squares and a few coins fell their way when the dwarf, after her dance with the bear, would pass the plate, gathering what each one's heart told him to give.

They bought a larger and deeper-sounding harmonica, they put a beautiful collar of live-oak leaves around the bear's neck, roses and bells around the bear's neck, all made out of paper, and one fine day Celestino came back with the ax.

"Let's go back to Quiavicús" was what he said, showing the ax to his wife, happy with his woodcutter's face, his back hungry to carry its good burdens of wood.

The dwarf cried and said to him: "If you go back you won't cut wood but snakes."

"That's not nice to say, but you've said it and let's find out."

Quiavicús, half rebuilt, received them with its new

houses, and in the countryside, the only thing that had changed, besides the beaches along the river, was the new-born volcano, converted into a tall, peaked, and disdainful important person.

"I have my deeds," Celestino said to his wife the day they arrived, "and I can claim that all of that volcano belongs to me."

"Do you still want to be rich?" she asked. "Don't forget that your ambition left me this way, this size, because of your ambition I was carried off by the hurricane and changed into the little shepherdess in the crèche and that's how I've remained, much to my misfortune."

"But, Catarina, who can ever understand you? Didn't you say that if I start chopping all of the trees will turn into snakes on me?"

"That's what I said, but it's better to chop down snakes than to be rich again, claiming that the volcano belongs to you and beginning to plant on it as long as it lets you, because it's still throwing off lava."

Yumí spent a good day in the woods. The leaves had not recovered their greenness, their springlike shine. They seemed condemned to an eternal autumn, toasted and life-less, and the trunks and branches still seemed burned.

With the first blow of the ax something black came out and spattered him, just like blood. Because of his doubts he went up close to see if it were not a rubber branch that he was chopping, but no, it was simply a carbonized tree, and when he shook himself there was no stain; he had been wet by the sound of a black laugh.

He remembered Tazol, the Mulata, and he went away from that tree that was laughing, was making fun of him, to look for another trunk; he could not go back to his place without his good burden of firewood.

He struck, but the ax sank as if it were in animal fat, not hard wood, and all the branches trembled, and each branch, all eyes, turned haughtily in search of who was hitting the tree.

Right there he forgot about his ax and he did not stop until he got to the dwarf and the bear. They were sitting down waiting for him. Coming in and telling them that they would go back on the road was all one thing. The bear stood up on his hind legs and applauded with his paws. The dwarf jumped up to kiss Celestino with her little lips, and the three of them, on their way already, stopped on a small rise that overlooked Quiavicús to look at it for the last time.

The Fly Wizard and the Boar-Men or "Sauvages"

One night while they were preparing to bed down under the ceiba trees in a large square, who could tell whether out of fatigue from a long journey along the bed of a dry river—sand bars, stones, dry grass that wrapped itself around their feet—or from remorse, since Celestino had confessed to his wife what he had never told anyone, or, if he had told it, never in such a thorough and raw form.

"I traded you to Tazol for riches on that cursed night when I played sick so that you would go call the constable, the soldier, and my friend. Tazol snatched you away and everybody, from the most important people down to the most humble, went out searching for you. But you really had disappeared and only I knew where you were, that is to say, that you were with Tazol, without knowing where and it hurt me thinking about how he had told me that he was going to punish you for having been unfaithful to me with our deceased friend Timoteo Teo Timoteo. But my wealth was of no use, I swear to you, no use, because I was desperate knowing that you were lost. And the only thing left to do was hang myself. I didn't do it, even when I had the rope tied to a tamarind tree with the noose all ready, Tazol appeared before me with a big box which had inside everything that I had had ambitions for all in miniature, and among all those many things, a little clay shepherdess that looked like you."

Yumí's words were like pitch bubbling out of the darkness, an interior blackness pouring forth, like a death vomit, and the ears of the little dwarf were soaking them up as she had the feeling that she was hanging in space, deaf, mute, ready for nothing. After a long silence a curtain of tears separated her from her husband, and she felt very far away, in the infinite loneliness of a being who knows that she has been betrayed.

Yumí stood up; he had been squatting. The resignation of the dwarf, who did not complain about anything to him, motionless, nailed into her joints, was unbearable for him— Ninilojita!—and he went off to look for a palm branch to sweep around where they would sleep, to drive off the evil spirits. And in spite of the sorrow with which he moved away from her, as he moved he felt relieved, without the weight that had been crushing him while he had kept it all secret.

"Bring me some dry twigs over here," his little wife asked him with a trace of bitterness in her small voice, "because we have to build a fire and heat some coffee."

And those sips, those first sips of coffee that they took facing each other, Yumí will never forget as long as he lives, and who knows but that he will still remember them when he is dead.

Catarina was drinking her coffee mixed with tears and he, almost unable to breathe, with the sadness of a condemned man, his lips unable to part, his mouth refusing to drink. But the need for something hot in that most bitter moment made him sip, and the more he drank the more full the clay receptacle seemed.

"We have to dance tomorrow," she said, but it would have been better if she had slapped him the way the Mulata used to. Only once, when he was cutting down a live-oak tree and it had hit him on the back of the neck with one of its branches, stretching him out on the ground like a toad, had he felt pain like that.

"I'm going to feed the bear," he answered, and he went off with his big cottony feet that tickled as if from ants, a feeling that was so certain that he lifted up one foot to see if they really were ants and not that inner tickling of cowardly blood.

They lay down, unable to sleep. They were part of what did not sleep at night. But closing one's eyes and stretching out one's body was enough.

"Watch out, there must be a 'sauvage' roaming around here!" Celestino said to his wife, but she did not answer him, and he added in an upset tone: "There must be 'sauvages' around here."

Fatigue and sleepiness conquered them. And when Celestino awoke the "sauvage" was almost on top of them, not because of them but because of the bear, who was already awake and about to leap on the strange apparition, an animal with hair like the teeth of a buck saw, little near-sighted eyes, short stubby ears, and two long tusks, one on each side of his snout.

"Sauvage!" Yumí scurried from under the covers, without the dwarf's feeling him. "You're not going to fight with my bear, you're going to talk to me right out."

And the Sauvage, who likes conversation with men because he seems to be able to fall asleep with it and get over-stuffed with a unique sweetness, immediately forgot about his quarrel with the bear, and both of them, as they drew apart, raised their hair and growled.

Sauvages are men who had been dancing disguised as wild boars to the rhythm of huge drums. While they danced they would drink corn liquor by the bucketful, a drunkenness that did not affect them by making them keep on falling down and getting up until they lay stretched out on the streets, but by making them jump and jump, higher and higher, which displeased Tazol and he enticed them to the sealed mountain where, poor fellows—they were unable to remove their disguises as wild boars and so they remained that way—and they bred their children that way with the wild sows that Tazol had given them.

"And what shall we talk about?" the Sauvage asked Yumí, squinting his little eyes beneath his black and wiry bristles. His two tusks, one on each side, seemed to be laughing at Yumí, with a laugh that ended in a point. The moon had its sad laugh that was round. The Sauvages had their laugh that ended in a point.

"Oh, Sauvage," Yumí sighed, "there are so many things

86

in this world that need to be cleared up, and Sauvages know so much more about them than men do!"

"I smell chicken!" The Sauvage sniffed, his head already raised and his nose moving around.

"Don't get the taste for chicken now that you're about to chat with me, Sauvage, and I'll promise you a hundred good hens if you get me out of a pinch I'm in with someone who is our common enemy."

The Sauvage acted as if he did not understand, even though he was quite aware of what Yumí was insinuating, more intent on the smell of chicken.

And he could not help himself. He left Yumí and went jumping off into the shadows up to a courtyard which he entered without making the slightest noise, holding his breath. Yumí went after him—how could he miss the chance to talk to a Sauvage?—and quicker than one could count, the hairy tusker decapitated three hens and got ready to swallow them with great delight, feathers and all.

But the dogs had awakened, and along with the dogs the owners, and when the Sauvage with one leap jumped over the fence beside the chicken yard, there they found Yumí, who after receiving a few blows on his back and head with the flat of their machetes right there as the owner and his three sons beat him, and being bitten by the dogs, was tied hand and foot and hauled off to jail as a thief.

The jail was one of those large crates in which merchandise from overseas is shipped. It was set up on a corner of the square with a grating for a door, through which the prisoners and the authorities entered and left.

They locked him up in there. The sons, machetes in hand, stood guard as sentinels so that the fellow would not escape while the father went to wake up the Mayor, so that justice could be done that very night. It was the custom to make quick riddance of chicken thieves, especially since this one had been caught in the act of eating them, feathers and all, a terrible outrage.

"Oh, my sons, my sons," the father exclaimed before going to call the Mayor and while he was locking up the grating with an enormous padlock, "eating a chicken feathers and all is pretty close to eating a person clothes and all, and the way we're heading, if the people in these parts keep on getting hungry, some day they're going to eat us all up!"

He made some other tremendous prophecies, like all old men, and ended up shouting, already on his way to where the Mayor lived, who was probably asleep.

"If the law refuses to do me justice, I'll take this damned fellow out and give him a bath in a vat of boiling soap, not just to take off his hair but his skin too, and that's how we'll teach chicken thieves a lesson."

The sons, while the father was coming back, walked around the box that had been set up as a jail where Yumí, hardly recovered from the blows he had received, was not lamenting his own fate, but the abandonment in which he had left his wife, that little dwarf whom everyone wanted to lay hands on and carry off home for their amusement, and the orphaned bear, who without them was destined to end up in a circus or a zoo.

"Huimi-huim! Huimi-huim! Huimi-huim!" Strange howling like that could be heard in the distance, then something like a bumpy kind of galloping, and still later the falling of something very large as it was dragged up to the edge of a precipice and let drop below, where it bounced around as it landed.

Yumí did not have time to reflect on anything. Beating about from one side to the other in the large box which was his jail, he barely had time to bend at the waist and put his head between his knees. But the crash was so great that when at last he was motionless, he was scarcely able to tell whether he was still alive.

Had it been the owners of the chickens who were planning to roll him deeper and deeper down into the canyons, jail and all, until they had finished him off?

And while he was meditating, aching right down to the roots of his hairs, he felt around for whole pieces of his body, fearful that something might be missing, because it was all bruised, his bones almost broken, his knees and elbows scraped. Fortunately no, he was whole, and he began to breathe with pleasure, if such a thing could be said in that extreme situation.

Suddenly he hunched over and buried himself in a corner,

88

horrified at thinking that sharp machetes were cutting through the boards, ready to do him in. But no. They were tusks. And by means of a rather large opening through which a man could pass, the Sauvage had him come out, the one he had accompanied to the chicken yard and through whose fault he was there.

"Flee! Run along that road!" the Sauvage warned him.

"I can't run away! I'm not going to run away," Yumí resisted, "because back in the square where you came last night I left my wife and my bear."

It was still the same night, but to Yumí it seemed that centuries had passed.

"They're all right, your wife and the bear. The one who's in danger of being cooked in soapy water is you. So run away up there and hide in the Sauvages' corral."

Grandmother Ha and the Hayumihahas

It was dawning on the mountain of the wild boars. A sun soaked in indigo, a land soaked in blue. Crags covered with blue-greenish lichens on which the tusks of the Sauvages had drawn capricious signs. Could that be their way of writing? Did they keep their annals in those drawings made with the tips of their tusks?

The Sauvage who had freed him, accompanied by an army of Sauvages, turned to follow him, went behind him, and as soon as they arrived, he introduced him to his relatives and friends gathered there that morning. An old wild sow, long-tusked, her two tusks in the shape of half moons, they were so old, thanked Yumí for having saved one of her grandchildren from death. The human smell had attracted the dogs, who forgot about the Sauvage smell. Besides, wild boars can fool dogs because they give off a pig smell.

"And before that," the young Sauvage said, "he stopped me from fighting with a bear."

"Well, because of all this I want you to leave me alone with him. What's your name?" the wild sow asked when all the Sauvages had left.

"Celestino Yumí," he answered without being startled that wild boars could talk, because he knew that it was a matter of dealing with human beings who because of their drunkenness had been condemned to remain with the disguise they were wearing.

"But," the grandmother sow added, "this is not the best place to converse in. I'd rather we went to one of the rooting places. It was abandoned some time back, but the dampness of the soil, where leaves and flowers are rotting, makes me feel better."

The sharp head and the narrow body of the great wild sow opened a way through the solitary thickets up to the rooting place, where she invited Yumí to sit down on a stone. In the distance one could hear the fighting of wild boars as they ran among the trees, jumping, rooting around, playing with the disheveled golden shoats, shoats so small that they had no tusks as yet.

"I can get a whiff of your misfortune," the grandmother sow said, "but ours is greater, dressed in this heavy, thick, dark brown skin, and always chased by hunters who like our flesh, not knowing that they're eating human flesh while they enjoy it grilled over a fire or cooked a thousand different ways."

Yumí's eyes clouded over with tears.

"Oh," exclaimed the long-tusked sow, stretching out her neck and shaking her ears, "if I could only cry! There are two things that we can't do no matter how human we may be—laugh and cry. My grandchildren at their parties shake their teeth, their tusks, and they imitate laughing, but how far that animal rattle is from real laughing, the soft laughing, the strong laughing of men, and as for crying, long ago, when I was a young girl, I used to prick my eyes to feel the water running down my cheeks and pretend that I was crying."

"What I do know," Yumí managed to say, more and more worried about the little dwarf and the bear abandoned in the square, "is that wild boars are very sociable."

"And that's why my grandchildren dare go to town, because like all who are young, they like contact with people; but they always run into bad luck, because they get hunted down or caught in cruel traps. But let's talk about your troubles."

"There's no way out of them," Celestino lamented, a little nauseous from the pig smell of the rooting place.

"We'll find a way out," the wild sow said, "just as long as you stick to my advice and swear here, by putting your hand on my right tusk, that you won't tell anyone anything."

Yumí, not without apprehension that the sow would bite him and that it would cost him his hand or part of his fingers, swore just as she had asked him to do.

"Very good," the old sow went on, "now get a thorn. There are a lot of them around here. There's one. And prick your upper lip with it and take that blood—a few drops are enough—and paint a red dot on your forehead and paint another red dot between my eyebrows."

And that was done too, very laboriously for Yumí, who was dying from lack of sleep, his bones and tendons aching, his face mashed in, one hand that he could barely move, and a foot that felt as if it had been unscrewed from its angle.

"We are sworn now, the man Celestino Yumí and the sow-woman Haularahaha by name. In our language, when we speak like human beings, the words have the particle 'ha' placed in front and two 'ha's' at the end. For us your name is Hayumihaha."

And after a brief silence: "But, of course, Hayumihaha, it's a question of having power over Tazol, the all-powerful. Of getting your wife, Hazabalahaha—last names are already gibberish by themselves; that's why we only call people by their last names—to be once more what she used to be, to leave her dwarf state behind and change into a normal human being."

Yumí, in whose ears the Hayumihaha was dancing around, promised the long-tusked sow, great tusky old woman, great old grandmother, that if she could work that miracle, he would change his name, adding the "ha" and the "haha" of the wild boars to his last name.

"My grandson, the Sauvage you met last night, went to a

91

good Christian friend we have near the village to ask him to go to the square and bring your little wife and the bear to his house. We will become friends and we will all live together. And who knows but that we may be able to cross the bear with a sow. How beautiful a bear-boar would be!"

"How kind you are! Taking care of my wife and the bear. How kind you are!"

The grandmother, after other circumlocutions—old people turn things over a lot before saying what they have to say, some turns in their heads, turning over themes that do not fit the case, some turns in their hearts, stringing together sentimental memories pulled out by the roots, until they finally turn loose what they are going to explain—when she had finished finally gave Hayumihaha the secret by which his wife could return to her natural size. He was so happy that he could not speak or thank her, and she put him in the care of a young sow who was betrothed to a Sauvage with bristly hair that grew even between his teeth and his tiny eyes, grayish, humpbacked, and she took him to the house of the Christian, where he found the little dwarf and the bear, safe and sound.

"Let's go," Celestino said, "let's be going," anxious to be able to put into practice the secret that the grandmother of the wild boars had given him so that Catalina would no longer be a dwarf.

"Yes, let's go," the Hazabalahaha woman answered him, "but first you have to thank the man who brought us from the village and put us up here in his house, hiding our tracks from people who were looking for us to throw stones at."

"Sir, good friend of those noble beings that are called wild boars . . . "

"Sauvages," the Christian corrected him, "and there's a good deal of difference. A boar-boar is one who always was a boar, but these others are Sauvages, human beings who remained forever dressed in the costumes they had once used in a dance."

"Sir, friend and companion of the Sauvages, God will have to repay you for the favors you have done us, because we are so poor that all we have is this tambourine and this flute."

When they left the place, the dwarf was no match for Celestino and she asked him why he was in such a hurry.

"Hurry," he said with husbandly ill-humor.

And the three of them went along a main road, bumping into loaded carts, empty carts, ox-drawn carts, wagons pulled by mules, men and women on horseback, Indian bearers with their burdens on their backs, woodcutters with loads of chopped wood on their backs, lumbermen who were carrying great long logs of wood between two or more of them, women with baskets on their heads, packs of stray dogs, flocks of birds that flew from one tree to another, and different colored soil, red soil with the smell of iron, white soil in rough clods, and greenish soil.

They walked all that day, they went through two towns, three towns, and at nightfall they were still walking. It seemed like madness to Catarina. All that walking and walking without any apparent direction.

Still, she did not complain, she did not want them to stop because of her size and her little steps, she had to take many for each step taken by Celestino or the bear, and who only knew where they were going in such a hurry!

The bear began to limp until he could not walk any more and he stopped, lifting up his front paw to Yumí, who without a word removed a thorn that had stuck in it with the point of his machete.

And they stopped there. It may or may not have been a coincidence that the bear had picked up a thorn in that place. For Yumí it was the sign the great Sauvage woman had told him about; they were already on the mountain that was called "The Devil's Turns" and there they would stay to sleep.

The little dwarf wrapped a piece of rag around the bear's sore paw while Celestino ran to gather enough wood, lots of wood, an unusual amount of wood, for the bonfire to warm the coffee and the tortillas.

The dwarf became alarmed at that great bundle of wood. It was too much. She wondered if he were planning to burn her or burn the bear. And in answer to her questions, Hayumihaha explained that there was frost in that place and it got very cold at midnight.

93

"But so much wood . . ." The Hazabalahaha woman could not get over her astonishment, and when she heard herself called that she asked Celestino to tell her why he was using that gibberish he had learned among the Habas now that they were about to go to sleep at the spot where the famous mountain of "The Devil's Turns" began to rise.

"Because of the favors they did for us," Celestino answered, "I swore that we would add a 'ha' to the beginning of our last names and a double 'ha' at the end. And the things that are going to happen will explain it all!"

"So much mystery!" the little dwarf complained, because how could she hold it in if her husband had traded her for riches once, might he not be up to the same thing this time?

The bear prudently withdrew from the blinding glow of the bonfire, the huge fire whose golden tongues of flame were looking for him and to which he playfully replied from a distance by sticking out his tongue and wiggling it in time.

"And now we'll put the coffee, we'll put the tortillas, we'll put the jerked beef on there."

"It's all going to get burned!" the dwarf shouted at him, jumping like a pygmy but not going near the fire so he would not push her in and roast her all at once. He was capable of wanting to bring her back in normal size out of her ashes, according to some words that had escaped him, that was what he was after.

But Celestino had already thrown everything on the bonfire, and in an instant the food was turned into ashes.

"Oh, Lord," Hayumihaha began to wail, "what will become of us, we haven't eaten for days!"

Since he was complaining like that, the dwarf no longer said anything to him, a stupid man deserves a silent wife; and then there appeared along the road a man of medium height with a bundle on his shoulder.

He stopped to ask them what was wrong and Celestino complained about what had happened. The coffee had left the pot as if volatilized, the tortillas and the jerked beef had turned to ash, they had nothing to fill their bellies with and they had not had a bite for days.

"You were wrong in spending the night here," that farmhand told them, "because in these 'Devil's Turns' many demons appear. Try, now that you have nothing to eat, nothing to fill your bellies with, to quiet your needs with some sleep; by sleeping you can eat, by closing your eyes you make hunger go away. Go right to bed and cover yourselves with your good blankets, because those demons turn people into ice, turn them into skin of ice, hair of ice, fingernails of ice, feet, hands, head, ears, nose of ice which fall into pieces, and they carry Christians off once they're shapeless like that."

The Hazabalahaha woman proposed going on, leaving that terribly unlucky place.

But the newcomer, squatting down with his back to a leafy *guarumo* tree, laughed and said: "Poo-poo, leave here at night? Impossible! I don't know whether you know where you are, but it's a much longer way back than going on ahead, and I advise you not to move away from your bonfire, it's better to bundle up well in your blankets and you won't have to worry that way."

"We don't have any blankets," Celestino explained, "because they took everything away from us back there in the town. Bad people in that town. They left us just with what we're wearing."

Hayumihaha tried to identify the farmhand with Tazol and there was no way he could. Not in his voice, not in his appearance, in no way did he look like Tazol. He was, simply, one of those storytellers who went along the roads looking for someone to talk to.

"Well, then, you'll have to cut some leaves to cover you up in your sleep, and also a lot more wood so that the fire doesn't go out and keeps you warm all the time and so that you won't be in the dark not even for a minute, because in the darkness you run the risk that the stone that made these nine turns will come rolling down from up above, run over you, and kill you."

"Is there such a stone?" trembled the dwarf, not so much from the cold which was beginning to show its teeth as from fear.

"Yes, there is," the farmhand answered, taking a piece of

95

wood with a spark crackling on the tip to light a cigarette that glowed in his mouth underneath his large mustache. Afterward, after lighting his cigarette, he said: "And didn't anyone in town tell you?"

"No one," Celestino said.

"They're very wicked! That's worse than stealing your clothes, because what's going on here can cost you your hide and your soul!"

Two smoke oxen came out of his nostrils and, while he savored the sharp aroma of the tobacco, he explained: "There isn't much traffic around here at night for fear of the stone. Because, as I told you before, suddenly it starts rolling downhill and finishes off anything it meets—trees, animals, people. That's why you can see so many broken pines, so many dehorned trees, broken rocks. And that's why these nine turns are also called the buzzard's turns, because that stone kills a lot of animals and many people get killed, and buzzards feed on dead meat. They have banquets around here."

"What misery!" Celestino sighed.

"But once it's down below, after rolling down from up there, how does it get back up?" the little dwarf asked.

"Ah, child," the farmhand lamented, "that's the saddest part! In order to get back up it turns into a man."

"Then is it a stone or isn't it?" Celestino made two question marks out of his eyebrows.

"It all depends. When it's a stone it's a stone; but when it's a man it's a man. And it was the thing that made these nine turns so that the Devil could play in them to his heart's content, could play hide-and-seek nine times, because I don't know if you noticed that every turn is a hiding place, the one ahead hides a person and the one behind also hides him, and you have to count them as you go along, because if you don't, the Devil, rascal that he is, might add more turns."

"Hayumihaha, you're a wild boar," Celestino muttered under his breath, "and if you're a boar, haboarhaha, why can't you tell whether this fellow is just a storyteller—one of those farmhands who because they are always wandering around alone along roads and through the woods, as soon as they see a fellow man they come over to talk—or whether it's Tazol?

"Moonteeth the wild sow informed you that a man would appear around midnight and it still isn't midnight, and that the man would be the guardian of the Devil's nine turns."

"Excuse me," the other one said when he finished his cigarette, "I didn't offer you a smoke because I don't know whether you want to fall asleep. I do, that's why I'm smoking. It puts my thoughts to sleep outside and it wakes them up inside. And here, as you can see, with a cigarette you have to give the Devil his nine turns of smoke, then the angel his seven smoke rings, and knock off the ashes from the end of the cigarette with your little finger so that the earth can have its taste, which it has for burned tobacco scales."

"Well, we don't smoke," Celestino hastened to say, not because the three of them, he, the dwarf, and the bear, did not really like tobacco, but for fear that Tazol would use a trick like that to put them to sleep.

Moonteeth the wild sow had warned him that if they fell asleep the guardian would carry off both of them and the bear.

But now that grandmother of the Sauvages, tusky and kind, was so far away that when fear emptied his chest and he felt his heart in the emptiness, his only consolation was to call upon her: "Grandmother Ha, help us! Grandmother Ha, defend us! Grandmother Ha, for my little wife who has suffered so much from Tazol, don't let him take us, let us be able to do this time what you promised me on the health of your hahgs!"

The dwarf, curious and imprudent, was doing a lot of talking to the stranger and she ended up asking him the secret of that stone that turned into a man and that man who turned into a stone.

The other one, after lighting another cigarette, his large mustache covering his lips that were like those on the snout of a wild boar—sometimes he looked like a Sauvage with black tusks—began to tell the story. The bear was dozing and Hayumihaha wondered whether that farmhand might not be someone sent by Grandmother Ha to look

97

after them. He rejected the idea. How could he trust what could be seen in that world they were in, where Tazol could disguise himself with those mustache-tusks of a Sauvage in order to carry them off and lose them in a hell worse than the one with that certain Mulata.

The Devil's Nine Turns

The farmhand, blowing the smoke of the Devil's turns out of his nose and from his mouth, his lips shaped like a funnel, the angel's rings, rings of white smoke that took a long time in breaking up, told the story:

"A lustful drunkard of the worst kind would always come back through these woods from his binges and carousing, complaining that he was a man. It would be better to be a stone!, he would repeat with every step he took, better to be a stone so that everything would slip over me and nothing would bother me! His name was Felicito, Felicito Piedrasanta. How strange life is, being named holy stone, the one who was going to end up being the Devil's stone! That's how it was. And for many nights he would shout through the woods: 'Why should only my last name be stone and not my flesh, my bones, my whole being? I would stop being a man, and I would be happy doing honor to my name!' Whip in hand, Cashtoc, the earth devil, appeared to him one very dark night dressed as a foreman, and without giving him time to flee or defend himself—drunk and all he was still dangerous because he was always armed—began to whip him until he left him stretched out on the ground and even then he kept on whipping him, although the Evil One tried to have the lashes fall in places where even if the sharp pain shook him he would not lose consciousness. And when he had whipped him for almost three hours, he pierced him with: 'Felicito Piedrasanta, do you want to be a stone?' And the fellow, his flesh torn by the lashing, bathed in sweat and blood, in saliva and tears, in the filth of leaves and sandy ground, dragged himself away, fleeing from the punishment, and answered yes, that he did want to be a stone. In that way, Piedrasanta said to himself, even if he beats me some more I won't feel the lashings. And he turned into a stone on the spot.

"One afternoon it was very hot, and the stone, with the deep voice of the living dead, began to complain about what he was, and mutter that it was better being a man, a thousand times better, because a stone got bored lying there and never leaving the same spot, not being able to move, bored and annoyed at watching all of nature living and dying, the trees growing, the animals breeding, the branches blooming, as they bear fruit, as their leaves fall off, the water flowing, the birds flying, and the animals walking with their feet on the ground, enjoying their freedom.

"'Ap! Ap! Ap!', Piedrasanta-turned-to-stone complained.

"'Ap! Ap! Ap!', an expression that must be 'oh! oh! oh!' of stones, calling on his torturer, asking him please to bring him back to human form.

"'I don't want to be a stone any more, no, no! I'm sorry, and for all that you must hate me, because I don't think you love anybody, I'll give you my soul, I'll turn it over to you, but bring me back to my real nature! I'm bored, I'm terribly bored with being a stone, without being able to yawn or stretch, having to conform not only to my boredom but to the boredom of the layers of dust that are petrifying on top of me and which are leaving me more and more inside, with little contact with what I used to sense was going on around me!'

"The Devil came up in a storm—it was hard to tell what kind of laugh was filling his chest, a laugh of black shavings, because it could not be seen coming out between his teeth as at other times—and he gave the stone an enormous kick, and that was enough for Piedrasanta to emerge from it.

"But as soon as the unfortunate drunkard was face to face with his tormenter, an earth-colored devil armed with a huge whip, his voice trembled and he said to him: 'If you're going to hit me, it would be better for you to turn me back into a stone, because then I won't feel the lashes.'

" 'It's not a matter of that,' the Devil answered him, 'I won't hit you, but I'm going to have you build me a road with nine turns in it from here to the top of this mountain.'

" 'But how can I do it all alone if you don't help me?'

" 'I'll help you with the tools, all sharpened and ready, so get to work or I'll whip you.'

"Felicito had no other choice but to start the job, but they say that when he finished the first turn, every time he hit a stone with his sledge hammer to split it, there would come out of his chest an 'Oh, how lucky you are to be a stone!', with no strength left to begin the second turn. Dead with fatigue, with no food except roots and leaves—the trees didn't have any fruit on them—he threw himself on the ground and began to shout that he had been better off when he was a stone.

"The Devil did not even bother to appear. Immediately Felicito began to feel fat, hard, and heavy, his vision clouded over, his hearing sank into a great silence and he was changed into a stone once more.

"But Felicito, who was a larger stone now, became tired of his weight and with his drunkard's voice—all he had left was the voice of the great drunkard he had been before, a holy calendar drunkard because he drank on Sundays and feast days of obligation and belched liquor on the other days—began to beg the one whom he no longer could tell whether he was friend or enemy—the Devil is both, friend and enemy accordingly—that he make him a man again and that at once he would begin the second turn in the road. The Evil One, anxious to have that malefic route where so many souls would get lost later on, came, kicked the stone, and Piedrasanta appeared.

"Beside him, alas, Felicito found brand-new tools. What seemed strange to him was the loneliness of the place. Nobody passed by there. Someone he could tell about what had happened to him. Someone whom he could ask to go to town and have nine consecutive Masses said for him, because in that way perhaps he could frighten off the one of the nine turns, now that he was about to begin the second one.

"It was harder than the first one, not only because of the

rocks and crags that he strained his lungs on breaking up, but because of the softness of the terrain which had to be filled in with his shovel. At the end of that second turn, feeling that he was dying, he thought about his great refuge and humbly, humbly, with the fading voice of a dying man, he implored the Devil to turn him into stone again and that he would remain stone.

"The other one did just that and Piedrasanta entered the mineral repose of a legislative session. He had made his request while standing, and on dropping down, dead with fatigue, he no longer could move, he was already stone. But this time something had gone wrong beneath his hairy hide and there remained in the sliver of his brain the fingernail of a thought which allowed him, even though he was the roughest of minerals, to think that he could not stop being human, even if he were a stone, a duality that to the great surprise of the blue powers of the Devil obliged the latter to return him to his condition as a man without being asked and whatever happened would have to happen.

"But this time, brought back to his being by the force of his own thought—the universe surrounding him had the smell of a festival about it—he was the master of a strange energy, notwithstanding the threats of the one who was demanding, whip in hand, that he start work on the third turn.

"Felicito heard his thought tell him not to worry, that it was going to help him and that with a calm heart he could begin his work without fear. What did happen was that it illuminated him inside and made him, instead of working primitively, take steps to make the job easier; he used a lever to move the boulders, but misfortune is always around, and when he began to sweat—there was no other explanation—he lost that little piece of thought that had been left in his hard head and then there came a general hardening, to such a point that when he finished the third turn and considered the six that were left, he stopped, motionless as a rock. Better like that, turned into stone for time immemorial.

"But during a banquet of hearts of yellow birds which the Barn Owl, in the company of the Seven Owls, had served Cashtoc, the red-earth devil, the latter confided to the owl that at the end of that third turn in the road where they were there was a statue that was human inside, a stone, a rock that was a man, the same one who was building the road, and he asked him to go and disenchant him.

" 'And how shall I do it?' asked the Barn Owl, basking in the pleasure of talking to the red-earth devil.

" 'Roosting on that stone, you will say that if underneath your feet, underneath your feet that are crosses with claws on them, there is a man, that he come out, and when you feel him move you will advise him, as something that belongs to you, to begin the fourth turn, since in any other way he will not become either man or stone again; I'm getting quite tired of his drunkard's whims, not knowing what he wants, whether to be a stone or people.' "

The farmhand who was telling the tale to Yumí and the dwarf excused himself for not going on with the other turns so as not to tire them, but he could not be silent, he told them, about what happened to Piedrasanta on the last turn, because between the fourth and the ninth, five times he became a stone and five times he got back his human state. The seventh turn was one of the most bitter. He could not divert a brook that during the night would wash away everything he had done during the day. What could he do? His refuge was to turn into an inanimate being, except that this time he was turned into a stone for almost a century.

"But I was going to tell you about the last turn," the farmhand said, without taking his eyes off the dwarf, which meant to Yumí that he wanted to carry her off. "Now that he was on the last turn, the earth devil had given more freedom to Piedrasanta since he was already finishing the work, and the man took advantage of it to summon the deer. As soon as the first one appeared, Piedrasanta asked him to go to the nearest village—nowhere is too far for a deer to go—and to beg the priest as a favor to do him the great charity of coming, and so that he would not get lost that he take a new road that made eight turns going up the mountain, and that there at the ninth turn, where he now was working, there would be waiting for him, who knows, either a stone or a human being. The deer shook himself as if electrified, electricity of the moon. The great wheel of cold pineapple was about to come out and everything began to be silent. The moon engenders fear on coming out, a fear that is mixed up with the touch of cold one feels when one sees it appear so round and beautiful.

" 'Where were you planning to send the deer?' The Devil appeared before him underneath the lunar light that was bathing his red flesh with the whiteness of bone.

" 'I wasn't planning to send him . . .' Piedrasanta lied.

" 'The deal was,' the other one said, his black horns reaching up to the moon, with his tail wrapped around his neck like a most elegant scarf, 'that when you finished the road for me, you would go back to your village and go on getting drunk and being a stud for women; but you can't trust humans, they're all traitors, some because of interests, some out of cowardice, and others because they have it in their blood. You did it out of pure cowardice, going around looking for supernatural beings to help you, when already with just the work of the nine turns you are about to finish you would have freed yourself from my claws with the lesson that somebody who changes into stone is not any happier. But no, you had to nullify the pact by trying to trick me, and the deer got away from me but the priest won't.'

"A laugh made out of the silver of the moon and the water of a wild river among enormous stones, stones that might have been human beings, was floating in the air around Piedrasanta.

"What could he do?

"He still had his legs and he could meet the priest along the way so as not to expose him to the Devil's anger.

"That's what he did. He put on his sandals and started downhill, which was why he had built the nine turns of the Evil One, and he was the first, the first human foot to run along them. But on the way he turned into a stone and, rolling, rolling with the impulse that was carrying him, he landed in a pool of water, where the road became narrow between some large mango trees. Half of his stone body went to the bottom, but the other half was at the surface of the water.

"And even though he was a stone, the Devil had left him with his senses.

"The priest, riding a mule, rosary in hand, began to climb along the first turn, and the second, and the third of that mysterious mountain, and there in the third turn, when the animal heard the running water, he went over to satisfy his thirst from the depths of a mirrorlike well that surrounded a stone, which was none other than Felicito Piedrasanta.

"While the mule was drinking, circles and circles of water around his nostrils and the noise of a liquid bray, the priest glimpsed a piece of gold at the bottom of the pool. He had his doubts. Maybe it was a reflection of the moon. He dismounted, so as not to remain in doubt, and he looked for a branch, cut off the leaves, and went poking around with it to see if the reflection would be broken. But it was no reflection at all; it was a piece of gold. Felicito, turned into stone, but with his senses, was witness without being able to do anything, and he heard the priest lift up his cassock to step down the bank of that pool of water, roll up his sleeve to sink his arm in and pick up the piece of gold. But what happened—head first and all at once in went mister priest, and soon after, because of the mule, they found out what had happened, and the sexton came, and seeing the lump of gold in the daylight, he also tried to get it, and he was carried away right there, and the choirmaster came, and the bell-ringer, and the same thing happened to all of them.

"Piedrasanta, turned into a stone, heard them first, then he saw them, and last of all he felt them as they rubbed against him before sinking into the current that became lost in a deep cave, the priest, the sexton, the choirmaster, and the bell-ringer.

"The water of the ages was wearing away the stone into which Felicito had been changed. One day some travelers found, as they leaned down to have a drink, a skeleton that was emerging from a large stone. It was Felicito Piedrasanta's. And they tried to carry it off, but the Devil would not let them. The stone and Piedrasanta belonged to him. A man begins to belong to the Devil as soon as he starts to drink. And God can do little against that because during the beginning of the world, the Devil challenged him, warning him that he was going to invent a drink against which divine power would be useless and with which he would be able to ruin anyone he wished. God accepted the challenge. The Devil built the first still out of his horns. And ever since people who drink have belonged to the sweet-cane Devil, because there is nothing that is more destructive to a man's elevated realm, the realm he has locked up in his head.

"Walking uphill, Felicito returned, neither stone nor skeleton—the Evil One has human flesh at his disposal and he had dressed him in it again—with the burden of the priest who had been buried there, the sexton, the choirmaster, and the bell-ringer, all through his fault, but when he reached the ninth turn, he made his wicked friend know that once and for all he wanted to be a stone. The Devil said that he would leave it up to him. You will be a stone when you want to, and when you want to be a man, you will be that. I give you this in exchange for the good road you have built me. And ever since, when up on the top of the mountain Felicito is bored with being a stone, he comes rolling down to the flat; at the first turn he becomes a man. He is the guardian of the Devil's nine turns and he's always around here. You see him as a man at the first turn. He cuts wood, always trees, he fixes the road. But suddenly he becomes bored with being a man and then he starts out toward the top of the mountain and as soon as he reaches the ninth turn he becomes a stone again."

The dwarf was sleeping and Celestino seemed to be nodding, without losing a glimpse between blinks of the person who was masquerading as a storyteller and could be Felicito Piedrasanta, guardian of the Devil's nine turns.

By the heat of the fire, so many coals, so much burning wood, so many flames, so much stubborn smoke, the person with the story lay down to sleep with his back to the dwarf, more likely to feign sleep, with his shirt lifted up in back to warm himself.

Celestino measured the distance between his wife's little back and the broad shoulders of that intruder who was sweating a viscous mixture of mistletoe and pine pitch, ready to follow the advice given him by Moonteeth the Wild Sow, Grandmother Ha, if the prediction were to come true.

When he has her back-to-back and tries to carry her off, you will grab her feet so that he cannot seize her, and

105

put all your strength into it until you get her off his back.

And it happened. With the half turn that the Devil's turner gave, he picked up Catarina, whom he clutched to his back, the instant in which Celestino, calling on the wild boars as he grabbed his wife's feet, had the presence of mind and strength enough to get her loose, get her loose, get her loose. And between the one who was struggling to carry her off and the one who was trying to keep her, the dwarf grew, stretched out, recovered her size, and when finally she got away from the back of the one who was rolling downhill, turned into a huge stone, she had come back to her normal size, she had stopped being a dwarf.

"Celestino!"

"Niniloj!"

They did not say anything else. In the midst of their joy she fainted, burned, skinned. Her back was one big open wound from her shoulders to the base of her spine. What could he do? How could he extinguish that livid coal? Cobwebs? Compost? Another care that would embitter them. The Devil's turner, unable to carry her off, stuck his stone back, that of a huge rolling stone, to the back of the bear and carried him off. Cobwebs and compost they used for flesh. They settled into a lean-to built by Yumí, who was helped by a milky reptile with green eyes that would paralyze his prey with hypnotic force, and he managed to catch rabbits, armadilloes, badgers, small animals they could feed on. Water. Ears of corn. Crickets. The convalescence was long, very long. The rapid growth of bones, muscles, tendons, nerves, everything, left her lying like an invalid night and day, and while new skin did appear on her back as it healed, it was as if the mud and cobwebs had remained under her skin, and there appeared there in a bas-relief of huge scars the face of the one who had tried to carry her off, Felicito Piedrasanta. They had to get out of there. They made themselves ready. A hammock, a jar, a pair of saddle bags, some rope, what they always took with them.

"Since I have to watch out for you as we go, covering your back, you go first," Yumí said to his wife; what was certain was that he was doing it so as not to lose sight of the face of the drunken Devil that she was carrying around

106

uncovered, because since her blouse had been burned, she could just manage to cover her breasts with a piece of cloth.

Going uphill, where they intended to reach the summit by passing through the Devil's nine turns, Yumí said: "The scars came out bad."

"Why do you say that?"

He did not reply. She did not know anything about what was happening on her back.

They climbed all morning, and at noon, about ready to reach the last turn and get over the summit, Celestino noticed that the face stamped on Niniloj's back had become jovial, smiling, mocking, and he was frightened.

"Let's not go on," he shouted. "At the ninth turn there we'll find the man turned into stone and he won't let us by!"

They turned back, and as they got closer to the first turn, as they were finishing the second, the face tattooed out of the flesh and skin on the Zabala woman's back was frowning, as if it were pouting, as if it were about to cry.

"Let's stop, Niniloj, let's stop," Yumí proposed, short of breath, "it's dangerous to go on; there by the first turn we'll find the one taking care of this Devil's road changed into a man! Remember that up above he's a stone and down below a man!"

"But if he's up there, he can't be here."

"Ah, we don't know that!"

What could they do? They climbed and descended without deciding to go through the first or the last turn, and, when fatigue got the better of them, stretched out on the ground, they could hear the steps of a man who was climbing and dragging his feet or the rolling of an enormous stone.

"Niniloj, I'm not crazy."

"Then what's wrong with you the way you talk to me from behind as if I weren't myself, as if you were talking to somebody else?"

"I can't explain who I was talking to."

"And I can't explain what I feel when you talk like a crazy man the way you were."

"But it's not being crazy, Niniloj, it's not being crazy."

"If you say so, then it's not."

"And what do you feel when I talk like that, when I talk as if there were somebody else between us?"

"I don't know."

"Try to think about it."

A Cabalistic Escape Through
the 9 of Destinies

They returned to Quiavicús strange and old. They seemed eternal. To those who wanted to listen, they explained how, in order to avoid the vigilance of the guardian of the Devil's nine turns who had them trapped, they had waited until he changed into stone and had rolled down eighteen times and climbed up on his own two feet in the shape of a man twenty-seven times. Between number 8 and the smoke (one), which add up to 9, Yumí had slipped off toward the summit through the last, the highest, the ninth turn, and between number 2 and the lid (seven) trips, which also add up to 9, Niniloj slipped off toward the valley through the first turn, going backward, arse-backward, on the advice of her husband, who, without saying why, recommended that she sneak out *recula reculorum,* he knowing (she had not and could not see herself from behind and he had not told her about it) that the Piedrasanta that was still painted there from the shoulder blades down would open the way for her. The magic music of number 9. If they had not managed that cabalistic escape by means of small numbers, Yumí would have had to have waited 162 years and escape from the nine turns by the 9 that those figures added up to, and Niniloj 243 years and also flee by the 9 that the figures added up to. Storytellers, they said in Quiavicús. He cut and sold wood and she, in a lean-to they had set up, bought corn and beans with which to sustain themselves with the little money that her husband earned. They had no ambition for anything more and when some curious neighbor woman would ask them if they wouldn't rather leave that place, they hastened to answer in one voice no, they were happy there. But they were old now, as some saw them, to work the way they did, but in compensation they had no children, that is to say, they had no compensation. But they had good answers on the tips of their tongues, and they answered that if the years were visible outside, inside their form was very young. But you don't even provide yourselves a good life, they would be told. And they would answer right off: A good life is life and nothing more, there is no bad life, because life itself is the best thing we have. You don't have any chickens, someone else would propose. Why should we, to eat? That's what they're for, but since we don't eat chicken, we don't need any, why chickens? And a small pig of theirs to fatten. What for? To sell him. Oh, but if we can't have one, we can't sell one! That was how they would go on, then, the man, old now, gathering wood, and the woman, old now, taking care of the hut. Why, of course, that's how we'll go on. That's why these villages don't progress, because everybody is like you, they're happy with what they have, which is nothing, and with their future, which is no future at all. Yes, maybe that's why, but we're already too old for progress, that's for young people, not people our age, progress. Sucker-fish, that's what you are, suckers! Yes, that's what we are. And lucky that you live off your work. That's what we live off. But you don't pay any taxes. No, we don't pay any. And don't you have any money put aside? No, we don't have any money put aside, we don't have anything. With us, as anyone can see, what we earn from work we eat. You don't even buy clothes. No, we don't buy clothes, we're fine this way, just the way we're dressed, with clothes that get old on our bodies. But here, according to what they say, a great plague will come some day and you'll die if you don't bathe, if you don't change your clothes. Well, yes, that plague will probably come and we'll die. Our time will come. And the worst is that you'll contaminate everybody. Yes, the worst is that we'll contaminate other people. They'll have to burn down your home, it's so dirty, with a dirt floor, no place to take care of your bodily necessities. Well,

109

we'll go somewhere else if they burn it down, and we have the woods for our necessities, why have a special place if the whole forest is for that? How old are you? We most likely can't remember. I'm very old and my wife is very old. I'm older than my wife. Were you born here in Quiavicús? Yes, right here. Did you get married here? Yes. All this information is for the Town Government. Yes, that's what it's for. But don't give answers like that. If we answered any other way you might get angry. We don't have any words of our own, and that's why we repeat the words people speak to us. Please . . . No, it's not because of pride. Then because of fear. We don't have anything, but since what people say who talk to us is nicely said, we repeat it. Are these really your names: Celestino Hayumihaha and Catarina or Catalina Hazabalahaha? Yes, those are our names. Did you live among Gypsies? No, we lived among wild boars. All of a sudden it's the story of Romulus and Remus, except that it must have been a wild sow who fed you with hog milk. Yes, that's how it must have been. But do you know who those historical figures were? No, but the one asking the question comes from the authorities and he knows it and that's enough. In this world it's not necessary for everybody to know everything. A few know and the rest are satisfied with listening to them. Do you have birth certificates or some paper that certifies that those are your names? We don't have any; during the earthquake in Quiavicús the roof of the church fell in on the priest's books, and we were buried there. That's why we don't have any birth certificate or any other papers. And are there neighbors who know you? There aren't any; they're still too young and we're already old as the hills. Did you live in hiding and is that why nobody knows you? No, we didn't do no hiding, but when you get to a certain age, going from children to grandchildren, the grandchildren no longer know who you are and they don't care, and then you stay away out of sadness. But just think how talking like that you make everything unreal; one feels that nothing exists, not the straw roof, or the cane walls, or the dirt floor. That's the way it is maybe. My husband was very, very rich and he isn't any more. I was a dwarf and I'm not any more. But that's already witchcraft. Who can you tell it to? But we're not witch doctors or witches. We want to be. You have to go to Tierrapaulita for that. Yes, to Tierrapaulita, let's go next month, if we're still alive. And aren't you afraid? Of course, but since we're already old, we have nothing to lose, and this wife of mine wants to be a healer-witch and I want to be a clairvoyant-wizard. A month later the shack was closed one morning. They hit the road before the rains began, in the beginning of June, at sunrise on one blinding day. The mist muffled the song of the roosters. A dog barked here and there in the distance. The ground was icy underfoot. Columns of black smoke came out of the ovens for baking bricks. A few carts. Some people on horseback. When they reached the stone cross there is at the exit for one who is leaving and at the entrance for one who is returning to Quiavicús, they huddled together. They had to cross themselves so that it would go well with them. But in addition, already thinking of himself as a wizard, Hayumihaha took the little coral-colored beans out of a knotted kerchief, little beans that are not for eating, that are poison, but which bring one good luck.

"Niniloj!" He had not called her Niniloj for a century, "We're doing well, but keep the baskets tight. Remember that we're carrying him in there and since he's in the shape of a cross he can't do anything to us."

Among the few supplies that the woman was carrying— tortillas, coffee, brown sugar, red chile, a jar, and a pine torch—there was a cross made out of dry corn leaves, *tazol*, corn is a god, *tazol* is the devil, but now in that shape, Tazol, tied to the cross of God, had lost his malignant powers, and he went along with them, perhaps to defend them, as they entered Tierrapaulita, the shadowy realm of black magic.

Yes, without saying so, they were bringing Tazol so that he could protect them; after all, he was a friendly demon, one with whom they had had dealings, and they had imprisoned him in the shape of a cross to make him fast so that he would not escape from them, because, being a devil and all, as they approached the labyrinth of hills in which Tierrapaulita lay, he began to get concerned, trying to pull back like a dog that was being led along tied with a leash.

"Even Tazol, who is a devil, is afraid to enter Tierra-

111

paulita!" Celestino exclaimed, anxious that in the face of such evidence his wife would desist in following the pathway that tied one hill to another and the other to another hill, a hill-tying road, because according to what people said, those hills were running away from Tierrapaulita too.

But Niniloj, the baskets firm on her body, tightly tied, an attempt to prevent Tazol's cross from escaping, would not return to Quiavicús without all the secrets of the healers. She already had a holy hand for the cure of cramps, sour stomach, tenesmus, but just as an apprentice, and she would return from Tierrapaulita an expert.

The Fly Wizard and His Wife Wish to Become Very Great Sorcerers

"Tierrapaulita!" they shouted at the same time; they could not believe it. "Tierrapaulita!"

"I shouted out of delight, Niniloj!"

"And I out of fright, Celestino!"

In the distance, among abrupt, dry, rocky mountains, they contemplated a mound of houses surrounded by an ancient Indian wall that had become a row of boulders with the centuries, and a moat, part barren and part planted with dwarf corn, with no way into the town except over a long and narrow bridge.

"What fright, Celestino!"

"What delight, Niniloj!"

And they said no more to each other, he in front, with the brim of his hat thrown back like a prolongation of his forehead, his machete in his bony hand, his pants and the sleeves of his jacket both short, and she with the baskets where Tazol was riding, without any power, changed into God's holy cross.

"Listen here, Celestino, the first little thing we must do in Tierrapaulita is buy the Prayer of the Lonely Soul!"

112

"That's for a fact."

"If I'd had that prayer and had brought some genista along to pray with, the Devil would not have dwarfed me, and that's why I want to buy it first thing, because at this point, an old woman and a dwarf again, what a jubilee that would be!"

During all of that they were going along so fast that they had climbed up the first streets almost without taking a breath, Celestino always in the van, as is understood, and Catarina bringing up the rear, but talking.

"As you can see, nothing is straight here, just as they told us. The streets are bent, like stone ribs, the houses are crooked, the square is crooked, and the church—ha! ha!— one tower this way and the other one the other way, and the dome looks like an accordion—some wind must have bent it out of shape!"

"Be quiet," Celestino stiffened her. "Tierrapaulita is the way it is because that's the way it is, and wherever you be!"

"Quiet with what you see, but the fact is that we're going to leave here, me with a crooked neck, just like treacherous guilt, and you with bowlegs!"

"I just told you, wherever you be . . ."

"The same as I used to tell you when I let you go to the fairs with your fly open, and you didn't pay any attention to me."

"And that was how my troubles started. Tazol, the corn demon that we carry imprisoned in God's holy cross, followed me night and day with that evil laugh of his, daring me to go to High Mass with my fly unbuttoned, because if I did, many people would sin, especially the women, and he would make me rich, and later on he made me the richest man in Quiavicús, which is what happened."

"Because you sold me . . ."

"But I'm sorrier than Saint Peter was when the rooster crowed to him, and don't keep screwing me with that, because what would you think if the rooster was screwing around with Saint Peter at the gates of heaven, crowing cock-a-doodle-doo, cock-a-doodle-doo at him. So not even the rooster crows at Saint Peter to remind him of his terrible guilt, and you won't mention my fly to me again!"

113

"I'll always have to tolerate you as a fellow human, because after all, when people get old in marriage like us, it isn't husband and wife any more, but just fellow humans."

Through the square, with its tilted ground and crooked houses, dogs were chasing each other, some crippled, others with zigzag skeletons, others warped, and others twisting on the ground with cross-eyed bitches.

"Let's get out of here," the Hazabalahaha woman complained, "because I'm already getting scared. The air is making us see things!"

And over by the church, as if spit up by the ground, the priest came out and passed close by them, one leg longer than the other, leaning on a twisted cane, one eye popping straight out ahead and the other one half dead under its fallen lid. His cheeks were ruddy with little veins and the stubble of his two-day beard was damp.

It was difficult for Celestino to hold his wife back as she looked all around for the street by which they had reached the square, ready to run away alone if he did not follow her.

And she almost gave a yell when the sexton came out. A little man with a broken spine. His hips were like pistols under his long-tailed jacket.

Hayumihaha went up to ask him, using that way to contain his wife, if he could get the Prayer of the Lonely Soul from him.

The other one raised his eyes, as if trying to straighten up, and out of his cucurbitaceous back he drew an affirmative nod, and with little steps went toward the church, not without turning several times before disappearing to signal with his hand that they should wait for him.

Inside the church everything was crooked. They went in stepping softly, following the sexton. An earthquake must have left it that way, off its axis, the central nave, the high windows, the dome, the main altar, and the side altars, and also the images at the stations of the cross, which looked more like playing cards than the steps of the passion of Christ done in lithographs with overgilded colors and frames.

Celestino—already nervous with the inclined floor, the pulpit that hung down over the congregation with its twisted

114

steps leaning against the oblique walls, the confessionals—rubbed his eyes and would have fled with his wife if the sexton had not appeared.

He came as if he were walking backward; he gave them the Prayer of the Lonely Soul, and then, looking at them sideways—he could only lift his head that way—with one hand beating on the other, both hands with twisted fingers, he reminded them that they were to make an offering.

"How much?" Hayumihaha asked, reaching for the red-leather wallet where he carried his money.

The sexton shrugged his unequal shoulders and grunted something like as much as you wish. Celestino gave him two coins.

They fled from the church, while the other one was hiding the coins in the bottom of one of his twisted shoes. He immediately came out to spy, suspiciously, wiping his dribbly nose on the sleeve of his long jacket, to see if the priest was coming.

"You can't leave Tierrapaulita without the other prayers," a woman came up to advise them, with a tricky look; half of her face was solid and turning into marble, while the other half, in contrast, was extremely mobile.

When the woman noticed that the pair of strangers was stopping to listen to her, she kept on talking: "Here in Tierrapaulita, if you look for it, you can find the Cross of Caravaca, which is the most effective of all known prayers."

"The one that interests us now," Celestino said, "is the Prayer of the Just Judge."

"The 'Just Judge,' you say? Well, I happen to have one and I can give it to you so you can pray. Come along to my house. It's this way."

And she went twisting along a street that was also twisting.

They were behind, one stuck to the other; only when they were very close together did they feel no fear.

They reached the door and waited there. Two invisible eyes that had no being weighed upon them from behind the hole-pocked boards of a window in the house where that woman had gone in. Through the other window, which was open, they looked inside. Incredible. Tilted from one side to the other were the seats of the chairs, the inclined table, a

115

sofa with two right legs and no others. And a mirror hanging on the wall that bowed from top to bottom, drinking in all of that twistedness.

The woman came out. Had she kept the prayer in the kitchen among the ashes? She came out, hair and clothes reeking with a message of food, onions, garlic, tomatoes, and half-cooked lard, and she gave them the Prayer of the Just Judge and the one of the Seven African Powers, a prayer that a sailor had brought her when she lived on the coast of the Atlantic Ocean.

"But now," the woman added—she moved only half her mouth; all the rest of her face was marble—"you most likely need the Prayer of the Holy Shirt and The Holy Crusade, and the main one, as I told you when you were coming out of the church, the Cross of Caravaca."

"And where can we find them, because now that we're in Tierrapaulita we want to get them all?" Celestino asked.

"It's quite hard to find them. But I'm going to give you some advice. Ask everybody who approaches you except Sisimite, who is an evil trickster, an impious fellow."

"And how can we recognize him since we don't come from here?" the Hazabalahaha woman ventured, feeling her dry and wrinkled legs trembling underneath her skirts and petticoats.

"How can you recognize him? I am a Dramatic here in town, Concepción Bocojol. It's easy to recognize Sisimite. Look at his feet, because he goes barefoot. He can do his mischief better that way. The big toe on his right foot is on the side all of us Christians have it, but he has the big toe on his left foot on the outside."

"Well, that fellow with his toes like that, we won't ask him," Hayumihaha said, "and God thank you."

"Shh! Here in Tierrapaulita none of that 'God thank you.'"

"You see, Celestino?" Catarina intervened.

"Here you have to say: Caxtoc thank you, pronounced Cashtoc. But I have the feeling that what you two are after is to get to be a witch and a wizard, and as everybody knows Tierrapaulita is the college town of wizards. Oh, but it's something that's hard to bear, unless you fall into the favor of All-Clothes-Twisted-Just-the-Same, who is the woman whose magic art turns everyone she touches into witches and wizards, an instant of such great pain that not everybody can bear it; most of them remain idiots for the rest of their lives."

The Hayumihaha couple, who were already becoming twisted—Celestino saw that his wife now had one eye higher than the other, and Catarina that her husband was going around with his nose twisted and turned up, as if it wanted to go visit his left ear—passed a message on to each other with a blink that it was urgent to find that famous All-Clothes-Twisted-Just-the-Same quickly, because that was what they had come to Tierrapaulita for, having gambled everything on everything, to exchange their simple natures for the complicated nature of a witch and a wizard. No question of going back to Quiavicús to cut wood, poorer every day with the little that the wood brought in, but to have it ever so nice, knowing everything the way people who know witchcraft do, with powders from a dead man's bones, the hair of a man who had been hanged, shavings from a raccoon's member, leaves of loco weed, garlic strung across the horns of black bulls, bitter honey from wasp ants, serpent skins wet with moon within and scaly with sun without.

"The address of All-Clothes-Twisted-Just-the-Same?"

"Yes, because if it all works out, she'll make us a witch and a wizard—at least me."

"And me a healer! Hey, there, why do you leave me out?"

"I think she can, that All-Clothes-Twisted-Just-the-Same can give that knowledge to both of you."

"And isn't it a power?" Celestino asked, a bit disappointed; what he wanted now was power.

"And where does power come from, real power, not the false power that humans deforce, do you know what *deforce* means? A Dramatic can talk with the people, and she doesn't have to put footnotes to her words."

She explained what *deforce* meant, but those people did not listen to her very much and they understood less, hanging on her words, nevertheless, not for those academic, grammatical, philological explanations, but to get the address where she lived and how to get to that mysterious

117

woman who was called All-Clothes-Twisted-Just-the-Same.

"The first thing is to get there as midnight runs down, which is before the twelve strokes, there where the world runs down and is going to fill up the hourglass with human scruff. Oh, but my Devil, my Cashtoc!, every minute I forget that I'm talking to ignorant people and not to Dramatics. I meant to tell you that you have to look for All-Clothes-Twisted-Just-the-Same before midnight. You have to go into her hallway when the twelve peals of the church bell are tolling, which only ring at midnight and are the only bells that can be heard in Tierrapaulita, because the priest found out that the noise of the bells twisted the houses and the streets even more and that they left the bell-ringer so crooked that to see where he's going he sticks his head out from between his open legs."

"And would you please," Catarina decided, "give us the address of that maker of witches and healers?"

"Ah, so you do want to be a witch and a wizard!"

"That's what we came for," Celestino clarified.

"That's what I wanted to know so I could write down your names, not in my ship's log, not in the black fable of Saint Dionysia, but in my statistics. A thousand and thirteen wizards and witches have already left here and an equal number of healers of both sexes. But I must ask you, before I give you the address: isn't your time limited?"

"Oh, no," Celestino exclaimed, "we left the way a person does when he's poor and alone, someone who doesn't leave anything or anyone behind, just a miserable hut. We left for the unending."

"Then the voice placement will be easy. Oh, excuse me, I'm a Dramatic and initiated in speaking difficultly. Let me explain. We all have the witching sound in our throats, the one that can produce enchantments, and just as a singer's voice is placed, All-Clothes-Twisted-Just-the-Same places those sounds called upon to break natural laws by a miracle in the apprentice of miracles, in its proper place, because all power is in words, in the sound of words."

The Hayumihaha couple did not understand anything that the woman was telling them, while she turned from one to the other like a drunkard, so that she could see who was passing by and greet them by name.

"Hello, Doña Crisinita . . ."

"Nice day, Melchor . . ."

"Holy and good"—mumbled—"Curtiembrita, give my best to your sisters . . ."

And the fact was that everyone who passed said hello, as if they were afraid of her, as if it were a question of one of Cashtoc's wives, which was what she was considered to be by a whole string of madwomen who moved about Tierrapaulita.

"Aha!" she exclaimed, sticking out her living eye—the other one was already like the eye in a marble statue—as she saw the priest coming along with his crooked hat, one ear very high and the other folded down to his neck, "And I suppose you're going to warn these friends in Latin—that Latin you speak is nothing but Latinized Spanish—that I'm crazy! Well, little Father, don't bother, here in Tierrapaulita we already know that there are more devils than holy water! I'll tell this dear and newly met couple that I'm mad, mad, mad, one of Cashtoc's madwomen, and that's why you too should pay attention to what I say, because I have the gift of prophecy, having come out of the cage of lions who licked at my body, along with the tremendous combing of my hair by the tigers with their claws."

The woman, with dislocated movements, tried to draw them toward her, but they took refuge behind the priest. .

"I didn't give them the address of All-Clothes-Twisted-Just-the-Same because, Father, you should know that these—"

"I know, I know," the priest said, taking off his crooked hat—the edge of the brim had fallen down behind—but when he left his head uncovered, the frightened couple noticed that his head had a twisting on the top part, as if when it left the ears it were twisted like a chalice which showed on top his tonsure instead of the host.

Celestino felt like shouting: "Uncle Priesty, put on your hat, you have a very ugly head, all twisted, like a two-story house where the upper floor is about to fall off, already at a tilt!"

"Well, as you've heard from her own lips, this Whorey is crazy. She says her name is Concepción something or other. On the column of the baptismal font there's a mark

119

that came from a great butt of the head that, according to some old people, this unfortunate creaure gave. Her godmother almost dropped her—it was the day she was christened—and it would have been better if she had been smashed on the floor, because then Tierrapaulita would have been spared another peaceful madwoman, which are the worst kind, because, oh Cashtoc—" the Hayumihahas were surprised to hear that not even the Uncle Priesty invoked God but Cashtoc—"you can seize the violently insane, tie them up, lock them up, give them injections until they go to sleep in a saintly way, but peaceful lunatics have to be tolerated along with all their inconveniences, especially the crazy women who persecute us priests with their logorrhea —the word was not made flesh but diarrhea—their desirorrhea, the desire to put someone in arrears who is not in arrears, their pissorrhea, because they just lift up their skirts and out comes the torrent, their imaginorrhea, because they live imagining things and imagining things."

Celestino asked his wife if she understood anything, and she answered that at first she made efforts to follow the Uncle Priesty in his Latins but that she got tired and let him go on alone without listening to him because she could have had a stroke if she kept on trying to concentrate on what he was saying.

While that woman disappeared, they went walking along with the priest toward the front of the church, and there Celestino took off his hat, which was hard to find because his head was getting twisted too, crossed his arms, had the impression that they were not very straight, and said: "Well, Uncle Priesty, since the fair in San Martín Chile Verde we haven't run into any pastor."

"Yes, Fathers are very scarce." The afternoon sun was giving an orange tint to the black hosts that were riding on the priest's nose in a pair of dark glasses that he had just put on. "And those of us who agreed to go out into the villages, well, as you can see, we've been forgotten, just as if we didn't exist as far as the diocese is concerned."

"And since you're the first Uncle Priesty that we've seen," Catalina ventured, before the monsignor could go on speaking, "we'd like you to give us some Gospel, because we're all kind of demonized, fighting against a certain demon named . . ."

Celestino nudged her with his elbow, and therefore she swallowed the name Tazol.

"I can't give you any Gospel. I can't do anything."

"Why not, Uncle Priesty? If it's because of the offering, we'll pay you."

"I'm all out of holy water."

"And haven't they brought any? Have they left you with a dry font?"

"And where would they bring it from if I had any way to ask them, because I'm besieged here by Cashtoc. A calf the color of a hill of rust, a hill of ironwood sawdust, gave me to understand in one of his tremolos. Instead of a choirmaster I have a choircalf, who does not low but blows, a low blow against the great musicians who wrote sacred music. The calf of the scriptures is the one who accompanies me on the harmonium while I say a dry Mass, *cantabile* and *gesticulabile*, because Cashtoc has left me without wafers or wine to consecrate."

"And why haven't you gone to the capital, Uncle Priesty?"

"Because, haven't I been telling you that Cashtoc has me under siege? The last time I tried to leave on horseback, by the last house in Tierrapaulita, where the road that leads to the bridge begins, the animal reared just like a demon and threw me to the ground with two broken ribs, which, since they are crooked bones, nothing is straight here, must have healed the way they were. I'll sneak out on foot, I said to myself, and since I've been wearing a cassock since I was fifteen, it would be easy for me to wear a woman's skirts without anyone's noticing that I was a male *eclesiastis consagratum obispum*. But when I got to the bridge, ker-boom, I slipped and half dislocated my ankle. I gave up trying to get out of Cashtoc's web. At night, with that stickiness of sleep woven with the eyelashes of effervescent widows, an untouchable net is drawn around me from which I can't escape, because I'm imprisoned in it like a cassock horse fly, with this hat that no longer can find any place to rest because it looks more like one-of the twisted tiles you see on the roofs of Tierrapaulita."

121

"Then, even if there's no holy water, you can say some of the prayers from the Gospels for us, Uncle Priesty—they would be of some help."

"But why bother with hypocrisies! You're hypocritical souls, because what you're after is to turn into a witch and a wizard, and that's what you were talking to mad Benabela about, she used to be called Macusa" (he had said another name but the Hayumihahas had not noticed it) "because peaceful madwomen like that like nothing better than to change their names—they think that if they change their names they become different people—and one day, without anyone's knowing why, they want to be Violas, the next day, or after a while, Violets, or even Cirfrusias, Cifernas, Tirrenas, Mabrocordotas, Fabricias, Fabiolas, Quitanias, Murentes, Narentes, Podáliras, Engubias, Tenáquilas, Pasquinas, Shoposas, Zozimas, Zángoras, and—and that's the end of the alphabet."

"Still, Uncle Priesty—" Catalina went close to the priest —"we would like to confess. We've been overdemonized, you can be sure."

"Oh, no, I've got enough demonized people here in town, in this Tierrapaulita of my sins, to have to listen to demonized people who came from other places! There must be priests in their confessionals who can listen to sins that are not all the same thing—the pleasure one gets during confession is in the variety of sins—while here in my confessional I only hear the same litanies of demons and women in volcanic activity. *Malayun, malayun famulas, finitas infernarum sirtes!* All of them possessed by the dark spirit of Cashtoc, some taking pleasure in their buttocks, others in their thighs, others in their milky teats, without no lack of those who let four fingernails grow so that they can lacerate themselves with them until their backs bleed, or males who pass hot pins through their virile members, *bilum metalis, sustratum ingredientes mean!*"

Night was coming on and Celestino and his wife escaped from beside the Uncle Priesty without saying goodbye, what else could they do, because he kept on preaching to them in an incomprehensible language and they were planning to leave Tierrapaulita that very night.

The Corn-Leaf Devil
Makes Mr. Fly's Wife Pregnant

Sunny saffron, hills blinking with fireflies, lardy darkness.

Catalina in front, Celestino behind, the latter was not very much in agreement with that flight, but she demanded it, they were going foot-why-do-I-love-you through the maze of streets in Tierrapaulita, anxious to leave as soon as possible the domains of Cashtoc, the Great Demon, before whom all the others prostrated themselves, even Tazol, whom they were carrying imprisoned in the cross of the cross-hung Lord. Alas, poor Tazol! A poor little playful devil, who didn't even make a noise in Tierrapaulita where the Great Demons reigned, among worms with feet, butterflies with tails of light, lightning flashes for omens, spooks or haunts.

Tierrapaulita disappeared, swallowed up in the shadows of the night as if it had sunk, and one would not have known that it existed except for the wicks of lighted lanterns and candles which released an earthy, dead light without reflection through the cracks in windows and doors, some cat sitting on some sill licking its electrified fur. Talking could also be heard behind the doors and a sprinkling of dirty words disturbed the silence of a corner with the passing of some mule drivers who were coming back from having a good time. And after that last revival of voices, nothing, the empty darkness.

Luckily they were already reaching the outskirts of the town and from the light of the stars they could make out the road and the bridge. Human eyes had never seen a road with more hunger than those of Celestino and his wife, who already felt that they were out of Tierrapaulita, fleeing, gobbling up that dark strip of earth with their feet, among

123

crags covered with ferns, trees with few branches, and telegraph poles with wires that Cashtoc tapped by sowing small
parrots all along the lines, so that on the following day
at dawn they could translate with their gabble and chattering
the messages sent to Tierrapaulita or originating there, or
everything they heard through those metallic threads, whose
sleeping vibration would perforate the foggy nights with
the noise of their witching language, dots and dashes, the
apple-orchard vagrancy of that fantasy of a world in
potential, of that colloid state of ghosts who carried dew-
drop hourglasses in their pockets.

As they were already taking their first steps toward the
bridge, Tierrapaulita lost behind, with its jumbled houses
and church, just as if the city had been left paralyzed in an
earthquake without ever falling down, in that great apo-
plexy of apocalypse, suddenly their hearts gave a turn, the
bridge had disappeared and there was nothing but the deep
moat. They had almost taken the step. What had prevented
them was hard to say. Their first thought was to go back
and warn the priest, in case he tried to flee, that the bridge
was missing. But why go back since the priest was following them, accompanied by the madwoman, the priest as
Celestino's shadow, the madwoman as Catarina's shadow.
Every movement that Hayumihaha made the priest would
make; every turn that the Hazabalahaha woman would
take the madwoman would take. They were their shadows,
perfectly outlined on the stone pavement by the light of the
moon that was rising, and while the madwoman was whipping herself with the hair lashes of a cat-of-nine-tails, the
priest was twisting away, dancing angrily with his black
feet, shoeless under his black cassock. As he danced he
took off his priest's hat that was soaked with dew at the
same time that Hayumihaha took his hat off his head to
scratch his skull and try to think properly about what they
ought to do. The Hazabalahaha woman, clutching his arm,
did not dare move. As a remote consolation she clutched to
her belly the baskets in which she was carrying the holy
cross made of dry corn leaves—that is to say, Tazol imprisoned in the magic of the cross-hung Jesus. For a few
moments she felt that Tazol was not moving around in
the basket but in her womb. Two, three times, on the edge

124

of the moat that was cutting off their way, among the streets of Tierrapaulita and on the road, she was on the point of confessing to Hayumihaha what was going on. She felt pregnant by Tazol. Something that never before had inhabited her belly was moving around, with little pecks like a blind hen, trying to turn around to get into a better position, which was impossible because membranes are membranes and they are not there the way they are so that a new being can do anything he wants to with them. The son of a devil would be a devil. She was out of breath. Tazol, the son of Tazol, had just given her a kick in the belly from inside which left her nauseous, seeing stars; her eyes felt cold and full of water, the cold of shells from which bullets are extracted, leaving them empty. The son of a devil would be a devil. She almost fainted, hanging onto her husband's arm. How horrible! The only time she had felt as sick was when she had been bitten by a *casampulga* spider, and so that she would not die from its bite, they had made her repeat *"casampulga," "casampulga," "casampulga,"* while a relative played on a flute to soften the poison and they prepared the antidote, which was a small child's feces. Pregnant by the Devil? No matter how tightly he had been tied to the cross of the cross-hung one, Tazol had good reason for going along so quietly, because he was penetrating her womb through her navel. That was how he got in. If it had been some other way, she would have felt it. But through the navel—oh, Lord, through the navel!

And not through the navel buried there in Quiavicús, so far away in her thought. Quiavicús, now that they were worse than lost in the edge of that moat, where they were being pushed by their own shadows, transformed into the priest and the madwoman. No, Tazol did not enter through the navel that was lying buried in Quiavicús, under the fireplace of three stones, in the shack where she had been born and where her parents had lived. The bandit had gone in through the dead navel that she was carrying with her, through the hole that only served as a lint-catcher, with some three old white hairs and the little fold of skin, like the fold of a corn-leaf cigar. The moat? Nothing worse could happen to her.

And sweating hot and cold, she was reflecting with

glimpses of memory and thought on how capricious the Devil is. Why had he not made her pregnant when he had had her in his power, when he had changed into a hurricane and had snatched her away on Don Agapito Monge's path, shaking her this way and that way like an opossum carrying off a chicken? She respected him then. Why, then, when he had her in exchange for riches, had he not done her that great damage?

She ought to tell Celestino about it. Right there, so that he would throw her into the moat, and with good reason, because being his wife, another had grounded her. But she stopped for a second time, considering the difficulties that the poor man was suffering in that cursed Tierrapaulita. She would confess to him later on. Now, with the moat, the madwoman, and the priest, and for her alone, Tazol's child in her womb, they ought to get back to the town. Waiting there would mean their end, they would perish, because with the blinks of the madwoman, silent now, just like her evil shadow, the breathing of the priest, the evil shadow of Hayumihaha, and the kicks of Tazolito in her womb, they would be pushed into the moat.

They could not flee any more lightly or more quickly, because their feet were not sufficient, cowardly mortals at the edge of the darkened hell, where now there were only coals and ashes, more frightful in its solitude and silence than an active hell.

But they fled without moving away from the edge of the moat, where—what were they waiting for now, what were their feet waiting for—their feet had run away from them, leaving them standing on their clothes.

Catalina squatted down, big-bellied, legless, as if she had to pass water, and she did, the water of a woman made pregnant by Tazol, and while she was doing it, with the hand that did not feel like touching and not finding any feet, she felt around for them and there was nothing.

From the ground she raised her teary voice, warning Celestino of what was happening to them, because he could not find his feet either. But they were not standing on their clothes as they had thought, but on some pegs without toes. Their feet had the same shape in back and in front.

"Oh, Hayumihaha, my little one will be born like that!"

126

"What little one?" Celestino asked.

"Tazol's," and she began to wail. "Why did you give me the basket with that cross made out of *tazol* to carry?"

And when she could speak, she told her husband that the Devil had entered her through her navel and that she was expecting a little devil.

Hayumihaha, with the tremendous proof of his toeless feet, formed by double heels, the same in front as in back, did not find his wife's confession tragic.

Because at that moment, jumping over the moat just like an acrobat, followed by a very dark animal, Sisimite, the little demon of the fields, landed in front of them, accompanied by Cadejo, his dog-lion-tiger-tapir-calf, calf because of his little horns and little hoofs, dog because of his faithfulness to the Demon—in other words, being a Demon himself—faithfulness to himself, lion because of his mane, tiger because of his bloodthirstiness, tapir because of his carriage, and with two hairy rings, like glasses, around his dreamy pupils of moon and water.

"Where are you going, people? People can't go along here!"

"We're going to Quiavicús," Celestino stammered.

"Going or coming?"

"Going," Celestino affirmed doubtfully.

"Coming?"

"No, sir," the Hazabalahaha woman, indignant because with her open hand she was trying to waft away the suffocating heat that Sisimite was giving off, "we're leaving!"

"It doesn't look like it. If you were leaving, you'd have to have your feet pointing frontward."

"We have," they both said.

"Hoo—trying to fool me! You could only be heading *recula reculorum!*"

"This is a fine thing that's happening to us!" Catalina said under her breath, and, turning to Sisimite: "Great Prince of the Woods, we're going in the direction that our faces are taking us, because our real feet ran away on us, and we only have these toeless feet of ours."

"No toes? Hoo, Wild Boars, ha, pa, you're Yumí, the one who came to be a wizard!"

Celestino's throat went dry. That guessing devil knew

127

and was making fun of his blood oath that had made him a blood brother of the Sauvages, or wild boars.

"No toes!" Sisimite emphasized. "Did you hear that, Mr. Cadejo?"

The animal with the skin of a hairy river that he alluded to snorted with carnival joy out of one of his flat nostrils and out of the other came the iciness of ash dust; he moved his horny head from one side to the other, as if gadflies of lighted tobacco were burning his ears; he made the hairy circles around his eyes spin like black sunflowers, and he sneezed to the great disgust of Sisimite, who was bathed in drops of saliva and snot, just as if Cadejo's teeth and very white corneas had been fragmented in the sneeze.

On the other side of the moat, where the bridge had been, three women of smoky sponge appeared out of the brush in the dark. They kept shrinking and growing.

The tallest of the three was weeping, with her hair thin strings of water that made her pale chick-pea-colored cheeks silver, her disconsolate cheeks, her discolored clothes, her feet of damp soil.

"She is Weeping Water Hair," the voice of the priest was heard as he followed Celestino like his shadow, "and she is crying over the men who die without having been hers, and no man has ever been hers."

"And that's why," the madwoman put in her two cents as she followed Catarina like her back, "in Tierrapaulita, among the mourners, there isn't anyone who laments the drowning of Weeping Water Hair next to the remains of a dead man."

"The rain weeps for men who die," the priest added, "or, rather, weeps for the same man, the one, eternal male who is repeated in all the corpses she accompanies wailing to the cemetery."

Siguanaba and Siguamonta were the two Siguanas or women who were beside Weeping Water Hair on the other side of the moat, getting smaller or growing larger, all accordingly.

Siguanaba, the warrior woman of solitary canyons, and Siguamonta, the warrior woman of canyons that are near populated forests, villages, or cities.

The two of them were on the lookout for drunkards who were apt to forget quite quickly that they were bipeds and start to walk like quadrupeds.

"The biped drunkard," mischievous Sisimite laughed out his explanation, "blows round farts, and the one who turns into a quadruped so that he won't fall down, square farts, which are hard to expel because they're the wrong shape. But the shape is not important, it's the stink—right, Mr. Cadejo?—and by the stink the Siguanas, Siguamonta and Siguanaba, can tell if the biped or quadruped has got drunk on corn wine or the harder stuff."

"And furthermore, besides smelling the drunkard's anal breath, these warrior women," the voice of the madwoman was heard behind Catalina, who in front, in her womb, was carrying Tazol's child, more and more restless, "they can tell whether the drunkard is carrying in his head the four hundred happy rabbits or the sad ones, laughing alone or weeping crystal partridges, as if from the still of their tears drops of liquor were flowing."

"Oh, woe!" complained the Siguana of the small gullies near inhabited places, "don't take it for ill that my body changes into a thorn tree the instant I give myself to the one who pursues me, dazzled by my beauty, attracted by the lodestone of my dark body, I am condemned to love with thorns, to wound what I desire, to scratch what I am searching for, to perpetrate the crime of crimes, carrying a man up to an orgasm and in that instant sink all of my vegetable needles into his flesh, the ones that collect their prey mercilessly, because they are poisoned with a substance that blends into one the convulsions of love and those of death."

"And those are the drunkards who are found in the morning among the thorn trees!" annotated the priest, letting out a yawn that he tried to catch in the hollow of his hand and put on like a skullcap.

"I am the Siguana of the solitary canyons, of the bottomless pits," the third of the three women said, as they grew large and small on the other side of the moat, "I am Siguanaba, the one who weighs less than air, less than smoke, the one who walks in the emptiness of her sex, the most solitary of pits."

"The man who goes after her is blind and falls into her pit," the priest sermonized behind Celestino; "she attracts him by her physical beauty, scarcely covered, and ready to turn into a vertical fall until he breaks his skull and body on the annihilating rocks. He falls and doesn't find love, but death, his eyes bugged out, his bones sticking out of his flesh, bloody vomit on his lips, his ears burst, and the noise of his fall among the leaves. How many men disappear from their homes and one fine day it's discovered that they fell off a cliff!"

Celestino withdrew his toeless foot, which from fear felt as large and heavy as a pile of dough, from underneath the toeless foot of his wife. Was he the only one to blame for the fact that they were going around with that affliction? Why blame him now that the heavens were sinking? Salvation? Ha, ha, ha, Hahg, ha, ha! Sauvation. He called on the Sauvages, his blood brothers, and it was of no use. No one answered. By his own means? But how, between the horror of the moat in front, and behind Catalina, the madwoman, and in back of Celestino, the priest, like their shadows, on one side the unstable, jumping Sisimite, accompanied by Cadejo, who yawned like a man and laughed like a crocodile, and on the other side, with the moat in between, Weeping Water Hair, and Siguanaba and Siguamonta on mountains of drunkards.

Catalina felt gas on her stomach, but although the parcel she was carrying was using her womb as a drum, he was beating it with the palm of his hand. It was not gas. She noticed that it was not gas. And she let loose what it was. The heir of Tazol, whom she was carrying in her belly, was talking to her from between her buttocks, with a compressed voice, as if he could not express himself well between those enormous cheeks that were inseparable because they were so fat.

"If you turn my Lord Father loose, the Great Tazol, leaf of flame of dry corn, I'll come out of your stomach like this wind and I'll get you out of here. Tazolito, your son, offers you this in thanks for your having given him comfort and a place to be born in. I entered through your navel; in your bosom I learned all of the desolation, anguish, and dark grief of the human fetus, and I will come out of here to free you both from the trap you fell into. So, Hazabalahaha, with your teeth and nails undo the cross of dry corn leaves in which my father, the formidable Tazol, is held prisoner."

Without consulting Celestino, who was being threatened by Cadejo as he bared his claws and teeth, ready to maul him, Catarina grabbed the baskets in which they were carrying Tazol, reduced to God's holy cross. She took out the cross, undid it, and . . .

"There's nothing like going out for a stroll with the Devil himself!" Tazol shouted on feeling himself free, incorporated in the wind, speaking to the terrified couple as if to close relatives.

Sisimite, as soon as he heard Tazol, a spindle of corn and wind, jumped four times from one side to the other, trying to enclose him in the cardinal points.

"Don't be afraid of anything, Sisimite," Tazol said, laughing his rasping laugh of dry corn shaken by the wind, realizing that the other one was enclosing him in the four leaps of the universe, "I'll not escape these limits, you don't have to imprison me in your delightful leaps! I came from Quiavicús to Tierrapaulita with these strangers who want to be a witch and a wizard and remain in our service. But before going on with this long explanation, I give my greetings through you, friend Sisimite, to the lord and master of these subterranean cities of Tierrapaulita, the Great, the Immense Cashtoc, feet of felt, legs of alum stone, face of obsidian, mask of jade, eyes of will-of-the-wisp, voice of registers so low that humans cannot hear, with his great rooster's crest hidden in the long locks of his shining hair."

Sisimite ran off with the greetings of Tazol, the cornleaf devil, in search of Cashtoc, the Great, the Immense, earth devil, through the subterranean cities of Tierrapaulita, that of the Ails, that of the Ugs, that of the Orms, that of the Oles, according to their inhabitants: snails, slugs, worms, moles, the deep vegetable cities, the cities of stone, all under the sway of the black fire of the earth and the white fire of the sun and, while Sisimite went and returned, Cadejo got the sense, the touch, and the smell of the afterbirth in which Tazolito had been wrapped up, as Catalina

131

covered it with custard apple leaves, preparing to bury it. Bury it? It was snatched out of her hands by that animal who hungered for placentas, breasts, navels, and sex organs, his favorite food.

"Great Evil-Doer . . ." the deep voice of Cashtoc was heard coming from the moat, greeting the newly arrived demon of dry corn leaves, "unconquered Tazol, olive-yellow one, specialist in idolatries and heinous sins—tell your protégés, those human beings that I see there and that I had destined to chatter on my horns, not to leave Tierra-paulita, where there will be no lack of magnanimous inopportunities which will change them into a witch and a wizard, the apprenticeship of magic and counter-magic, long and difficult."

"Great Cashtoc! Immense Cashtoc!" Tazol answered, "who made your bracelet from the coils of a serpent pursued by the wind that I stirred up, I am the one who plows with the wind, thanks be given to you from all of us who praise you, and we ask you to stop being hesitant and accept a diving-suit that we have put together from the hard shells of scaly insects so that you can dive into the humble pots of our fireplaces, insignificant particles, molecules, atoms of your great infernal cauldron. And in proof of the wish that Celestino Yumí and Catarina Zabala have to serve you, there has been born to us a second Tazol, a bastard who will cause much damage in the world."

"Now," Yumí protested in a low voice, nudging his wife, "the rich one, the all-powerful one is going to be you!"

"And are you jealous of that? You're not jealous of me, of my body! Oh, Celestino, why did you give me those baskets to carry on my arm like a pair of man's baskets made out of maguey, when you knew that there was danger since Tazol was there inside!"

"He was tied up, crucified with the Lord."

"And he got into my belly just the same and left a son of his there! And you're not jealous of that! Not of that! Of my power, of my wealth!"

"You said that he got in through your navel?"

"Yes, that's how it was. I swear by—"

"Cashtoc!" Yumí interrupted her, fearful that there,

132

where even the priest swore by the Great One, the Immense One, she was going to mention God.

"I swear by Cashtoc!"

"Then how can I be jealous? Jealous of your womb?"

"Jealous of everything!"

"Of everything, no, because Tazol put his child in through your navel, and it's from the belly on down that a person gets jealous about!"

"You barefaced thing! Jealous of that, when you traded me for riches?"

"Hee! Hee! Hee!" laughed Yumí with the yellow laugh of envy.

"I mean that if it hadn't been the son of Tazol and my navel, you wouldn't have been jealous either."

"No? But a person gets jealous from the belly on down, I told you. The door of the house is what you guard, but since the little *tazol* got inside of you like a chigger through the fold of your navel, the best thing was to let him stay inside of you and take shape there."

"*Para in eternum . . .*" trailed off the voice of the priest through the holes of that sort of mesh of a confessional which covered his face like a perforated mask.

"Did you hear what the devils were saying? What they need are the wombs of sterile women where they can deposit their offspring, because the population of the world is growing and there aren't enough malignant spirits. And that's a fact. A little devil, once he's born, will never die."

And after a good while, trying to forget, to chat, Yumí added: "What will the devils call you, that's what I wonder."

"Giroma!"

A little shout was heard from the voice of the rodent Tazolín, holding Tazol's hand as his father strolled next to Cashtoc, the Great, the Immense, the Invisible, along the edge of the moat, into which had fallen Weeping Water Hair, Siguanaba, Siguamonta, Cadejo, Sisimite, the madwoman, and the priest.

"Giroma," repeated Tazolito, "which means rich woman, powerful woman, mother of all magic!"

The Great Fly Wizard Is Turned into a Dwarf by His Wife's Vengeance

"Will you love me if I'm dwarfy?" Celestino ventured.

"And so . . ."

"It happens here that now that you're a rich female and mistress of silver hells, where they cook gold untold, ask Tazolito, your son, to turn me into a dwarf in revenge for what Tazol made you go through because of me."

"You're the one who said it. I'll ask him. You sold me and you bought her."

"Who?"

"That one . . . and if what you want is for me to sweeten your ear, well, I won't sweeten it . . . skeleton of gold," added the laughing voice, slightly touched with bitterness, to remind him that the other one had loved him more when she found out that he had golden bones, thanks to Tazol, so that she would get everything when he died, his wealth and his bones. The poor thing did not know that someone who has a skeleton of gold is not mortal.

And it was all in an instant (one who stops being what he is does not believe it), he gesticulated, he moved, he would have run away, but what for, his arms, little arms now, almost touched the ground with his hands (he saw them, a baby's little hands), and his legs, no longer than the distance between some thumbs and forefingers, were little legs, and his head, a little head, and his face, a little face, a little face across which his first big dwarf tears were flowing.

"Don't cry, Papa Owl!" intervened Tazolito, who had been hunting deer and, when he heard weeping at home, he had come right back.

"And why shouldn't I moan and cry, my son," replied Yumí, getting a good dose of common sense from the insides of his heart, because he ought to try to be the putative father of that little demon, "why shouldn't I cry, son, if your mother wanted me to be a dwarfy, and I was? The ground is so close and the sky so far away, oh . . . boo-hoo-hoo . . . oh . . . boo-hoo-hoo!"

"The sky will be close again and the ground far away, with these stilts," Tazolito consoled him, offering him a pair of stilts, "and you won't be Celestino Yumí any more, but the famous Chiltic."

Chiltic, no longer Celestino Yumí, held back his sobs, while Tazolito was saying: "Giroma, Chiltic, and Tazolín, a new family of acrobats! The famous, the formidable Chiltic will do the stilt dance in public squares, on the roads where teamsters stop for lunch, to the rhythm of the music played by Tazolín, the musician who can play all instruments, from the tri-lis-fus of the penny whistle to the tri-tri-pi-trin of the guitar, and the drum, and the flute, and the shell, and the ocarina, and the rope marimba."

"And won't there be," the first time that he was speaking with his little mouth, with his little dwarf words, "some instrument that imitates an owl sound?"

"I won't have it, Papa!" the angry Tazolito jumped almost thirty feet high and when he came down he was choking words, on the verge of whipping his progenitor, that unfortunate and detestable dwarf, with a corn stalk.

"And what's all that about, what's this about music that imitates an owl sound?" interposed Giroma, with a last shred of pity as she saw her dwarf husband, with the stilts between his legs, shivering with the coldness of fear, which cannot be saved as it enters and leaves the body.

"Owl music is the music of the instruments of carnal love!" Tazolito explained, going over to kiss the forehead of the beautiful Giroma before asking Chiltic to get up on the stilts. They only had a little time left, if they wanted to get away alive from that place they were bound into, on the edge of the moat, between it and the walls of Tierrapaulita.

The dwarf made thirteen thousand faces, gestures accompanied by the grimaces of a man with a mustache, as he got up on the stilts, horrified that not even as a dwarf had he got his toes back. He still had, like the one who had been and perhaps still was his lawfully wedded wife—could that

135

Giroma be his lawfully wedded wife?—feet with heels in front and in back, could Catarina Zabala, the Hazabalahaha woman, a deer-woman, be that big woman called Giroma?

She was. Because of that foot business she was, without any doubt, the one who had made him unhappy with her public belly, a stranger's child, the child of a devil, putting horns on him, and reducing him to the state of a dwarf, minimal and horrifying, just like a fetus with a mustache.

Yes, by that doubling he could see that she was the same one, and as for him, that defect of toeless feet, more like little hoofs than feet, was announced as a great attraction in the places where they did the "stilt dance," now that he, Giroma, and Tazolín were covering the towns in the region of Tierrapaulita, not the underground ones, the outside ones, the ones that climbed from the sea to the sky along high land, higher and higher, story upon story, applauded everywhere, anticipated everywhere, even though no few people accused them of being devils or sorcerer's apprentices, as marvelous and bad-smelling acrobats.

From the "stilt dance," the "chiltic" or "chitic," the playful dwarf, witty, sly, with his own and other's buffoonery, took his name. They paid him honor; sometimes he would dance it solemnly, pretentious, stiff, like people from cold regions; sometimes with a great wind in the stilts, with drunkard's legs, like people from the coast; sometimes he would go into imitations, in which he had no equal. The "dance of the gnome," gnome-monkey, a jolly little monkey who mimicked, an affliction turned into a joke, a dance of his forebears from the days when trees walked and grew at the same time. The "grasshopper dance," with the execution of a hop, skip, and a jump with the stilts held together, in time to the earthy cricket music that Tazolín would imitate on the ocarina. The "cockroach dance," hard to do and heroic, because he had to follow the indecisive flight of the pursued roach, here, there, there, here, a trick that made people at the fairs go wild, ready to undo their kerchiefs to leave some coins in the plate that Giroma was passing, not satisfied with her richness and power, and who exploited Chiltic and Tazolín, since she kept a good part of those donations for herself.

But Chiltic knew other dances, and he danced them at

nightfall, between night and day. Crafty dances, in which he exhibited his first abilities as a wizard. When he danced the dance of the "hummingbird," at the high point he would raise his stilts and remain motionless in the air. In the great dance of the "pierced quetzal," Tazolín would shoot metal-tipped arrows that he would catch on a small marimba of magnetized metal keys that he wore as a necklace. Arpeggios before the music filled the air. Nothing audible. All enchantment. By means of the quetzal pierced in that dance, they would cross jungles, woods, mountains, horizons, distances.

But in a minute Chiltic would abandon those abilities of a wizard for the most audacious of acrobatics.

The women closed their eyes, the men looked at him worried. He was dancing with the stilts along telegraph wires. Everybody was thinking about the icy anguish of that life in jeopardy, if he fell, he would be killed; the suspense, the silence with which they watched his telegraphic dance would be followed by fiery applause, wild shouts, and tumult, because they all wanted to hold him, touch him, find out if that daredevil were made of flesh and blood.

A large yard. Hungry animals and packs of hounds. Dogs and bitches who only ate when some noise managed to break the silence, for then they could eat with their ears, and in order to eat more noise, they would bark, they would bark interminably. From the door of a kind of kitchen a shadow of soot with hair from a broom came out and threw them a piece of smoke, smoke that smelled like fried pork, a gesture, because the shadow that came out to silence them only made the gesture, after which paws and famished snouts would jump around without finding anything on the ground of the yard that was covered with weeds; nothing but the smell, because Granny Soot, from her miserable kitchen, only threw them the smell.

The maddened packs turned on them as they came in, asking for lodging in that yard, and they would have bit them—that was what it meant to be a foreigner—if Tazolín had not stepped between. He stopped them with his diabolical power, but Chiltic had jumped up on his stilts with one leap, not noticing that the doorway was quite low, and he hit his head on the roof of old, worm-eaten beams, which sounded as if it had not been he but the big house which had cracked its skull. For a long time the dust of antiquity rained down on them. Each little grain of sawdust was the start of a story that had come out of its hole of silence, each little grain of dry wood, now just the bone of a log, worm dust.

The fairs get most lively when night begins, but the dwarf Chiltic only knew that from second hand. Afraid that they would steal him from her or that he would get lost, he earned so much, Giroma would lock him up every night behind a wall of stones and mud. And this time, in that yard, his wife locked him up with a loaf of stale bread and a jug of water. His wife?

He felt horror when he said it, because she was, no doubt about it, his wife was the bedeviled Giroma, mistress of Tazol, and not just through the navel, even though in order to justify herself she had confessed to him that in those moments of tricky pleasure, with the devil on top, but without appearing to be anything like a man, a being, a body, she had felt as if decapitated, her headless body fidgeting on the ground, the twin summits of her breasts shaken by a tremor that knocked down villages, opened crevices in the earth, uprooted trees, changed the course of rivers, made lakes emerge, rolled the clouds around, and turned the moon the color of black pepper, as it hung there suspended in the green-blue atmosphere.

And in that duty she was surprised by the shouts of Tazolín. He was calling her with shouts to tell her that the rascal of a dwarf had run away. He had lifted up the bricks and fled from where they had left him under locks, dogs, and the naked eye of Granny Soot; she only slept with one eye because she spent the nights in the kitchen, with a broom as her lance, fighting off those who in her imagination were coming to rape her. Nobody came near her, except the dogs, who satisfied their hunger by licking her, while she would cry like a little baby, trying to defend herself, to protect with her long-nailed hands that combination of wrinkles, gray hairs, skin, lumps, moles, which below her belly, between her legs, the tongues of the dogs were fighting over. And that was how she celebrated night after night, and that night with even more attention, what phosphorescence had those travelers brought, those strange acrobats?, her silver wedding anniversary with the dogs, among long-tailed rats that only peeped out with their little eyes, and very prudent cats who followed the spectacle of the covering of the old woman by the pack from up on the soot-covered beams, sometimes meowing, sometimes quiet, sometimes jumping from one place to another, gold-filled eyes, spectral, they would break the compactness of their black hides, shaken by electrical discharges, every time the old woman would moan with just a touch of life, no longer defending herself now, given over to her sex organ, which was eating itself up.

Cats with much of yawning monkeys about them, and something of bats in their ears, just the eyes, the teeth, a tongue, the claws.

Suddenly, one of those elastic shadows left the mother beam with one leap and dropped and let drop in the darkness—no one knows from where; perhaps from one of the kitchen shelves—a bag of flour, which, when it fell on Granny Soot, bathed her face in white. And there things went, bingety-bang, bingety-bang, bottles and cans falling, the fleeing of meowing, weeping cats, hair on end from fright (Granny Soot with a moon mask?), and the scattering of the hiccupping dogs, as if the crickets they had collected as they sniffed among the grass and stones were chirping in their insides, and when they ran away, because they were so skinny, they went whirling in the wind, just like butterflies.

"Flying dogs," Granny Soot repeated as she tasted the flour and thereby made her lips look like a clown's, "flying dogs, did you ever see anything like it?"

Hee! Hee!, her secret. Keeping the dogs hungry and anointing herself with leftovers from the meal, all over her body, so that some would lick her teats, others her belly, others her legs, others her buttocks, others her back, and the most lustful her parts, sprinkling her with their urine, their red organs sticking out, somewhere between being devoured and being kissed, because sometimes they would bite her, tooth marks that she had not been able to remove, even with thistle water.

She lifted up the thin serpent of her arm. It hurt her. Her arm, her collarbone, her neck. A stiff neck? Hee! Hee!, she had her secret, her lovers. Vanilla extract? If she were to get up and stoke the grills. Cook some more meat and anoint herself, so they would come back. She relaxed, looking cross-eyed, full of a vanilla smell. The bottle must have broken. Damned cats. That's all they're good for. A pain in her coccyx? As if the dogs' snouts had beaten her. But, what a smell of vanilla. The perfume of mourning over the saving-up of love that I did, it was unsavory, like a fool, mourning over amorous waste, about which I used to say, if I didn't save it, I wouldn't have it tomorrow. Wouldn't have what? Everything ends with old age! What would have become of me if I hadn't had this bunch of hungry mutts? "Unsavory" is saving the things that give pleasure in love. Except that Granny Soot had found out too late.

The dogs ran after the dwarf Chiltic, who had escaped from his confinement and who was running through the streets, chased by the canines, stilts, what's the use of feet any more? But another pack cut off his path, and when he saw himself surrounded he put the stilts under his arms like crutches and climbed up a pole and started running along the telegraph wires. The dogs barked, shrugged, got into fights of twirling knots, among pieces of ears that were torn out by ferocious bites.

And that was how Chiltic, the dwarf, escaped from Granny Soot's lovers, wise in the ways of fooling people, because he had already left the angry Giroma and Tazolín, alarmed at his flight, telling people to look for him with a wild broom that sweeps up dead men's saliva, the same as it does the saliva of the living, because they could find him by his saliva, since men go spitting along the street.

Chiltic reached the fair, dragging his stilts, with the healthy intention of getting drunk. The ones who found him drew back respectfully, some pointed at him, others followed him, and soon his presence was celebrated with bravos and applause. They were not looking at him in his dimensions of a dwarf, but in his grandeur as a hero, someone who could remain motionless in the air, without support, someone who left them speechless while he danced along the telegraph wires on his stilts, from pole to pole, balancing himself. They had seen him with his stilts, balancing along the wires that were trembling like swallows, without losing the tempo of the *son* that the musician with the ocarina was playing. They smothered him. Chiltic soon realized that if his admirers kept on surrounding him, they would crush him. They all tried to push and elbow themselves close to the one who was smiling at anyone who would smile at him, answering in monosyllables or jokes anyone who spoke to him, and defending himself from those who were trying to touch him, take him by the hand.

He was saved by a leap. One leap and up on to the stilts. Which was what everyone was waiting for. Between seeing him on the ground, like a great flea, and contemplating him up there, they preferred to see him over their heads, how well he deserved to be above them, that fellow who risked his life as he earned it, dancing on the wires.

And that was how he was able to get away from the elegant places and take refuge in a grove of evil death, an eating place for poor people, where they sold domestic liquors. Nobody recognized him in that badly lit shack, full of smoke and drunkards under full sail or with their sails half raised. He was afraid. One of the drunkest came staggering over to fix his eyes that had been crystallized by alcohol on what seemed to be a vision out of a nightmare. His drooling prevented him from speaking. But with signs, the man asked him if he was really as small as that, or if his drunkenness made him look like a dwarf. He touched him to make sure that he was really there, and he laughed with a spongy laugh that went back inside of him when he saw that Chiltic's little head only reached halfway up the back of the chair and that his feet barely stuck out over the seat. He looked more dead than alive. The paleness of a suicide. He stopped and gave a shout, "Long live the Blessed Virgin!" before going back to his place.

"Duwarf!" an old half-breed of Indian and Negro grubbed in his ear, "listen to my voice, which is like a mirror, when you listen to it, look into it, and when you look into it, spit out your anger, so that tonight your joy will be clean! Duwarf—" the old man came closer to Chiltic—"I'm

141

a spiritualist, and I can guess what's going on with you!"

The dwarf was going to ask him to go away, but just then the drunkard came back, bent on removing the old man, who tried to shake him off, shouting at him: "Don't butt in, you bloody drunk!"

"Saint Something, right? Saint Something, and not like you, you bearded old shit Noah!"

"Don't curse!"

"No, sir. Praised be the Patriarch!"

"Who saved so many animals!"

"Drunken animals, you understand, because the old man liked his nip, not like you, whiskers, who ever since you got mixed up in the spirit business stopped drinking! Spiritualist!" The drunkard drew back to contemplate the old man from sufficient distance. "The only spirits you know come out of a bottle!"

"Look out, you'll crush him!" The old man pushed the drunkard, who was about to fall on the dwarf.

Chiltic, while they were arguing, got out of the chair and with one leap was up on his stilts, ready to flee, but the drunkard managed to grab him off his high masts, and if it had not been for the spiritualist he would have flung the minute piece of humanity that was Chiltic onto the floor, although the impact would have been minimal, because the floor was covered with drunkards sleeping it off.

But the bloody drunkard insisted, and Chiltic, about to fall down, let go of the stilts and remained hanging from the ceiling, among Japanese lanterns, chains of colored paper, boughs of green pine, and *picaya* leaves. And then the unholy drunkard started. As if the danger were giving him its smell, he gave a real twist when he started to try to climb up on the stilts. The spiritualist closed his eyes. They would be the death of him. One push, another push, and he took off like a rocket, his shirt tails in the air, his hat back over his ears, but he had taken longer in getting up than in falling down among the bottle-suckers, where he also stretched out at full length.

The old man placed his shoulders so that the little shoes of the doll Chiltic could stand on them as he let go of the ceiling, but no sooner did the old man feel the contact of

142

the little burning soles, which stopped his blood from flowing, than he realized that Chiltic did not have any toes on his feet.

Ashen, transported, convulsive, the old spiritualist felt touched by the Devil, and his legs were not enough to get him away, shouting down into the town toward where they had the animal fair, so they could give him black mare's piss to drink, the blacker the better. But nobody heard him, neither the human lights of the blinking fires, nor the fleeing stars which were deserting the heavens.

Chiltic sneaked out almost immediately, before the others could discover his spark of a devil, dragging his stilts and the damned desire to get drunk, which he had not been able to satisfy. But as he was leaving, he noticed that the drunkard who had dared to profane his stilts was sleeping face down, with a bottle that was lifting up his jacket, like a pistol in his back pocket. Chiltic appropriated it. He needed to drink, drink, drink, feel human, be the one who went to the fair in San Martín Chile Verde with his blinking fly in a pact with Tazol, his first deal with the Devil and one that had become endless, or in that other famous fair, when he was rich already, when he met, for the delight of his eyes and the eyes of his friends and everyone who looked at her, that certain Mulata—what a female!—but, like all great females, how distant in bed! Yes, yes, he had to drink, drink, drink, and forget, drowned in a sea of booze, what he was: a strange acrobat in a fair of strange people, stone people, wood people, white-earth people daubed with colors, skin, eyebrows, eyelashes, a man's mustache that was just like a brush, and words like echoes in an empty skull.

Chiltic, looking for a place to lie down in, put his hand on a thorn bush and heard a repressed laugh.

Hey! he said to himself, the Prickly Pear Bird is laughing at me, and he became a little tender and loving, wanting to see if the one whose spines he was tickling was laughing at him because he was doing it.

But it was not the Prickly Pear Bird. And when he heard the laugh again, and when he touched the largest of the

143

wrinkles or ditches of spiny bristles, he thought he recognized it, although he was afraid that it might be a hedgehog.

"Sauvage!" he shouted. "Sauvage, my old friend! The last time we met, my wife was a little dwarf. Now it's me. Life's like that. But tell me, where are you going, what are you doing around here?"

"Nothing special. Living. I came to Tierrapaulita looking for somebody to cure my earache. I was getting the song of a goldfinch."

"The milk of a woman dropped into your ear . . ."

"They already did that."

"And your mother, the Sauvage with the tusks of white smoke, how is she?"

"A *salve* for the jewel she is at her age, a Sauvage, still a Sauvage! And now, let me ask you: What about the bear?"

"The bear?" And when he said it, Chiltic did not think about that beautiful, childlike beast but about the Mulata, covered with hair down to her feet, the dark skin of a sleeping star covering her hardened flesh, her thin legs, her round buttocks, her pointed breasts, all in the ideographical image of *oso*, bear, just the way he saw it: between the two hoops of the *o*'s, a gigantic felt *s,* crossing and recrossing for the whim of that fruit of fire in such delightful surroundings. "The bear?" Chiltic repeated. "Tazol stole him in the 'Devil's turns.' First he tried to snatch away my wife, who was a dwarf then. The Evil One stole people from behind, with his back daubed with infernal pitch, but that time, when he already had Catarina stuck to his back, I pulled and pulled on her little pieces of dwarf so that I made her legs grow longer, and I not only stopped him from carrying her off, but I got her back to normal size. Pleasure mixed with fear, frightened and happy at the miraculous growth of the one who had stopped being a dwarf, made us mad with joy, we embraced, we kissed each other, we looked at each other, and when we looked up the bear was on his back, waving his paws, stuck to the back of Tazol, who, as soon as he got him up to cloud level, turned him into hail."

"And that bottle?"

"Cane liquor!"

"Are you going to turn it up?"

"While I was looking for a place to do it, I leaned over on you, my friend."

"And those stilts, Yumí?"

"Oh, I'm not Yumí any more, and much less Hayumi-haha! That was when I lived in . . ." And he sighed, and in the sigh he could be heard to say Quiavicús, the way the expatriate, the exile seems to say when he sighs, even though he does not speak, the name of his land, "now my name is Chiltic, the stilt-dancer."

"How lucky! How lucky to walk on stilts and be able to go to chicken yards and pick hens like ripe fruit, so that people on the ground can get them."

The invitation could not have been more blunt.

"If you want, let's go. I'll go with you," Chiltic proposed.

"To a chicken yard?" the Sauvage asked, because he could not believe what he heard, and his earache had gone away with the pleasure he felt.

"Yes, let's go, I'll pick you a lot of chickens."

The Sauvage in front, his all-powerful head opening fields and darkness, and the little dwarf on his stilts, following with leaps and bounds.

That was how they reached a chicken yard guarded by mastiffs with red hair and phosphorescent eyes.

Chiltic began to pick sleeping chickens out of the trees. They did not even peep, because before they could peep, the wild boar had put them out of their misery.

The dozen and a half outside dogs—there was another dozen of little lap dogs—let their ears prick up with the first sounds, but when they heard the tempest that was lashing the hens better—they were falling out of the trees and there wasn't the slightest wind blowing—they threw themselves onto the bulk of the Sauvage and a strange creature that was following him and whom the packs dared not approach, even though it had ended up on the ground, fearful, milling around, weeping with the pleasure of having to bite, as could be seen from the movement of their tails. What could they do? In an instant, Chiltic gathered together the feathers that the Sauvage had been dropping as he ran away, while he fled—he was chewing on the last chickens—and he stuck them to his body with his saliva of anxiety, the thickest of glues, and he waited.

The dogs surrounded him, and the best hunter among them took him by the neck and returned him to the chicken yard.

Why, Chiltic complained, dressed in feathers, is this son of a hunting bitch bringing me back to his goddamned chicken yard? What an evil foot I have, to fall into a jail made out of double metal mesh!

He stopped his complaining when he saw the one who cleaned up the chicken yard coming, a scurvy old man with one eye missing, and instead of running to meet him with the other chickens and hens, he stayed with some roosters who were drinking water, and just like them, as he picked at the water, he lifted up his neck.

The old man was surprised at the size of that chick drinking water among the roosters, and he spat. His mouth watered at the thought of such good prey in a cloud of saffron rice with hot peppers. Less wary than the dogs, he picked it up by one foot—if he had had two eyes and less desire to eat it along with some rice he would have noticed that it had no toes—and he took it to the cook. She, congratulating herself at having such a gallant animal in her hands, weighed it and hefted it; tying its feet, she hung it on a spike, head down, so that the blood would go to its head and the body would be empty of that sustaining liquid.

She went to work scrubbing some frying pans, washing some pots, all in order to gain time so that the animal that they were going to eat would have its blood all in its head, and also so that she could boil water where, once she had wrung its neck, she would have to bathe it so that she could pluck the feathers off.

"Poor animal!" the old woman exclaimed, unhooking it from the spike where she had it, and she looked for the neckbone to break it, so she could wring its neck.

At that instant, with the old woman leaning over and to the side, ready to twist his neck, Chiltic asked her: "Are you going to kill me?"

The old woman dropped her catch and ran shouting out

146

of the kitchen, falling down and getting up from fright, and the dwarf, as quickly as he could, ran away as fast as he could run, picking off the feathers by the handful, and along with the feathers pieces of his puppet-sized clothes, until he met the Sauvage, who gave him back his stilts.

But the man who cleaned the chicken yard was not going to accept the loss of such a beautiful chicken, and he grabbed the cook by her gray hairs, as pale as her bleached hands, threatening to put her head in the boiling water in which the dwarf Chiltic had been on the point of being plucked, and he would have done it, if a ray of sunlight, coming through a hole in the roof, had not painted on the soot-scaled wall of the kitchen the picture of a wild boar with laughing tusks being ridden by a small Christian who, because of the feathers he still had on, was easy to identify as the little rooster that had spoken to the old woman.

Why did you not confess your dark sins last night?

Kneeling at the confessional of the firmament, tightening her silent lips to the thousands of little golden holes that opened onto the ear of the priest of Tierrapaulita, the un-sooter of souls, whom on that Christmas Eve Huasanga had helped with midnight Mass, dressed up as an acolyte, without her ever having been baptized, with the same little flesh and little bones with which she had come back from limbo, where she had taken a vacation when she was dead.

"Dwarfy! Dwarfy!" The priest of Tierrapaulita, the spreader of solace, the slave-driver of demons with a dry holy-water sprinkler, ran after the Sauvage and Chiltic.

"Dwarfy! Dwarfy!" the priest shouted at Chiltic, "I have a little woman your size, and I want to establish a breeding place for dwarfs, so I can sell them to courts, seraglios, and circuses."

"To hell with her!"

"Cursed blackness, my marrying a dwarf! It would have been better if that one-eyed man had eaten me along with his rice! And to a dwarf my size, the hell with her, at least!"

He began to laugh, thinking about the picture of Huasanga. A big flea with a large head and fat behind, her little

147

snout sticking out, a place for words to hang on, and her miniscule eyes stuck way inside.

But why not let his wife, the powerful Giroma, find him married to that minute and frightful creature?

"Preternaturally, I unite these dwarfs in matrimony," shouted the priest of Tierrapaulita from the main altar, "but first, for the third and last time, with the word handed down by the Holy Catholic Church, I ask whether among those present here there is someone who knows of any cause or impediment to why this marriage should not be carried out."

And after a prudent silence.

"Do you, Huasanga, flea dwarf, take Chiltic, the stilt-walking dwarf, for your lawfully wedded husband?"

"I do, Father."

The priest, with his cape and three-pointed cap, gave a final flourish to the ceremony with a harangue for all the dwarfs in the world, asking them to multiply, and getting down to particulars, with his eyes set on Chiltic and Huasanga, he said: "Pygmies, no addition: body to body, total pleasure! No chilling subtractions: contraceptives or abortions! Much less, long or short division! Multiplication— twins, triplets, quintuplets!"

"What a punishment," Chiltic was reflecting, "to be a bigamist involved with dwarfs and full-grown women all the time! First that certain Mulata and the Zabala woman, his wife, who was a little dwarf then, and now, his wife, the powerful Giroma, and this smallest of dwarfs, Huasanga."

It was too late for the Sauvage, a wild boar with tusks of ivory from the moon, to warn him not to get up on his stilts.

When the Sauvage, his old friend, reached the scratching place where the feast was locust soup, the guest of honor seemed terribly beaten up and drunk, Chiltic, on his high masts, already dazzling those who were there in his honor, and he was dancing the "scissors dance" as a farewell to the guests, opening and closing his stilts as if he were snipping to pieces the last moments of the party, which ended with the shout of the Sauvage warning him not to get up on his stilts.

It was too late. The terrible and impetuous Giroma had demanded that Tazol transform her unfaithful dwarf into a giant, the only way she could get him away from Huasanga's love.

And the finale of the "scissors dance" was no longer being done with stilts, but with the legs of a giant, the other items having disappeared into a pair of extremely long pants, and the toeless feet were encased in huge shoes.

A Woman's Jealousy Turns a Dwarf into a Giant

The Giants received the new Giant on a mountain of flags. A battle against hair. Giants and Gigantics were fighting against the hair that was coming out of them, unmanageable, furious. Like cutting down trees. Like cutting down ceibas. And are not ceibas trees? No, they are stars, they are giants with leaves, with hair. No one knows who planted them. They were not planted. They fell. Meteors with light for hair, like Giants.

The fight between the Giants and their hair would never end. Hair, beards, and hairy fuzz that covered them from their shoulders on down, as if they were bathed in cascades of shadow, a shadow which was spread over their arms, even the backs of their hands had gloves of fuzz that could be combed, their armpits were blinded by hair, their chests were like carpets, sweaty navels were invisible, and there were tresses between their legs.

And that Giant stink even reached Huasanga, impelled by her bridal desires, even though her forehead barely reached a foot below Chiltic's knee.

"My Gigantic," she squeaked at him in the frying talk of her great desire, "I don't know what's happening to your Huasanguita, but I want to try a Giant!"

A rumbling of mountains. Calling someone a Giant who

was only a Gigantic. Giants are Giants. The four most gigantic Giants: the Giant of the Wind, Huracán; the Giant of the Earth, Cabracán. There are many Gigantics. All those who do the Dance of the Gigantics during religious festivals.

And that was why the earth rolled and trembled, every time that someone with magnetized teeth, the teeth of lodestone, like Huasanga, would confuse the sacred Giants with the silly Gigantics.

Did she do it intentionally? Was she looking for the destruction of Tierrapaulita to avenge herself on everyone and everything?

What was certain was that she was jumping like a flea, repeating over and over: "I want to try a Giant! I want to try a Giant!"

Huracán, the Giant of the Wind, could not bear such disrespect, and with his lips still wet from a rich mixture of cocoa and corn that he drank as refreshment he began to destroy everything he found in his path. Eucalyptuses fell, banana groves fell, avocado groves fell, sapodilla trees fell, balsam trees fell, cedars fell, araucarias fell, pines, cypresses, falling to the ground with their heads of green comets and their long tails of branches and birds.

"I want to try a Giant! I want to try a Giant!" the dwarf insisted, each time more lively, more demanding, fingering her long hair, as if she were milking the black rain of her head, the liquid mirror of the strands of her thought were giving a lifelike reflection of the happiness of a wedding night with the cyclopic Chiltic.

Giroma, the powerful umbilical mother of Tazolito, warned by the Grandmother of Giants of the earthquake that was menacing Tierrapaulita—Cabracán was already waking up—took the imprudent dwarf by her little arm, dragged her away from on top of Chiltic's foot, and away from the houses of twisted stone that were being shaken by rumbles and cracks, and threw her into the depths of a cesspool for rain water and the kind of waters that are passed.

"A dwarf who does not respect the Giants and, with evil intent, provokes them into duels of love, aware that they are great makers of catastrophes," Giroma said to herself, in

150

order to excuse her vengeance and her jealousy, "deserves to die here."

And in that cesspool—mud, garbage, small shadows of a toad, toads, ferns, dry branches, spiders, cobwebs, angry flies, hungry pigs—Huasanga would have perished if the sexton had not come to her aid, necky, hair, bony, with his twisted spine, in search of the mushroom that made hunchbacks straight.

"Is it a child?" he muttered the words, but his surprise grew as he heard her calling for help with shouts which were not those of a little girl but of a full-grown woman.

He jumped into the cesspool before the teeth of the hungry pigs could reach her, and he snatched her away from the power of those beasts all covered with rotting mud, certain that she was the incarnation of the spine-straightening mushroom and not the tricky dwarf that the priest had given to another dwarf as his wife.

Now he had it, now he had the famous mushroom in the form of a little mud woman! What was lacking? Possessing her? Making her his? Yes, the magic . . . sexual . . . there, underneath the thick reeds . . . But he did not get to do it—thousands, millions of flies were carrying her off, insects of dream and rain, which come down from who knows what empire.

He spit out blue-winged flies, stone-legged flies, greenish horse flies, and bloody horse flies of lust, as he went after that one who, in spite of obviously being an old woman, by her size gave him the feeling of possessing a girl in puberty, an attraction which was doubled, multiplied, by the pestilence of the mud, a maddening aphrodisiac for him, even though he repeated to himself that he ought to proceed slowly, because that little figure might very well be the straightening cactus of twisted thorns, and if he made her his she might fall apart at once in his hands.

From among the buzzing of the wings of the thousands of black insects which were covering Huasanga her little voice came out.

She thanked the sexton for having saved her, and since his bestiality and unhealthiness were not hidden from her, she invited him to leave the earth with her and take a little stroll through space.

The sexton accepted, and enormous iron-clad flies got into his clothes, his shoes, his hat, and he had the feeling that he was being lifted from the ground.

Seas, mountains, clouds, rivers, lakes, everything was passing under his feet. Night came, and they felt the warm breathing of the stars on their shoulders. Still, at every moment, the sexton kept on trying to get over to the little cloud of flies in which Huasanga was traveling, a face or mask of a spider with teeth, hooded eyes, lips of old sealing wax, which he did not see, drunk with the pestilence that was filling all of space for him.

He should be punished! sentenced the oldest of the flies in the ear of the dwarf with lodestone teeth. He rescued you disinterestedly enough, the insect went on with his buzzing voice—flies speak with their wings—but then he became poisoned!

The flight was arranged so that the flies who were carrying him let him drop onto the roof of the church in Tierrapaulita, so that he would not fall too far, a mercy that they did him for the favor he had done the dwarf when he hauled her out of the cesspool, and that was how the perverse sexton hit his bones between the bell tower and the dome, one night in April, half rainy and full of barn owls, with a blow that left him one-legged, more crooked than before, and with a trembling manner, given to flatus, and with the mania of smelling along corners and walls, broom and creoline in hand, looking for the smell of urine and more, if there was more.

Giroma, powerful in all places because of her tiger-striped navel, with the fingernail-fold of the Devil's cigarette, returned; she was wearing so many necklaces that she made more noise than a river, looking for Tazolito, her son. She wanted to tell him, and she was already laughing to herself, imagining the faces that little devil would make over the debasing punishment she had given to Huasanga, mistress of the flies who, after they got rid of the sexton, made the little dew flies come to clean her off, the wasps, holy executioners, so that they would perfume her, and the fireflies to curl her hair, until she was transformed into a cute doll.

But what was happening to Giroma? Why was Tazolito

152

laughing? Was she stuttering? Yes, she was stuttering, just like everybody else, because her jaws were shaking in rhythm to the movements of the earth, which were shaking Tierrapaulita until it made the houses in the streets go up against one another, just like fighting cocks, as if the streets would close up, and just as they met they would straighten up like drunkards and continue standing, perplexed, more crooked than before.

And all of that because the Giant of the Earth had taken a few stretches as he woke up when he heard his younger brother, Huracán, jumping on one foot among the trees, just like a boy, among the immense ceiba trees that were closing their eyes, closing all their leaves, and letting themselves fall, abandoned to their weight of vegetable stars, the weight of pieces of straw for the Great Giant, who, when he saw them fallen, dragged them off, changed them into fireplaces with green flames.

There was not a white road left or a bone that was not bloody. The lustful dwarf had confused the Giants with the Gigantics, the Giants, who were the four sides of the square face of Cashtoc, the Great, the Immense, and the Gigantics, who were now getting ready to dance, not with the sound of a celebration—they were not in Tierrapaulita to celebrate —but in compensation for the insult that had been made to the other ones.

The Dance of the Giants and the War of the Wives

The Dance of the Gigantics began with a storm's rifle-shooting, bull-horned cloud-butting, thunder-hammering, rain-slapping, hail-scratching, rock-kneeing, reed-cuffing, and tree-elbowing, as they fell into seas of pulp-leavings and leaves; in the town they were not doing better, images christing and sainting in the shadow of the church that was

153

rainy with worm-croaking, door-knocking, door-slamming in taverns and kitchens of the houses, where, half invisible, there could be heard the panning, jarring, brooming, and heeling, yes, stepping, the stepping of those who were walking or rolling leglessly, arm-lacking, in the courtyards, next to the clothing that had fallen from the roping, and flower-pot-breaking.

But the Gigantics—the face of Cashtoc on which they were dancing was square—were wearing the burning skin of nettles, and their four masks were facing, at the same time, the Four Giants of the Sky, enough to calm the furies of the elements.

Their masks were four.

The one of the face. The mask of the Golden Moor. Blue eyes, brows like blond mustaches, teeth of silver, lime and carmine on their cheeks. The one behind, the one of the back, the one that is never seen and goes with us, a mask of the carbon of a fragrant wood with luminous moles. We know from it that we are absent from what goes on behind us, followed by the seeds of sleep in the great darkness of life. The mask of the right ear, over the right shoulder, the slingman, a blue maskarell, or mask in the shape of a swell or sea shell, and the one on the other side, over the left shoulder, the shoulder on which the blow gun is carried, the mask of joy, the smile from one corner of the mouth to the other in the growing quarter of the moon.

Four were the masks of the Gigantics who celebrated the arrival of Huasanga, half naked, with a phosphorescent breech clout. Who, better than she, the guilty one, to assuage the wrath of the Giants of the Square Face of Cashtoc, the Great, the Immense Earth Demon. She came on the hand of a monkey who was a little taller than she, a figure with very long arms, almost dragging his hands as he carried them loose, a head like the seed of a sucked-out mango, feet turned in, tail of a playful reed. The small eyes of this companion of the dwarf's, focused closely on what was below and in front, and sunk deeply upward, gave him the aspect not of a simian but of a little skull made out of the hairy pit of a plum cashew. With his right hand he held the little hand of Huasanga, whom he was taking to the dance, and his left hand he stuck into his mouth until he touched his teeth with his fingers, roasted peanuts that he chewed quickly as he threw back his head.

But everything was not all dance in that emergency. The half-breeds, dumfounded by the thought of death—the telluric danger was wrapping them up in its invisible power —got drunk or went to confession, or both at the same time, when, drunken and desperate at having to end their days in Tierrapaulita, they realized that they could not flee, that it was inevitable that they would end there, they shouted or babbled their sins in the taverns or on the street corners.

The priest's eyes were turning into pills in the shadows of the confessional, which he had scarcely left, relieved because that woman who smelled of carnal sins—it was no fun for him now that he was old, senile, and gouty— had finished confessing, and he could go out and breathe a little air and have some fun, like a little boy, with the antics of the Gigantics, even though it was hard for him to stand in the main door of the church, knowing that it looked out on the main square, or the square face of Cash-toc, the Great, the Immense, the destroying demon of man and everything made by man, the enemy of life, without being the friend or partisan of death, since he did not propose to end creation but to wipe it out, what good were human creatures, what good was what had been created, what good was existence.

A shout interrupted the dance.

"That Gigantic is mine!" shouted Huasanga, running after Chiltic, the dwarf who had married her and whom, so they could steal him from her, they had transformed into a giant as tall as his stilts.

When Huasanga let go of the monkey's hand, he fell apart. He was made out of flies, who separated and flew after her. And more than once, as a part of the dance, the flies would separate and reform in the body of the monkey, which made everyone laugh.

The squabble began, although it looked more like a pantomime.

Giroma stepped into the dwarf's path. The Gigantic was hers. The flies came together, compressed, and formed the monkey, who protected Huasanga, but as soon as she left him, he would disappear, converted into a handful of flies.

"They're making fun of my mother, the powerful Giroma!" Tazolín said to himself and entered the fray.

He had never fought before, much less against an enemy who took shape and then lost it.

But that was why he was the son of a demon.

For a beginning, the other one gave him a loud slap with his long monkey's hand, a treacherous blow, which the infuriated Tazolín immediately returned with blows that only succeeded in scattering flies, who played dead, to get up again, fly, and reform the group that made up the monkey again, whose hand, in a fist now, gave Tazolín a violent blow on the nose, his bloody face crashing into that of the priest, toward whom, pursued by Tazolín, the flies had flown.

"Insolent boy!" the priest protested, not knowing whether to take out his handkerchief and clean the blood off his cheek or chase away the flies.

He did not do anything. Paralyzed, motionless, he saw how, as they mounted together again, they stopped being flies and formed the body of the simian. He crossed himself and held Tazolito back.

"Don't do anything else!"

"I'm unconquerable, I'm the son of a devil, the son of Tazol, and that monkey can't hurt me!"

"Calm down! That monkey and all monkeys, according to the demonomantics of Tierrapaulita, are the angels that Cashtoc uses in his tricks."

The dance of the Gigantics had not been interrupted, in spite of the row Giroma had with Huasanga over Yumí or Chiltic, the former called out Yumí, or Hayumihaha, to attract him, and the latter, Chiltic, both with reason, the Stilt-Gigantic, very tall stilts with pants on, who had the strange appearance of a bird on a screen, or of an anopheles with legs of yellow thread.

"Whose were you? Whose were you? Who did you belong to?" Giroma shouted; and as she complained she remembered that she was Catarina Zabala, the Hazabalahaha woman, except more powerful and with more money.

156

"I'll give him back to you, you're a devil like me, but you're a fool," Huasanga said, one eye out and the other sunken in. "I'll give him back to you as soon as you can prove it!"

"There's the proof, right on your arse, you bitch!" And Giroma gave her a kick with her toeless foot, something like a piece of meat that had been spat out, and continued: "He's my husband, and I, Catalina Zabala, proved it when I was a dwarf, and I want to prove it now that he's a giant!" The cleric raised his hands to his frozen ears and squashed them as if they were toads. Don't listen! My God, don't listen! The black of his cassock showed along the edges of his fingernails. But how can I avoid hearing such cursing, since I'm besieged here in this land by the most perverse of demons! A primitive devil with mineralized insides, a square-faced devil whom a ceromantic of Tierrapaulita, dropping wax into water, advised him to get rid of through a pact with Satan, the Christian demon. But who could make that pact? Who dared? He trembled. Make a pact—he, make a pact with Satan? And how could he make a pact, even supposing that he decided to do it, since he had no link with anything pagan, and least of all with that other devil, just as jealous as ancient Cashtoc about being the only one to be obeyed and the only one to be depended on, like the heart's blood, by all who fell into his domains.

He wrinkled his brow, the beating drums were booming out his thoughts. Near and far, the dance of the Gigantics continued, and the fight between that opulent woman and the frightful dwarf, aided by the monkey made out of flies.

Someone came looking for the priest. Something about some coconuts. It must have been the moment. Some were dancing and others were fighting. The women over the Gigantic, and Tazolito and the fly-monkey over them. He slipped out the main door. It was the moment, it was the moment...

Huasanga, hurt more from the kick than from her stay in the cesspool, and since she was very small, went up to Giroma and with one big tug pulled off her sex, a terrible vengeance, the worst thing that can happen to a woman. How unprotected! How orphaned! Tazolito, at his mother's tearful pleas—her sex was her power, and now she felt

157

weak and unhappy—went after the dwarf, but he could not catch her, fighting with the fly-monkey, who was a monkey just as quickly as he was a cloud of insects that made Tazolito blink, cough, and sneeze.

Wooden drums, tunnels of unending echoes. Leather drums, bellies of resounding wind. Sea shells with a prophetic howl. Tortoise shells. Empty gourds. Cane flutes. Jingles. Ocarinas. And the Giants and the Gigantics dancing, thanks to their four masks, they had their faces turned at the same time to the four extremities of the celestial quadruped who was covering Cashtóc's square face—the square of Tierrapaulita—easy to recognize in his invisible presence, for in his chest could be heard the magic face of the makers of sundials, and around his neck like that of a hanged man the necklace which roared, announcing destruction.

A spectral hour. Is it daytime? Is it night?

The last golden cloud, the first stars, the first vampire. And the dance of the Giants or Gigantics, with no beginning or end.

Devils Here, Devils There, Stop and Hang Up in the Air

Tazolito called the centipedes, fastened them to his sandals, and went skating off along all the roads in search of his father. It could not be. His mother dispossessed by that vile Huasanga, and he tricked by the fly-monkey. So much skin had been torn off that his hands were like a painter's gloves soaked in the colors of rage, sadness, and desperation.

Somebody. A slight chill over the water and over his skin. A rattlesnake was slipping along the surface of a brook. The whole creek bottom, that bottom of bewitched land, rolled over and came out to contemplate with its mud eyes the passage of the snake.

"You must know, Cascabela," Tazolito's voice stopped the snake, "that I'm searching for my father, the one who wears a cape of gleaming corn leaves, handsome as an ear of yellow corn. And you must know, Cascabela, that my mother was robbed of what is most precious in a woman."

"And that's why you're looking for your father!" rattled the rattlesnake.

"Who but he, the imponderable sorcerer!"

"A great devil, a great devil, but how can he intervene, if he had nothing to do with such a precious part?"

"Then where did he engender me?"

"Through the navel, young sir, through the navel."

"And where was I born from?"

"Also through Giroma's navel, and her scandalous youth irritates us all. Your mother, before having you, was a barren and poor woman named Catarina Zabala, of the Quiavicús Zabalas. But your father, the great Tazol, was always in love with her, and he even made a deal for her with her husband, a certain Celestino Yumí, who is going around as a giant now."

"Well, that's why I'm looking for my father, Cascabela. He must know about what has happened. What the trick Huasanga played means for our house."

"The most dangerous dwarf I've ever known. Not just your mother. She does the same thing to all women. She lies in wait for them on the streets in the dark and snatches away their sex."

"They told me that my father is with Cashtoc, but I don't know where . . ."

"That's how it seems. They're hidden someplace in Tierrapaulita, and when devils go into hiding, something big can be expected."

"But the Gigantics are still dancing in the square."

"I'm going now, Tazolín, and if you want to know where your father is with Cashtoc, ask the whitest squash you meet, it has to have a spiny green stem and thirteen waves on its bald head."

And the rattlesnake went off, following the current, without sinking, sounding her precious little bells in time to the flowing of the river water, which could also be heard rattling.

Tazolín—disgust had made him lose his divinatory powers—felt around among the cornfields that all smelled like his father in the ears of corn, in search of the white squash with a spiny green stem and thirteen waves on its bald head.

He felt hunger, that indefinable hunger that a devil or son of a devil feels, because everything in a devil is like that. If he feels hunger, it is an endless hunger, if he feels thirst, it is an endless thirst, if he feels sleepiness, it is an endless sleepiness, if he feels hate, it is the same, and the same if he feels carnal love, because he cannot feel any other kind of love.

And not a single tender ear. Something was moving. A worm. But a worm from the ground, one of those who have legs but do not walk, dragging themselves along on their backs. He followed it along. It climbed up a stalk of corn and slipped in between the covering of an ear wrapped in purple leaves. Tazolín ruined the worm's banquet. It had been ready to gobble up a nest of corn worms, when the other one, hungrier than he, took them for himself, just as they were, raw, with the taste of an uncooked tortilla, chewing them with both cheeks, a suppuration like white lard showing in the corners of his mouth.

And after he had fed himself with worms, he saw with the eyes of a worm where the squash was that he was to split open and ask the seeds where his father was hiding.

Lifting it up with both hands, with one blow he split it open on the ground, and the little seeds were swimming like tiny wasps in the ooze from the squash.

He frowned, thinking about the fly-monkey, but almost at the same time he made a happy face; each one of those little wasps was a small flying devil, talkative and active.

"Where is my father?" he asked them.

"He's with Cashtoc!" the buzzing answered him.

"I know that. What I want to know is what he's doing, why he left my mother all alone, why he's hiding."

"He's hiding with Cashtoc in the church."

"In the church?"

"They're on the lookout for some contraband."

"What kind of band?"

"Contraband, some smuggled holy water." And they

160

added, no one more in the know that those wasp-devils, "The priest received three bags of coconuts, and Cashtoc, who sees all, smells with his eyes, hears with his eyes, feels with his eyes, and everything he hears he sees with his ears, smells with his ears, feels with his ears, and everything he smells he sees with his nose, hears with his nose, feels with his nose, and everything he feels he sees with his touch, hears with his touch, smells with his touch, discovered that those coconuts are coming loaded with holy water."

And the truth was that in the church where Tazolín betook himself the great devils were gathered, from the hierarchy, among whom he found his father, to the lay devils, the former with enormous pyramids of very hot chiles, green tiaras, yellow tiaras, and the latter with simple clerical bonnets of sweet peppers. Their rank was measured by the bite of the fire of the hot peppers that covered their heads.

What were they to do? How, with what powers, could they find protection from those coconuts filled with holy water, an ecclesiastical wile used by the archdiocese to bring that anti-diabolic liquid into Tierrapaulita?

"It's a religious secret!" Tazol exclaimed, and wrapped himself in his cape of white corn leaves, with the noise of a sleeping cornfield that is being awakened by the jumping of the birds.

Outside, the dance of the Gigantics, without beginning or end, was continuing on, and Chiltic was dancing among them *ad pedem literrae,* according to the priest, and with great, great inventiveness in the judgment of the despoiled Giroma, whose eyes did not lose a single movement of the Stilt-Giant, because she was still in love with that cause of her latest misfortune, the worst of her misfortunes, brought on by his still being bigamous with a dwarf and a normal woman.

"We have to tell this priest fellow, I deduced from what I have heard," intervened a shepherd devil, the kindest face in the infernal world and the bloodiest of all of them, "that this is already going too far."

He lost the floor to a drunken red devil, his tail stiff, his horns erect. He proposed doing away with the little priest. A poison that would tear his insides out.

"In the name of Cashtoc, the Great, the Immense," an-

161

other devil interposed, "it's a well-known fact that our colleague here, who used to be kicky, is getting hardening of the memory, and at his age—he just turned seven thousand two hundred—he's not up to this. And hardening of the memory is the same as becoming undeviled, because it's a well-known fact that poison . . ."

"What do you mean it's a well-known fact that poison!" shouted the red devil. "We have to get rid of him, because with just one drop of holy water there won't be even a shadow of a person possessed or in the devil's power in all of Tierrapaulita."

"I'm against it!" howled another devil with the snout of a coyote from the choir benches, his eyes bloodshot with sealing wax instead of blood. "The priest is very useful to us, and why should we want him dead, because a dead person is no good for a damned thing!"

"Stop thinking in terms of punishment," the superior voice of the invisible Cashtoc, sustainer of the reverse side of creation, could be heard. "What a complex of stupid devils, who only think about punishment! What is under discussion is how to get possession of the goods, with what power, because some spell will have to be used!"

"Unruly priest, what a surprise he's going to have when he finds out that we've discovered him! And don't let him know anything, because with us it's the act that will tell him!"

"How do we get possession of the goods, that's the problem!" Tazol added, crossing his hands of roasted corn on his corn-leaf vestments.

"On every coconut we'll put one of these things a woman has that can't be mentioned in polite society," the shameless Huasanga dared to say, "and as a sample," she added, "here's my latest theft, it belongs to Giroma."

Tazolín would have jumped on her, but there was his father, who was the one who was challenged, and next to the dwarf the fly-monkey gesticulated menacingly. Against his wishes, Tazol did not move. The rattlesnake was right. The only thing that concerned Tazol about his powerful mother was her navel.

"I'll be damned!" muttered a blasphemous devil, his topaz pupils folded under the big lashes of a person pos-

162

sessed. "Maybe this wretch is giving us the key."

"Let me have the floor." The dwarf raised her voice of a piccolo that was out of tune. "And first of all, let Guguaso shut his trap; he has to carry a pouch of camphor so that he won't chase after me at night, forgetting his business, which is sweeping up the laughs of dead people along with the laughing and weeping of a cypress!"

"Put a *lox* on every coconut?" a big devil who spit out burning copal between laughs and grimaces asked in a mixture of Spanish and Quiché. "Ha! Ha! a *lox* on every coconut—great idea, great idea!"

"And since coconuts have little holes . . ." the dwarf advised.

"But, dazzling Cashtoc," dared Hierbero, the herb-devil, "in our copal, in reseda, genista, rosemary, tobacco, four-leaf clovers, restharrow, marjoram, vanilla, balm gentle, ivy, cress, vervain, rue, pepper, before accepting this formula of a feminine sex organ for the coconuts, which are asexual, we should try first to find the enchantment which will take away the essential virtue of the water which fills, in the place of coconut milk, those cavities of white meat."

They were all silent as they listened to Cashtoc's herbalist speak, tall, long-haired, aquiline nose, with a double necklace of black vulture feathers around his muscular neck.

"Holy water," he continued, and drew two enormous transparent flowers, similar to glass chrysanthemums, out of his breath, "cannot resist the attraction of these flowers, suns which can attract through the double shell of a coconut, or through a mattress, or through a skull, and draw out the power there and dissolve it in the atmosphere, where its action would be harmless."

"I doubt it!" insisted the lippy dwarf as she twisted her nose. "Turn holy water into thought? What I propose is better, because without changing it from its liquid state it would become something else, if we stuck that unmentionable of a woman to the coconuts."

"More diabolical! Yes, more diabolical!" the opinion of some.

"More perverse! Yes, more perverse!" the opinion of others.

"Hierbero's idea is alchemy!" exclaimed Tazol, the pock-marked demon, each mark on his face a kernel of corn.

"And the spell would go," the herbalist continued, from the ink stain of his bluish face, his teeth white lightning, "the spell would go: transparent flower! Crystal flower! Sun turning with the sun without being a sunflower! By your virtue guarded in light, extract from the water which fills these coconuts, the Christian power, a sweet and brackish power, and replace it with the non-taste of pure lymph!"

They did not discuss it any more. They approved with a show of tails the use of the alchemy of Hierbero, necklaces of mourning wings, to deprive the holy liquid of its potency, and also Huasanga's perverse trick, which would give them a chance to scandalize and make fun of the priest, who, waiting for the late hours of the night to take the holy water out of the coconuts, had come back to the door of the church to follow with his old man's eyes, the staring eyes of an old man, only old men no longer even blink, the dance of the Giants, for that was how he said it, Giants, even though Cabracán might make that strange Tierrapaulita fall into pieces, and Huracán might demolish the cathedrals of the jungles.

"I'll go get . . . I'll go get what I get—" Huasanga got up; she still seemed sitting because of her size—"because I can't pull those big flowers out of my breath like Hierbero." And she left, followed by the laughter of the devils, who enjoyed her joke, followed by the fly-monkey, wearing her riding costume: a small pearl-gray hat, breeches that were also gray, with pearl patches, short boots, a vest that was buttoned tightly over her doll breasts, a whip in her right hand, gloves, and in the cuff of her linen shirt, fastened with two small mother-of-pearl buttons, a scented handkerchief.

Even in windy people you can tell chocolate from ambergris, Tazolín thought as he went up to his father, who was farting and brushing his teeth—he had spoken, and words are the dirtiest things there are—with a curved brush of seven colors, a rainbow from which were falling like drops of foam: quetzals, hummingbirds, peacocks, and birds of paradise, or, as the demons said, of "what good was all that had been made."

Without waiting for Tazol to finish his washing, Tazolito

164

brought him up to date on what was happening to his mother, despoiled of her sacred fire, of her sex, by the turbulent dwarf.

Tazolín had never been so close to his father, and he was looking at him, admiring his pock-marks. Each mark on his face and on his hands was a kernel of corn.

And along with it all, he told him about the fly-monkey.

The other one added the pock-marks of his teeth to the pock-marks on his corn-ear face when he laughed; he touched his son and said to him: "Mr. Everything-at-Once, it's easy to see that you're young, but with the years, with the centuries, you'll see how they go about cutting off our souls and our bodies, making firewood of us! That's why you have to renew yourself! And happy are humans, who are cut off by death when they get old, and are sown into the ground to come back to life again! And as for the light stolen from Giroma by Gusana, the worm—" he made the mistake on purpose—"I never glowed in that light, not even when it was traded to me for riches by her husband, Celestino Yumí, in Quiavicús; the lantern of her navel was always enough for me!"

Then he changed the subject: "It's getting dark. It's absurd for it to get dark! It makes no sense! It makes no sense when the sun comes out, reaches noontime, and then goes back to hide! It ought to come out for good and never leave again! A fixed sun, like the one that illuminates Cashtoc's breast, where it is eternally daytime, or unending shadow, like the one that darkens Cashtoc's back, where it is eternally night!"

The dwarf had come back. She was carrying the female sex organs like a string of onions. The water had been separated from its holy power by Hierbero, double necklace of vulture wings, and the dwarf ran to stick those female parts on each coconut, where there was a sign of little holes, and the devils hid in wait for what would happen.

Coconuts, Devils, and
the Smuggling of Holy Water

The sexton began to stroll through the sticky darkness of the humid night, waiting for the priest, who was backing up, step by step, so that no one would notice in the square that he had left the dance of the Giants—he still said it that way, Giants—when he went into the church, where as soon as he was inside he dropped the heavy beams across the doors, locks and bolts, and more locks and bolts.

"Let's get a large pine torch so that we'll have plenty of light, and some jars to hold the water in the coconuts."

"And what's the water for? Ah, Father, you want to pass it off as holy water! Baptizing with coconut milk? Sprinkling the dead with coconut milk? Using the sprinkler's rain to wet the dry earth of the graveyard during each response with coconut milk?"

"That's it. It's just the way you say. Coconut milk must have some divine virtue, that's why God has kept it isolated in that round universe covered with a hard shell, almost bone, a hidden vegetable cranium covered by a second shell of woven filaments."

Only the priest knew that it was holy water and that that very night he would be able to free himself from the terrible inferiority in which Cashtoc held him besieged in that town of secret pagans, Tierrapaulita, where now the thunder of the big drums was reverberating as it accompanied the slow, the heavy up-and-down of the Giants' feet—he still said it that way, Giants—to pacify earthquakes and hurricanes.

"Let's have a smoke," the priest said to the sexton, and he took out the cheap cigar that he had kept half smoked in one of his pockets and he brought it close to the embers of the pitch torch which was burning with a reddish light, scaly, smoky, and smelling of turpentine.

The sexton then lit a cigarette of purple corn leaves and strong tobacco.

The smoke, as it spread out along their clothes and faces, seemed to bring them together, and with that the priest took on courage, and taking the jars—the sexton carried one, along with the pine torch—they went out to the corridor of the cloister where the coconuts were strewn on the floor.

"They have to be opened," the cleric said; "this afternoon I took them out of the baskets to have them closer at hand. I have two machetes hidden here. Do you know how to open coconuts?"

"Who doesn't! And the coconut head of a Christian even better—" the sexton spit out a stream of black tobacco juice as he said it—"and the machete makes the same sound, chomp!, when you chop off the top of a man's coconut and leave his brains hanging out!"

"Don't say such horrible things! Here I am laughing, in spite of how afraid I am that Cashtoc will discover us. Sometimes fear is laughter. I'm only laughing because of the surprise that everything natural and supernatural in Tierrapaulita is going to have! The demons and these idolatrous Indians, resistant to the true religion, because always, even though they come to kneel and light candles, they still bear arms in the legions of Cashtoc, the devil of the earth, made out of this earth, fire of this earth. All of this has to be reformed *a fundamentis*."

"Father, let's open the coconuts now. The machete is sharp and it's eating up my hands, as if it wanted to scalp the heads of devils."

"Perhaps there won't be any need to use force, because let me tell you: in order to put in the blessed liquid—" whoop, his tongue had got away from him!, but he corrected himself—"that fresh and bluish liquid which, like a secret spring, has God or the Christ child enclosed within its sphere, finger marks were left on the hard shell, because you surely know that during the flight into Egypt the holy family, attacked by the thirst of the desert, in an oasis found

167

these blessed fruits, more blessed now to me than ever, and that the child Jesus, when he opened them, left the mark of his divine fingers, little holes that we will unplug with the points of our machetes so that we won't make too much noise."

The marvel-of-Peru vines, Don Juans during the day too, were climbing up with the wavy movement of serpents of air and strong perfume to hang like curtains made of green and flowers along the roofs and walls, curtains that hung down like an embroidery of shadow and light over the floor of the corridor where the coconuts were, in the light of the moon that was peeping out between the towers of the church with its white back all tattooed with scars, souvenirs of the amorous whipping that the sun had given her on blind nights when the stars were dark, asking her to come back and fulfill love face to face.

A rooster crowed, but when he realized that it was not dawn, but the light of the moon and the glow of a torch, he swallowed the cock-a-doodle-doo with a reverse sound, ood-eldood-a-kcoc, ridiculous and forced.

The priest and the sexton, who was in charge of the light but who, since he could not get closer, was looking more intently, with the glow of the flames lighting him up, drew back, half seeing what they could not believe, and the priest was gazing on what looked like a diabolical nightmare.

Out of each coconut, through something feminine that cannot be seen without sinning, the water was pouring out and wetting the floor.

"It's holy water!" the priest shouted, revealing his secret to the sexton.

"How can it be holy? Can't you see that they're women taking a leak?"

"Get away! Get away from me! Why did you say that? Why didn't you let that devilish vision be undone? Now, now it already has the flesh of words."

"Ah, but this time the devils can't get the best of me! Have I only got one arm? Don't I have a machete in my hand? And I'll start with one of these dirty sows who came here to piss in the cloister!"

And he jumped forward with his machete in hand, he dropped the torch, which was giving off tongues of golden flames, as one who was going to destroy with the blows of his machete the lewdest of the coconuts, the one with Giroma's sex, and that was when the devils laughed.

The cas-cas-cas-cas-cade of Cashtoc, deep, subterranean, a laugh of iron that softens as it cools, a cas-cas-cascade of metal and hollow-sounding beams, was joined to the convulsive, coughing laughs of devils poisoned by tobacco, or the asthmatics who, when they laugh, drown in dry pools, to such a degree that in order to get their breath back they have to move their bat wings, which also sound like dull laughter. Tazolín, who was also laughing, saw the awful Huasanga mounted on Cadejo, wearing her riding outfit. Cadejo, when he laughed, showed his teeth, just like golden railway ties along which the endless trains of his laughter were running. There was Sisimite, the dog-killer. Every malignant spirit kills something. The wolf-killer, a big, seven-wolf-killing-with-one-bite-every-night devil. The husband-killer, a little devil who was laughing with the movement of his ears, husband-killer because he was a louse who took care of old-timers who married young women. The louse, with his carnal bite, left them in their graves. The wood-killer, a vegetable devil who dried up trees, laughing next to Tazol, with an austere, desolate laugh. And the butcher devils, the slaughterers, scalded with the fire of the blood that was on their faces, hands, arms, and clothes, and formed a kind of hard-kill crust of scabs and wounds, laughing not only with their large mouths but with all the bloody stains that covered them.

The priest did not wait. His eyes, rolling with fear, saw the machete of the sexton lifted up against him, sharp as a razor, and he fled into the darkness, as if he were escaping into his immense cassock, changed into the total darkness of the parish house, the sacristy, the church, until he went out the main door, and he did not come back in, beams and locks fell when he opened it, because he had no strength in his legs, which doubled under until he was on his knees, with a round plate in his hands, and on that plate the head of the Baptist, cut off with one slice, bleeding, between his pale ashen lips the enormous teeth of a beheaded person which were also laughing.

The Gigantic who gave it to him—the beheading of Saint

John was the high point of the first part of the dance of the Gigantics—was wearing sacred clothes, with the sacred colors, with fringes representing the days of the sacred month.

And he could not help taking it (he felt that the sexton had cut off his head, that it was his own head that they were giving him in a plate dripping with blood), because it was the sacred custom to give the parish priest the head of the Baptist, the cranium of a large, bearded, long-nosed doll, with mussed-up hair, eyelids like the lid of a tomb, and the sweat of death simulated with drops of wax, while the giant drums, like the giants, were silent, and in the silence, in the majesty of the silence, the Gigantics saluted the stars that had turned to bone.

Over the sexton, they left him for dead among the coconuts, the devils passed, anxious to go out and celebrate on the square the decapitation of the Precursor, rolling in a tumult with green women, heads of coconuts, breasts of coconuts, bellies of coconuts, who were doing the dance of the palm trees with the movement of their arms.

These green beings, females with coconut heads, coconut breasts, coconut faces without eyes, without mouths, were showing off their perfections, naked, opulent, hospitable, worthy of the earth demon, the Great One, the Immense One, in the light of the stars that were banished from heaven, and when they fell they dragged along down their little tails of shining zoösperms.

The priest closed his eyes. He clutched to his lean and bony chest the head of Saint John, the size of the world, cut from the only living palm tree in the desert.

A shell horn cried nearby. Another cried far away. Another farther away. The four corners of the square, twisted by the earthquake, also cried like shell horns. And the main door of the church, converted into a shell horn, also cried beside the priest, who was squeezing the head of the Prophet, closing his eyes as tightly as the finally fallen lids of that figurehead, icy, fuzzy, with his skin of earth with scales of word, sweat, and dust put on.

"Who formed his mineral face? Who formed the stones?" the priest was repeating. "The desert," he answered himself, "the desert, layer upon layer of sand and silence, made it grow from the outside, and that was why no dead man can be silent with him to whom death came from outside and not from within."

A palm tree that was waving its branches rhythmically, just like a woman, like a Salome with many arms, her waist with all the flexibility of a rush, a body made from the coils of a snake, snatched away the head of the Baptist from the priest, just as the sexton, crawling like some kind of vermin, came out to join him, missing his right arm. He touched and retouched his shoulder to no avail. It was not there. The priest, when the sexton came over and confided his fear that he had lost his arm when he had decapitated that coconut head, touched him and said: *"Ego perdidi prae sulutum,"* using his Latin so that the other one would not understand what was in it, I am losing myself.

The drums were sounding with the continuous hesitation of beaten leather, accompanied in the background by the wail of small flutes, the sound of dripping water, the dance of the palm tree with the head of John among its fluvial, lacustrian, oceanic branches—hair of agate daggers, funerary rattlesnakes, atmosphere of alchemy—as it ran, without finding an exit, from one to the other of the four corners of the square, the four cardinal points, among the Gigantics, dolls that were lying half dead from fatigue, and the priest, who was sitting on a step in front of the church, his clerical bonnet tipped forward, leaving his tonsure half-covered behind, as he lamented not having been able to smuggle in the holy water, into the ear of the sexton, who, because he had lost an arm, was kneading and kneading the empty sleeve, as if from that effort of massaging that piece of cloth it would grow out again.

But the sexton left his ear and went out to meet the silence that was painted with stars, where the shouts of a palm tree with many arms were bubbling as it danced with the head of the decapitated giant, converted, among the branches, the hands with thousands of green fingers, into a livid star that was dripping blood and the sweat of fire. Her voice could be heard, and another bold voice that wailed:

I see you as you face the body of the sun,
yellow liquid attacked by fire's water,

now as ashes scattered by the wind,
torn out with diamond sparks
from the clean roots of the shadow!

I see you bathed in your red, reluctant blood,
sponged like honey from among the bitter strands,
the petrified machinery of a sea ghost,
a blinking, mauled desert, you yourself,
facing the jingle bells of dew
that sow the sex of the demanding suttler dame!
I see you and I cannot tell whether you are medal or rudder,

in your skin of old rags,
starched by the sweat of sweats,
erect, virile, with nothing but your head,
never appeased,
with the look of the one who swallowed the thorn
to plow his heart!

You fill your lungs with the multitude
that lazes under the sun
and washes itself at night
with the smell of salt and onions,
of trodden grass,
of the warm hollow an animal
leaves as he gets up sleeping.

Oh, dull and drab! The points of my breasts,
toasted to gold, enter your dead man's eyes.
Will your pupils suck my lonely milk?
Even dead, you slip out of my grasp!
Do you love the earth more?
Why do you not stand still in front of me,
head without a body?

Oh, dull and drab! I open the folds of my tunic
so that your head may sleep upon my naked thighs,
and I mingle your hair with my hair,
overcome on top of you who possess me
with your body in the tomb
and your head on my legs . . .

172

Oh, blind!
Oh, sweet!
Oh, only one!
Oh, dull and drab!

My feet play with your head,
your beard tickles my soul,
the cold edge of your forehead,
the great ivory tears of your untouched teeth
of a chewer of herbs . . .
I am going mad! . . . I had wanted you warm
as the froth of boiling milk,
and for you to bite my toes like a slave,
with a shuffle of sandals.

Oh, dull and drab!
When I put your head to my ear,
I can hear your breathing of the sea
in the depths of the desert,
and I shake it as one shakes a sea shell,
and I shout, an avaricious woman with an empty grasp,
where are my star eyes?
It is frightful to shake your head
and not hear your stars knock together!
You path like darkness . . . let me!
Your hairy chest and wheel of teeth . . .
Let me pour out into the river of my weeping!
Your hands have swollen into sails!
I could have fit into your hands like water
that quenched your lightning thirst,
or barley that cocooned your hunger.
Let me! Heavy as the darkness and just a head!
Let me swim out of your hair,
like a castaway caught up in weeds and water,
but who surfaces at last . . .
your surface is heroic!
Let me crawl out of the caverns of your eyes,
fleeing from the paths in your inside
where corpses start to walk!
Let me come out of your lips
like the sand of the desert that curses
me in the depths of the seas . . . let me . . . !

The great drum of the skin of the night, the great drum of the skin of blood, the great drum of the skin of clouds, the great drum of the skin of forests, all recovered their throbbing brilliance at the feet of the Gigantics, stretched out in the tangled dance of tasting or biting the ground, according to whether they danced on their soles or on tiptoes, without breaking the movement of the obsidian hoops of the black drum, the coral hoops of the red drum, the copal hoops of the white drum, the jade hoops of the green drum, hangmen's nooses that in superimposed sonorous circles rose from their feet all up along their giant bodies until they came off over their heads, and woe to him who, when he passed the noose of sound around his neck, became confused in the dance, closed his eyes right there, lost his breath, and remained hanging in the infinite night.

Cashtoc, the Great, the Immense, the demons of the earth and the wind, Cabracán and Huracán, the devils of the umbilical grain, Tazol and Tazolín, and all the working devils of Tierrapaulita, Cadejos, Sisimites, Weeping Women, Siguamontas, Siguanabas, Elfs, Siguapates, Mirror Serpents, Popiques, Malinalis, little devils of the bushes and little devils of the air, were watching the spectacle, eyes and teeth, tails and horns, motionless as if magnetized.

Another Episode in the Dance of the Gigantics

Tazolín, the umbilical son of Tazol, twirled his sling and sent a stone in the direction of one of those dancing mastodons, a Gigantic who fell flat among the jumbled complaint of the drums and the shuffling of everybody. Only Giroma, the powerful Giroma because of her riches, the sad one, dispossessed of her light, of her sex, ran to lean over the newly fallen Gigantic.

It was Yumí, and she immediately began to shout to

heaven for help, unprotected in the night, where the echo of the drums had just been extinguished and the stars were going out from the breath of the wind, like lighted candles.

Stretched out, the body of the Gigantic Yumí, whom the priest and the sexton took to be Goliath, was growing as the night grew, already immense in the silence. And Giroma felt that she, a woman of flesh and blood, was not the widow of Goliath, according to what the priest and the sexton had been talking about. The widow was the night.

The dead giant grew and the night grew. The giant grew more and the night grew more.

The earth and the sky gave way for that long mountain to fit in the darkness.

The Gigantics wept for him with tears of stone, leaning over the body of their companion who had been killed by the stone of a small boy, in a kind of dance of posthumous homage, a dance in which they raised their eyes of monsters who were suckling from the sap that was falling from the stars.

"Dead! Dead!" Giroma was repeating to make herself believe it, moving her hands that were edgeless razors along the fallen body of that mountain range that was growing, growing . . .

And with every stretching of the Gigantic—for Giroma, that hill was still Yumí, her husband . . . what an idea, bringing a mountain to throw down in the square!—Tierrapaulita was rocking on top of the hammock-earth, and the church was creaking, just as if it were about to collapse.

One-armed, trembling, the sexton went over with his voice of a dried-out tubercular to tell them not to touch, not to move the Gigantic Goliath, because it was written that his weight would sink the world.

"Not touch, not move my husband?" Giroma stood up over the body of the Gigantic on whom she had been raining tears, and added her protest: "Where did such a fine messenger from Huasanga come from?"

"Madam, the fact is, if they move him . . ."

"The fact is, if they move him," she offered, "and how can we avoid moving him, since we have to bury him!"

"I don't know," the sexton excused himself, "but what

175

we will know if they move him is that he'll bury all of us in a wink of the earth, which will open and close."

"Our Lord has hidden his face from us—let us hope that it is only for a moment . . . *in momento indignationis absondi faciem meam parumoer a te!*" said the afflicted priest, the ground wavering under his feet, wavering and shaking in a sinister combination of tilting and balancing.

"These people don't ask for confession! Savages, ask the Father to absolve you!" shouted the sexton from behind the priest, who was running from one extreme of the square to the other, tormented by the continuous trembling of the earth.

"Why should they ask, since they know that nothing is of any good against their demons who are persecuting us— hurricanes, earthquakes, the destruction of everything and the annihilation of human kind!"

"Father! My God! The earth is opening up!"

"Memento homo quia pulvis eris!"

"What possessed you to speak Latin to them—ask them, ask them not to move the Gigantic—they didn't pay any attention to me!"

"Oh, my son, by speaking to God in the divine language, perhaps he will remember us!"

"I don't care whether he remembers or not!"

"Blasphemer!"

"Blasphemer or not, what's urgent is for you to ask them not to move the Gigantic; if you don't, you'll be *pulvis* head first underneath the ground!"

"The earth is opening up!" The priest fell on his knees to the ground that had been softened by the tremors, next to the sexton. "Lord God, have mercy! I broke my fast, that's true, with chocolate and peanuts! I smoked when I woke up, before saying Mass, I filled my stomach with smoke, when I should have only sucked on the cigar and blown it out my nose, avoiding its serving as a perverse food! I wound up more than one prophetic holy woman and more than one of them went around announcing that the earth would be converted into a cemetery of unburied corpses, ready to revive when they heard the trumpets of the Last Judgment!"

176

His voice was suddenly cut off. He stood up and went on: "Sexton, don't you hear trumpets?"

"Yes, they're the trumpets of the Dance of the Gigantics. They're announcing the death of Goliath."

"Oh, Malachi!"

"Let's go to the burial," the sexton proposed, his feet on the quiet ground; it seemed impossible to them that the extremely long tremor had passed, "because we're all out of tobacco."

"Get thee behind me! I will not smoke again until Cashtoc frees me from the clutches of Cashtoc!"

"Father, watch what you're saying!"

"Yes, only the Devil can free one from the Devil!"

"Giving up tobacco? That's all right; but that doesn't mean that you don't have to accept what they offer you so you can give it to me. I'll smoke until the all-powerful Lord thinks it proper to get us out of here!"

"Do you doubt, then, that it will be soon? Why do you want to store up tobacco?"

"What I doubt, Father, is your will to abstain from a delicious cigar, and that's why I haven't offered not to smoke until we leave, but to smoke until we leave Tierra-paulita!"

"But, sexton, that offer presupposes, implies—do you understand me?"

"Completely, Father, except when you speak Latin, because then I'm tempted to answer you in the pig Latin of the altar boys who assist at Mass."

"You understand, then, what I'm trying to tell you. In your promise is implicit the belief that we are never going to save ourselves, that we are never going to leave here, because if that were not the case, you would not be planning to build up any supply."

"Let's go to the burial," the sexton insisted. "They've already taken the corpse away. He's a mountain. It took thousands of them to put him on their shoulders."

"You go and tell me about it."

"Millions of ants moving a mountain . . ."

"You go and tell me," the priest repeated. "I'll stay in the square, over there under the bandstand, protecting myself a little from the night dew. I don't want to expose myself to their asking me to read the response for a giant who was not baptized."

"And we don't have any practice in the matter of reading responses for giants, and it would not be looked upon well if you were there; besides the widow, there's his other widow, Huasanga."

"Go ahead—the time has come for the pygmies to bury the giants!"

Who goes with you?

Your dreams were cut off, and life continues as it goes.

The widow of a giant, dressed in obsidian, with no other jewels except the stones of the great ages!

A widow dispossessed alive of the skin of her husband whom they tore away from you like part of your skin, while lost in your ears without human limits was the rolling of the earthly drums and the black voices of the heralds of destruction who raised their hands to their brows as they bowed before your Goliath, fallen like a temple without wings!

And it was during the dog days, in the last bath of the golden salts unhooked from the burning torches like pieces of forgetfulness that are consumed alone.

The widow of a giant, the white owl had descended from the belfry to drink the oil from the lamps of eulogies and navigation!

The shadows pass, but not the one of the lost love, the shadow that chills, a spectral shadow, an ancient sponge that sticks to the face like a mask!

Giroma—Catarina Zabala your real name—call the four hundred gravediggers with copper skins, tattooed with symbols and with your word of diamond which breaks up into a tear, ask them to help you bury your giant, without waking him, because he would wake up as a dwarf, as you had wanted, when by your powerful will he was changed into Chiltic!

Do you hear?

The Four Hundred Young Men were already talking on the terraces, in doorways, in front of the church, in the squares, and they came up on tiptoe to the one who, by playing Goliath in the dance of the giants, lost his life, struck by Tazolín, the son of his wife and not his, with a pebble that was put in the sling of the little umbilical devil by the vengeful Huasanga, the one who had torn the sex off that widow, that double widow, without husband and without sex.

The giant fell down in the middle of the dance, with its four sacred masks, in time to the throbbing rhythm of the great black hide, the great red hide, the great white hide, the great green hide, the four drums, nocturnal, bleeding, cloudy, and like a mountain, and without the earth's sinking, no one would have been able to move the coprse, except these four hundred pall-bearers.

Get your sex back? What for, with the giant dead. What for, if you're bandaged up in mourning?

Night, the widow of the sea, will understand your white betrothal to the Four Hundred Young Men who are carrying Yumí on their shoulders, Yumí or the dwarf Chiltic, converted into a giant, like waves that on their shoulders are holding up the largest vessel. They, your Four Hundred Husbands, in place of the giant, will undo your hair gathered into a single braid for the blackest of mourning, will touch your breasts, will kiss your navel, and on your skin of butterfly wings, where you had your sex, they will pour a covering of live-oak ashes, the most chaste of ashes.

But where are they taking him, what tomb will fit him, if standing up he is taller than the night and lying down he is as broad as the sea?

Will they roll him up to bury him, like the great serpents, who after they are dead keep on breathing through their horns?

Will they cut him into pieces?

The axes are ready. Four hundred chops into Yumí's flesh. Four hundred pieces of his giant's body. Four hundred eclipses.

A *chimán*, a sorcerer with a face of bluish bone, interposed himself between the four hundred axes already in the air and the body of the giant. His luminous hands, rings on the tips of his fingers, around his fly-wing fingernails rings sparkling with fish hooks, and he stopped the butchering of the one who, in spite of his four faces and his look of a serpent-corpse, was none other than Yumí.

"Don't chop him up! It's useless!" Chimán shouted. "His pieces will come together, he can be rejoined, and he will come to life again."

Huasanga was laughing as she heard the widow weeping, without the latter's being able to hear who was laughing, because the former had made herself invisible.

"And I get nothing from stopping them from chopping him up," Chimán added, face of bluish bone, "and I may even be going against my own interests, since I'm traveling around buying heads to sell to Cal-Cuj, who, locked up in a cave, feeds himself on human heads. His cacao claws are bloody. The killer of sons. He's eaten them. The killer of wives. He's eaten them. An evil creature with red eyes, grandfather and father of discord, insult, calumny, an anonymous letter written in blood. My interest would be for you to let the four hundred axes fall on this gigantic body, because I would be left with the beautiful head to bring and sell to Cal-Cuj."

"Are you looking for heads?" the one-armed sexton intervened.

"But not yours. Your flesh smells too much of incense, and that's why Cal-Cuj barely tasted your arm, spit it out, and threw it in the garbage."

"In the garbage?" The sexton opened his eyes wide. "Where, where is that garbage dump?"

"It's underneath a tree where so many monkeys are hanging that it doesn't seem to have leaves, but tails."

"Take him there, Chimán!" intervened the invisible Huasanga. The sexton was trying to find out who was talking. "Take him there, Chimán, Carved Flint, Valiant Hunter, Weaver of the Message of the Speaking Jaguar! Take him there and he, in exchange for his arm, will give you another head, the head of another giant, a certain John, who was beheaded in the great dance of the giants at the request of a lustful sinner, a good dancer, with teeth on her sex!"

"Do you have that head?" Chimán asked, all of his death-blue face turned toward the sexton's face.

"I know where they hid it. The tremor of the earth made the dancers run away. It's magnificent. Enormous. Crowned with tendrils and striped like a tiger's head, that was how the lips, painted with annatto, were cleaned by the one who

180

demanded that they behead him as she caressed him after he was dead."

"It doesn't matter. Stuck in his cave, Cal-Cuj, a jackal who devours human heads and flesh, won't see it. I'll sell it to him by the pound. You say that it's big. When heads are small I deal with him by the lot. But when they're big, he takes them according to weight."

"But it's not a head."

"What do you mean, it's not a head?" the cutting voice of the invisible thief of women's sex intervened.

The sexton was going to explain to Chimán that it was not a real head, but the head of a dummy, a Gigantic from the dance of the Gigantics.

"Yes, it's not a regular head, I was going to say," the sexton picked up in passing, "but a head that must have a lot of meat and bone, because it weighs so much that I can't lift it with just one arm."

"Maybe it's still attached to the neck of the victim. Maybe it isn't completely separated."

"Ha! It was a brutal cut and that's how I lost my arm."

"Oh, you were the one who beheaded him?"

"But I thought it was a coconut."

"What, what, what?"

"Oh, Chimán, what pleasure to speak to a person like you who understands the inexplicable! If you only knew what was happening to us . . ." The sexton turned his head all around and went over to the great ear of the wizard, the ear of a deaf beggar who eats with it the few sounds that silence gives him as alms. "Cashtoc, the Great, the Immense," he went on with his explanation, "has us besieged, the priest and me, in this place that ought not be called Tierrapaulita but Tierramaldita, accursed land, because we have no holy water. To get out of that situation, Father proposed to smuggle in the holy liquid, and he ordered several loads of coconuts that would be full of holy water; but Cashtoc's partisans found out about it and on every coconut, when we were getting ready to draw out the precious liquid, they had put that part of a female that cannot be mentioned, and what did we see, what did we see, Father and I—the coconuts changed into urinating women. Indignant at such a trick, beside myself, machete in hand, aimed at one of those coconuts, but in the maneuver it was my arm, I put such effort into its decapitation . . ."

The sexton took a breath: "I lost my machete and my arm, and when I got to the front of the church I found the priest with a plate in his hands, and on the plate a head, the head of a giant, the head of Saint John the Baptist, ready for you, Chimán, to carry off to that Cal-Cuj, just as long as you give me back my arm, take me to the dump where Cal-Cuj threw it.

"If you'll just wait here for me, because it's not mine. First, logically, it belonged to the giant and now it belongs to the dancer who asked for it from the twinkling stars on this endless night. I'll have to sneak it off, steal it, do you understand?"

They had abandoned the head on the steps of the church during the tremor. The sexton would risk anything to get his arm back. He wrapped it up in banana leaves, then in salt leaves and rags soaked in chicken blood. In that way Chimán would think that it was real. The smell of blood would stop him, eager as he was to be in the good graces of Cal-Cuj, from unwrapping it. The main thing was for him to give him back his arm, and put it back on, that was why he was a healer with the greatest magic. After they had it all agreed on, with that head of a big doll from a religious play.

"Let's get out of here! Let's get out of here right now!" the sexton quickly said in the ear of Chimán, who was happy as he felt the bulk and smelled the pleasant odor of blood. "Let's get out of here, because we run the danger that they'll take it away from us!"

"With ten petals, like my fingers, shall be the friendship between us," Chimán offered, with the head of the dead man on his shoulder, followed by the sexton, who slyly asked him if he could go with him to where he had to meet Cal-Cuj.

"I'm not authorized to show you the way—" that was the answer the sexton had expected, the one he wanted— "and it would be better if you went first to the dump to look for your arm. I'll take you another time. You can also hunt for heads for Cal-Cuj. He pays very well. By the lot or by weight."

"And this one, how much does it weigh?" the sexton asked for something to say.

"I estimate six pounds. A very fine head."

"Yes, very fine, and I think that it has enough meat, cartilage, and bone. Cal-Cuj will enjoy it."

"Part of it he eats raw, and part cooked with sweet corn."

The dump was seen among some rocks, bushes, and trees that were half dry, covered with *micos*, little monkeys with very long tails, intelligent, howlers, ready to give battle, prepared to defend the sacred garbage of Cal-Cuj from those talking birds, as they no doubt viewed Chimán and his companion, who had to raise his one arm to protect his face from the green fruit and broken branches they were throwing at them.

Chimán gave them some peanuts. A scramble. Bites, shrieks, blows with their tails, slaps, scratches, just enough time to recover the arm that Cal-Cuj had not eaten because it was the arm of a censer bearer.

"Oh!" The sexton almost fainted when he felt Chimán sticking his arm back on with monkey spit; he did not know what to say, and he stammered with emotion: "How can I thank you, who have your face to the sun, your face to the stars, your face below the earth turned toward you, the shadow of a black bird on the stone table!"

The sexton soon realized that it was not he who was speaking through his own lips, because the one who used complimentary speech like that was Huasanga, the nonpareil.

"I'm going. Don't follow my tracks. You'd get lost. I'm in a hurry. I have to reach Cal-Cuj's cave as soon as possible with this great present, the head of an illuminate, a precious stone that is weighed as a precious stone, a quetzal feather that is weighed as a quetzal feather, a dream of dreams, a bearded man with pheasant eyes."

The impatience of the enchanter to reach the cave of Cal-Cuj, Face of the Death of Heaven, Drunken Owl, Slim Shell of Black Ears, was the same as that of the ex-one-armed sexton to get away from him, now that he already had his arm, before they could discover his trick of having given them, in place of a real head, a head of rags, cardboard, and clay, with the teeth of a dead man and the beard of a goat.

The sexton trotted down the mountains that after the burning-off looked like the rumps of immense monkeys with hair of burned gold.

"Tierrapaulita!" he shouted when he saw at his feet the town that had fallen out of the sky like an old denture.

And he raised his two arms, the old one and the one that Chimán had just attached with monkey spit, endowed, he had told him, with the strength of an arm of the sea.

In the meantime, the enchanter continued step by step along the path of sand and stones that were crumbling, toward Cal-Cuj Mountain. The mountain was also known by the name of its only inhabitant, the Devourer of Heads.

Chimán was no longer climbing. The head weighed so much that he could barely take a step, and he was on the point of sitting down and unwrapping it, because more than the head of a man, even if he were a giant, it weighed like that of a lion.

But he had to arrive before nightfall, and there was nothing to do but gather his remaining strength and keep on climbing.

"Cal-Cuj!" he shouted, exhausted, at the entrance to the cavern, feeling around among thick piles of straw in which the wind of the summit was coughing, sneezing, making all the noises of a rheumy old man.

"Cal-Cuj, you of the Braid of Birds, you of the Tattooed Heart, listen to your Chimán, who brings you a great present! Listen to him, before the empty darkness snatches away from him the noblest of human heads! Weigh it! Weigh its silence without muteness, its clarity without light, its thought without bones!"

The echo repeated the words of Chimán in the cavern as the only reply.

"Cal-Cuj, leaving me like this in the loneliness, exposed to the terrible, monstrous darkness, a sharp wheel without claws, without face, without feathers, unique, fatal, with the weight of flowers, of clouds, of stars, of precious perfumes for the god that has his side open!"

And raising the head, the smell of blood waking him, perhaps, he shouted louder: "Some sign, Cal-Cuj, some

184

sign! Bring out your balance for weighing heads in your deformed ginger hand, the balance of the four cups, and put in any one of them, in the black one, in the white one, in the red one, in the green one, the weight of night, the weight of day, the weight of blood, the weight of trees, so that you will know how much this head weighs!"

Taking refuge up on the bandstand of the main square in Tierrapaulita, where, before Cashtoc, the Great, the Immense, had begun the destruction of the town, concerts had been given, the priest heard the steps of the parishioners who, without doubt, were coming back from the burial of the giant, indifferent, ragged, and not once, but several times, he went over to the railing with the urge to preach them a sermon that would make them tremble, repent, drop to their knees.

But the fear that they would stone him dissuaded him from it.

Nevertheless, the Holy Spirit was more powerful than his fear, and in the middle of a great shake of the earth, a tremor, he started off vehemently. He did not get through many words. A roar rose up from that accumulation of ill-tempered, wrathful people, some armed with the Holy Hemp Rope, the lash for bad interpreters of God or the devils.

The entrance door to the bandstand, locked on the inside, resisted the rush of the mob, but already some of the more agile were climbing up the walls and reached the railing which enclosed the narrow space in which the priest would have to defend himself, an attitude that he rejected, kneeling down, lowering his head and waiting for them to decapitate him.

Decapitate him? No. Whip him with the Holy Hemp Rope is what they proposed to do, if the sexton had not come to his help. He came around one of the corners, and when he saw the danger that the little Father was in, he stretched out his right arm and from the distance of several yards he took the bandstand in his hand and lifted it off its foundations, with the priest and all of those who had him cornered, cowards, who, when they felt the bandstand rising like a balloon, jumped and almost killed themselves.

The priest, meanwhile, ran from one side to the other of

185

what was no longer a bandstand, but the basket of a balloon, but not of a free balloon, rather of a balloon that an all-powerful hand was guiding.

The toothless roofs of the houses of Tierrapaulita—some were already just beams without any tiles—the knock-kneed towers of the church, the twisted streets, the moat without a bridge, the walls, all passed under the flying bandstand where the priest was traveling on his knees, giving thanks to God for having saved him, not so much from death as from the testicular flagellation with hemp ropes.

But he raised his head and noticed that the one who was carrying him in the air was the sexton. Impossible! It could not be! He rubbed his eyes until they almost came out and stood naked on their lids in order to believe it. And he did not believe it, and he would not have believed it yet, if the other one, with his powerful right arm, had not deposited the bandstand on a hill in the outskirts of Tierrapaulita and come over to greet him, pale and smiling like an acrobat who had taken the death-defying leap.

Renegade! he was on the point of scolding him, with the greasy volume of the *Divine Office* all ready to throw into his face, but he reined in his character of a crotchety old priest, ready to listen to the sexton, who was slipping into his ears the idea that, in order to free themselves from Cashtoc, the Great, the Immense devil of red earth, one of them, the only church people there were in Tierrapaulita, would have to make a pact with the one who was not only a demon but something worse, an infidel demon, a pagan demon. As could be seen, he had been one-armed, and now he had his two arms and the strength of a giant, that sexton of his, negligent and traitorous, and he had gone ahead and made a pact secretly with Cashtoc, in the den of the four dancing voices.

"And now," the sexton said, "I'll fly to Tierrapaulita and save the church!"

The priest became doubly alarmed. What that reprobate had said meant that the church was in danger, but his haste in accompanying him meant that he was already making the pact.

The church was dancing like a giantess to the rhythm of

186

horrid-sounding subterranean noises, beats from the drum of the drummer devil.

The church was dancing and the square was dancing. The square was dancing and the houses were dancing and the mountains were dancing. The mountains were dancing and the trees were dancing.

"The Holy Shirt of the Son of the Living God . . ." the priest was reciting the Prayer of the Holy Shirt, stuttering without stuttering, his jawbones clenched and his hair standing on end like the comb of a rooster before a mirror, while the demonized sexton was encircling the church with his right arm, which in exchange for the false head of Saint John, Chimán had stuck back on him, so that the church would not fall down.

"But a thousand times better on the earth!" The Father was upset and now reciting the Prayer of the Great Power of God, effective against earthquakes, as he affirmed that it would be better if the church fell to the ground than be saved by that demonized man, as much of a greeter as he was false, in the midst of the catastrophe he was making little signs of greeting, a cabalist from whom he quickly ran away, as from Cashtoc himself.

But the sexton ran to catch up to him, carrying the church in the air like the bandstand with his powerful arm, shouting at him: "Don't leave it behind, Father! Can't you see how it follows you? The church is following its shepherds! Shall I put it down on this hill? Would you prefer it farther away?"

"Put it back in its place, let's not make any bargains!"

"All right, and then let's escape from Tierrapaulita! That deep moat is the limit of the domains of Cashtoc, who asked Huracancito to carry off the bridge, so all right, I'll put down my arm so that you can cross and I'll escape right behind you!"

The proposal was tempting. But that was the sticky part of the Devil, the tempting part.

What better bridge than that arm that had saved him, making the bandstand fly like a balloon, from the debasing whipping, and which defended the cracked structure of the house of God, now in its place again, from the volcanic angers of a rebellious earth?

"Hey! hey! hey!" secret voices resounded in the cleric's brows. "Now you're deceiving yourself, which is the Devil's own way, he doesn't deceive, he lets the interest deceive the interested party."

Because that was the other side of the coin.

Was not Cashtoc's ultimate desire to finish him, not to kill him—that would have been the least—but to keep him alive in the infernal palaces of his volcanoes, make him travel awake through that underworld of volatile caverns that disengage like gigantic vampires, and fly from one side to the other underneath the terrestrial crust, or carry him to the moon, where he would find the ashes of everything created, or to the sun, where he would find the great condemned ones?

"Let's try. Try to cross over," the sexton proposed, stretching out his powerful arm from one side of the moat to the other.

The ecclesiastic refused, drawing back, with his hands lost in the pockets of his cassock, moving his head from one side to the other on a neck which, without the white collar, gave him the look of a madman, but the sexton whispered in his ear: "After us there will be no Devil in Tierrapaulita, because we will return with holy water, a good supply of hosts, lots of wine, and we'll invite the Prelate, so that he can do battle along with us. But we have to get out of here!"

The Battle of the Heads

Cal-Cuj, at Chimán's call, weighed the head which the other one announced with so many exaggerations on his scale of four balances, and it really was a matter of something superior to anything his appetite had imagined. It weighed more than night, more than blood, more than the clouds, more than the trees, weights that were put as counter-balances on the black disk, the red disk, the white, and the green.

While he was weighing it, his mouth was watering and he was imagining a most glorious banquet.

From his most hidden of stills he would draw out his best liquor, he would light his lamps of rose-perfumed oil, and he would go down to the Great Idol to give him some of the blood of that princely head to try.

But the first thing, as in all banquets, was to get drunk. The liquor, poured by the glassful, did not take long in going to his head, nor did his mouth take long in opening slightly with a smile of hieroglyphic teeth, ready to sink themselves into the first bite of what his whole being was craving.

The face at his feet was bloody, the chicken blood that the sexton had put inside the large mask with bushy eyebrows, lashes spread wide, a few stingy hairs.

The smell was perfect. In the oily light that was coming from the lamps and floating loose in the airless cavity of the cave, what a beautiful piece of human being: pale as a sunset, sandy hair in curly ringlets, nose in a sharp hook, lips to be kissed while they slept.

Cal-Cuj, drunk to the point of falling down, stretched out on a mat and brought over the face of the head that he was going to nibble on, smear over his mouth, and he kissed and bit it at the same time, but in one of those bites he let out a terrible ouch!, he had just put his teeth into something that was clay, starched rags, and very hard cardboard.

A laugh from the pain of a toothache that generations would hear until the end of the world, on the top of Cal-Cuj Mountain, the tail-lash of a comet imprisoned in the heart of the mountain, and a roaring around in search of recovery so that he could stop that frightful laugh, and he was laughing from both pain and rage, which was the same thing as he caught on to the trick of which he had been victim.

He lay on his back, rolling around, resolved not to let anyone pull his leg. Pull his leg, his arm? He remembered at once the arm of the sea with occult powers that he had

189

given to Chimán, so that he could exchange it for that accursed head.

The gray-haired priest, receptive to the words of the sexton, return and expel the devil from Tierrapaulita, crossed himself, began to recite the prayer of the Seven African Powers and started out on the bridge formed by the other one's arm.

But what was going on?

Halfway across the arm, halfway across the bridge, the strength went out of it, its rigidity, its substance, and it was changed into a cloth sleeve from which the priest would have fallen into the bottom of the moat if he had not managed to grab the branches of a guava tree.

The danger of death facing the priest made the sexton forget the loss of his arm for a moment, the second time he had lost it, and more painful now, since it was a question of a magic arm.

With his help—he had used his belt, and sometimes he was helping the priest and sometimes his pants that kept falling down—the priest managed to climb out, and they both stayed there as if seasick, the cleric stretched out on the ground—the great fright had still not passed—and the sexton trying to hold back the tears that were wetting the empty sleeve of his jacket.

Far from there, but not too far, Chimán was waking up to the pecks of a big ugly bird called the Bean-Cracker. It was pecking him on the ear, and each blow could be felt by him, even though half asleep, as if bone dice were rolling around inside of his ear, the square little words with which he was being called by Cal-Cuj, who was part of Cashtoc, the Great, the Immense.

"A pain in your heart for calling me with the Bean-Cracker," Chimán said to himself, "and I tremble to think what I will find burning on the tip of his tongue!"

And he set out for Cal-Cuj Mountain.

"A bad sign," Chimán said to himself, seeing white stones pop up in his path, "because he's so hungry that he's sticking out his teeth at ground level. If the head I brought him didn't satisfy him, where will I find more heads?"

The voice of Chimán doubled down over his chest, like part of his face, his chin, the few hairs of his beard, and, silent, he reached the summit of the mountain, where Cal-Cuj showed him his broken teeth.

"And I thought, Holy Wizard and Lord of the Four Masks, that you were sticking out your teeth along the road from hunger."

"I was sticking them out from pain. I showed them as white stones on the roads so that I could get some relief, because, pretty as you came and threw me that head, which I paid for at the price of gold, it was not a real head, but a big rock."

And after a long silence: "How will I get my teeth back? When will I get my molars back? How will they grow out again? From what roots? I don't want white teeth, but blue ones! To bite like the sky! To bite like the sea! That's what I want!"

"But that sexton won't get away from me! Watch me urinating rattan vines here!" Chimán shouted. "I'll bring you his head for you to eat, cooked with amaranth and squash seeds, because you won't like it raw, the way you didn't like the arm I brought you."

"And which I gave back, at your request, Chimán, changed into an arm of the all-powerful sea!"

"Because it tasted like the flesh of a censer bearer."

"But now, Chimán, my Chimán, with the hunger and rage I have, even though he smells of incense, I'll stuff both my cheeks with him."

"After all," the priest consoled himself, not far from Cal-Cuj Mountain, on the rim of the moat, leaning his head on the sexton's shoulder, every time that Cashtoc fooled him in his attempts at flight, the years rained down on him, "after all, the arm that wizard gave back to you, and I feared you had made a pact with the Devil, helped you rescue me from death and flagellation when you made the bandstand fly, and then your arm saved the church from falling down when it was dancing like a giantess. What more can we seek from the Lord, sinners that we are? He saved my life and priestly dignity so that I could go on fighting against Cashtoc, even without material weapons, since we're even dispossessed of holy water, and he left the

191

church standing so that services could still go on."

They returned to the parish house when night had already come on, time to go to sleep, but not with that intention. They had to stand watch, if they did not want to be surprised by Cashtoc, the Great, the Immense, who did not sleep with both eyes, either by day or by night. While the sun was up, he kept his black eye of a dark cave open, and when night fell his glowing eye of a jaguar.

But their eyelids, little scales on which the head of sleep was weighed, were giving in, the counterweight of their pupils was not enough, and the momentary image of death which robs man of his senses fell over them.

A little stream of ammoniated, copper-colored liquid, which in contact with the air becomes a solid vine, was flowing, while Chimán, there in the distance next to Cal-Cuj, who could not find any relief for his broken teeth, kept on pissing vines and pissing vines, all that was needed to travel over hills and valleys to where the sexton was.

The little liquid snake stopped beneath the cot where he was sleeping with a heavy snore, and it climbed up the scissor legs, divided into four little serpents, and, turn upon turn, it coiled around the body of the man, covering him down from the shoulders, his arm, the empty sleeve, his hand, his chest, his waist, his navel, his legs, his thighs, his ankles, down to the tips of his toes, his buttocks, his crotch, his sex, his waist, his navel, his chest, his arm, his hand, and his shoulders, and then once more from top to bottom, and then once more from bottom to top, with the mechanical precision of thread turning on a spindle.

The priest woke up, anxious to tell how he had freed himself from a horrible nightmare, his heart, like a giant, jumping in his breast, his forehead pearled with ice-cold sweat, his mouth dry; but, whom could he tell it to, because beside him, in the next cot, instead of the sexton there was a decapitated mummy.

"Oh, no!" the cleric shouted, and jumped out of bed in shirt and shorts, more gray than white, and in some places grayer than gray. "There's no better exorcism than a good beating!"

And he began to beat the leaden mummy at the same time as he hurled the vilest insults against the Devil.

But it was like beating on a tortoise shell and the spell remained, without Cashtoc's coming out to defend himself with his numerous hands of fire, even when they lost contact with his legs, and his legs with his feet, and his feet contact with the ground, remaining as if in the air.

"Dominus mecum!" were his last words before falling silent, swallowing as he did the insults which the gears of his thought were grinding through up to his rigid lips, incapable of articulating a word.

Under the sexton's cot was his head.

No, it was not his head—it was another head, more voluminous, wrapped in leaves, dirty with earth, stained with blood, bitten, just as if some alligator had begun to eat it!

And he did not have his cassock on!

He slipped it on as best he could. That armor was good for something, even though it was so threadbare that his legs could be seen through the fabric.

The blue clarity of volcanic ash that was coming in through a high window promised a rapid dawn that he had not expected there with that beheaded person wrapped up in layers and layers of silvery vine, lunar, and the head of a giant with woman's hair beneath the bed.

"The first thing you have to get out of your head is that you have a head!" he repeated, turning around with his cassock on now; when he put it on, he had not felt his head.

The church had filled up with people with tadpole eyes. Those Tierrapaulita people, who never spoke or moved.

What were they waiting for?

Those in charge of the dance of the Giants were looking everywhere for the head that had been sliced off in the sacred pantomimic memorial of the beheading of the Baptist, and they thanked the Father, who showed them where it was, scratched and battered.

But the sexton was not the only one who was missing his head that morning; all of the saints in the church were too.

"Oh, wicked Indians!" elucidated the cleric, out of control, "because this is not the work of Cashtoc, but of the Indians! If it had been Cashtoc—" he was weeping bigger and better—"the church would smell of powder farts, but the stink is that of a public pissery—the unbearable stench of a wet Indian, of damp vines!"

Which of those shaggy parishioners, spread out on the pews of the church with the pleasure of their heads, scratching away at their lice, among the headless saints, would clear up for him the mystery of the disappearance of the holy heads, except that of Saint Dennis, who held his in his hands; they had cut it off, but neither stupid nor lazy, he had picked it up.

And hadn't they probably done to him just what had happened to Saint Dennis the Areopagite?—the doubt entered him—hadn't they cut off his head just like the sexton, and what he was probably carrying now was just a talking head?

"Father! Father!" There came up to speak with him some women who were bulky, heavy-browed, squat, with ears of jerked beef and a rain of earrings of gold and precious stones.

When the priest came to, the first thing he did was raise his hands to his head. What joy that they had not stolen it!

Those big women, the confiscated goods of the church in its old age, accused Cal-Cuj and Chimán of that bloodless decapitation, with the added insult of wrapping up the sexton in tree-killing vines.

"And something worse," the priest added, regretfully, "because they were taking him away piece by piece, first his arm, then his head!"

"But the cockfight man has come," those women informed him, and since the cleric pretended not to understand, or because he really did not understand, they affirmed, surprised, "this morning the cockfight man arrived."

"Poorly done," shook the voice of the cockfight man in the square of Tierrapaulita. "The parish priest should make a pact with the Devil when it's a case of a Cashtoc, a Tazol, a Sisimite, Siguanas, Cal-Cuj, and Siguapate, all the more so if they're awake, and from what I can see they're not asleep, because there isn't a house that hasn't been cracked, Huracán and Cabracán! They're demons of the earth, indigenous, terrible, millenary!"

"But you, kind sir, if you wanted to, you could mediate."

"Me?" laughed the important person, hiding his teeth, which were the only ugly thing about him, teeth of dirty marrow. "With all my heart, but you have to remember that I'm a bit of a devil myself—ha! ha! ha!"

Those who were talking to him, half-breeds with mustaches, assimilated Indians, but still beardless, were thinking, while he was laughing: He's not a bit, he's a full-blown devil!

"Anyway," he said, going toward the front of the church, "I'll help you," and he said subtly, "I'll help you if the priest will back me up."

"You don't need advice, but right now you could win his favor by helping him find out where the heads of the saints that were stolen last night are hidden."

"It won't be easy."

"For someone for whom nothing is impossible?"

"It might seem so, but respect for the impossibles of ones like Cashtoc is what keeps the peace between us."

"Your worship knows what he's doing, but the saints can't go on that way without their heads."

"Unless it was a church in the shape of a cheese, the kind they build today, where they only have statues of decapitated martyrs on the altars. Saint Osita, Saint Dennis, Saint Laurianus, or—" with full rascality now—"if we put animal heads on the saints."

"Animal heads on the saints?" The half-breeds with mustaches and the simulated or assimilated ones were scandalized.

"The consternation among the hosts of Cashtoc, the Great, the Immense, would be indescribable. The heads of their guardian spirits on the bodies of saints?"

"And the surprise of the priest would be unimaginable!" the others vouchsafed, blinking to protect their eyes with whispers of shadow before they became blinded by the flinty fire that was coming out of the skin of the cockfight man.

"Saint Joseph with the head of a tapir! Saint Louis Gonzaga with the head of a snouty pig! Mary Magdalen with the head of an iguana! Saint Sebastian with the head of a wounded stag! Saint Francis with the head of a tame coyote! Saint Dominic with the head of a sheep! Saint Pascal

195

Baylon with the head of a monkey! And the Apocalyptic woman, the Conceived one, with the head of a dove!"

And as he was saying this, the cockfight man crossed the threshold of the main door, and there were the saints with those animal heads, as ridiculous as they were strange.

The priest gasped at that diabolical and satanic spectacle, an *Ecce Homo* with the face of a screech owl, and, *prae manibus,* an Infant Jesus who looked like a fish, but at that very moment he had his revelation, he reflected that it was not part of the workings of the earth demons, destructive powers, shattering, brutal, but was the low comedy, without grandeur, of the captain of the rain of accursed angels that fell from heaven.

And, while he was getting his breath back, he lost his mind, and with his mind, his speech. He tried to protest violently, and he could not find the words, reduced to gesticulation, without much emphasis, because he felt his heart weak and his blood like the chaff of silence in his veins.

But the promise of the cockfight man. The hieroglyphics burned, the chocolate turned bitter in the cups, the music of the bone instruments moaned, the maguey plants sweated, pecked by red-eyed thrushes, and suddenly the decapitated ones recovered their true heads, the atmosphere of fire had been broken like a mirror of dreams.

The priest, recovering his senses, his words, his chest, his breath, applauded, just like a wild little boy, before each restored image, the Christs with old hair, the smiling Virgins with the face of Virgins and not gazelles.

Only the mummy of the sexton, invisible under its leaden armor, hard as a vegetable tortoise shell of tree-killing vine, was still without its head.

"We will carry him to the *pulcrus,* like the relic of a martyr," proposed the cockfight man.

The priest nodded in agreement, and off they went to deposit him behind the main altar, helped by the mustached half-breeds, among the blinking of the lighted candles in the hands of women, old men, and children, accompanied by the buzzing of voices reciting the response.

The Earth-Born Devils Abandon Tierrapaulita

Cashtoc, the Great, the Immense, gathered together his legions in a house without a roof, without doors, without windows, on the outskirts of Tierrapaulita, the depopulated and destroyed Tierrapaulita. Which was the door through which he had entered? Which was the window out of which he had leaned to call his people? They were invisible. His floating voice and nothing more. His briny steps were reproduced upon the leaves. His followers did not appear, and the minutes were falling stars. He howled like a hungry coyote, he hissed like a serpent, he beat his wings like an owl with chick-pea eyes, he shook his quiet wings, he sent the trees off in search of the giants. From the earth surface of a giant to his interior is a distance of more than a thousand leagues, and that is why they are slow with their replies. Their delay was unheard of. The others were already there. Huasanga, mounted on Cadejo, wearing Giroma's sex in the buttonhole of her riding jacket like a flower. Sisimite, on the money wheel, a monster with sharp ice and fire on his coin edges. All of them, the visible and invisible *coleletines,* or demons of the air, *milaniles,* or little devils of the brush, protecting their bodies as they came close to one another, because in the darkness and among devils, they eat each other's bodies.

No one dared speak. The summons of Cashtoc, the Great, the Immense, always alarmed them, but this hasty summons with ventriloquist echoes resounding across the mountains had startled them. Because they had dominated Christianity. In Tierrapaulita the parishioners would hang to the wizards and the temples where they burned *pom* resin before the idols, and secretly fed Cal-Cuj, the devourer of heads, and worshipped Tazol with corn masses, and danced serpentine beneath the moon, why did he call with such great shouts for all of them to come.

Cashtoc spoke when the giants appeared, their backs darkening the four celestial windows.

"The Christian demon has arrived," he said, "and we must abandon Tierrapaulita—that is to say, after sacking it, without leaving an inhabitant or building whole! For us, to conquer is to destroy, to conquer is to depopulate! We are leaving because the aims of this Christian demon, who was an angel and has not lost his divine soapiness, clash with ours, his aims and his methods, and we could not live together without the whole thing's becoming a pleasant lunch among devils!"

And with a lumpy voice in his throat of earthy crust: "Creation was dust and dust will be all that is left of the cities we destroy! No more cities! No more men, who are nothing but the look of beings, like a clay mold, crumbling by itself, or a wooden one, hanging from the trees like an ape! Real men, the ones made out of corn, have stopped existing in reality and have become fictitious creatures, since they did not live for the community, and that is why they should have been suppressed. That is why I annihilated them with my Major Giants, and just as long as they do not reform, I will annihilate all of those who forget, deny, or reject their condition as kernels of corn, parts of an ear, and become self-centered, egotistical, individualists—ah! ah! ah!—" his laugh turned inwardly—"individualists!—ha! ha! ha!—" he laughed outwardly—"until they finally change into solitary beings, into puppets lacking any senses!"

The sulphur pits, stars of fire tongue that had fallen at the feet of the volcanoes, followed the voice of Cashtoc like sunflowers of smoke.

"Plants, animals, stars—they all exist together, all together as they were created! It has occurred to none of them to make a separate existence, to take life for his exclusive use, only man, who must be destroyed because of his presumption of existing in isolation, alien to the millions of destinies that are being woven and unwoven around him!"

And after a pause, giants and earth-born demons savored with attentive ears his silence, which is the dust of sound.

"Therefore," I repeat, "man must be destroyed, and his constructions wiped out, for his presumption of singularizing himself, considering himself an end in himself!" the shout of Cashtoc rushed out, an echo of rocks which break away, and then it continued on with the hoarseness of a rain of earth: "Different, quite different, are the strategy and tactics used by the Christian devil, the son of slyness! This crafty foreigner conceives of man as the flesh of hell and tries, when he does not demand, for the multiplication of human beings, who are isolated like him, proud like him, ferocious like him, finagling like him, devilishly religious like him, to fill up his hell! That is why he undid the mirror vapor that the Heart of Heaven had poured over the sexes, a mirror vapor in which man and woman, in the magic instant of giving life, left a copy of their images mixed in with the new being, whose navel they offered to the community, meaning by it that this one would not be alien to the existence of all, but part of their existences, which at the same time are part of the existence of the gods!

"The more men, according to the Christian demon, the more men for hell, and thereby his interest in propagating the species which we are bent on destroying!" concluded Cashtoc, the Great, the Immense. "For *his* hell, which they confuse with the fire of the volcanoes which my Giant Cabracán keeps lit; not our Xibalbá, our hell, the one of deep darkness which binds the eyes, the one of white forgetfulness which binds the ears, the one of green absence which binds the lips, and the one of red and yellow feathers which binds the sensibility."

"And why, Lord, don't you match your fighting cock with his?" Tucur, the owl messenger from Xibalbá, ventured to ask.

"My cock, thirteen times champion over the most artful deities, plagues, fevers, droughts, famines, whose spurs have served to make fire every time the gods steal fire away from us, would lose his plumage, the proud standard of his comb and beak, the flute that lets out his first greeting to the day—how could I risk him, O Giants!, O Tucurs!, with the cock of a foreigner who ties to the spurs of his cock curved razors that could shave the air if it were bearded?"

"Where will we go?" asked Tucur, an owl with drunken feathers.

"Where does the scorpion who does not burn go?" said the tongue of Huasanga, her mouth sown with little laughs.

"We have to carry off the priest!" Cadejo proposed.

"You peeped too late!" intervened Siguapate.

"He's not ours," Cadejo insisted, raising his nasal voice, "but we already have him tamed, and he will surprise the brutal devils."

"You peeped too late!" repeated Siguapate, a ghost made out of sand and water, who added ironically, "The Angel of Light invited him to play cards, along with a few drinks of anise and some Havana cigars!"

"Yes," affirmed a life-seeking elf, bowlegged and with the teeth of a manatee, "the priest is already on the side of the cockfight man. He won him over by getting back the heads of the saints, and if he isn't already, he'll look the other way at the methods the one who was Angel for a Day wants to use to propagate the human species!"

Siguamonta stirred it up: "No wandering or sleep when men and women come together in bed. 'Married?' the curate will ask, curing himself in his own health. 'Married by the Holy Mother Church,' the other one will answer, putting him to sleep, because, with the whole world turned toward lust, toward procreation with lust, nothing about a religious wedding will matter, for it will be a question of increasing the possible candidates for hell."

"Giants," the telluric voice of Cashtoc thundered again— the houses heard him with their foundations, the trees with their roots, the sea with its depths—"forward! Let the column have an honor guard of giants! Let that Gigantic who played the role of Goliath in the dance rise from his grave! Toward the back side of these mountains, which are our volcanic backs, we abandon Tierrapaulita, depopulated and almost in ruins. Someone else will come to throw you from your homes! On the arm of a certain Avilantaro, audacious man, the Christian demon comes and with him, alas!, let us be sad, the ones who will demand generations of men without any reason for being, without any magic words, unfortunate in the nothingness and the emptiness of their ego."

Giroma, the powerful one whose unhappiness over the theft of her sex had no limit, the young umbilical mother of Tazolín, who on the opposite side of the coin had an old woman called Catalina Zabala, supported by the Gigantic who had played Goliath in the dance, and who was none other than her husband, Celestino Yumí, and by the imperishable Tazolín, cat claws, went along as the only woman of human kind in that caravan of cliffs that were turning into clouds, of sun tigers that were heading toward the white plains of the salt flats.

"Is everybody coming?" Cashtoc asked. "Are the dancers of the Dance of the Cux and the Iboy coming? Is the stone that roars coming? Did you forget the annatto, the great chile, the calaguala fern, the copal, the cress, the ginger, the tamarind, the mint, the pepper, the soap tree? If we haven't brought them, we'll have to go back for them before my Giant Huracán knocks down the white ceiba tree!"

Tucur, the owl with drunken feathers, proclaimed: "Before the black ceiba tree was knocked down, the bones of the dead fled from Tierrapaulita."

"And the yellow ceiba tree fell down—" Cabracán's great buried voice was an earthquake—"before leaving, I cut it down with my yellow-edged axes, that immense tree of sun spiders!"

"They have only the green ceiba left," Cashtoc announced, "to give shade to those who are ours, and remind them that the only way out against the one who dominates them is conspiracy! They are not ceibas of peace, they are ceibas of war!"

The dwarf Huasanga, riding Cadejo, the Elfs, Siguamonta, Siguanaba, Siguapate, Sisimite, the Weepweepweeping Woman, all in the cortege stopped to listen to the rain of horned angels that was falling on Tierrapaulita. Such different demons! All angels, all made in heaven. And with them, overland, there advanced for the taking of the town legions of shadow-makers, endemonized and undemonized people, necromancers, astrologers, alchemists, sorcerers with theurgical mirrors, horoscopists with wandering looks, palmists who, when in addition to the lines of the hand read the veins in the leaves or hands of the trees, doubled as botanomantics, with no lack of people who consulted

201

fate in people's navels, ophalomantics, who proclaimed Tazolín as their patron, or fortunetellers, who guessed the future with cards or decks of cards, or the readers of backs, or spatulomantics, or lithomantics, attent on stones, or those who read the future in excrement, just as long as the feces were fee ¢'s or $'s or serpents that were coiled or loosed or combined among themselves like Arabic letters.

Left there was Tierrapaulita, from which, when Cashtoc and his cortege had left, the priest fled too, riding a black mule with eyes as red as radishes. And all that the little Father would tell the Archbishop seemed so small, what he would say in the audience that would be granted him, about his calvary in a town which, when he had arrived to assume the parish, was in the power of demons of red earth, of dry corn leaves, of sweet cane, and of terribly destructive giants.

His Grace, a man with worn-out patience, folded his hands, twisted his mouth, frowned, bored by the detailed account that old rheumatic parish priest, deformed, with one leg longer than the other, was giving him of his fight with the most primitive forms of the devil in Tierrapaulita, the most pestilent witchcraft, the fiercest hatred of God, the worst superstitions, and once in a while he would scratch his back on the worn-out back of the large chair he was occupying, before putting on a worn-out smile which meant that the audience had ended.

In the curia no one listened to the tales of the priest from Tierrapaulita. For the young seminarians serving in the cathedral they were the senilities of an old man. The hallucinations of an exorcist who had been worn out by his duties, according to his peers, the brilliant, virtuous, and veteran canons who asked him if hell was located in Tierrapaulita, which, joking apart, brought on a serious discussion as to where it was located, whether in the center of the earth, as had been declared by the Council of Trent, or everywhere, as the Jebbies maintained as they tried to do away with that hell of subterranean dungeons by means of a modern theological concept, so modern and advanced they were that it was ridiculous to them to conceive of the souls of reprobates chained around the terrestrial globe in order to make it spin, or to hold that it was the influence of that unconsumed infernal fire that made the seasons change. But, of course, in order to agree with that priest who had just arrived in the capital, poor, like all village priests, they unanimously accepted the idea that one of the mouths of that darkest cave was in Tierrapaulita, where on dark nights the wrinkled earth would let loose the muteness of heaven and the howls of the condemned with flame-shaped tongues, with their hair in the shape of snakelike shadows, their complaints as rumbles, and their groaning in torture as the shaking of the earth.

"All these clergymen who leave the capital come back from their villages either dreaming or frightened," one of the chamberlains commented in a loud voice in the ear of His Grace, who was deaf and was getting deafer, just as he was losing his sight, his hawk eyes, because only with the eyes of a hawk can one get to be a bishop, and his smell, chocolate no longer smelled good to him, and his taste, to such a point that his great weakness, fritters, tasted like old corn pap to him with his false teeth. "Such a priest! Such backwardness!" the chamberlain went on in the ear of His Grace, "coming here with his stories of giants, as if this were the age of Enoch, of dwarfs, giant snakes, basilisks, and boar-men—ha! ha! ha!—boar-men! Such a priest! Believing that natural forces, earthquakes and hurricanes, are the work of the Devil, even though in all of that he keeps company with none other than Thomas Aquinas, with all due respect for Saint Thomas, whom I put ahead of all the philosophers, and I tell people: 'Not Saint Thomas, Saint Promise.'" His Grace did not catch the pun. "And then, in a different order or disorder of ideas, those absurd mystifications about coconuts with urinating female sex organs, and that sect of worshippers of the Bad Thief."

"The Devil would not be so primitive in our time," deduced another of the curials; the hawk eyes of His Grace, as they peered through the worn-out lenses of his glasses, gave him his consent to keep on speaking.

And the one who was speaking continued: "If the Devil were the way that old priest paints him, it would be easy to reduce him to impotence. Against the demon of earthquakes,

203

reinforced concrete, and against hurricanes, the planting of high-crowned trees to break the violence of the winds."

"And where does it all get us?" asked the chamberlain, who had been the first to cross lances with the ancient priest who had returned so undone from Tierrapaulita. "It brings us to the fact that the clergy is missing opportunities to put an end to all of these terribly primitive manifestations of the Evil Enemy."

"What makes it difficult," sighed the curial as he spoke, "is doing battle with the Lucifer who has become involved in human progress, marvelously adapting himself to modern customs like all of us, and partly because, as I see it, the Devil, by means of original sin, enters into the natural formation of man, sixty or seventy per cent, and I'm being conservative!"

"What's your name, Father?" the Archbishop, with his worn-out voice, asked the priest who had just spoken.

"Mateo Chimalpín," the other answered, not surprised that Monsignor did not remember his name, because his memory was worn out too.

"Welll . . ." His Grace wore out the *l*'s while a page knelt to place the menu in his hands, which Monsignor celebrated with a brief applause in which he only tapped the tips of his fingers, but it was a meaningful gesture, meatballs and saffron rice.

"Welll . . ." His Grace repeated, "Father Chimalpín will be named parish priest of Tierrapaulita, and I hope that he won't come and tell us any fables about devils."

And he said no more, because his voice was worn out, and a somewhat worn-out rocking chair was waiting for him in the garden, where he would have the meatballs for lunch, and he would not have to get up to wear out his siesta, for he could stay there rocking with a movement that was wearing, that was wearing, into which His Grace, a nod here, a nod there, did not like to put much effort, and also out of fear that he would wear out his slippers with the silver buckles.

And on the same black mule on which the priest of Tierrapaulita had escaped from the domains of Cashtoc, coinciding with the diabolic changing of the guard, the millennial moment of the abandonment of a town by the

earth demons in favor of the Christian devil, with the same
Indians accompanying him, and following the same moun-
tainous course, Father Mateo Chimalpín set out for those
regions of black tempests of high magic, after he had knelt
to receive the blessing of His Grace, and had worn out his
amethyst ring with a sonorous kiss, which, if it was not the
fire of everything created, was as enthusiastic and animated
as the singer of Masses who was off for the first time to
take up arms against the Devil, far away from the capital,
and he himself extinguished it, once he had given the kiss,
so that the fire would not spread, as he made his lips into
a candle-snuffer.

The last words of His Grace were from Saint John
Chrysostom: "Remember, Father, that 'most priests end in
perdition.'"

He took along as sexton and secretary an old drop-out
from medical school, capable of effecting cures and with
some practice, and with a scientific base better than most
doctors, and in a foot locker on the back of an Indian
bearer, the heavy artillery he would use against Satan: the
complete works of Saint Thomas Aquinas, a *History of the
Church in the Indies,* by Fray Diego de Mendieta; the
Criticón of Baltasar Gracián; the *Apologetics* of Bishop Las
Casas; a book of sermons by various preachers, Bossuet
foremost; the *Compendium of Moral Theology,* by Father
Larraga; and, to the Greater Glory of God, books on
cataclysms, hurricanes, predestination, devil worship, not
to mention the *Manual for Exorcists* of Fray Luis de la
Concepción, the Holy Bible, and, for light reading, the
Apocalypse.

Wizards, Witches, and Spooks
Return to Tierrapaulita

Celestino Yumí and Catarina Zabala, who were already on
their way to becoming a great wizard and a great witch—
they still had to go through some more magical transforma-
tions—thought that they ought to abandon the caravan of
the Earth Giants, carriers of green plates, and the Sky
Giants, carriers of blue glasses, and, without taking leave
of Cashtoc, the Great, the Immense—how can anyone take
leave of the one who is everywhere; you say goodbye to
someone who is leaving or staying behind, but Cashtoc continued to be present in every place where there was witchcraft—they left, accompanied by Huasanga, a spiderlike
dwarf, who, so that she would not get into any further
trouble with those who were already such principal sorcerers, and feeling herself menaced by tarantulism, gave
back to Catarina Zabala, the double of the youthful Giroma,
the feminine timbre of her voice, as she had already been
speaking hoarsely, by restoring the sex she had snatched
away, and with it there returned her tone, her animality;
accompanied by Siguamonta, the ghost of a woman turned
on a pole of orange wood, her hair in a rain of flint that
could be combed and her great category of a female for
howling drunkards, whom she attracted with her lodestone
sex, as they became converted into silent, rigid, and blind
metal dolls; accompanied by Siguanaba, a vision who appeared floating, footless, legless, with only her thorax, the
emptiness where all the shadows joined to form her clothes,
woman with three heads, the one she bore on her shoulders,
and the two which were round breasts, lightning rods that
attracted the staggering drunkard, coming up to her only
to fall into the sexual emptiness of gullies; accompanied,

furthermore, by Cadejo, tattooed with circles of mockery, four times four-footed, with his sixteen paws, four of red wood, four of shadow, four of people, and four of the Devil, his hoofs that were combs of alum stone to entangle in horses' manes and in the hair of uncombed women; by Weepweepweeping Water Hair, rain which weeps for men who die, which weeps, rather, for the one, the only one, the eternal male who is repeated in all the corpses that she accompanies to the graveyard, proud of the pricks of her tears as they wet her body and converge toward the mortuary fuzz of her pubis of an orphan, a widow, an abandoned woman; and also accompanied by the Chief Elf, with a phosphorous smile, Mongolian eyes, hair of crow's feathers, teeth of chalk, godlike, bachelor, and bisexual, and by lesser elves, vulgar and exhibitionists in parks and markets.

All this legion of spooks and spirits abandoned, along with Celestino Yumí and Catarina Zabala, the tail of the comet of water and fire that Cashtoc was dragging along toward the high mountains peopled with caverns, to return to Tierrapaulita, followed by Sisimite, jumping, jingling, feet on the moon, feet on his feet, which with his own feet were multiplying and disappearing, and Siguapate, a demoniacal monkey who throws earth into the eyes of travelers so as to rob them of their hearts, for which they call him "ingrateful Maker of Ingrates," to rob them of their memory, until they get lost in nothingness, and to pocket their sacred organs, to annul generations in their germ state, like a "Great Seducer of Death," with whom he fornicates through the holes of the iliacal cavities, leaving her like a chopped-off branch of neverlasting, with her skull eyes imaginatively closed, and condemned by that youthful concubinage to use her scythe only in the harvest of old men, since Siguapate has decimated other beings before they were engendered, alive and just as they were in the liquor of life of their progenitors, and that is why there were no children, why there were no young people.

A light drizzle was wetting the houses of Tierrapaulita, the houses, the streets, the trees, when the great sorcerers Yumí and the Zabala woman and their companions returned, and as soon as they reached the town they dis-

207

banded, each one to his nocturnal duty, after greeting Sombrerón, a dwarf with a square for a hat, pulled down to the green trees of his ears, almost putting out the street lamps of his eyes, a mouth of a dry fountain, hands like the front of a church, with steps that looked like fingers, without knees or legs, just a thorax sitting on his feet of black oilcloth and, therefore, a jumper and a dancer. In Tierrapaulita they also greeted Tatuana, limestone, featureless and, still, such a good sailor woman, compass eyes, fingers with the pulsation of a watch's second hands.

Tazolín, the son of Tazol and the navel of Catarina, when she was the powerful Giroma, caught up with them, crying kernels of corn, and asked them if he could stay with them, his parents, in Tierrapaulita, and not with his grandfather, Tazol, in the mountains.

He liked to chatter so much, and there in the country he couldn't, it was all loneliness and birds who couldn't speak. Better there in Tierrapaulita, playing and chattering and laughing, watching out that his finger was not grabbed by the blue macaw, husband of the red macaw, a present from the two mirrors of trickery which Tazol had given to Yumí and Catarina as he tried to lose them.

"Fine," the two sorcerers said, and in the back courtyard of their house they locked up the grandson of Tazol in the company of the macaws.

Tazolín, without knowing that they were teaching him to be a trickster, passed his time amused by now-you-peck-me-now-you-don't, among the blue lightning bolts of the male and the red lightning bolts of the female.

At night he dreamed that all the stars were pecks of golden macaws who were pecking as they tried to hurt his little fingers and could not, and with that dream of a little devil trickster from the sky, he was condemned to be pecked to pieces by those birds of white fire.

And so it happened, and the son of Tazol and the navel of the powerful Giroma, pecked to pieces by the rainbow and the constellations, fell to earth like a child with a grandfather's beard, a corn beard, the seed of wild corn.

Without Tazol's grandson, Celestino Yumí and Catarina Zabala presented themselves to the Christian demon, and

208

they were the first in Tierrapaulita to call him by his name: Candanga. This nickname kept his name secret, and only they and Saint Zachary had ever been able to guess it, Saint Zachary by his sense of smell, which was devilish, that was why he was disguised as a saint on altars, and they because they were already on their way to becoming great sorcerers.

Candanga, A Christian Demon in the Land of Infidels

"Breeding tiiime! Breeding tiiime today! Breeding tiiime!"

Darkening and shy was the Tierrapaulita night. The streets dark and damp. The houses sleeping one against the other like white hens.

"Breeding tiiime! Breeding tiiime! Breeding tiiime today!"

Anyone who was not talking stirred nervously in bed beside his wife, and the women, disposed to fear, let their eyes walk through the darkness as they bristled, smelling of nocturnal sweat, or they tightened their eyelids, the petals of shadow that became great, immense, while outside.

"Breeding tiiime! Breeding tiiime today! Breeding tiiime!"

It meant . . . it meant . . . The gossips, without undoing the knot with their morning sneeze, were content to cross themselves, and what good was further explanation.

"Breeding tiiime today! Breeding tiiime! Breeding tiiime today!"

Married couples, people living together, those who were sleeping with a woman, no longer just gave a turn or half a turn in bed when in their wakeful sleep they heard that call of the Evil Enemy, but would roll around, contracting, stretching, using strokes of the hand to invite their companions to comply with the vendor's chant with that bitter and yet sweet debt they owed each other.

"Br . . . ee . . . ding . . . today!"

No, they could not even hear him any more. What he was shouting had them terrified.

It was whispered about that among the remiss, those who did not respond properly to the call, that they would have the Devil's rooster turned on them, and it would be the rooster who played the male. And that was why, at the sound of the first "Bree . . . ," the women would uncover them-

213

selves with quick hands which they would then place over their breasts, because in that business of children, the best thing was to make the most of it, because it was not right to make their husbands wear horns by lying with the Devil's rooster, who did not wear horns but spurs. With no Gypsies having been around, it was already said that some women had already begun to bear tar-colored children with red lips and tongues and white teeth. No other Gypsy than Candanga, the Christian devil, who would mount his rooster on his natural concubines, the hens, a roosterism that spread to every woman who slept with a man, even though she was already on her way to becoming petrified resin, if she could not make her man comply with the command of "breeding time."

Candanga, whose prominent knees made him so ugly that he hid them under garters of precious stones, explained that he had found that marvelous treelanded region almost without people, the inhabitants of Tierrapaulita and its rims decimated. Earthquakes, hurricanes, plagues had been used by Cashtoc in his policy of annihilation, so that He, the Devil of the True God, would not find a living soul.

Therefore, as the concessionaire of that human flock that had remained and had been further destroyed by the Lethe-bearing waters of Spanish baptism, his policy was re-population, a policy which he hawked about, because the Devil's pulpit is the street, with mysterious and lascivious shouts, trying to get a checkmate before he even saw the game, since the priest, new in town like him, was using the threat of exorcism and excommunication against the pos-sessed people who were complying with the command of that bestial vendor's shout, that meddlesome boar, dog vomit, wild mule, swine-snout rooting around in excre-ment which he eats with both jaws, both nostrils, both eyes, because all of him is besmirched up to his ears, corpse-maggot, pustule-pus, two-headed snake, shadow-crab . . .

No one had eyelids for the nights any more, the intermin-able nights of Tierrapaulita. There were neither eyelids or pupils for the eyes of the poor people, the most credulous, eyes in the shape of garlic cloves strung together like tears born out of the gratitude of the flesh in that saying and making of mine-on-yours which they were obliged to do by that howling shout that beat against the large doors of smithies and taverns, against the wooden-flute doors of the new houses, where people with money lived, against the ship-skeleton doors of merchants and pimps, and against the crossed-wood bars of the barracks, the church, the jail, and the old cemetery.

"Breeding time! Breeding time!"

The prosperous people of Tierrapaulita, less credulous, listened to it far off there, more awake than asleep, and such immense fissures in their sleep, in the sleep that was forming into a ball in their heads, on their cushions, cushions and pillows which were part of their heads, heads with brains of wool, brains of straw, brains of feathers, brains of pillows, with sleep in a ball all covered with hairy leather and which, when that tremendous shout was heard in the middle of the night, would leave them like a cat in the shadows as it followed the cats which were dropping off the roofs of the houses in Indian file, their fur standing on end, wet with dewdrops, who cleaned themselves with their little towel-fabric tongues when they reached the kitchen and made themselves comfortable next to the fire, snuggling into a stone bench, into the corner oven on the wall that was black with soot, disheveled, scaly.

"Breeding time—mmm . . . mmm!"

The street dogs, noses on the ground and tails between their legs, scratched at the doors with their front paws, asking for help. From door to door, whining, bony, with fear on their faces, their teeth cold, as horned bats passed on the frightening shout, the invitation to breeding, which also made the dogs shut up in yards and courtyards go wild, anxious to hunt down the sound, the echo of what was neither sound nor echo, but an audible spell, which some people, the priest among them—he was brand new in the place—maintained was the voice from the charnel house, an archaic expression that the Father used as he tried to make a reference to carnal lust and Charon's ferry.

But woe to them who heard it in their cups, because in a town where there is no other diversion except getting drunk, they were not the minority. They became covered with goose flesh, sweaty, and they drew their wives to them, drunkards that smelled of urinals, with the threat that if they did not submit, the Devil would father their child.

"You can't hear it any more, it's already passed by," the women would say in defense.

But, as if Candanga in person had been waiting for that moment, when they came to the "already" he would thunder out: "Breeding time! Breeding time! . . ."

The howl of a coyote hungry for souls, not meat, remained as if suspended over their heads, waiting for the reply which could be nothing else except the one they had at hand in the intimacy of what no longer seemed to be their bedroom, no matter how they recognized it with the touch of their eyes in the semi-darkness, no matter how much they heard the dogs running around in the yard, barking, howling, but rather a space which formed a whole with the depths of the night.

Out of the roots of that same shout, being peddled now in a low voice, there came the terror that crippled them, that cramped them, that made them measure, using their marrow as a rule, the risk that bordered on the mystery of life of not fulfilling the macabre invitation to breed, because, after so much time together, with grown children already, once more they had become the playthings of their natures, he a drunkard, and she with the liquor of weeping that bathed her small pupils, knowing that the Devil was converting them into the material of human propagation.

From the profile of the very high mountains surrounding Tierrapaulita, all splendor, a circumcised splendor, without clouds, and from over there, from that sublime erection of peaks, to the most feminine curves of the neighboring ranges, the music of the sky and fossil reeds playing over on their flutes of fossil cane the sounds of the old Caribbean Sea and its white hair of foam.

And such a tropical nature of live coals that had eyes, we know from those eyes that the night can see; the silences with ears, we know from those golden earrings that hang on invisible ears that the night can hear; of the live coals of some metal burned up in the cosmos, and we know from its sleepwalking light that the night is full of absent people!

216

Father Chimalpín Challenges Candanga

Only now in Tierrapaulita had they begun to learn the name of the new parish priest, Mateo Chimalpín.

As a student in the seminary in Santiago, he had learned by heart a famous sermon that was a model of sacred oratory when it came to doing battle with the Odd Angel. And that immortal piece had come back to him like pearls, pearls or drops of sweat, as he dug it out of his memory in the pulpit of the church that was crowded with people, from the rich seated on their *prie-dieus,* down to the poor seated on the floor.

Almost leaping from the pulpit, he shouted: " 'Tremble, oh imperishable monsters that bring sex into the field of battle against God! Tremble, oh monsters more furious than Arians and Circumcilians, than Priscilianists and Donatists, than that whole swarm of ancient locusts' " (to make it comprehensible he said grasshoppers) " 'and scorpions, who have risen from the depths of what has been forgotten, from perdition and from death, to lay siege to Tierrapaulita!' " (He allowed himself that freedom, because the sermon he was reciting had said Holy Zion!) " 'It is true that you are monsters even more ugly and abominable, more feared and daring! It is clear that you are the very Troglodites of Ethiopia that Pliny spoke of, with no respect for any law, but living like beasts, living in caves, eating meat that dripped with blood, and not recognizing any bond with society. It is true that La Mettrie, Hobbes, Toland, Collins, Volston, Tyndale, Diderot, Voltaire, Rousseau, and so many others that I do not have the time to name them, who were their disciples, all ended up, some attempting revelation, others natural illumination, peopling

217

that isle of Atheism, comparable only to Tierrapaulita'"
(he permitted himself that exemplary addition), "'an
island described so well by Cardinal de Bernis, an island
that God reduced to ashes, as he will do with Tierrapaulita,
if you do not mend your ways and not listen to the shouting demon. Awake, my children, awake from what Fred-
erick II plotted in Berlin, along with Alambert and Voltaire,
and from the rivers of blood which their partly realized
plans have caused to flow!' "

In another sermon, or, rather, a lenten talk for men only,
Father Chimalpín prepared to face the Odd Angel, whether
he was that tyrannical voice, invisible as the night and untouchable as the wind, which invited breeding, or the cockfight man called Candanga, blue-eyed, always wearing spurs,
who gave free rein to his goatish instincts, without breeding,
because the Devil lacks the liquor that gives life.

"This twisted and deceiving agitator," he made clear to
the men who were listening to him, stiff-headed, greasy-
bearded, some wearing the medals of various religious
brotherhoods, "in his diabolical crusade in favor of copula-
tion, uses a great deal of propaganda, no product can be
sold today if there isn't any advertising, and the Church
could use some; he uses plenty of loud propaganda to wake
up men's and women's instincts, their baser instincts, as he
incites them to breed, because he doesn't say *brood*, extremely ambiguous, disconcerting, and part of his great evil
power as a creator of ambiguities.

"Precisely, my brothers in Christ, where the ambiguity
lies, the unclean scrofula, the demoniacal cancer which
grows a tumor on the souls of those who fall into his nets,
of those who let themselves be trapped by the shout of his
propaganda, which does not induce the propagation of the
species by the will of beings who love each other, but from
fear, from the terror sown by his howls that come from
the pits of hell, and that is why it is heard tell that they have
opened fissures as deep or deeper than those opened by that
terrible native devil Cashtoc, now gone from here, but
making his way in other towns during Lent with the doll
called Mashimoón."

The Odd One did not even respect Holy Week. On Good
Friday, after the Tenebrae services, oh, how opportune it

was for the priest to remember that stanza from Jerónimo de Cáncer:

> *By then upon Mary,*
> *the sleepy eyes were cast,*
> *by then from out the shadows,*
> *the final psalm at last.*

Because Candanga did not even respect that day of silence, and he obliged Father Chimalpín to preach from the steps of the church, while inside, a solitary, deserted candle burned.

"Since I have come to Tierrapaulita to chain beasts and to give battle, and for no other reason, I jump into the arena of the circus, waiting like a new Ursus, all the muscles of my soul tense, because with my frail body and my poor bones, I could do little to defend the Church against the horns of the bull, the Devil, that is; here I am, with the help of God, inveighing against that perverse profaner of Good Friday!

"I challenge," he continued, with the gestures and expressions of a man possessed, "the magicians, the wizards, the sorcerers of Tierrapaulita, they say there are great ones, and Candanga, that half-breed demon, a mixture of Spanish and Indian in his human incarnation! I am ready here to give battle on any ground to that Evil Enemy Angel, to his followers, and to those who still serve Cashtoc, a devil who never spoke, the opposite of this carnival chatterer, this hawker of the easiest of all merchandise to sell, sexual merchandise, which, when advertised in the wrappings of his shouts of fear, becomes something even more exciting."

When he had finished his challenge, he threw down a purple glove that belonged to His Grace and which had come along in one of his pockets—oh, the carelessness of chamberlains!—waiting for Candanga or one of his wizards to appear and pick it up.

A pock-marked Indian, little versed in the duels of chivalry, thinking that the little Father had dropped the purple glove, picked it up and brought it to the sacristy.

And the sexton questioned him at once: "Are you a wizard?"

"No, sir, how could I be a thing like that!"

"Then why did you pick up the glove?"

"Be . . . Because I wanted to! And now you have it back!"

"No! No! No! It's not a question of having it back!"

"What else is it, then?"

"Father will tell you."

"I'll wait for him here awhile, then."

"Awhile?" the voice of the sexton came out, while he said to himself: Oh, Jerónimo, Jerónimo, why were you born on the day of the Slaughter of the Innocents by Herod, as he adjusted the dark glasses on his nose, upset at being in a town so full of enchantments, serving as squire to Father Chimalpín, who had brought him along as a sexton, and not as a Pancho Santo, a holy belly, as they ought to call the Sancho Panzas of combative priests.

"I'll wait awhile," the Indian repeated.

"Not awhile! You'll wait until he finishes. He's having dinner."

"But when I said awhile, I meant that I'd wait all the time he takes in coming, because when somebody like me waits for such an important person, the time spent waiting is always only a little while, it's never much, and please grab this glove because it must belong to a holy hand."

"Wait until Father comes and give it to him."

"Just as you say, I'll give it to him, then."

"And can there be any greater liberty taken than for a person to come to church on Good Friday with an open fly? And me here like a celestial pimp!"

Why did the Indian fumble with that business of "celestial pimp" and the allusion to his open fly? Could the sexton have discovered who he was? None other than Celestino Yumí, the great wizard into whom Candanga had entered when he heard the challenge that Father Chimalpín had hurled from the steps of the church as he threw the glove in his face. Hidden in that emissary, he was going to answer the daring challenger. Yumí, with his sprinkler mask which, instead of little holes, had pock-marks, acted as if he did not understand the "celestial pimp" business—it would have let the sexton know his name, and in that way take over his person—and he hastened to correct the outrage of

220

his open fly, at the same time as he said, as no one should say: "It shouldn't bother you, if you're a man, that is," and he added muttering, "or maybe you can pretend."

"A man?" Jerónimo de la Degollación attempted a chilling smile.

Father Chimalpín could be heard coming from the parish house. Jerónimo had time to go over and look at the Indian in the light of the lone candle that was burning because Jesus was dead that night, and closely examine the cabalistic tattoo of smallpox scars which formed a constellation on his face.

The steps of the priest were disappearing in the shadows, as if instead of approaching he had been going away. The truth was that he had approached on tiptoes and was hiding, waiting for Jerónimo de la Degollación de los Niños Inocentes to receive the glove that the Indian had insisted on giving him and which he refused to receive.

The purple glove of His Grace, thrown by Father Chimalpín from the steps of the church as a challenge to Candanga, the cockfight man, the "breeding time!" man, was also destined for the sexton as an undemonizer, because it was a holy piece of clothing which would oblige Jerónimo de la Degollación to show himself in his second and demoniacal nature that had got control of him, by means of a wandering malignant spirit, a certain certain Mulata who had got into his body.

A glove, which is a hand, but an empty hand, had a special meaning in the art of exorcism, and Father Chimalpín was waiting, on his knees now, with his rosary in his hands, Hail Mary after Hail Mary, for the sexton, who, as he felt, was badly illuminated by that evil female, to take it and rid himself of that pestilence of effeminacy, because, according to demons who know about incubus and succubus, when the woman whom the Devil puts there, introduces, into the human mass of the male is flesh and blood, incantation results, and when she is not carnal, but a simple spirit, effeminacy results, precisely what was happening to Jerónimo de la Degollación.

Oh, if he would only take the glove in which Monsignor had left the shape of his hand and expel from his body the certain Mulata who had got control of him by the light of the moon, which, immense, almost round, and bloody, was lighting up the holy season of Lent!

The apprentice exorcist, who had combed his lashes so much with so many complicated texts about spells, and who now was feeling a bit like Father Ciruelo of Salamanca or the Canon Montearagán, was far, far from knowing that the two highest infernal powers were facing each other, Candanga and Cashtoc, hidden, disguised in the Indian with the healed-over pock-marks, and the sexton with his teeth of an alum moon and the manners of an old maid.

The diabolical contradiction. The demon of heaven in the possessed Indian, and the red earth devil, changed into the certain Mulata, in the half-breed sexton.

"Breeding tiiime! Breeding tiiime!" resounded the Tempter's vending cry, despite the fact that it was Good Friday night.

"Breeding time!" the sexton burst out, and while the echo was still ringing loudly outside the church, he added: "You can tell a bird by its feathers, it's easy to see that this Candanga is just as vulgar as the people he manipulates, whores, cuckolds, and mixed couples of man and woman, when the best kind is a pure couple, man with man and woman with woman."

And after a pause, he asked the pock-marked Indian what his name was.

"I'm going to call myself José Quiquín, José my first name and for a last name Quiquín."

"How pretty! What a nice sound, José Quiquín!" the sexton broke out in flattery. "And what have you been in your life? What have you been? Do you mind my asking?"

"I was a woodcutter."

"Oh, a woodcutter!"

"Then I was very rich."

"And you no longer are now!"

"And then I was a dwarf."

"What do you mean, you were a dwarf?"

"Yes, I withered and dried up."

"And what did you do as a gnome?" Jerónimo twisted; a demonized person can feel the spirit that possesses him

222

like an immense belch, air that he cannot expel, either above or below.

"I danced."

"My, how wonderful."

"I did the 'Stilt Dance,' and they called me Chiltic . . ."

"Chiltic! Chiltic! Go on, tell me more! What were you after you were a dwarf?"

"A giant!"

"A gi . . ." Jerónimo de la Degollación de Herodes lost his voice, his whole being was the certain Mulata, and after a moment he added, ". . . ant! Oh, love!"

The Indian thought that he had heard him ask for the glove, and he handed him that purple shell that had the sweat and the hand movement of His Grace—Father Chimalpín, who was following the scene, said to himself: Now I've got her, the product of my exorcism by means of an object charged with antidiabolic electricity—but the sexton very carefully would not receive it, took away his hands, which were the copper color of the moon, which Yumí had only seen on the certain Mulata.

The priest let it be known that he was coming. The noise of the clapper of his legs and feet beneath the bell of his cassock.

"I was asking this Indian," Jerónimo de la Degollación de Herodes hastened to say when the pale face of the priest came out of the shadows, "why he leaped to pick up the glove that was thrown, after the death of Jesus, as a challenge to Satan."

"It was quite bad what I did, Father, what I did, because I thought you'd dropped it," and he held out the purple glove, which Father Chimalpín received, "but how was I to know that you'd thrown it on the ground as a challenge, like the challenges you see in plays, and I should have left it thrown there until the Devil with Eleventhousand Horns grabbed it."

"Eleven . . . eleventhousand horns . . ." the Father repeated inside and out, "it means that you, sir, Mr. Froth, Mr. Froth who puffs up the way it does on boiling milk, will have to realize that it's not so easy, the way it is with a bull, to take the devil by the horns, because there are eleven-

223

thousand of them . . . eleventhousand! O, Lord God of the visible and invisible universe, give me sufficient strength to take Candanga by his eleventhousand horns! But where am I going to get eleventhousand arms, eleventhousand hands."

"They'll come out of your body!" the one with the pock marks told him, an Indian with hair like a vulture's neck, and Chimalpín began to feel with horror arms emerging from above and below his own arms, like a Buddha, fans of different colored arms and different colored hands that formed an immense peacock tail on him.

But they were not eleventhousand, they were still not eleventhousand, and they had to be eleventhousand, if he wanted to take Candanga by the horns.

And going mad, he felt more arms emerging, not just near his arms now, from his armpits and his shoulders, but from his ribs. One arm, two arms, three arms from each rib. And from the space between his ribs. And from his waist.

But they were not eleventhousand, they were still not eleventhousand, and they had to be eleventhousand, if he wanted to take Candanga by the horns.

And, as if by enchantment, arms began to emerge from his ears, and each one of his hairs thickened until it became an arm. From his tonsure there was a flow of arms, a flow of hands, a flow of fingers.

But they were not eleventhousand, they were still not eleventhousand, and they had to be eleventhousand, if he wanted to take Candanga by the horns.

And while he was thinking and saying all of that, his teeth grew long, and out of his open mouth leaped arms with hands, some in the shape of molars, others like elephant tusks, others like walrus tusks, all arms, ivory arms, bone arms.

But they were not eleventhousand, they were still not eleventhousand, if he wanted to take Candanga by his eleventhousand horns.

And his eyelashes grew long, like trembling hairy arms, black, with crystal hands, they might be described as the large tears of illuminated spiders, and his eyes were there with the strange ring around them of little arms that had rainbow-colored myrtle hands.

He took out his handkerchief with a pile of fingers which were fighting, like playful little serpents, to take out that piece of perfumed linen from the bottom of the pocket in his cassock, which had sleeves all over it, sleeves and more sleeves, and more sleeves, sleeves from which arms were emerging by the hundreds, just like bunches of fingers instead of bananas.

And when he dried his sweat with a single handkerchief raised to his brow by nearly fifty-five thousand fingers, they could not all touch the handkerchief, which corresponded to eleventhousand hands, he started to run off toward the baptistry in search of holy water, and, God in Heaven, his legs were also arms, arm-feet, feet-arms, and he looked more like a tonsured spider moving on thousands and thousands of hairy extremities.

A Battle Between Two People Possessed by Opposing Demons

Neither the sexton, Jerónimo de la Degollación de los Santos Inocentes, nor the Indian, who said his name was José Quiquín, noticed what had happened to the young priest, who, when from the dark hands of the latter he had taken the purple glove of His Grace, embroidered on the back with a tassel of wheat in glowing golden thread, had fled toward the baptistry, changed into a spider wearing a cassock from which eleventhousand arms were emerging, just like fuzzy legs. He fled into the shelter of the darkness, swallowing his own heart, as he realized that by trying to snatch Tierrapaulita out of the clutches of Lucifer, by throwing in his face, which is the public square, the challenging glove, and by trying to trick the sexton into taking it in

225

order to bring about his disenchantment, demonized person that he was, rattling as he walked on those forks that had five prongs or fingers, he was dragging along all the waste of all souls, the waste with which the flames of hell were fed. From a delucifier he had changed into a luciferized person, and that was why he was going for holy water, eleventhousand arms in movement, just like the legs of a spider, out of his great black cassock.

"Where do you stay at night? Where are you going to sleep?" Jerónimo asked the Indian with the eleventhousand pock marks, he could not have had any fewer than eleventhousand scars on his face, and neither the latter, as he paid attention to the question, nor the former, as he tried to penetrate the mystery of that mummified Indian, realized that Father had run off to the baptistry not on two feet but on hundreds of paws.

"In Tierrapaulita, I stay wherever night and sleep catch up to me."

"What do you mean?" the sexton asked; he had heard a kind of weeping from Father.

"You keep on walking and walking and, if you're sleepy and it's not night time, you can't lie down to sleep, because if you go to sleep during the day, you run the risk that flies of the sun will shit on you and make you sick in your deepwater eyes, and if it's night time and you're not sleepy, well, why go to bed, you keep on walking and walking."

"And when sleep and night both catch up with you together in Tierrapaulita, where do you stay, where do you sleep?"

"I used to on the porch of the Town Hall, but one night my sleep was so deep that I woke up in a barrel of whitewash they were using to paint the building with. The Mayor and some other drunken buddies threw me in there for fun, and when I woke up I was drowning a white fog."

"A moon fog," Jerónimo asked, "from the back side of the moon?"

"That's most likely what it was, fog from a cloud that had its back to the moon," the Indian José Quiquín threw out, like someone who gave no importance to what he was saying, with the feeling that this Jerónimo de la Degollación was none other than the certain Mulata who had slithered

226

into someone who had been drowned in a glass of moon the size of a woman's divine back.

"It's not a dangerous fog, the one that doesn't show its face!" The sexton was still playing.

"Right now, no," Quiquín sighed, "but the danger is later on!"

"Later on?"

"Yes, later on, because you keep on looking for that face, and while you look for it, that image you adore, you lose your heart and your senses."

(. . . which is what might happen to me, the Mulata said to herself, and Cashtoc was wrong, if he'll pardon me, to choose me to be the person through whom he would confront the devil of heaven, Candanga, aware he would be cased up in the body of Yumí, or maybe he didn't know it—what is clear is that all that separates us is a mask of dried pock marks and the dirty hide of this feminine sex . . . sex . . . sexton.)

"And how long were you stuck in the whitewash?" Jerónimo asked.

"I don't know. I could feel the lime burning my eyes and I ran to dunk my head in the public fountain, and the women who were washing there ran away shouting: 'The White Corpse! The White Corpse!' " That was what they shouted.

"And did you revive when you washed your eyes?"

"I splashed around in the water. When I woke up, when I opened my eyes under the clean, transparent liquid, the fog wasn't there any more."

And, after a pause in which both possessed people sized each other up, the Indian, who was none other than Celestino Yumí, very old now, older than old, added: "After that I tried to sleep by the entrance to the market, but you have to keep in mind that sleep must weigh something for your lids to fall, not just to put its shell over the seeds of your eyes that feel hardened with tears of sadness, but to cover you all over, down to your feet."

"Why? Why? I don't understand!"

"Because by that entrance there, moving in all directions, like shadows dying of hunger, there are beggars, cats, and dogs, who rummage, the first with their hands and the sec-

227

ond with their paws and noses, through the remains of meals, chicken skeletons, tamal leaves . . ."

"Please, don't go on!"

"And among so much filth, I found a bear one day!"

"A bear?" was asked, no longer by the sexton now but by the Mulata, and Celestino Yumí could just make out the tone of her always haughty voice.

"Yes! A white bear, clean!"

"As if it had been part of the fog!"

"Exactly, as if it had belonged to the fog! But it had only been a dream."

"A dream?"

"A dream that the Devil who made the drunkard who turned into a stone, and when he was a stone he wanted to be a man, and when he was a man he wanted to be a stone, make the road with the nine turns, had carried him off stuck to his back. Such times! My wife, the Hahahahaha —" he pretended as if he were laughing at Catarina Zabala under the eyes of his former mistress—"was a dwarf then, and the woman who owned her dressed her like a doll, with one color for her dress, her shoes, and everything for each day."

The sexton, the Mulata, rather, afraid of slipping into sentiment and ending up confessing who she was, which would have given the victory to Candanga, and it was better to continue the infernal game of who was burning whom, cut him short: "Well, from now on, what did you say your name was?"

"I'm going to call myself Blas Pirir now. I used to be called José Quiquín, but now my name is Blas Pirir."

"Such a man!" the sexton twisted around, wasp-waisted, female roundness, the flexibility of a vine, and, while he raised his arms to put his hands on his head, added: "Such a difficult man! Now you're not the one you were, but Blas Pirir."

"Yes. Blasito Pirir, another one of my friends carried off by smallpox. And I have other names. All belonging to companions who shuffled off. I was the only one left behind, pock-marked." And he raised the tips of his fingers to the round little scars on his face, arranged in the shape of an astral cabalistic sign, the way the fire copal had left them.

"Well, Blas Pirir, from now on, be careful, from now on, when you come down out of your hills, no business of sleeping somewhere else. Straight to the parish house, where we will always put you up. It's a work of charity, undressing the naked!" He laughed at his ambiguity, which was not so much of an ambiguity, all in all, he would undress that Indian who was materially naked, covered with ragged pants and shirt. "And if you're hungry, you'll eat here with me. What a piece of mercy, taking food away from the hungry! And it is, because if a person is unaccustomed to eating . . ." And he laughed again, he was laughing like the Mulata with her frozen hailstone teeth. "And you'll go to bed—what was your name the last time?"

"Blas Pirir, but I'm no longer Blas Pirir, I'm Domingo Tuy."

"Oh, my, oh, my! Another companion who died of smallpox? They passed away and the survivor remained with the weight of their names."

"And that's why they haven't passed away. While I'm alive and use the names they used in life, they haven't died. It's a form of logical magic. And it's not I, my dear sexton, who bear their names. It's they, their names, syllables and sounds, that bear me, and take me back to before the holy *kak* or holy fire, to happier times."

The pock-marked Indian stayed there looking at Jerónimo de la Degollación with all the little eyes of his blind scars.

The thousand looks of night from the face of a man, a thousand looks that the sexton returned with his two tiger pupils, the eyes of that certain Mulata, who despised him for having lent his services to the Great Increaser of Men.

"Breeding time! Breeding time!" The nightly invitation of the street vendor's shouts on the streets of Tierrapaulita to couples so that they would come together and breed on that Good Friday night.

"Breeding tiiime today! Breeding tiiime today! Breeding tiiime!" And the Son of Man was dead.

How could someone take a woman to have children if God was not alive?

"Your real name, what is it? I mean your real name, the one you received at baptism."

229

"My real name is: He who was born with the arrow of his cactus thorn."

"But that's not a name."

"It may not be a very Christian name, but it's my name."

Jerónimo de la Degollación de los Santos Inocentes por Herodes Antipas—his real name was no shorter than that of the Indian, face of a mask punctured by smallpox—felt more and more feminoid, more of a sodomite, the certain Mulata was already in possession of all of his parts, and while poisonous women's hair was circulating through his veins instead of blood, he asked with a tongue spongy with pleasure whether as a child he had not sinned against nature, trying to condemn himself along the road of monster-breeding.

"I did . . ." Jerónimo confessed, inciting the Indian to confidence; "according to my horoscope, I was born under the medieval sign of those vomiters of a very black sky who crown Gothic cathedrals, who are neither male nor female, neither animals nor men, neither angels nor devils, with their maleness uncontained, gargoylish pouches . . ."

But he suddenly remembered that he was there as a succubus, and that his carrying on was that of a male who became a gargoyle when he felt his virility empty, a gargoyle who just as quickly thought he was a lion, a winged lion, like a demon for whom thought was heavy and he had to support himself with both his hands on his chin to hold up his head, a gargoyle who in summer died of thirst, the thirst of a stone, and in winter got drunk on rain water.

Jerónimo came back from his slaughter, which was what he called his thoughts, and he found himself facing the little eyes of a cold vampire of the one who was none other than Celestino Yumí, whose bat teeth did not seem to be laughing, but were half opened so as to catch in flight the return of his breathing which was striking objects that could not be seen, and that aided his navigation.

The certain Mulata was losing ground, either from the sexton's lack of control or because Cashtoc was not helping him, and he was on the point of turning to the Supreme Maker of Ambiguities, the Demon who included all Demons, and asking him how was it that Celestino Yumí, an

230

Indian, was possessed by Candanga, the Christian Tempter, and he, who was a man of the church, was playing succubus to an aboriginal devil.

"Yes, God Chac will reward you," the marked face said with a very distant voice, "every time I come down from my hills to Tierrapaulita, I will come to stay in the parish house, if I don't disturb anyone. A little corner will be enough for me."

"Disturb anyone? A little corner?"

The certain Mulata he had in him could not bear any more, and he took Yumí's (that really was his real name, but he had not wanted to say so) hands and raised them to his cheeks to make them the mirror of caresses; but the quiet, indifferent hands of the false smallpox victim, vulgar, callused, could not manage a caress, even under the impulse of those fond fingers.

"I'll stay there on the floor, when you give me a place to sleep, God Chac will reward you," the Indian said, while the other one let go of his hands, indignant at his indifference of a sorcerer who was prepared to best him.

In contact with the hands of the sexton, which had the warmth of the Mulata's, Yumí felt that he was losing his control over his rivers of rubies.

"There on the floor," the Indian was going to repeat, but the sexton cut him off.

"We'll give you a bed."

"Better just a mat for the sleep on the floor that will be slept when I'm asleep!"

"A mat and on the floor? That will never do. What was your name?"

"Genitivo Rancún."

"Well, Genitivo Rancún . . ."

"In the hospital, if I may tell the story, they put me in a bed and boom!, I got onto the floor, and the nurses said: It's the fever that did it, in his delirium he thinks that the cold floor is ice water; but I came out of it, because sleeping in a bed was more likely to kill me."

"You have two ways of talking."

"I don't understand. I only have one way. You can see my tongue, it's just one."

"But it speaks two different ways. Sometimes like a peasant, and other times like an educated man. Did you ever belong to a brotherhood? I'll bet you did!"

"No, I didn't. I'm poor, right? In order to belong to a brotherhood you have to be quite rich."

"And weren't you rich?"

"Yes, very, very rich, but I was telling you that I saved myself from death because even in the hospital I wouldn't get into a bed, an animal with four legs that doesn't walk, and just because of that, because it's an animal that doesn't walk . . ."

"Tables have four legs too," the sexton clarified, contradicting those wandering theories, "and you eat on a table."

"I don't do that either! I eat on the floor."

"But you sit in a chair."

"I don't do that either! Never! I sit on the floor! A chair reminds me of a table, a table of a bed, and a bed of smallpox! That's why I sleep, eat, and sit on the floor! But it's at night when you shouldn't lose the I of the earth. Even though in the daytime . . . In the daytime you get the I of the earth through your feet, but at night, people who sleep in beds, please tell me, how can they get it. And when you have the I of the earth, it means losing your own I, being relieved of it during the night."

"And when you were married, how did you sleep?" Jerónimo attacked, one could almost hear the tone of the Mulata's voice.

"Oh, well! With a woman yes, you can sleep in a bed, because if the only real and true thing there is is the earth, a woman is the shirt of dreams that the earth puts on. A shirt of water, if she's a woman as fresh and good as the rain. A shirt of mirrors, if she's a woman of the sun, a strong woman. And a shirt of forgetfulness, a shirt of erased faces, if she's a moon woman, a seashell woman with precious holes."

"Did some woman erase your face?" The question was quite direct, and Celestino Yumí, incarnated in the crafty Indian all covered with scars, answered: "A certain no-account . . ."

The Mulata was on the point of leaving the sexton's body. A certain no-account? She . . . a certain no-account? She did not do it, because Jerónimo with his possessed voice hastened to say: "On the porch there's also a hammock where Father takes his siesta and where you could sleep."

"Hanging?" the Indian reacted. "Never! For a person to be air, atmosphere, darkness or light from above, clouds or rain when he sleeps? A person who sleeps hanging will be ruined sooner or later. It's enough for us men not to be the truth, without hanging while we sleep!"

Saint Badthief's Devotee and a Huge Spider of Black Rain

The only visitor who came to the church, which was kept wide open on that shadowy Good Friday, was Gabriel Santano, the druggist in Tierrapaulita. He was a devotee of the Bad Thief, the materialist who was crucified, the one who was called Saint Badthief by those who followed his doctrine of not believing in heaven or the hereafter. From one of his pockets Santano took out a sponge, and from a little jar he took a cathartic paste made with *tereniabín*, not to help the saint die well, but to help him defecate, because in the statue he was portrayed, the vengeance of idealistic sculptors, not as someone agonizing on the cross but as a dry-belly man, a graduate in constipation, in the last stages of a lengthy cramp.

"Glory to thee," Santano prayed to him, his voice shrouded by the sacred fear of matter, "because in thee we recognize the one who proclaimed the greatest of human freedoms: the freedom to doubt, and because you died proud of being mortal among immortals!"

Year after year, the druggist of Tierrapaulita would fulfill his promise of visiting Saint Badthief on Good Friday, during the solemn hours of that solemn and solitary night. He was the only crucified figure to whom no one brought candles, or incense, or flowers, or cypress branches.

233

In past years Santano had had time to croak at him, as he imitated the ravens, or to move the black sleeves of his cone-shaped tunic, just like the wings of a vulture, but this time he barely anointed his lips with the peach paste. The church was filled with noises, and in the baptistry, weakly lighted by high large windows, with open eyes, even open mouth, he surprised a gigantic spider who was drinking the holy water, and beyond, in that door that opened into the sacristy, the sexton, looking like a woman, in the company of a man scarred with pock marks that were dark little points and glowing little points.

What was he to do?

He still had a rabbit's weapons, but his curiosity was greater than his fear. How could he leave without knowing who that spider was, dressed in a cassock, and with thousands of legs—who that glowing woman was, with a mane like a horse, with little hoofs almost, the feet were so small, and who was that ancient man marked with old signs of smallpox?

Outside the infamous vender's cry burst forth: "Breeding tiiime! Breeding tiiime!"

But how could anybody take a woman to procreate, if God were dead, if the Just One had expired between the weeping of Saint Dismas and the insolent laughter of Saint Badthief?

"To nothing with what can breed nothing!" Gabriel Santano began to shout, but nobody heard him; the priest, or spider with eleventhousand legs, was still drinking holy water in the baptistry, and the sexton and his companion had disappeared, heading toward the parish house.

"The coconuts were here," the Indian peeled by smallpox pointed out as they came to the courtyard of the parish house.

"What coconuts?" asked Jerónimo on his own, getting ahead of the Mulata, who, as the envoy of Cashtoc, knew quite well what it was all about.

"Oh," Yumí, the envoy of Candanga, reminded him, "that's right, there was a different priest in those days and a different sexton. Some coconuts in which they tried to smuggle in some holy water. Ha, ha—on every coconut the dwarf Huasanga, hahaha, hahaha—" he was laughing and

234

could not speak—"put the sex of a woman, and it really was the slaughter of—"

"Herod? Be careful with my relative, the heroic beheader of children!"

"No, the beheading of Saint John!"

"Oh, such divine times! Beheading! Beheading!" As he said that, the sexton took the Indian by his old-looking waist; it was no longer the firm waist of a strong male that she (the certain Mulata was still incarnate in the sexton) had known in his good days.

Along a passageway they came to a small courtyard covered with an arbor of flowers in the form of a spur. Spur-jabs of perfume spurred the night in that weepy corner of sweet dampness, an improper setting for the diabolical memory of that Indian with a face of motes in the eye, the holy dew of pale lentils.

"Yes, sexton, yes, smallpox is holy fire, and that's why, among us, we call it the 'beautiful-fire-of-the-lord-God-Christ'! And lost is the man who doesn't call it holy! That happened to me, when I was healthy, with a face that had no sunken freckles. But then it happened—I only said 'smallpox,' I'd forgotten the 'holy'—and in a minute there I was, shivering with fever, and when night came on, in the darkness, it broke out on me. It's holy, but it's horrible! Let me tell you that I saw my childhood friends, the ones who had grown up with me, expiring, rotting, burning up, because the holy smallpox is not a fire that purifies, it's one that makes everything rot, eyes, lips . . ."

"Breeding time! Breeding time!"

But how could they have children if God were dead?

And, after the vending shouts had passed, the Indian with the voice of a cracked bell closed his eyes as he said, as if he himself were speaking in the darkness: "And while they were dying, under the holy flecks of fire stone, pulverized lightning stone, José Quiquín—"

"But that was your name!"

"I am José Quiquín, I am his name! He died, but I am his name and that's why I'm still alive, just as I am also Blas Pirir, Genitivo Rancún, Evaristo Tupuc, Diego Zim, Santos Chac, Pancho Tojonabales, Chilano Canul! And while they were dying, silent, tongueless, they had already

235

been spat out in pieces, the pus of the pustules pouring down over their faces, as if it were the weeping of milk trees, the weeping of metal in white fire which was turning them black, black as burned-out ashes—ashes instead of tears, ashes instead of pus, ashes instead of eyes, ashes instead of sex, ashes . . . ashes . . . hide and hair . . . ashes . . . ashes . . . the flock of vultures was dancing with rage on the metal roofs of the wards, maddened by the pestilence of living and dead people who, before turning into ashes, were in their last agony the food of postulary flies, those tiny flies, frantic flies who were stealing their touch to carry off on their little feet and wings."

"Horrible! Horrible!" shouted Jerónimo de la Degollación as he opened the door to his room, a broad, high, echoing room, on whose threshold Cashtoc, in the person of the certain Mulata put into the body of the sexton, was on the point of being defeated by that painting of the last smallpox epidemic.

But a match, a green candle lighted, and two half-glasses of cane liquor, tossed down inflexibly, without blinking, without breathing, calmed the internal and external battlers, the Indian and the sexton, Candanga and Cashtoc, the one with the necklace of red ears of corn, the color of blood that a bemooned woman has.

"Breeding tiiime! Breeding tiiime!"

But how could anyone give life that night if God were dead?

The Chamber-Potters and the Fight Between the Hedgehog and the Spider

From the shadows that were not being pruned by the flame of the green tallow, the Indian could see the sexton approaching, covered from his shoulders down by a very long and ample heavy black cape, as a music box turned out a kind of dance in three-quarter time.

The one with the cape was wearing in addition a hat that hid his face under its broad black brim.

To the rhythm of the music, slow and stately, moving so that he would not interrupt the couples dancing, he came over to where the candlestick was, opened up the bottom of his encaped darkness, and asked the candle if it cared to urinate some light, offering it a porcelain chamber pot.

Everything remained in darkness while the candle, under the cape of the Chamber-Potter, was urinating a golden light.

"Thank you, my lord Viceroy," the voice of the sexton wrapped in that dark cape could be heard, "you have urinated a golden, frothy, festive liquid that will be used by this humblest of Chamber-Potters to mix, along with some small-leaved sweet basil, the most aromatic kind, into the morning chocolate to be served to my lady Viceroy, because it so happens, God save us, that she has begun to look with feminine famine at your royal coachman."

Then he came to a mirror, stepped back, and drew his cape about him with the crick-crack of a double lash.

"No, my lady marchioness, if you wish to relieve yourself, please look for the ladies' Chamber-Potter. He will kneel at your feet and receive your esteemed liquors."

Jerónimo de la Degollación was going through all those steps of a courtly comedy and explaining that in other times, during the colonial period, at balls given by the nobility in immense palaces with endless salons, attended by hundreds and thousands of guests, the height of courtesy was to have circulate among the gathering a goodly number of Chamber-Potters, under whose ample black capes ladies of quality could urinate silently and maidens, too, could make a flutey sound as they produced their lakes of beer.

"Do you understand," the sexton said, with the useless smile of a beheaded person showing between his teeth, "what the role of the Chamber-Potter was, the Perfect Chamber-Potters, those who swore a Gospel oath in a solemn ceremony to guard their professional secrets until

237

their deaths and went to their graves without revealing what they heard, smelled, and knew, because there was no lack of impatient heirs, ready to empty out their sacks of gold in order to find out whether the uncle from whom they were going to inherit a large fortune urinated in a stream or in drops, comfortably or painfully and already with the fetid odor of a kidney being stabbed by a nephritic stone. And even more tempted by gold were the Ladies' Chamber-Potters, because by the sounds, according to the occult science of the Normans, there was a way of telling whether one's betrothed was a virgin, or whether the 'Gothic lady' who was passing as a noblewoman could be discovered to be a parvenu by the copiousness of her rains, or whether the distant mistress of one of the Governors, by her babbling, the nervous babbling as she relieved herself, had confessed that she was about to fall into the arms of that infantry captain who, they said, had swum over from Spain, because the brigantine which was bringing him took on water (a different kind of water) off the coast of Hilueras, and that gentleman and three Franciscan monks had saved themselves by swimming ashore."

The Indian had not expected the sexton to score on him like that. The latter continued: "A Prosecutor of the Holy Office for the Mainland, the Islands of Barlovento, and the Philippines, was going out of his mind trying to discover whether the granddaughter of the Chief Mayor, the Count of Tapia y Centeno y Audomaro, used a chastity belt. The aforementioned person had arrived for Easter, and his coming was celebrated with great fervor by the colony, which drafted a letter of thanks to the King, where it said that they were all content and happy to know that now there would be someone who could hang, fry, and flagellate, jail, excommunicate, and exile, in the wink of a take-those-gods-away-from-me-and-give-me-the-other-god. But what an Easter for the unfortunate Chamber-Potters, those walking urinals with long and thick capes, because the Prosecutor was convinced that they could clear up the mystery, reveal whether that maiden had her parts imprisoned in the cold device, almost funereal, even though, iron and all, in contact with them it warmed up and became sweet.

238

"Chewing on the quill pen with which he had just signed the sentence of detonsuring by fire of a priest who had been soliciting in the confessional—they were to open a hole in his skull, where his tonsure was, until they could see his brains boiling, all in order to frighten the Chamber-Potters —the Prosecutor of the Holy Office was thinking more and more about the granddaughter of the Mayor and Count, not with very healthy thoughts, not very sane or saintly, although he pardoned himself with the excuse that since the death of his wife he had been living in continence, which, if it were not too difficult in the frigid climes of Navarre, became next to impossible in the Tropic of Cancer, among men and animals maddened by the furor of a land that one could venture to describe as a uterine oven. And therefore, in spite of his strict abstinence," the sexton went on, "since he was dominating his urges less and less, despite cold baths and camphor rubdowns, he decided to ask the Count Mayor for the hand of his grand-daughter."

Let's see who's confusing whom now, Jerónimo said to himself without relinquishing the floor: "But the Prosecutor of the Holy Office had it in for the Chamber-Potters, because he had not been able to get out of them, either by bribery or threats of torture, whether the little Countess, whom he had watched in more than one ball as the Palace Chamber-Potter lent her his services, used a belt like that, not that the Chamber-Potter looked at her as the lady used his cup, because he remained hieratic, his head high and his arms raised to cover her completely, forming a kind of tent, but because, as the Inquisitor said, they have more opportunity for knowledge than bleeders or the people who apply mustard plasters. The Inquisitor of the Palace Chamber-Potter also inquired whether in the act that was of such little quantity the little Countess would empty herself from the angelical little opening or the cavernous and ephemeral opening, since by the shot one can tell the caliber . . . the Prosecutor of the Holy Office gave himself away when he interrogated the Chief Chamber-Potter, spreading his investigation to other principal ladies, trying to learn which among them drank almond liquor, a generous wine, vanilla water, orgeat, or intoxicating punches, because if a liquid that enters the body comes out on the face, where it either refreshes or alters it, it also shows its origin as it comes out in the smell, color, and substance of the urine.

"The Chamber-Spotter," the sexton went on, playing with words like a good demon, "refused to inform him, obliged as he was by his oath sworn on the Holy Gospels not to reveal the secrets of his profession. The Prosecutor of the Inquisition told him that he had the power to relieve him of that oath. But the other one felt that besides his oath there was the honor and dignity of his profession as a Chamber-Potter at stake 'What honor and diginity!' the Inquisitor roared. 'Honor and dignity in a chamber pot? You'll talk under torture!' 'Applied to the man, not to the chamber pot!' the other one replied. The Prosecutor clenched his senile fingers of pale lime around his gold-plated medal on which a green enamel cross glowed at chest level. And at that signal a group of men with tunics and hoods over their faces appeared. Only small holes for the eyes and a wet stain on the cloth where the mouth was. They seized the Chief Chamber-Potter, who was sentenced *Christi Nomine Invocato* to be burned at the stake, not in his solemn black cape of a High Chamber-Potter but in the blue garment of a convicted penitent, for having sustained that the Earth relieved herself of her pregnant urine into the sea that received her rivers with her Chamber-Potter's basin with a turquoise top and a silver rim."

Demoniacal, delirious, hallucinating, the sexton, none other than the selfsame certain Mulata, cut short the story and, opening his cape, he came impetuously toward the Indian in whom Candanga, the Christian devil, was incarnate, using the pretext of presenting him with the basin to despoil him of his male attributes; but the other one, in less time than it took for the cape to blink over his person, grew quills out of each of his pock marks, turning into a ferocious hedgehog.

Jerónimo de la Degollación tried to flee, covering his face with the stinking basin like a military helmet, and wrapping his body in the Chamber-Potter's cape, but it was of no avail; he was attacked by an enveloping cloud of quills that gave off sparks, smoke, fire, and the ashes of burned tortoise shell. When the hedgehog left him, and left him for dead, stretched out on the floor, his cape in shreds, tatters, and out from his hands, his poor hands, his bloody fingers, scratched and rescratched.

A desperate battle began in the church. Half rising, all ears, Jerónimo was trying to get up, anxious to know what was happening and to help Father Chimalpín, no doubt being attacked by that devil's hedgehog, but he could not find the door in the darkness, and he ran, more with his hands than with his feet, bloodying the walls until he finally found the way out and . . . he lost his speech, when he appeared in the church, and with his speech, his tongue, and with his tongue, his breath, and with his breath, the thing it was, the certain Mulata, who left him, a simple sexton once more, and in the light of the sanctuary, from the sanctuary lamp, a reddish blinking, a blinking of blood spattered by the red oil, he watched in horror the combat that was taking place between the hedgehog, with his erect quills, and a giant cassocked spider with eleventhousand hairy legs. The spider moved its legs, like fingers on a keyboard, trying to trap the cruel spiny demon, who would escape by rolling into a ball, unwinding immediately, and returning to the attack with all the points of his quills directed at the spider's eyes, which were shining like drops of dream water behind the falling and straightening of his extremities.

Another shadow approached to watch the fight. Gabriel Santano, the lone devotee of Saint Badthief, and even when he saw himself armed with a crossbar, ready to take the side of the cassocked arachnid, whom he saw simply as Father Chimalpín, fighting with a hedgehog, he could not decide, afraid that in the confusion of the struggle the blow might hit the priest and not the animal.

The certain Mulata, invisible, freed herself from the body of the sexton when she found out that the one who was fighting with the priest was Yumí, and she put an end to the battle, changing into a blinding fog which immediately became a cloud and then a porous stone, so as to immobilize the contenders, and she did it just at the moment when the spider with eleventhousand arms was grabbing the demon of eleventhousand horns which had turned into quills on the hair of the hedgehog Indian.

Degollación, more tatters than clothes and cape, more scratches than skin, climbed up with the druggist Santano, who had not let go of the bar, to send the bells flying, thinking that it was already Easter Sunday; but up above his hands froze, his fingers grew, hollow fingers, and he began to ring for Requiem Mass for the accursed souls of that accursed hell of Tierrapaulita, where one not only heard the shout "Breeding tiiime today! Breeding tiiime today! Breeding tiiime mm-mm!" but the answer that they were obeying the Devil's order that night, that night of all darknesses, when Jesus had died.

"Breeding tiiime today! Breeding tiiime today! Breeding tiiime!"

"We're trying," peasant voices coming out of bedclothes graves.

"Breeding tiiime! Breeding tiiime today! Breeding tiiime today!"

"Heh, heh, heh," an alcoholic voice, "it's pretty good!"

But how could they have children if God was not alive?

The church was filling up with cursing witches and wizards. They were attending a Mass for the dead being sung by a spider dressed in a black chasuble from which arms poured out and rested on the altar, opening and closing on his chest when he turned to say *"Dominus vobiscum,"* and raised on high every time he said *"Oremus."* The spider with eleventhousand arms. Five thousand five hundred large fingers made the sign of the cross on his forehead at the Gospel, and with eleventhousand hands and one hundred ten thousand fingers he elevated the dead host, the unconsecrated host, to the noise of the silver chains of the censer bearers, who were giving breath to that most holy moment with the smoke of their censers, while there was spitting by the garlic-chewing wizards, the rue-chewing wizards, the tobacco-chewing wizards, and the *chacs,* or herbalists, who chewed maddening poisons.

In the front, toward the center, facing the main altar, on a *prie-dieu,* that Requiem Mass was being heard by the certain Mulata, dressed as a dead bride, and Celestino Yumí, that rich fellow with whom she had only been married in a civil ceremony during the Fair of San Martín Chile Verde and who now, corporally present as a porcupine, was

242

taking her as his wife, and with the shout of "Breeding-timetoday!" that echoed through the empty streets he buried all his needles of delight in her dark flesh, right there in the church, during the wedding Mass that was a funeral, pricks to which the Mulata, beautiful, like the back of the moon, responded with a roaming of her white eyes over the faces of the wizards chewing garlic, rue, tobacco, chile, mullein, clinging to the marital beast who did not soften his spines, but made them harder and sharper in the huggle-snuggle of the amorous game, in which she felt that the luminous spines were coming out of Yumí's golden bones —a sun that was so internal, a light that was so deep . . .

"This is my hour of heaven," she exclaimed happily, "my strange hour of heaven!" without being bothered by the broken atmosphere of the wormy eclipse. Yumí's presence had ruined her. The Devil of Heaven never should have used it (why did he do it?) to confront her (was the light disposed that way, eclipse at midnight?), to confront her with her up . . . (the word fell apart) updoubleset—that was what Yumí was, her updoubleset, her double not being upright—they would punish her—she deserved it—every-thing had collapsed, and if Candanga pardoned her, the Devils of the Earth, never, and they would have their vengeance, laughing at how badly the adventure had come off for the Christian Devil, the one that she, the spirit of them, the spirit of Tazol, had loaned herself to in the game.

The sexton, Jerónimo de la Degollación, in the meantime had tied all the ropes from the clappers of the bells to his wrists, as if he were going to pull some mules by their tongues, and he rang the alarm.

Tierrapaulita!!!!
Tierrapaulita, get up!!!!
Tierrapaulita, wake up!!!!

The bells seemed to be saying that over and over. But nobody came. They were all afraid of meeting the Devil at night, only Catarina Zabala, when she remembered that Yumí, her husband, was walking in the streets, woke up Huasanga, the sex and nexus-stealing dwarf, only sex is nexus, whom she had kept in her service in spite of her having been her rival, her husband's wife, when Yumí had been a dwarf, out of pity and because still alive in her

243

memory was the time in which she, traded to Tazol for riches, had also been a dwarf in the house of the certain Mulata. But they had not been great sorcerers then. Now they were, and the proof of it was that she took down a star and put it on for a skirt, then she covered her chest with magic necklaces, and beneath her blouse concealed a necklace of dried worms so that she would not be drooled on. People can trick someone with their drool and slaver. The visible loops fell down in the strands of rainbow to her hanging breasts, broken by age.

The light of Catalina Zabala, as she filled the main door of the church with her presence, burned the eyes of the cursing wizards, visible and invisible, who looked at her as their eyes burned; what was really happening: the surrender of the Moon to the Christian Demon, for that was exactly the role that Yumí was playing: representing Candanga, dressed as a hedgehog in his wedding to the certain Mulata. And if the Christian Devil had appropriated the moon, where would the witches and wizards, the sorcerers, the herbalists, the enchanters go?

The monstrous spider with the eleventhousand arms, with a tonsured little head that came out of his belly, around his navel, lowered his chest, put on the funeral cape, and began the Latin words of the response, indifferent to the battle going on among a crowd of men and women dressed in yellow, with bunches of yellow flowers in their hands, who had been awakened and brought together in the church, not by the bells of the alarm but by the powerful *teponaguas*, drums made out of hollowed trees. Candanga and his people were defending their right to punish the certain Mulata, now that, abandoning the body of the demonized Jerónimo de la Degollación, where she was in the service of arcane plots, she had revealed herself, the way a photograph is revealed by exposure to the light; but the chewing wizards would not listen to them, their teeth armed with the most biting of peppers, red chiles, green chiles, ready to chew them and spit that burning saliva into the eyes of the Christian devils. They raised their hands, painted yellow like the flowers of a dead man, straight toward the West, toward the villages of vegetable memory. Their vengeance against the Mulata would have no limits. A black sea without beaches, their vengeance.

"Malcam!" . . . *"Malcam!"* . . . shouting those words, seconded by thousands of voices that repeated them, all people with yellow-painted hands: *"Malcam!"* . . . *"Malcam!"* . . . they went away with the Mulata as their prisoner. They would take away her magic, her magic clothes with their symbols and colors, just like the ones worn by all the women gathered there, and the most daring of them tore off her clothing of a woman condemned to lose her magic, the green embroidery of the cosmic tree, while another violently tore off her skirt, the zigzag lines of the rain, and another the snakes of clouds of blood and orange braided in her hair, and another one tore off the circle of the lunar sign embroidered on her back. But those were only the external signs of the magic that protects a woman, and thereupon Huasanga, the thief of female sexes, snatched away that trap with little lizard holes, to the great joy and thanks of the Zabala woman (who kept the Mulata's sex as an ocarina). *"Malcam!"* *"Malcam!"* *"Malcam!"* With the shouts of *"Malcam!"* *"Malcam!"* the Mulata, dispossessed of everything, was dragged away by the green sorcerers, flesh of green tallow, hair of green mildew, eyes of dam water, and green teeth, to the Cave of Flints, where they would make her walk barefoot over pointed stones, grief on the tips of flint, and sleep on thorn bushes that would remind her dark sugar skin, when she had been herself again, of the thorns of that love of hers who had been disguised as a hedgehog. In the Cave of Flints the desolate chant could already be heard . . .

Two eyes, no!

Let her have one eye!

Let her have one eye!

Let her have one eye!

Two lips, no!

Let her have one lip!

Let her have one lip!

Let her have one lip!

Two hands, no!

Two hands, no!

Two hands, no!

Let her have one hand!

Let her have one hand!

Let her have one hand!

Two legs, no!

Let her have one leg!

One leg and one foot!

One leg and one foot!

Two ears, no!

Let her have one ear!

Two teats, no!

Let her have one teat!

Let her have one teat!

Let her have one arm!

Let her have one eye!

Let her have one hand!

Let her have one leg!

Let her have one ear!

Let her have one foot!

A Woman Cut in Pieces Keeps on Moving, Like a Snake

From the exit of the Cave of Flints, through gloomy canyons, the Mulata went moaning on her way back to Tierrapaulita, with just one eye, just one lip, just one arm, just one hand, just one breast, just one leg, just one foot.

She was weeping and saying: "I'm only half of what I was! Half of the certain Mulata! A woman lives the best she can! Who put this crown of thorns on me, these porcupine spines? What other queen do they want! All right! They left me with a whole heart! I'll keep on raising the devil and God with things! Why did they leave me with a whole heart?"

Caring for a smoking mirror, a mirror of colored metals,

a large surface covered with holes that was being fed from behind with the smoke of aromatic plants, Catarina Zabala was waiting, in her role of Giroma once more, the powerful Giroma, by a pool of water which she fed with mosses, flowers, the blood of small birds, the half that they had taken away from the certain Mulata, and her sex, and she had brought her paralytic husband there, Celestino Yumí, who had managed to emerge from his hedgehog shape, but not from the stony immobility which the Mulata in the shape of fog had cast over him and Father Chimalpín, a spider with eleventhousand arms converted into a shower of blood, so that she could stop the terrifying fight from going further.

And she left him there to watch floating by on the water, now an eye, now a breast, now a lip, or the sex of that marvelous creature, the bronze color of the morning star, lunar back, black hair, the navel of a sunflower, thighs made from the silky stone of a secret quarry, shoulders of white lilies that would rise up to climb along the curve of her neck and drop down to join the torrent of her lowered arms as it opened into her hands and the rivers of her fingers, those rivers through which she entered everything.

"Oh! Oh!" moaned Celestino Yumí, paralytic, in love with those fragments from heaven, "the only consolation is that jade breaks too, gold breaks, a quetzal feather falls apart, we're not on earth forever."

Huasanga made fun of him: "I remember when you were the dwarf Chiltic! I remember when we got married! We split up when you grew and grew and grew until you reached the size of a giant. The size of you on your stilts!"

"My heart will go off," Yumí went on, without listening to Huasanga, "like wilted flowers. Oh, I hope it's soon! Oh, I hope it's soon!"

"The priest," Huasanga insisted in her babbling, "wanted us to have children! That crazy priest that left Tierrapaulita when his face began to look like a moldy padlock, the one who bred everything: chickens, canaries, ducks, squirrels— ha! ha!—he married us so he could breed dwarfs for circuses, courts, and harems."

"Her eye," Yumí sighed as he saw the round, naked, most beautiful pupil of the certain Mulata float by, "is passing in the water like the heart of a bell bird, and her lip, like the petal of a blooming poppy, and her round breast, like half of the world that was her empire!"

"But you didn't get me pregnant, eh? You didn't get me pregnant . . . and I grabbed your giant foot, shouting as loud as I could: 'I want to try a giant!' and because of that, because I wanted you to make me pregnant, it all ended up with your wife's, the powerful Giroma from then on, throwing me into a cesspool, so that the hogs would eat me, but that twisted sexton pulled me out!"

"Can men be truth, perhaps?" the paralytic murmured as he watched half of his love floating in the water, "Can things be truth, perhaps, is what we do certain, perhaps?"

"And you should be thankful that Giroma didn't throw this one into the cesspool but into clean water, fed by the poisons that keep life going only so that it can suffer!"

Then, with little dwarf jumps, she came over to the paralytic and said to him: "Do you know something? The pieces of the Mulata that are swimming around in this bluish pool, now a breast, now a foot, now a buttock, now an arm, still have feeling, and you could communicate with her through them and advise her that if she wants to be what she was again, she should ask the help of . . ."

Huasanga stopped herself. Catarina Zabala was coming to get Yumí, and she carried him off like a piece of furniture, as he turned his statue eyes in vain toward the dwarf.

"I brought you some marzipan," the Zabala woman told him, "the most delicious marzipan there is, the kind you like—skeleton of gold, and don't get alarmed, because the secret of your bones is only known by me and that certain so-and-so with half of her whole and half of her quartered."

But Yumí was not listening to her.

What humiliations the Mulata, one-eyed, one-armed, one-legged, suffered in the house of the witch Giroma, the Casasola, the lonely house, as they called the mansion situated on the eyelid of the town!

She made her wait outside in the yard, in one of the back courtyards, among clothes hanging on the lines that were dripping dirty water over the drying racks, slippery with soap, next to vultures that were disputing cats with open

248

bellies, more flies than cats, the sacrifices of the sorcerers. The intestines of a white cat are good to check nighttime flatulence, and the paws of a black cat, cut off during a full moon, are good for evil work, because when they are given to people so that everything will come out well, it all turns out just the opposite.

In the courtyard, among garbage and trash, the Mulata was waiting to be received by the powerful Giroma. What a nameless humiliation! Pots with a fermenting brew placed on top of parrot feathers were receiving the green fire that made the fertilizing essences in scum and top scum boil in a trembling way, the fertilizing essences that would assure those about to be married that their children would not be mute, but would be as chatty as lorry parrots or the smaller kind. In other pots there was also boiling, not over a symbolic fire this time but over a grill of live-oak logs, the great stew of snouty fetishes: raccoons, rats, coatis, foxes, squirrels, the only thing to be used against impotence in the male, also recommended for feminine sterility.

The Mulata—she was just one eye, just one lip, just one arm, just one hand, just one ear, just one leg, and just one foot—slipped off through a mouse hole into the Courtyard of the Puppets.

Hundreds, thousands of unpainted wooden dolls, carved out with a machete, long-legged, short-armed, a neck that was too distinct from the thorax, almost a prolongation of the chest up toward the flat head, cut off at eyebrow level, and above the negation of a chin were the mouth, the nose, and the eyes, all close together, as if they liked to see and smell at the same time.

"I, who sold my flesh to the riches of the sun," moaned the Mulata as she considered her present situation as a thin serpent, holding in her single hand of crooked fingers one of those puppets, dolls of roughly carved wood, some light as the air, carved out of balsa wood, and others heavy as a cross, carved out of gallows wood.

She did not go on. What good did it do her to complain to little wooden statues, like votive offerings, having marked on their bodies the sign of the sick part of the patient, so that, with the care of a dark wizard, they would be cured?

249

But she, a cloth of star tears, how could the miraculous puppets cure her if she lacked half of her body and the dampness of her sex?

The certain Mulata, one-eyed, one-armed, one-eared, with a harelike mouth, and one-legged, slid off toward the room where the Masks of the Interpreters were hanging, and on the left she came across the Mask of the Bold Interpreter, the one who upset everything, created to confuse, with his eyes of a handless clock with Roman numerals. Time will end when all clocks eat up their hands, this clock time, because the other kind will never end. The Bold Interpreter lives outside of time because his eyes have no hands, just round pasteboard pupils with numbers. Or it will end when clocks get fingers and put their hours, minutes, and seconds ahead, because, judging from the haste with which they go along, they have an urgency to arrive, where?, wherever clocks arrive, if one hour follows upon another, if one minute follows another, if one second, in the unending chase of the blood of its mechanical emptiness, follows another second.

On the right, the Mask of the Interpreter of Slaves was hanging. His teeth, not tightly closed, were shaped in a bite, next to the Mask of the Interpreter of Stutterers, with his black face and stars twinkling on his forehead blackened by the tar of shadows. All the stammering of Night, the Mother Stammerer, and all the stammering of the Stars. Stutterers or stammerers spoke through that Mask, without the suffering of having to say things with twigs of words.

In back, the Mask of the Interpreter of Drunkards, fearsome, changing, a meeting of missed meetings, an involvement of uninvolvements, and enchantment of disenchantments, and near that festive false face the Mask of the Interpreter of Beggars. The round mouth of a pot to cook men in, like an immense cavity that had taken over its chin and barely left room for the eyes. Its unwashed ears, like a beggar. The uncut fringe of hair, like a beggar. Its lice, like a beggar.

"Who has suffered a greater humiliation," the Mulata was repeating to herself, one-eyed, one-armed, one-legged, with a harelike lip, with only one ear, like a chamber pot, "to be received by dolls! She? She, who had had Celestino Yumí at her feet! Yes, yes, it wasn't painful, she congratulated herself at having whipped him, scratched him, and never given her front to him for his amorous pleasure, because she had always given him her back, like the moon to the sun! Treating her like that, Catarina Zabala, who had been *her* dwarf, her diversion, her doll, day after day a different dress, until she got tired of her and the bear appeared! But oh, my blood copal, that wicked witch, being my favorite dwarf, Monday I dressed her in red and rubies, Tuesday in green and jade, Wednesday in blue and turquoise, Thursday in white and diamonds, Friday yellow and topaz—was that it?—she knew my weakness for splendor, for greatness, for dazzling things obtained by inhaling the fragments of a smoke plant that changed my body into airy moss, and it was childishly marvelous, when in place of an ear I would put on a star fish and I could not only hear the sea but had it inside of me, weeping pearls and spitting pink little sea shells. I did not think that, dwarf and all, she loved the one I did not know was her husband, the then powerful Yumí, with the magic of wealth, the *tazol* of his cornfields was changing into gold, and that ruined me. Without dying, the smoke draws us along its thread bridges and over those bridges of thread more delicate than eyelashes, we reach the lunar cave which the Grumpy Bird guards, and there I locked myself up with her to talk with an ancient colony of white water lilies. I was talking and the dwarf was laughing at the concept those flowers had of humans. We seem so ugly to them. And why do you smoke that diabolic plant? one of the water lilies asked me. Because it's the only thing that gives me faith! I answered right away. And that was how it was. I smoked it to have faith and presence. Outside of its airy mosses everything seemed past and uncertain to me. And that's why, I added, those of us who smoke it end up like swimmers who barely move their arms, who barely keep their heads above water, breathing those last little bits of air which will perhaps allow them to reach the shore of the present-present. How difficult to conceive, without smoking this smoke plant, of that present that I speak about, so present that the present itself seems to be past. But the water lilies began to fade, and I saw myself surrounded by trembling faces. The dwarf had fled.

251

With the help of the Grumpy Bird she had closed up the entrance to the cave with the cheek of a hill. I did not become alarmed. I took a new hollow stem, I put some of the divine plant in it, there was fire there, and I lay down to smoke until the Moon returned. The pulsation of return time startled me. She was coming back. My blood began to flow backward. I licked my lips. Icy licks. I licked my eyelids as my eyes spun. I could hear them spin. It was tremendous. Spinning around the Moon. Her whole back and, behind, the shadow of Yumí. Not drunk, but not in complete control either. Halfway, as when I met him at the fair of San Martín Chile Verde. Now we were facing each other again, he the incarnation of Candanga in the body of a pock-marked Indian—they must have given him a quick case, judging from his scars—and I in the body of that repulsive sexton, representing Cashtoc, none other than Cashtoc, the Great, the Immense.

"But first I ought to tell . . ." She went over to the Mask of Copals, among whose Sauvage teeth something was moving, a piece of white copal, no doubt, she could not see so well with just one eye. "But first I must tell that before this meeting with Yumí now that to avenge myself, shut up in the cave, I unleashed the most fearsome cataclysms. Earthquakes, mountains sinking, and, by forced marches, the displacement of a crust of lava that covered all the rich lands of that man who, poorer now than in his days as a woodcutter, only had the dwarf and the bear left to earn his living with, as he had them dance in public squares."

But she went closer to the Mask of Copals, and it was not chewing a piece of copal, but between its motionless teeth of a wild boar, of a Sauvage, dressed in white, Huasanga was calling her over there.

The secret that this dwarf who was a thief of sexes had not been able to confide in the ear of Yumí, the paralytic, she deposited directly into the ear of that unfortunate one-eyed, one-armed, one-legged woman who was showing her upper incisors like a hare, and with just one breast dancing under her blouse as if looking for its companion.

"Don't tell anyone that it was my advice, the powerful Giroma would never forgive me, and nothing about a certain Mulata, with that mayor there the name you will have to use is Yapolí Icué, for whose steps the plain will be narrow, the hills not too difficult, and the rivers not too deep."

Juan Buttonole, master of magic, received the visit of that half a woman as he sat in his black feather chair, adorned with small mirrors, surrounded by children who were playing at killing each other with short machetes, for their parents and grandparents had sent them to find Juan Buttonole so that he could teach them to fight with thunderbolts. The small machete-wielders found Juan Buttonole, not in his chair of black feathers, as Yapolí Icué had just found him, but on his blue bench, and they said to him with their little voices, with children's voices: "We bring you these five pineapples, eat them and your head will become filled with freshness. We bring you this, Juan Buttonole, in exchange for what you will teach us. We want to learn from you how to fight with thunderbolts of gold that looks like caramel and is shiny." "Did you bring your machetes?" asked Juan Buttonole, master of magic, who was dressed like a blue turkey, his arms covered with blue wings, like armor of feathers, and he scarcely turned around as he asked them if they had brought their machetes. "We brought them, Juan Buttonole," the children answered him, "and before leaving home we honed them on grindstones white as grandfathers' beards." "Very good, children," the great blue turkey answered them—that was how Juan Buttonole, or Juan Nojal, master of magic was dressed—and he added: "I was your age when my mother put a curse on me for having contradicted her while she was sewing a buttonhole on my shirt. 'Buttonhole,' she said, and I stubbornly answered her: 'No, Mother, buttonhole, no.' And between 'buttonhole yes' from her and 'buttonhole no' from my stubbornness, she pricked herself with the needle and the point of it went on along the rapid rivers of her blood to wound her heart. In her death agony, she cursed me with the name of Button . . . no . . . hole, or *no . . . ojal*. And her curse turned me black inside. In my loneliness I made friends with Manilaní, the devil of the bushes, and, taking pity on me, Manilaní indicated that I should speak to Jel, the devil who distributed

253

the realms of witchcraft, because they could give me some territory where there was a need for a sorcerer. 'Do you have a crown?' Manilaní asked me. 'I don't have anything,' I answered him. 'I have my feet, I have my hands, my eyes, I have my head.' 'Very well answered,' my friendly adviser was pleased, 'you have life and you are not proud, and because of that answer Jel will have no trouble in giving you a magic kingdom.' And he gave it to me, here on this hill, from where I have dominated the needles of fire that stick into the flesh of the clouds, the trees, animals, people, everywhere, like that accursed needle that stuck into my mother's flesh while she was sewing me a buttonhole. That's what I am, Guardian of the Needles of the Storm, and from what I hear there are children with short machetes, honed on the white beards of grandfather grindstones, who want to fight with thunderbolts. So be it." And it was. Those children do not return home. They stay on as skilled machete-men in the escort of Juan Nojal. And their parents and grandparents do not miss them because they can see them fighting with thunderbolts every time there is a storm.

And the certain Mulata came before that lord of magic under the name of Yapolí Icué and dressed as Tipumalona, or wearing the dress of the wife of the demon Tipumal, whom the Mulata had met while she was looking for the Guardian of the Needles of the Storm.

Tipumal and Tipumalona were bathing in pools of water vapor, their bodies naked, their eyes naked, his shaved head round and the same size as the breasts of the woman, which were floating upon the sulphurous water that stank like rotten eggs.

The Mulata, in spite of her one-eyedness, her lack of a lip, her one-armedness, her limp, her unearedness, made Tipumal restless; he was a devil of corrosive and rapid lust, not accustomed to going without satisfying her, and with that intention he took his wife, Tipumalona, by the neck and sank her head in the water that was yellowish with sulphur, ready to drown her. The constables would find a floating or a sunken corpse. But the certain Mulata, on to the intentions of that evil sulphurous and pestilent devil, when she noticed that the unfortunate Tipumalona was drowning, the last bubbles of her breath mixing with the water vapor, shamelessly lifted her skirts and showed Tipumal that, besides being one-eyed, one-armed, one-legged, uncared, and with a mouth that had no upper lip, she lacked her perfections, stolen in an evil hour by that vile Huasanga, even though now she had to thank her for the advice of sending her off to Juan Buttonole, master of magic.

When he noticed that serious deficiency, Tipumal, a devil with stallion blood, a demon who roared and cried like a man who was after women, let go of Tipumalona, who abandoned the depths of death for the surface of life, and she offered the Mulata her dress, so that she could put it on and flee, all of which happened in a matter of seconds. What was certain was that Yapolí Icué presented herself before Juan Nojal dressed as Tipumalona, which is wearing the clothes that mountain ranges wear when the sun goes down.

"Yapolí Icué," Juan Nojal said, settling into the bottom of his black-feather chair, "how incomplete you come before the presence of my painted heart!"

The Mulata, appearing to be even more unfortunate than she was, let out short complaints, showing her single eye, her single foot, her solitary teat, her ear . . .

"I'm not referring to that, Yapolí Icué," said Juan Buttonole, master of magic, "but to what cannot be seen! To that precious throat that is an object of love, to that box of red flints that the moon spreads out month by month, to the virgin offering, to the wrinkled sea shell, to the serpent-star, swallowing and sustaining, the one that orders a life worked out on axles of hope, the great butcher woman, a dream that hangs down from the heaven of the mouth of perverse people, a noose around the neck of a man who is alive, and bad and barren, like the flesh of flies, for those who take it in the place of pleasure, of pastime . . ."

Shared silence is the tastiest of breads. That was what Juan Nojal thought as he became silent and felt that horrible woman grow silent, that woman who was only her half, but much too present, much too vital in that caricature half. Carrion without an odor, a leper without leprosy, half a corpse, shadowed by the light of evening which was joining

255

the branches of the pine trees closer together, like the brows of beetle-browed pagodas.

"A bad business, what those great wizards did!" Juan Buttonole said when he got back the words that had been lost among the butterflies of his flitting thoughts. "But Yumí no longer has any power. She's the powerful one. Leave me alone tonight. Go sleep next to those maguey plants that have an intoxicating smell. And come back tomorrow when the dawn laughs down on this corner where I have my black-feather chair. I'll be somebody else, because every day I'm somebody else. Nobody goes to bed and gets up the same once he's gone through sleep. Can you hear it, deep down? Don't get nervous, it's the mass of a torrent that pours down with jasmines of foam."

Possible but not easy. And possible only as long as she followed the exact words, syllable by syllable, of the advice of Juan Buttonole. A woman of her stature, more or less, and somewhat thin, so that they could both fit into the same dress, or, rather, into the blouse and skirts of Tipumalona, which were what now covered the certain Mulata. She went among deer hunters, bluish, distant, armed with their bows and arrows. So distant that they did not manage to see her. She winked. Her eye was so powerful that it brought everything close up. And therefore it seemed near to her, but she had to walk leagues to reach the place where a woody woman, with skin like dry cow manure, a shaved skull, was shooing flies away. She had intended turning her path so that she would not pass close to that woman who was being devoured by some kind of teary salt, some kind of thorn bushes, and some kind of sun with flies. She shuddered. If it meant that, getting into the same clothes with that human skeleton, she would rather stay the way she was, one-eyed, one-armed, one-legged, uneared, showing her teeth in an unending smile for lack of an upper lip. There was still time. She was still far away. But her steps were drawing her fatefully on against her will. Did that woman she was approaching know? Was she waiting for her, or was she always there on the edge of the road? Had anyone ever passed along that way?

The skeletal woman, unaware of the intentions of Yapolí Icué—the certain Mulata still had to keep acting—

put her hands to her face, laughing and laughing, unable to hold herself in, happy to find someone else more unfortunate than she, half a woman, and she thought she must have drunk some mushroom juice, and she went over to touch her.

Yapolí Icué would also have liked to laugh at her, at her skull, which was what it looked like under the skin that was nothing more than a plate of moving mirror in which the play of her articulations was reflected, her jaw on her condyles, her arms on her shoulders, her elbows, her knees, and the perceptible movement of her ribs in time to her breathing. But how could she return the insult of the laugh, laugh at her, when her lack of an upper lip always made her look as if she were smiling?

With her eye, Yapolí Icué calculated whether that woman could fit in with her, the two together in the blouse and skirt of Tipumalona.

But how would she tell her, how would she propose that mysterious transaction?

"The one up there who takes care of the thunderbolts sends me here. He's like all solitary people, the master of his face and his heart. We have to be sisters in the same clothing. Together, very much together, just like sisters in the same clothing, just like sisters who might have been born stuck together, so you will make up for the arm I lack, the leg I don't have, the ear, the eye, the lip. You will stick out your face, and I'll stick out one leg and one arm and my hand, which is all I have left."

"What for?" The skeletal woman was interested in such a strange proposal, and because it was the order of the one up there in charge of thunderbolts.

"To take a fortress with no other weapon except a broom."

"A broom?"

"A broom made with the hair from a dead man."

"And how will we sweep? It's not easy. It's a science."

"Yes," Yapolí Icué recognized, "it isn't just ordinary sweeping, but Juan Nojal told me how we should do it. The chicken feathers will retreat. They don't like to be swept. The skin of ripe fruits will cling to the ground. They don't like to be swept either. And let's not even mention pieces

257

of paper with writing on them. They turn over with every sweep, all their letters headfirst. And the peelings from onions, cabbages, carrots, radishes, lettuce, potatoes, beets will play among themselves under the impulse of the broom and try to get away, but they'll come back, stuck to the broom itself."

"Yes, yes," the skeletal woman thought, blowing on her cold hands as if to warm them, "that isn't ordinary sweeping. The broom makes the sound of kisses on the ground, a new broom, and that's bad, very bad, because a broom has nothing carnal about it, it's made out of wood. It doesn't have anything carnal. Being carnal is part of life. You only hear kisses when it sweeps."

"But you don't have to hear that sound, Juan Nojal recommended to me," said the Mulata, who was none other than Yapolí Icué, "because if you hear it, the sound of the broom joins in with the air underneath, which always whistles when sweeping is being done, and who could ask for anything better?"

"From what you say," the skeletonized woman gummed, "we're to enter a fortress where trash and dust reign. And how can we avoid being separated, even though we're stuck in the same dress?"

"Juan Nojal gave me this hemp rope. We'll tie ourselves together, but first you have to tell me how many deer skins you want for the favor I'm asking of you. Going along, becoming one person with me, sweeping up in that house of evil cursing witches and wizards."

"The hard thing will be getting out of here, not getting into that fortress."

"Why?" inquired Yapolí Icué in agony.

"We'll have to be strong. Not listen to the proposals of the devils, because around here there are many devils who lust after deformed women. They'll climb up on our shoulders and offer to make us pregnant from behind. Hunchbacked women are made pregnant with the children of devils like that, and it gets into a hump and there's no place for it to get out. And, ugly as we are, with a pregnancy on our backs—but I shouldn't laugh, because a woman's laugh is absorbed by the little sand-grain devils."

"We'll get out." The Mulata appeared sure of herself.

"I've seen myself in such cockroach rags lately that nothing frightens me any more."

And while they were escaping out of those high mountains and Tierrapaulita began to paint itself out on the bottom of the valley, she brought back to mind the Requiem Mass of her marriage to Celestino Yumí, sung by a spider with eleventhousand rains, a black cassock, and an alb that was also black, a complicated fabric woven out of spider webs, dark, the maniple and the stole made out of women's black braids, and the funeral chasuble out of rasping dry leaves, leaves that autumn starches with its pitch of breakable gods.

"Breeding ti-iiime," she had heard while she was being married, and she had felt the desire to have a child by Yumí, to throw herself on the floor, right there in church and beg Celestino to make her a mother ("Breeding time! Breeding time!" was still being shouted outside), right there, giving him her front, not her back that was like the Moon, in the struggle, and she would have done it, at the request of her navel, which, like a clock of hives, tick-tock-tock, was ticking in her womb, showing that it was time to catch a nebula of progenies.

But they were already in front of the mansion of the great sorcerers, and they had to tie themselves up and put Tipumalona's blouse and skirt on together. From the broom, people would know that they were offering a sweeping. And that was how it was. Neither the powerful Giroma nor Huasanga suspected that hidden in that double woman was the certain Mulata.

The Devil of Heaven Proposes Insuring Peace

Bat-flapping, church-sacking noises, dew-dripping, such clear, fat drops, cat-walking, a kind of lost talking, twanging, stammering, yammering, and the thrashing of a dying person, door-knocking, dismounting of riders, carting of things, chattering of teeth, all in the ears of Gabriel Santano, the druggist devotee of Saint Badthief, all except the chirping of the bird he was so eager for, to make him realize that he was on earth and not among the murmuring of the other life.

"Oh, gray bird with the step of an old woman!" Santano begged. "Oh, gray bird! Oh, wake-up bird, what are you waiting for, land on the roof and greet the sun! Hurry! Hurry, dawn is on its way! Hurry, before the rice bird sings and starts the day off with a bad omen! Sing, gray bird! Don't you hear the *co cotli . . . coco . . . co cotli . . . coco . . .* of the doves and the *cuitlacosh . . . cuitlacosh* of the ash bird?, which is not a good omen either."

In the end and in spite of his crossbar, he too had to face the hedgehog, the infuriated spiny beast, he saw green, he saw fields of prickly pears, clouds of prickly pears with spines that stuck out, he saw barbed wire, battlefield wire that twisted under war's fire, and, as he laughed like the Bad Thief, he, Gabriel Santano, saw the crown of thorns of Our Lord passing over his body like a wheel of prickly teeth, wounding, but not too deeply, and he saw the thorny branches of rosebushes that had no roses, the nightmare of that demonized hedgehog, a large-headed beast with great, scratching bristles, a long nose for rooting, small Chinese eyes that were visible in the light of the clarity that was emanating from the tips of his quills, a pachyderm electrified with lightning bolts, one that would have put an end to his human sack of skin and bones that smelled of remedies if it had not suddenly turned again to put everything its quills were capable of into the battle with the cassocked figure, which looked like something in a black sack, which the sexton insisted on saying (and now Santano was seeing him that way) was a spider with eleventhousand legs, against whom, ignoring his small starfish size, the porcupine, or corpupine, as Gabriel Santano called him, was engaged in horrifying battle, changed into a rain of spiny hair, of butting needles.

. . . the spider was moving his legs, his thousands of hairy legs, trying to seize the eleventhousand times horned one by hair and horns, and he, Santano, stood with his bar ready, unable to intervene for fear of hitting the little Father and not the evil beast, so close they were in combat . . .

. . . still, was it the cleric or not? Where could he have got arms and more arms, so many, uncountable, just as uncountable as the number of hands struggling to trap the ugly little spiny beast that was escaping from his thousands of moving fingers, fingers and hands (the spider's legs), which the porcupine was pricking, wounding, scratching, so that in the end blood was showing on the eleventhousand extremities of that big hairy spider of darkness that was damp with the sweat of a dead man . . .

. . . the fight was getting boring, or so it seemed, and Santano moved with the bar from one side to the other, resolved to hit the corpupine, but the fear of making things worse, giving the priest a whack, held him back . . .

. . . and neither of the two showed any sign of fatigue in that battle without quarter, with waves of quills against hands of sand, and just as the waves on the beach escape from the sand that thinks it has them trapped, so out of the grasp of that strange soutaned sand escaped the quills of that animal, who would leave the hands and leap at the face, the crackling of a cloudburst accompanied by the sowing of drops or smallpox marks that stayed with the priest, trembling on his cheeks, his forehead, his nose, his throat, his chin . . .

. . . Santano suddenly pinched himself, in the dozing of dawn he remembered that he had gone to sleep, as the weightless spider, silence is weightless, was climbing like a woolen spider to take refuge in the transept of the church, pursued by the corpupine . . .

But why didn't the gray bird with the step of an old woman sing? Gabriel Santano wondered, afraid to start the day with the memory of the night before, Good Friday night, when he had been witness, only he had gone to the church to visit Saint Badthief, to the sulphury expulsion of a female from the body of the possessed sexton during the fiercest part of the battle between the priest-spider with eleventhousand legs and the corpupine. That female, who was none other than the certain Mulata, had thrown over the

261

maddened porcupine the water from the clepsydra that she carried in her deep eternity, water or moon mist, which had immediately hardened into stone . . .

. . . the church had filled up with cursing wizards who were blinking as if they were punctuating their thoughts with eyelash commas, some maddened by the parasitic noises of their insides, or instincts, which are the insides of the soul.

Santano found himself on his feet, so real was his memory, climbing up the spiral staircase leading to the belfry, no matter what bebell him; the sexton was already beating at the bells with their enormous clappers, and Santano was changed, crossbar and all, into the metal of some deeply human quality, into the intimate and certain metal that was expanding out in infinite navigation across the rooftops, up to the mountains, in a call for help . . . for help . . . who answered the bells and their wavy questions? . . . what bundles of carnal bodies, floating in the shape of clouds, cast off toward the voice that was invisible but ever present in the shadows of the night? . . .

. . . everything was vibrating, everything was moving, immense bites of great and small stars that within the eternal wheel were trying to grasp the causes and effects of the fragmenting of the swallows who, as they fled from the belfries, ended their triangular flights in the nearby cypresses; immense bites of the silence that served to brand on the surfaces of eardrums pierced like sea shells the images of the sound the church produced as it leaped exactly like a gigantic cassocked spider into the nocturnal shadows, with eleventhousand towers, eleventhousand belfries that moved like prehensile trunks after the peanuts of the echo, which the mountains were cracking and eating, leaving nothing except the empty shells of sound, and sounding, nonetheless, the way that silence sounds when storms have passed . . .

No, no, it's worse than hell! This absolute certainty that there is nothing, really nothing . . . (Gabriel Santano had returned, on his way back from the belfry, to stop in front of Badthief) . . . nothing about what had been said . . . he would laugh with the laugh of a materialist, a village positivist, the birisible feeling of a double laugh in his hands, as, like laughing teeth, his fingers clenched the bar which he was gripping in a desperate grabbing for something, while he came face to face with Candanga himself, dressed the way people are, pale, mercurial, without his rooster, or with the rooster changed into His Grace's purple glove that Father Chimalpín had thrown in his face as a challenge . . .

"He said so much when he challenged me!" Candanga complained to Santano as he stared into the startled face of the pill-pusher with his blue eyes of a celestial animal. "He lost his breath! He unloaded on my person all the insults an exorcist has! Bah!" He shrugged his shoulders. "Time-worn insults, and he was so worked up that instead of shouting *iconoclast* at me, he said *iconoblast,* a term more fitting for my predecessor, Cashtoc, the red-earth devil, a blaster of churches and saints!"

And, while the other one went on with his falsiloquy, Santano said into his ear: "No, no, my state is worse than hell, this absolute assurance that at the end of life there is nothing, absolutely nothing!"

"And why was he insulting me?" Candanga was saying. "Because I was going around hawking and inviting couples to breed, to get rid of all that fear of the flesh, so that they would keep on reproducing it in millions of photographs. Only the first parents were authentic, all other men and women are photographs that are taken from orgasm to orgasm, based on previous photographs and paradisiacal images, with no change in technique: a *camera obscura,* a shot, a sensitized plate, and the image of the new being. When he finished his challenge, he invited me to remove the malignant spirits from the world. This young Chimalpín, ignorant like some priests, doesn't know that I have already taken them away and that I've put robots in their places, my present functionaries."

And without pausing, he went on: "I did away with a few malignant spirits, a greasy and illiterate bureaucracy, and substituted them with robots who have their own heating system based on incandescent flesh, radar like bats, atomic powder to wash their teeth of fire which consume all metals, even titanium. Oh, no, that poor Father Chimalpín is thinking with his rear end instead of using his head! And what,

what is modern life, progress, civilization, if not my *I* in the dust of words?"

Santano felt that the Devil was carrying him off. Without moving from where he stood, he was being carried off. How could it be explained? Quite simple. Just as when the moon seems to be running among the clouds and a person who watches it feels that he is going along with it. Was he carrying him off to hell? Hahaha! Santano laughed at hell. The nothingness after death that was expected by all who believed as he in Badthief was worse. He shook his head. Drive away thoughts. Not to think. But it is impossible not to think. It is nothingness. But how sweet it would be not to think. Nothingness. Sweet nothingness. In one of his pockets he found the vial of bromide. A good dose. He had brought it to church on Good Friday. So many women got fainting spells. But the potion did not manage to stop his trembling. That slight and profound trembling of living matter in the face of nothingness, the absolute negation, which for the Sophists was only *flatus vocis*. How can one imagine nothingness? By emptying one's thought of all thought? Only in that way was it possible to conceive of the not being that awaits man after death, in his complete and total extinction. And that was why Santano was laughing, now that the Angel of Evil Light, alias Candanga, was carrying him off to hell, which, compared to nothingness, was just a bad joke, something that was not serious, and because he was going in the company of one of God's great vanities, the Devil, still a jollier companion, in spite of his being the executioner of souls, than Saint Badthief, the first materialist saint, in whose hoot at heaven all hope had died.

But he did not carry him off to hell.

The President of the Insurance Company peered over his antediluvian glasses, left over from the days when women darkened their eyes, pince-nez with a black ribbon that plumbed down his cheek and sometimes would get entangled on his hawk nose, and he could only free himself from its tyranny by looping it over the flap of his ear; he was peering and trying quickly to classify his new client, who was accompanied by a druggist who said that he had a business in Tierrapaulita, a client who, without batting an

264

eye, told him in a most solemn way that he had come to insure hell. (I wonder if nothingness can be insured, Santano stuttered to himself.)

The President of the Insurance Company bit his tongue and, along with his tongue, the black silk ribbon which had fallen off his ear, but he had already asked: "Against fire?"

"Just the opposite," the client answered, more and more serious.

The President of the Company meditated before he went on, with the rapidity of one who has everything prepared, the lightning surgery of an insurance salesman, what organ to go after, what weak organ has suggested to the client the idea of insuring himself and insuring his property. What would have to be done, the insurance man asked himself, a document in his hand, to draw up a policy, not against fire but against the extinguishing of the fire? And, all of a sudden, the sally of an accomplished salesman.

He took a form out of one of the drawers of his oversized wooden desk; the new client, whom he had taken to be a Hindu, had asked him on the telephone to be received in the office where the old desk was and not in his new office, since a part of his beliefs was not to do business near metals, although the truth was quite different: as an uncreated demon, he lacked the insulators that his robots now possessed, and he ran the risk that if he sat opposite the metal desk it would start to give off sparks as if it were electrified.

The President, a man of clock time, consulted the timepiece on his wrist and—horrors!—the most perfect Swiss movement, self-winding, a musical chime to awaken him, a calendar, sweep second hand, fluorescent numerals, had stopped, nor were his intercom and telephone working.

Isolated, completely isolated in that rear wing of the Insurance Company building, where the old offices with wooden desks were, he was face to face with a client who had come to insure his property not against fire but against the possibility that the fire that was consuming it would be extinguished.

He took out the form and asked the client to fill it out, while he would consult with the home office to see if he

265

could insure against the extinguishing of fire. Without trying to, he had hit the nail on the head.

"That's it, that's what I want," the client said enthusiastically, "insurance that the fire will not go out once it's been lit! Neither armistice nor peace treaty! The total annihilation of man and the reappearance on the face of the planet of my finest moments, those periods of human infancy that I recall with sadness, when, over thousands of years, on a chunk of cooling earth, there rose up an endless desert that was being consumed in flames a piece of earth's crust that sank so deep that there is no mind that can imagine it" ("To nothingness," Gabriel Santano said to himself as he listened) "and mountain ranges emerged. And since that period when the earth was growing cold, growing cold, I've always had the idea of insuring my property against the fire's going out."

And with the full power of his voice: "Isn't it stupid for there only to be insurance against fire, when there are more things that can cause disaster by its going out?"

"If you'll permit me," the President of the Company interrupted as he lifted the black ribbon that had got caught in his eyelashes like a fly up to the flap of his ear, "if you'll permit me, a life insurance policy is never useless, in addition to your policy against the fire's going out—" very logical, the President said to himself—"now that they're taking uranium out of the earth . . ."

"I can guess your thoughts," the strange client interrupted the rapid flight of ideas in the President's head, "now that they're extracting another earthly substance from my property, without its bothering them that the earth is still growing cold, that metals show them their snuffed-out eyes, and that my hand has stopped imposing the movement of rotation on the worlds. Another idea. Haven't insurance companies ever thought of introducing on the market policies for gods about to fall into disuse? Any god, even though he knows that millions of people believe in him, can fall apart at a given moment, and he should insure his divinity. If Buddha had carried insurance when Brahmanism broke out uncontrollably in India, the insurance company would have had to pay the living Buddha for the ruin of his divine enterprise. This brings us to the time I fell

266

from the Earthly Paradise, when I was not insured, and if you have the time, Mr. President . . ."

"In an insurance company time is eternal."

"I'll explain to you the reasons for my fall. Everything they say around here, or what is said by Justin, Tertullian, Athenagoras, Clement, Cyprian, Ireneus, Gregory, Epiphanius, Leo the Great, Petavius, and Tommy Aquinas, are hickish fibs that I have to go around correcting with my own words and in person, because the press, lackeys of heaven's imperialism, would never allow me to clarify my black legend, because those press fellows are even blacker, and because more than one religious trust that is not insured, as was the case of Buddha in India, would collapse spiritually and economically if I were allowed to speak out. Yours truly, knowing that we would smother in an ecstatic paradise—nothing is more loaded with despair than permanent happiness—suggested to the Creator, in my role as Guardian of the Nebulas and Mathematics (it took sixteen thousand years for my word to reach his ear, and his answer took sixteen thousand years coming back), that we should capture the cosmic substances that were spinning free, capriciously, without king or master, outside his small creation, his small space station with its own atmosphere and light from outside. He did not accept my proposal. Those substances would disturb his esctatic world. I insisted. My calculations again reached his seashell ear, which opens on the bottoms of the seas, sixteen thousand years later, the auditory distance that separated us, and the figures almost arrived too feeble for his electronic brain. And I did not know how to interpret his reply. It said: 'Night Letter. To: Mathematical Archangel. Clarify term distance' (say!, I said to myself, for the first time now I can use the speed of light, not the speed of sound that we had been using until then), 'what system calculation used. Insist my lack interest all existent beyond my planetary station.' I replied at once: 'URGENT. To Divine Ruminant . . .' (But, urgent as my message was, I knew that when it entered the motionless atmosphere of Paradise, where everything that had life was wound up the way toys are, and they all walked in fear that they would run down, since they did not have the key to wind themselves up with at hand,

267

running down is losing one's memory, and although memory was not necessary in Eden, as far as movement was concerned, it was, because somebody who lost the key with which he could re-member himself, no longer *remembered*, and he ran the risk of remaining motionless forever) 'URGENT. To Divine Ruminant. While preparing resin discovered plant . . .' (Soul, no more, my archangelic prescience made me put the NO in the middle of that phrase. Soul NO more, but I gave more). 'While we were preparing resin, I discovered a small plant that told me it was the only intelligent vegetable, with the secret of the movement of the planets.' That was as far as I wrote, because the Divine Ruminant, chewing on a cloud of copal that was whiter than his beard, deigned to come in person, ordering me to show him where that plant was. 'A vegetable that can think, a bush that can think—' his sandals of sonorous foam sounded on the floor of stars—'should be torn up by the roots.' And divine hands went to work, he tore it up before turning invisible. The only activity, the only diversion in that calm paradise was making one's self visible and invisible, crossing and recrossing the transparent separation between the invisible and the visible. I suffered, as an archangel suffers, for the plant that had been uprooted, whose leaves had turned yellow, toasted in the sun, always perpendicular there—we formed night by running dark cloud clusters over rails of rain—and that greenish yellow of the leaves of the plant was becoming golden yellow, and later on a fiery brown. I pulverized it in the cup of my hand and, attracted by its biting perfume, I brought the powder up to my nose and once, twice, three times, I sneezed loudly. But when the sneezing had passed, the scandal of the first sneezes that had been heard in Eden, that was not all. Such a feeling of pleasantness, of euphoric well-being! Other colleagues tried those powders, absorbing them directly from the hollow of my hand, and even though a small bit of mucus slid down from their noses to their lips, they had the ineffable sensation of feeling themselves more archangelic. And the Lord himself tried it, without disliking it, a mysterious satisfaction that made him order the plant burned because tearing it up by the roots was not enough. The smoke from the leaves which were burning with a great show and which we were inhaling as we breathed inundated us with an unknown delight, that of a deeper paradisiacal sensation, and even man, a creature of dark dreams, began to dream like us, with his eyes open, in a white dream of smoke, smoke like curled wood shavings that let me capture matter that was running free. I would absorb the smoke through my nostrils as it burned in a brazier, and I would release it through my mouth in the shape of rings that, as they kept on growing, would not lose their make-up that was both fluid and rigid. And that was my sin. Capturing planets or sunflowers that were producing all around our ecstatic paradise the blinking of the motion of the universe, with no lack of those whose gaseous state had not come to its term, like that ball of fire around which the little smoke ring can still be seen spinning. And perhaps something even more transcendental. With those little rings of dreaming smoke that were coming out of my mouth, I managed to capture the time that was roaming about loose, ransom it from eternity, where it was no longer time, but eternity itself, and bring it back to the cage of clocks."

He refreshed his memory a moment before going on: "The Lord called me before his throne. His feet were shining white, like newly drawn milk, and, fixing his great golden eyes on my lidless ones, he ordered me to cast into the abyss the few seeds of that smoke plant that I had left. In my archangel's mind there was floating, the navigation of a dream, the vision of a burning place of emeralds that was beginning to rise up out of the oceanic shadows, and temptation led to disobedience, I changed my flight away from the fiery abyss, and I threw the seeds into the vegetable world of that continent that was rising up. And I fell head first after the seeds, along with my angelic legions, surrounded by thunderbolts, lightning, thunder claps, a rain of sparks from molten metals that burned us until our color was changed into the amber skin we now wear, and waves of atomic dust, as they say nowadays. We called it dragon dust then. How long did it take us to reach the earth? It's quite easy to calculate. The length of time it takes the light from the most distant star, and we came from much farther away, and not at the speed of light, but at that of our weight, since we had lost our luminous condition as arch-angels, and as soon as I reached it, with the last sparks of my fingers, as my body lost its flame and the glow of my legions was being extinguished, I managed to give the seeds of the smoke plant the speed of light as I threw them into the burning place of emeralds and jade, which, as I fell head first, badly wounded, I dreamed of finding, and I would not have found them because of the rains of colors that followed, if the little hummingbirds, who can perforate starfish before they harden, had not saved them and hidden them in their enchanted palaces, and it was useless, therefore, in order to do away with the mysterious plant, for the earth to remain submerged in black ice for centuries, the congealing of darkness, because alongside those same small seeds, hummingbirds were hidden, and they kept them at rainbow temperature under a laughing light with the little motors of their moving wings.

"And I found them in the power of some terrible Giants, Cabracán, Huracán, Zipacnac, who were under the sway of a shadowy Cashtoc, seconded by a court of wizards, sorcerers, and malignant spirits, soothsayers and spell-casters, men made out of corn, not like our man, that unfortunate clay doll who had been expelled from Eden for having complained to the Lord for having given him a companion made out of flesh and blood and not out of the smoke of that fabulous plant. A smoke companion, whom he could rule with his breath, the way zephyrs do sails; he would keep her in spindles of smoke thread, spindles that are now called cigarettes; and he would absorb her through his mouth and nostrils, and fill himself, through her, with a peace that would change his poisonous thoughts into the arterial joy of reality made into a dream.

"I went up to the Giants, Demons, and priests of that green burning place, to demand that they return what I considered to be my plant, or my sole, for some reason my deformed feet had been made out of two of their enormous leaves, and, knowing with whom I was dealing, I used that ambiguous word and asked them to give me back my sole, because without those soles I could not walk on earth, where flying was not in style.

"The Devil cannot be deceived. Let those who hear him

be deceived. But there were no greater punsters than those Giants and Demons.

" 'Who plants his soles?' The skull of a mountain shook, Cabracán, pretending to be angry, but deep down inside he was enjoying the play on concepts.

" 'That cloud over there is the one who plants his soles in a storm.' He pointed at a carbon-black cloud on the horizon.

"Everybody was laughing before long. Huracán, limping, came over to shake my hand. Cabracán moved a crag toward my right hand, a crag with very long fingers. And they invited me to talk about the smoke plant that they called 'tobacco.'

"I swore by the red flower with five fingers, the flower of that plant that they called 'tobacco,' that it was mine, that I had stolen it from Paradise, and had cast it into that burning place of emeralds and little jades at the speed of light so that its seeds would not be lost in starry space, and I explained to them my delay in arriving centuries later, because I had made my descent with my legions at the speed of our weight.

" 'He's come to take it away from us!' they said among themselves with voices of alarm.

" 'No, my dear demons, I take it away and I leave it, I leave it and I take it away! Its use must be spread among the poor clay men, my men, sons of that Edenic pair expelled from the Garden of Delights, and who feel like orphans without the companionship of the white smoke of that solanaceous plant which—I like the name—I also call *tobacco*, because, poor things, all they will have left in the end is the black smoke of death.'

" 'Impossible!' the voice of a priest with a mineral appearance crossed with mine. 'One cannot divulge what is sacred, and that plant is sacred! Let us throw out this imposter who has come from another planet to steal tobacco from us!'

"Anxious to recover the smoke plant, my legions formed around me, awaiting their orders, imbued with astral silence, some of those legions would take on the shape of nebulas and perforate hills and mountains until they would destroy Cabracán in his subterranean caves, others had pockets of immense spatial emptiness, great pouches in which they would imprison Huracán until they could destroy him. We really came from very advanced worlds.

"I calmed my legionnaires down. The giants were not the ones we had to worry about, it was the smaller devils, headed by Cashtoc, the Great, the Immense. It would be better to leave for now and return later.

"I came back alone. The giants looked at me with their eyes of beautiful children. The smaller demons were not there. They had gone off to stand guard over the places where they had their tobacco plantations.

"I turned the conversation toward the ways one could enjoy the smoke plant. As I had done in the beginning, they lit bonfires, and when the fires became reduced to coals, they would throw the tobacco leaves into the fire, absorbing the smoke through their mouths and noses until they became intoxicated.

"I made them aware that with such a primitive system they were losing a lot, and I told them how I had perfected a way of enjoying tobacco that was so direct and intimate that it could not be improved on.

"Curious, like all giants, they brought me some rather long leaves that were neither too toasted nor too damp. I removed the veins and cut the leaves into strips, which I rolled patiently until I had a large cylinder, just like one of their giant fingers. I lit it at one end and I raised the other extreme to my mouth.

"They began to laugh with their great mirror teeth, teeth in which I saw my image reproduced for the first time, no longer that of an archangel, but of a man with a face of asphalt, traces of hair standing on end in the place of a beard, a mock beard that turned upward instead of being combed downward. And how many times was I there in that multiplication of my figure on the teeth of the giants, who kept on toothing the jingle of a laugh that had no end? They would drop teeth from laughing so much, and others would grow out, and others, and others, all for the same torrential laugh, clean water mirrors where my image was being multiplied, wrapped in smoke like charcoal that was being extinguished.

"But trying was better than laughing. Each giant took his

tobacco wrapping (they called it *puquiete*), lit it, and brought it up to his mouth. And that was when I won, because after a rapid 'Ah! Ah! Ah!' of pleased satisfaction (they had stuck the *puquietes* in backward, with the fire inside of their mouths), their eyes began to cry, the hummocks of blind earth of Cabracán and the great eyes like torches in the wind of Huracán. I paralyzed their jaws so that they could not spit, and I held back their blinking and their weeping. I wanted them to see me laughing at them, at their immense suffering as giants, and as one Cabracán, kicked about, seeking the help of the earth, and the other, Huracán, flapped his wings, seeking the help of the infinite, I could feel them sinking. Only when it was sunk, buried, would the fire burning their mouths go out, down until the only thing showing would be their top hats in the form of pyramids and craters through which the smoke of the fiery material they were smoking and the black tobacco drool of lava that they were chewing was escaping.

"Cashtoc, Tazol, and other demons of soft stone, frozen, disagreeable, with their careful hair styles, characteristics, and clothing, sat down around me with an indifferent air.

"With so many devils there, I meditated, it was going to be a very difficult business.

" 'Tobacco brings us together again!' I said as I nodded my head, my tall golden horns shining, and opened three of my red wings over my lean body, because a green mist had begun to fall, just as if instead of clouds pine trees in the air were losing their needles.

" 'We know what's being deviled here,' they answered me, 'propagating the use of the smoke plant among men, to which, Most Illustrious, Ambidextrous, and Handlehanded Candanga, we, the demons of the magic world, are opposed, because of the damage it will cause the human species. Tobacco must return to its sacred use.'

" 'I don't understand . . .'

" 'Why did you appropriate the plant? Did you guess what was hidden in it? What was meant to be the most divine of plants was changed into a poison!'

" 'Poison? Quite the contrary. Man would be the most unfortunate being on earth without that plant, with its broom of white smoke that sweeps away his worries, that accompanies the person who feels alone, alleviates the one who is worn out by his work, and gives patience to the one who waits. And besides, what does it hide, what secret thing is hidden inside of it?'

" 'But you know all about that business of a rib, your God could not find any other place to draw a woman from, and you fell down to earth with a bone between your teeth like a dog.'

"I held myself back, trying to ignore what they were saying:

" 'If you had not intervened, getting one-up with your discovery of the smoke plant, where you knew woman was contained—why give man what was just a mouthful for archangels? you said to yourself—God would not have turned to the bone-shaving that a rib is.'

"Overcome by rage, I raised my hand which lit up with the red whiteness of the target against Cashtoc's huge jade head, but I withheld my blow, all ready to slap him, reflecting that I had not come to fight with those infernal creatures from a green inferno, but to convince them to give me back my smoke plant.

" 'Why do you toy with me, knowing that I am a bull?' I shouted.

"Cashtoc covered his skin with broad yellow spots that alternated with black spots, and above the snorts of his mouth, which had grown terribly toothy, were the long whiskers of a gigantic cat.

" 'I see what you are. A jaguar. What good will come of our fighting?'

" 'Just for the sake of fighting . . .'

" 'But only under the prior condition that since one of us will be annihilated in the struggle, it could be me or it could be you, you order them to return to my legionnaires the plant that I stole from Paradise so that they can propagate it among white people.'

" 'It would lose its magic value as a plant of enchantment.'

" 'Oh, Cashtoc, beloved old jaguar, lay down your weapons at the foot of words, which are much more claw, more fang, more fearful than my horns and your spots of a golden beast, and let's talk. Tobacco is a magic plant for your priests, who, under the intoxication produced by the smoke, can attain the supernatural, but there is another magic: that of the person who expels the smoke and converts it into love, into friendship, into the bond of union between beings, and my proposal is for the smoke of the smoker who expels it after having enjoyed it, to be the bond of true peace among men.' "

And after a brief pause:

"But, sir—I remember now that I am in the office of the president of one of the strongest insurance companies—tell me: Could your company insure peace? How many millions would it cost to insure it? When the policy was paid, you would make it your business to see that there would be no wars, because, in the case of a threat of war, the insurance company would have to pay a fabulous sum, greater than all the possible profits that would be made by war industries, and peace would be saved forever. That was how it was done on the planet we inhabited before . . ."

The President of the Company blinked and, with the rapid blink, one of his lashes drew toward his hooked nose the black ribbon which was hanging down from his pince-nez as a sign of extreme elegance. He raised the ribbon with the back of his hand up toward the flap of his ear, he scratched his chin, just as if it were tickling him as his beard was emerging, and he repeated: "Insure peace? It was never proposed to us before. We hadn't even given it a thought. It would be a question of looking into it. Considered as a transaction for an insurance company, it's quite possible. But not only us, because even though we're one of the strongest companies in the world, we would need the co-operation of other companies in order to insure peace. The peoples of the world would stand as a security on the market to underwrite the payment of the policy. But—" the President of the Company took off his pince-nez and, leaning back, added—"you haven't told me how you got the terrible earth devils to give you back the smoke plant, tobacco, that is."

"Not until centuries after, many centuries, when I arrived with Spanish navigators, soldiers, and monks during the Discovery and the Conquest, did they give me back tobacco, knowing that it would be their vengeance against the white man, who would cling to it the way they would to the teat of a woman of smoke; the white man, who was no longer that light breeze flower who had left Paradise, but a long-legged creature bursting with blood and thirsting after toxic things, without worrying, no matter how much he was warned by philosophers and wise men, about the fact that the poison would kill him, as long as it alleviated the weight of life, false illusions which induced him to defend it as part of his happiness when he felt strong and healthy, and when he got sick and lost his drool, as the only thing to take along into death. Madness! Tobacco was madness, the complement of the newly discovered species, and more than one bewitched king, tobacco chewers, lost themselves in my cauldrons, the prey of vertigo and nausea, royal garments and all, the yellow color of a sand spit, edged with foamy lace. One king ended up with bluish flesh and a smoke skeleton."

"English?"

"No! That unfortunate English king took on a childish hatred of the sacred plant and made it fashionable to condemn it, all because after smoking it he vomited for several days like a pregnant woman. Sir Francis Drake would have done better to have opened his king's chest, so that smoke and vomit did not come out together, and not that of the pirate whose trachea he opened with one thrust, curious to know how the smoke came up the throat. But it is not a question of Tobacco but of Tierrapaulita, where the demons of the green burning place hid the smoke plants. They kept the city in bondage, and now that they have given it back to me, I find it depopulated and destroyed. The Earthquake Giant and the Wind Giant abandoned themselves to a game of fun for them and of death for humans. The fun game that the Earthquake Giant played with the Earth began with a soft hammock movement, which the excited Giant then followed with rapid shakings and jerkings, up and down, down and up, a convulsive trembling, a supreme pleasure and an orgasm for him, and for the Tierrapaulitans, the ruins left by an earthquake, which was the moment when the Wind Giant jumped forth to dominate light and darkness at the same time, with a most turbulent attack as he mixed night and day, roofs up in the clouds, stones along with furniture, uprooted trees along with the ceibas that are not supposed to let themselves be uprooted, with nests and hives falling about, honey and pigeons covered with ants, blind lizards, hairy caterpillars, hairless snakes, and frothy vegetable creatures . . .

"And how depopulated I found Tierrapaulita!" Candanga raised his voice, without paying attention to the loud laughter of the earth devils.

Hailstorms . . . loud laughter . . . Cashtoc was laughing like a duck . . . "Oac! oac! ha! ha! . . . oac! oac! ha! ha!" . . . and Tazol, in a higher key, also with the laugh of an aquatic bird . . . "Achee heehee cheekcheek! achee heehee cheekcheek!" and the laughter of Siguapate and Cadejo . . . "Cuachiton-ho hoho! cuachiton-ho hoho!" and the little laughs of the Siguanas . . . "Conix-hee! conix-hee! . . ."

"So depopulated . . . so depopulated," the Demon of Heaven insisted as he shouted to make himself heard over the infidel devils, "that without losing any time I started a repopulation campaign, the essential base of everything I planned to undertake afterward. In this campaign, which I only carry on at night, couples are reminded that they should procreate, with the laconic demand of: 'Breeding tiiime today and right away! Breeding tiiime!' because if it were not that way, my insurance friend, there would not be too many here for you to insure, nor would I have anyone to lead off to my opulent ovens as condemned people disguised as laborers. Flesh, bones, and a soul are all necessary to keep the machinery of the world moving in war the same as in peace. I wanted to insure both things, the duration of my fire and peace, and it seems to me that insuring peace is more worthwhile. I aim to change this Tierrapaulita into a people factory, which is the finest industry a nation can have, but now let me get back there with this friend who is here with me, Gabriel Santano, a devotee of Saint Badthief, who may have come to you to insure the nothingness that is smaller than the antimatter represented by one tenth of a thousandth of a millionth of a second!"

No Dawn in Tierrapaulita

Alas, it was not dawning, it would never dawn! Candanga
had not allowed, would never allow dawn to pass until he
was satisfied with his pasting together of men and women!
New beings are stuck together with human paste! No, no, it
will never dawn before the song of the bird of ill omen
comes—the sexton was saying all of this to himself, tormented by nightmares, as he moved himself, cot and all, on
top of the bed of Father Chimalpín, who woke up at once,
not daring to open his eyes, certain that the tight canvas
wing was one of the wings of the Evil Angel. How could he
look at him and not have his soul blinded forever? It was
better to feel him as he squashed him, pasting him like a
postage stamp to his creaking army cot. He had fallen
asleep. The devil never surprises people who are awake. But
how could he not help falling asleep, since he had not closed
his eyes once since he had arrived in Tierrapaulita, tormented by that evil-making shout that in the darkness demanded the propagation of the species. Demoniacal? No, it
could not be entirely demoniacal, and that was where the
poor Father was confused. Demoniacal was the other part,
the use and abuse of all the means invented to keep carnal
pleasure without complying with the divine mandate to
increase and multiply. A danger? The divine precept a
danger? Then what was satanic about that fallacious shout:
"Breeding tiiime! Breeding tiiiime!"? He had better rectify
his concepts. There was no sin in advising the growth of
families, but in the scandal of that voice in the shadows that
aroused instincts of bestial recreation, not the simple drive
of virility on the part of the male and Christian esteem on
the part of the wife, who gave no more participation than
that of a passive sleeper in whom the miracle of the repro-

278

duction of life would take place. That business of "Breeding tiiime!" aroused in the female instincts that made her shake the male awake, and in the male that monstrous voluptuousness that was the child of imagination, which is the child of the Devil, the breeding place of poisonous thoughts, wormlike caresses, perturbed contacts, the adhesion of body to body, with a clutching at the bestial act. A person is not a Christian just because he is one; a person is a Christian because it implies loving more, loving more is giving one's self more, is reaching, through that giving, everything that surrounds us, a nursery of happiness where one fulfills everything, without the diabolic shout of the aroused exigency, the carnal flame that breeds nothing but ashes. Children of ashes are those who are not born out of love, but out of machinery in motion, and since the latter are every day more common than the former, the world is being covered with ashes, and therefore we are opposed not to the multiplication of the human species in Tierrapaulita but to the industrialization of the species with the command of that satanic shout.

Alas, it will never dawn! the sexton repeated to himself, his ears like cold feet, his feet like distant ears, separated from his everyday self by torrents of the water of crushed glass from piles of sandpaper that made a chill run up his spine, made him clench his teeth that were on edge, and not listen to Father Chimalpín, who, without making the slightest movement, was complaining under the canvas of the cot that he thought was Satan's wing, the wing of the Evil Angel up against his cassock, his cassock up against his bodily person, his bodily person up against his soul, even though the last might well be the most impersonal for him, loose like a Venetian blind made out of small glass tubes waving in time to his own breath. Oh, the soul, the soul, and woe unto those who seek support in it, because it is just like trying to lean up against the rain!

Father Chimalpín, under the diabolic wing, really the scratchy canvas of the cot, felt, for a few moments, his eleventhousand spider arms, his flat face, chinless and covered with caterpillar hair, his clerical bonnet, just like a black star on his horns.

It was not dawning. First the bird of bad omen would

279

come, the rice bird, to gargle his remote fire-sausage voice.

Pray, pray to "Saintend," a saint who ended nightmares and tended a person against wrong steps, but this time, what could "Saintend" do, since hell has no beginning or end, and what good was "Saintend," because a person who fell under Lucifer's wing had no hope for his punishment to end, because it was endless. Give himself over to the Devil, to "Saintendless"? Emerge alive from under the canvas wing that was materially squashing him, as he had emerged alive, he remembered far away from there, from the Requiem Mass he had sung when changed into a horse spider with the eleventhousand arms and the eleventhousand hands of the devil himself, tangling and untangling themselves as he took the chalice, the holy form, the missal, with his real hands, with his real fingers, fighting against the thousands of extra hands and fingers, and as he swallowed what was there as part of a moan that was gloved in sleeping skin.

It was not dawning, the sexton was thinking, unhinged on his cot, without the courage to move, change his position, fearful that when he did Candanga would carry him off beyond the surface on which he was lying, outside of time, the way minutes were counted in the *tero . . . tero . . . tero . . .* of the *tero* birds, among the plaintive songs of the birds of the morning mystery that no one had ever seen, that no one knew, the flapping of the fussy dawn bird, who was swinging on the eyelashes of silence, as the firmament covers its blackness with the ornaments of dawn.

Horrors! He had served as acolyte in the Mass sung by Father Chimalpín, who was being toasted from the front by the enveloping and maddening flames, where those without eyelids like him survive, because he could no longer feel them from having opened his eyes so much in order to believe what he was seeing, and hearing, awake in his sleep or asleep in his reality: turning to Father Chimalpín, turning to the faithful, and saying: "Breeding tiiime!" and the answer: "We're already at it." No, let it not dawn! All the roosters luckily seemed to have died during that Good Friday night from the breeding plague. Let it not dawn! Let it not dawn! If a moment ago, as he changed his position

280

to find out what the Father was complaining about—nothing important, who doesn't complain under the wing of Satan, who doesn't cry like a mouse in a trap!—he had wanted reality to surge up and sound in all its shapes and colors, now, painful and quiet, he thought that even if he were completely paralyzed, that even if they buried him in the posture of a tadpole, it would be better, it would be preferable to the day's returning, because with what shadow of eyelids that were alive within and dead without would he be able to cover, erase the frightful reality that awaited him.

Better a nightmare. Pestilent and rocky, a nightmare would partially explain the superficial clarity that was trailing in through the cracks in the doors, contradicting his black water eyes, as he breathed with great heaves, his mind exposed to laconic rays of thought, filthy, hiccuping with his empty stomach. And his eyelids? There is something worse than hell, losing one's eyelids! What could he cover them with to keep on dreaming or pretending to dream the punishing nightmare of what the light was revealing to him? The Father, under the weight of the fallen cot, having wet his bed perhaps, to whom would it not happen, with Satan's wing on top of him? Let it not dawn until he got a grip on his self, he, the sexton, fighting against passing from nightmare to madness, as he felt his cot stuck to the back of a great hairy spider that had disputed the dominion of the church with a hedgehog of fire!

The light was being sponged up, sad, without the birds of dawn, without the gibberish of the *sanate* birds, or, rather, the satans of birds. With almost the same letters, the name of the bird says so. For all the mystery there is shut up in words, one still could not speak, except with fear.

Under the canvas of the cot, a sail detached from the mainmast in the storm of the dream, there was moving about—glugluglu—a great black wool spider defending himself against the hedgehog, immobilized, trying to tire him out, or electrified, just as if he were made of wire, attacking with rapid and mortal discharges in the midst of the shapes of ghostly saints on the altars covered with purple

281

rags, and the bruises made on the eyes of the witnesses with pulmonary breathing—the druggist Santano and he—by every thunderbolt of the dizzying fight.

Father Chimalpín, with those eternal infants that hands are, fingers at play, the fingers will always be ten children, was touching himself with a dissimulated not-wishing-to-do-it, up and down his arms, and how happy he was to know, to feel, that he only had two. Soon, however, he became uneasy. Where had he dropped the eleventhousand arms that he had asked for from the Most High Lord of Heaven in order to fight Candanga, the devil with eleventhousand horns, who had come at him, changed into a hedgehog with eleventhousand quills, hard as bristles, sharp as thorns? But what could he do, what could his arms do, which would serve him now to push away the wing of Satan that was crushing him, without killing him, the policy of the devil, poisoning and sustaining with the poison, crushing the human being, just like a cockroach, without putting him out of his misery, so that he would commit blasphemy.

The hedgehog was Candanga, the sexton was thinking, desperate at not being able to get rid of those macabre ideas as he tried to weigh his situation. Dropped into Tierrapaulita, not to sop up a few ounces of gold but to hide himself from those who knew he was a failure, he could feel his flesh beginning to dry up into trash, the eve of his turning to ashes . . . trash . . . ash . . . a simple play on words, almost the same letters . . . almost the same letters . . . For all of the mystery there is shut up in words, one should not use them except in fear. Yes, yes, yes, the hedgehog was Candanga, the cockfight man. But what did it matter to him whether he was or he wasn't, since what he wanted was not to return to the nightmare of remembering it . . . save himself, awake now, so that memory would install itself in the anchoring place of his mind and digest what had been lived or dreamed, a digestion that means going on living, based on unforgettable juices, the past torment . . .

The pock-marked Indian had come into the church to return the lilac glove of His Grace, a glove which Father Chimalpín had thrown from the front of the church as a challenge to Candanga. And as soon as he had mentioned the devil of eleventhousand horns, seeing arms and more arms coming out of the priest on all sides, until he changed into a spider with thousands of legs who fled toward the baptistry looking for holy water to bathe himself in so that those diabolic arms would disappear. And, while the priest was taking a bath in holy water, water on hot coals, he, Jerónimo de la Degollación, felt himself growing feminine, a smiling sodomite who tried, in the role of a Chamber-Potter, to make that Indian, who was none other than Candanga, empty the contents of his diabolical wizard's bladder into his pot, and he haired over in such a way that from every one of his smallpox scars there grew a quill, and it was a question of Saint Hedgehog, first against him, stringing his quills into the first cape of a dream, a dream from which he awakened asleep, defending himself like an automaton, no longer a woman, the woman he had been carrying inside of him had fled, but Jerónimo de la Degollación, alongside Santano, Saint Anus, the druggist, who had himself a crossbar, following the combat between a black cassocked spider and that animal with fire quills . . .

He remembered now that he was awake. It was not so much of a nightmare after all. In between the legs of the cot, crushed by the canvas, Father Chimalpín, with his eyes closed, thought that it was a wing of the Angel, and the sexton, who saw it with his eyes open, more and more open, did not believe that it was the parish priest. And he did not hold himself back. He stood up. And, dream or reality? he took a hurried close look at what from a distance had seemed to him, and . . . and . . . and—he drew back with a shiver—it was the pock-marked Indian, but it was also Father Chimalpín.

The latter, sensing that someone was walking close by, had no doubt but that the devils were coming to carry him off, trapped as he felt himself under the wing of the devil, and he closed his eyes tighter, shaken by a tremor of his body which made his teeth chatter . . . yes, yes, . . . let him be carried off, let him be carried off to hell, cassock and all, but let him not see it.

"Father Chimalpín . . . it's me—Jerónimo! Is that you?"

"Yes, it's I!"

283

But how could it be Father Chimalpín, all pock-marked? It could not be him, even if he said so.

"Father! Is it you?"

"Yes, my son, it's I! Where are we?"

"It can't be you, Father!"

"Tell me where we are, and anything will be possible!"

"Touch yourself!"

"No!"

"Touch your face!"

"No! I already know that we're in hell!"

"What you don't know, Father, is that you've had small-pox!"

"Smallpox?"

"Yes, your face is covered with dry scars!"

After a pause, the priest took out his right hand, the sexton took away the cot, and, without opening his eyes—he did not dare, the devil might be imitating the sexton's voice—he passed his fingers across his cheeks, his forehead, his chin, his nose . . . then the other hand—oh, if he only had the eleventhousand hands that could squeeze thousands of fingers on to what was his inexplicably pock-marked face!

"Why, yes, it seems that I've had the holy smallpox," he confided to the sexton, after rubbing his face over and over again, doubting his own touch. Hoping that he was not entirely awake, and that those scars were part of his nightmare.

"Why did you remove Saint Caralampio from the church?"

"What do you mean, why? Because he wasn't a saint."

"It's horrible, Father! It's horrible to look at you and remember . . ."

"Remember what? Saint Caralampio?"

"The pock-marked Indian who picked up the glove you threw from the steps of the church . . ."

"Oh, yes, that farmer!"

"He'd been pecked with smallpox just as if a hungry hen had been at him, just like you."

"It can't be . . ."

"It looks as if he even got in under your skin."

"That fellow?"

284

"He pecked you with his quills," and, after a pause, the sexton added in a low voice, "it was hedgehog smallpox."

The priest jumped. His eyes open, hair with eyes on it, an eye on the end of every hair, fingers with eyes, an eye on every fingernail, a nose with an eye that distilled mucus, on the sides of his mouth, on the wrinkles, two eyes, on his ear lobes, like earrings, two eyes. He jumped over to the piece of mirror that he used to look at himself while he shaved with a straight razor, and—no doubt about it—he was actually covered with round scars, made with a punch.

He could feel the mirror liquifying on his cheeks and running down like cold weeping as he looked at himself under that shell of a mask.

"Oh, Jerónimo!" he muttered, swallowing his image with the little saliva left in his dry mouth, it was really his face, that mask of a punctured mummy, "we must call the doctor, because I have been scarred outside by the black poison, and inside I have it in my cold purgatory . . ."

The sexton, a shadow projected by the facets of the sun that were passing through the eyes of the locks, was picking fleas, a trapped flea thundered between his thumb and index finger, staining his fingernails with blood; he pretended that he did not hear, in spite of the poor Father's lamentations.

"Oh, slave prison, jail of the eleventhousand scars, of the eleventhousand holes where slaves like me lie imprisoned, slaves bathed in the pus of Caliban! We have to call the doctor, Jerónimo! My skin was impenetrable, but now how will I be able to keep the secrets of confession if my interior can be seen like water through the holes of a strainer? Go get the doctor, tell him that the parish priest of Tierrapaulita was not bitten by smallpox but by the moths of protohistory! Do you hear me? Don't you see that with your flea-scratching, the satisfaction of a dog, you're increasing my worry, because it occurs to me that you were the accomplice of those who did such harm to me, and I'm afraid that from every one of my scars there will emerge the tooth of a comb, and what will this poor cleric be then, the image of a hog adorned with spiny armor."

"The doctor will probably refuse to come."

"Do you think he's afraid of catching it? Go and tell

him that it's dry smallpox, burned out, the kind that only left ashes on my skin, ashes with little holes like the marks of raindrops."

"It's not out of fear that he won't come. He's a layman. Laymen are less afraid of contagion than we believers. It's my belief, Father, that the fear of God they inculcate in us as kids makes us afraid of everything."

"Then he has no reason not to come, if he's not afraid of a person who woke up with smallpox scars, dressed with little holes of silence."

"He won't come because he's afraid or because he's not afraid, no indeed, but first, because his eyebrows are growing, second, because his eyebrows are growing, and third, because his eyebrows are growing!"

"And fourth . . . be quiet, in the name of God, you jumbler, you gossip, be quiet, what's wrong with him that makes his eyebrows grow?"

"It's obvious that you've never seen him, Father. Poor doctor! It's pitiful to see him with two curtains of straight hair, almost blond, dirty, hanging down from his eyes to his knees, just like the branches of a weeping willow!"

"And why doesn't he cut them? Aren't there such things as shears?"

"Because it makes them grow faster, which is like pruning branches of rain. And besides, this man who could come walking on the hair of his eyebrows will refuse to visit us and prescribe for you because he's an atheist, anti-*Deus*, anti-Us, and the last time, when I got a whitlow on my little finger and went to ask him to cure it, he told me that he did not cure church people, because if We, if we all died, so much the better!"

"And what possessed you to talk like a bishop? We here, we there . . . If the doctor won't come, he'll be breaking his Hippocratic oath . . . we'll tell him . . ."

"That's what a gentleman he was talking to threw out to him when I went to him about my whitlow, and he answered that he had, in fact, sworn to cure any self-moving human being, except priests, monks, nuns, sextons, and poor people. I swore, he said, with that mental reservation, not before Hippocrates, but before all the hypocrites who were my teachers!"

"You refuse to go call him? Then I'll go myself."

"No, Father, don't expose yourself. It's better to call the healer!"

"The healer? I'm no Indian, and who knows, Jerónimo de la Degollación de Infantes, if that healer of yours isn't the very one who made the doctor's eyebrows grow out in a rain of burning hair, since he uses the excuse that he's a freethinker for not visiting us, when the truth is that he's trying to avoid it so that we won't see his eyebrows change into the urine of a young colt . . ."

"Last night . . ."

"There wasn't any such last night! Last night was hell, I was in hell, that's all!"

"Hell, here in the church?" the sexton ventured.

"What's strange about it, sinner that I am, if, just as the sea comes out of its depths, there burst forth out of the ground the eye of the devil, without horizons, bent, infinite . . ."

"And the hedgehog?"

"What hedgehog? I'm the hog . . . I sinned, Lord, I sinned . . . *mea culpa!*"

"And these scratches?" The sexton showed the priest his hands, combed with scars as if he had fallen into a thorn bush.

"We won't tell anybody anything about it!" Father Chimalpín whispered. "I'm all scratched up too. About the hedgehog and the scratches, nothing; it would cause a scandal in Tierrapaulita, and Candanga would be the winner!"

"And how can you hide your tattered cassock?"

"I'll put my new one on."

"And the scars, Father? The smallpox scars . . ."

The parish priest could not articulate a word, contenting himself with running his fingers over the countless little dry holes from his cheeks to his forehead, from his forehead to his nose, from his nose to his chin.

"Go on, go call the healer," he finally said, "and don't ring for Mass!"

"Mass? Oh, Father, you already sang it last night! A halleluiah Mass and a wedding Mass, in which a hedgehog and a Mulata were married! Oh! oh! oh!" The sexton began

287

to dance, lifting his feet and letting them fall like lead, like boards, and shaking his hands on the shreds of his pants. "Oh! oh! oh!, smallpox for you, Father, and delight for her, because you can't tell me that a woman who chooses a hedgehog for her husband isn't full of lust. It was attended by the shadows of lunatics who came out of a burning asylum, their hair giving off smoke, and your reverence didn't say *'Dominus vobiscum!'* but 'Breeding tiiime!' "

"Quiet, in the name of God, quiet, because while you talk, the smallpox comes to life on me, burns me, insufflates me with its purulence, and I'm going to go mad or twist about like someone who's been insulted!"

"The mass of a huge spider and wizards! Joining in matrimony a Mulata and a hedgehog, a certain Mulata! But that's as far as it went. A great big woman appeared in the main door of the church—it had to be opened wide to let her through—a big woman, who carried under the canopy of her skirts, embroidered with glass dew, a dwarf who, with one bite, snatched off the certain Mulata's sex, among the little laughs of the demons of the air and the pasty laugh of muddy water, the she-devil of the plains."

"Quiet, please," the priest managed to beg, his face marked with smallpox, his cassock in shreds, like a kite in mourning, "slaughter of my sins, go get the healer!"

Jerónimo took one of the blankets, wrapped himself up in it, and, slippers, why do I love you, off he went in search of the healer, his hat turned down over his eyes, his unsupported chin a punctuation mark that was biting him as if ants were walking around his neck.

"Lord, oh good Lord," he was saying, "what will we do if Father can't get rid of his scars!"

The Magic Broom

The half of the certain Mulata, made whole by the skeleton woman, went on with the sweeping of the mansion of the Great Sorcerers, and she raised so much dust with the broom made from the hair of a dead man, gray dust, yellow, sticky, that she looked like a she-devil navigating through a cloud of fire as she struggled to keep her loose hair behind her own ear and the alien ear, with her shirt tails hanging outside the sash that was barely holding up Tipumalona's wide skirt, and her sandals were falling off her own foot and the alien foot. Desperation. She had swept the courtyards of the house, where only the stones were left showing, just like teeth.

"*Tachito-oo-ee-ah! . . . Tachito-oo-ee-ah! . . .*" the song of the bird who accompanies travelers could be heard, and she had the impression that the "*oo-ee-ah! . . . oo-ee-ah! . . .*" was putting distance between her and the broom, the broom and the ground of the courtyard that she was sweeping, or she and the skinny woman who was making her whole.

"No, no, no . . . travelers' bird, *Tachito-oh-oh! Tachito-oh-oh!*, don't take me away, don't carry me off with your sad song of the roads incomplete and without my name as a woman, my occult name, because without it, without my sex, I'm nameless, I have no name! Let me stay here, travelers' bird, because I have to get it back, because it was stolen from me by a sex-stealing dwarf in the service of Giroma, Catalina Zabala, while I was being married to Yumí in a Requiem Mass celebrated by a priest who had eleven-thousand arms! No, don't take me away along lonely roads, lonely travelers' bird, I have my struggle with me, my battle with me, the fountain of my temples which feels like coltsfoot to me, my heart's breath, only burlap and rotting blood now, and all that urges my poor, dispossessed self on, the thing that gives the taste of being to existence. I will defend my presence here and I will not let myself be taken away from the courtyards of the house of the Great Sorcerers, Yumí and Giroma, travelers' bird, hen of blue lake-water metal! Sing your mournful refrain, travelers' bird, the music of a glass of lake water where the fingers of the wind draw out the sound *atotolín!* . . . *atotolín!* . . . *atotolín!* . . . , the sound of your name, from its sharp and slender edge!"

"It would be better for me, for us, to stop sweeping," the certain Mulata said to the woman who was making her whole. "We run the risk of passing through the tail of a comet-broom made from the hair of dead stars, pulverized by us, who form one single sweeping-woman! Oh, but if we don't sweep, the sorcerers will not come out of their nocturnal house to see who is sweeping their courtyards, perforated by a thousand little holes!"

"At night the Zabala woman," the Mulata advised the woman who was making her whole, "gives her paralytic husband back his movements and gives free rein to her instincts, but Yumí, enjoying what is mine without my being there, sinks the real part of amorous contact, as his virile iron becomes hot, into the little oven they stole from me, hot coals that light up more when that woman tries to put them out with her blasts of jealousy, as she realizes that he is enjoying me in her person, thinking about me, creating me in his thought, partly in his memory—there was reason for my being his wife—and partly in his dream, there was reason for my being the beloved image that entered through the fontanels of his soul before the shell of his skull was turned to bone with the paste of eternity."

The Mulata took a breath.

"But it was useless trying to put out the bewitching fire of the sex that had been stolen from me, unless the Zabala woman swallowed it on the advice of Huasanga. Only by the wife's swallowing the sex of the mistress can she end it. And that is the danger. Not being able to stop that witch of a woman, who had a son by the Devil through her navel, from eating it like a raw oyster and taking possession of my sexual attraction."

290

The half of the Mulata made whole by the bone woman was sweeping up the sound of her lamentations. Nothing could be heard near the house or inside the courtyards of the great sorcerers. She was sweeping up the light. She was also sweeping up the light. Very little of the large house could be seen any more. And she was sweeping up reality. Everything would lose its consistency around her broom, in front of her broom, underneath her broom, behind her broom. It seemed to follow it about, but in dreams. Sweeping up reality is daring, but sweeping up what remains of it in dreams is madness. Reality, light, sound all having been swept up, the broom began to sweep up dreams, shadows, silence, and around and inside the house of the great sorcerers a total emptiness was created, impossible to be conceived of by a human mind. Neither sound, nor silence, nor light, nor darkness, nor reality, nor dreams . . .

The skeletonized woman who, in order to make the Mulata whole, was sticking out her face, one arm, her hand, her leg, and one foot, spoke:

"If they give you back your sex (blood of cacao its announcement, virginal blood its announcement, the child of your blood its announcement!), if they give it back to you wrapped in soil, will you take it?"

"If they give it back to me wrapped in soil, I will take it," the Mulata answered; "I will wrap it in the soil that is the skin of the earth."

"If they give it back to you (it is fire, it is a serpent, it is a devourer of men!), if they give it back to you along the road of married couples, will you take it?"

"If they give it back to me along the road of married couples, I will take it. I will wrap it in the husband, who is the skin of the wife."

"If they give it back to you (populating the earth is its role, creating creators is its role!), if they give it back to you wrapped in water, will you take it?"

"If they give it back to me wrapped in water, I will take it. I will sate it with the water from the well of my joy!"

"If they give it back to you (lust is its use, perversity is its use, shamelessness is its unchaste use!), if they give it back to you wrapped in man, will you take it?"

"If they give it back to me wrapped in man, I will take

it. I will wrap it in his skin, in his pleasure, in his light!"

"If they give it back to you (whose is it? . . . not God's . . . not the Devil's . . . not yours), if they give it back to you wrapped in dreams, will you take it?"

"If they give it back to me wrapped in dreams, I will take it. I will wrap it in the blue paint of my lashes."

"If they give it back to you transformed into one of the rings used in a ball game, will you take it?"

"If they give it back to me transformed into one of the rings used in a ball game, I will receive it. One of the players will pierce it with his sure shot."

"If they give it back to you soaked in hummingbird blood, will you receive it?"

"I will receive it trembling like a sterile woman who cries when she feels herself wounded by hummingbird blood!"

"If they give it back to you wrapped in words, will you receive it?"

"Yes, because its perfections are so many that all it lacks is speech, and it has been said that man and woman understand each other best when they speak with their parts!"

"If they give it back to you (land shell, sea ocarina, offering of all hours!), if they give it back to you wrapped in the ephemeral, will you take it?"

"If they give it back to me wrapped in the ephemeral, I will take it. It is strung along its days, drying out like warm dew. I will wrap it in the shadow of the moment."

"If they give it back to you wrapped in the eternal, will you take it?"

"If they give it back to me wrapped in the eternal, I will take it, alas, I will wrap myself up with it in death."

"If they give it back to you wrapped in smoke, will you take it?"

"If they give it back to me wrapped in smoke, I will take it, perfumed like an idol, if it is storax smoke, like a lover's signal, if it is the smoke of golden embroidery, preserved against all evil, if it is tobacco smoke, summoned to prolong pleasure, if it is the smoke of a heart toasting on a slow fire; but I would rather wait for the smoke of cooking that comes from pots of corn and beans, the smoke of a

292

house, the smoke of every day, and I will wrap it in that humble smoke!"

But with all the shouting of the broom, what was the use of so much trickery, what was the use if after sweeping up everything, sound and silence, light and shadow, reality and dream, and its being the mansion of the great sorcerers (the mansion of the great sorcerers was neither in sound nor in silence, neither in light nor in shadow, neither in the real nor the unreal), nobody came out through the doors of sleeping flint, nobody appeared at the windows of awakened glass, and only a green frog jumped out of a drain and came over to be swept up, a mysterious challenge that made her go back in her thought to the hill where Juan Nojal lived and consult him in that breath and return to her person, knowing what she had to do about the frog: spit out her teeth, her teeth, which loosened and jumped out (alas, poor certain Mulata, without teeth!), but as soon as she spit out incisors and canines, others grew in, which she also spit out, waiting for those that would fill her gums again, which she also spit out. Her teeth formed little piles of laughter. The frog opened his immense half-moon mouth and tasted that corn made out of laughter, he was eating it kernel by kernel, to give it back at once in silent vomit. Corn? No! Minute skulls of bone. The Mulata did not wait for any explanation. Quick as a flash, with the hand that was hers, she put her teeth back in her gums, little skulls of white bone with the gleam of ivory, and when she saw the frog extend himself and contract to continue on forward, she let out her first skull laugh, a laugh that opened one of the giant doors to the large courtyards.

The boards gave way, swollen, damp, encrusted, held up by wooden hinges, into a hallway with a jointed floor and arches with large masks that were weeping tears of rain water which thirsty ants were carrying off in Indian file to their holes, a thirst that immobilized the fierce vipers without eyelids in their lairs, luxurious as jewel boxes. In a jewel box of emeralds, a black snake with orange speckles. In a ruby jewel box, a yellow snake with a hairy, greenish little chin. In a diamond jewel box, a green viper, small stag horns, eyes of blue drool, a tongue as black as his poison.

293

In a rainbow jewel box, a water snake, like a coiled turquoise. The frog stopped and behind him the Mulata, who was making the skeletonized woman whole, and the broom made from the hair of a dead comet. Scorpions the size of dogs approached. They barked like dogs. Their tongs, the conquerors of stony places, dirty with names of river mud, moving compasses on the fine sands of sleep, were opening and closing the parentheses of death. The frog immobilized them with his moon eyes. Dog-scorpions and snakes that the certain Mulata, without letting go of the broom, touched nine times, until she possessed the nine sensations of touch and found herself with her body asleep under her awakened skin, half of it, what she was, face to face with the scarlet jaguar on the obsidian shell of a tortoise of black gold honey and eyes with lashes. Through the lens of her touch, only her touch awakened, she asleep, the reality of the pool where the Zabala woman had sunk the half of her body that had been cut into pieces came on so suddenly that all of her was erased. She did not know what had happened. What had happened to her tactile surface, the one that was awake and facing that mirror of water where the parts of her body were floating? What had happened to the remains of her sleeping body which she had stuck to the woman who was making her whole? What had happened to her? What had happened? Where was she? Oh, yes, the scarlet jaguar was chewing the air now, the transparency of the air to which she had returned from the water, whole now in the diluted light, the skeleton woman in the pool!

"Where are the great sorcerers?"

They were probably at the foot of the cacao tree, drunk from the smell of chocolate, among large and small parrots and macaws, their velvet navels under the care of horoscopists, their teeth doughy from eating corn bread, and in their hairy armpits, disguised as eagle owls, the interpreters with painted tongues, green the tongue of the one who spoke Quiché, indigo that of the one who spoke Zutihil, red that the one who spoke Cacchiquel, white that of the one who spoke Quekchí, yellow that of the one who spoke Mame, purple that of the one who spoke Pocomame, black that of the one who spoke Poconchí.

Above the look of the great wizard Yumí, paralytic, motionless, peaceful, shining, the oblique looks of the Zabala woman, a great jealous witch who was peering into the look of the master of the house to see whether those eyes, a depth of round reeds, were taking pleasure in the vision of what had not been given to him as a husband when he had married the certain Mulata, he had only had her from behind, as the sun did the moon, and now she was offering herself to him, but she did not have the body of the other one, which was isolated, powerful, nocturnal, prehensile.

"Celestino," the Zabala woman said, "come out of your complacent pleasure! Do you know that I can hear things being done and undone in our house, do you know that I can hear them sweeping up our sound, our light, our reality, our dreams?"

"It's the rain." Yumí half closed his eyes, his eyes of the sharpened metal of an ax.

"Rain, at this time of year?"

"Who can take away the wetness of broken mirrors in the middle of summer . . ."

"You're still complaining because I ordered your mirrors broken and their pieces buried in the blackest earth, where shadow and darkness are most mixed up, so that you would not see yourself reflected in the thirteen mirrors as when you were married to her whom you desired so much! Cheat! Ingrate! Why don't you look at me? Why are you breathing hard? The stars will help me! The flies will help me! You will fall with your head cut off by an invisible ax during the night of your conquest, and you will turn into worms! And I, why did I steal what burns my hands now? Who induced me to carry, hidden under my clothes, between my legs, the great Huasanga, the sex-stealer, so that she could snatch it away from the bride during the requiem wedding Mass sung by that spider with thousands of arms, since, if it had not been snatched away, at the shout of 'Breeding tiiime!' it would have bred, and in the birth, leaving me a Yumincito, it would have died? Jealousy blinded me and now, how can I make that living matter which is burning, separated from the body where it had been, disappear? Bury it? No, if it were buried, it would keep on living from its substance as a fruit and it would rise up just like a tree of forbidden fruits, and its multiplication would be like that of the thirteen mirrors where you used to re-create yourself!"

Catarina Zabala, unable to speak—lips with an edge of jealousy cannot articulate well—passed the back of her hand across her forehead, pushing back the hair that had fallen over her eyes like strings of fishhooks trying to catch her first tears, those that she had sworn not to let flow, and which were now pouring out uncountable, along with her sobs.

To unmake Yumí, that was what she must have wanted, but so as to remake him clean of that shadow, of that mangy presence of the Mulata, who did not let her see him as he had been before, a simple woodcutter, before he had exchanged her for common riches with Tazol, or afterward, when he had lovingly rescued her from her small size of a clay shepherdess.

"Where is it? Where does she have it hidden?" the certain Mulata, whole now, was asking of the frog who was jumping ahead of her agitated steps, because what good was it for her to have recovered the half of her body which had been swimming in the pool if she still had not recovered that perfection which is not painted between the thighs but is sculptured under hills of blackness?

"I advise you not to speak to the sorcerers," the frog stopped to tell her. "It would be better to steal it."

"Everything will be possible with your help," the Mulata said in desperation, "but there is still the danger that Catarina Zabala, on the advice of the sex-stealing dwarf, will swallow it like an oyster so that she can make herself mistress of all my mystery. And that was why she ordered the mirrors broken. Reality was not enough for the master of the house. He wanted it multiplied."

"Prostitution!" the frog jumped, choking.

"Why, if it was only I?"

"Ah, but the perverse Celestino Yumí did not think so, because in the thirteen mirrors it was you multiplied by many others, because he saw you, or he saw them, whole around your sex, or the sexes that were multiplied in the mirror, he saw thirteen whole women!"

296

"But I was still the only one for his desire."

"That's why—" the frog took another jump—"jealousy has no reason for existing, because even though a man covers several women, manages to cover many women, which happens among us frogs, male and female, the woman whom he sees, the one he hears, the one he feels, is always only one, one who is always all of them."

"Oh," the Mulata exclaimed, "you think like a cold frog! That one is the one we all want to be!"

The opening of the frog's mouth looked like a tear in an old and greasy rag. A little toothless laugh, hollow.

"But no one can be that one," he suggested.

"Will we arrive in time?" the Mulata asked.

"In time for what?"

"In time so that the Zabala woman, the great witch, will not have swallowed it. What would she have to complain about if it became part of her person? She would be both wife and mistress."

"We have to hurry," the frog said, jumping more quickly.

"Do you want me to carry you?" the Mulata proposed. "I'll carry you and you can give me little kicks to tell me if we're going in the right direction."

"That's a good idea," the frog accepted.

The Mulata picked him up and with his legs he guided her through the silent labyrinth of corridors, courtyards, passageways, stairs, rooms.

Yumí, who had recovered his movements—only his paralytic's clothing kept the shape of his body—took a blow-gun, and the Zabala woman helped him prepare the game bag in which he would bring back his catch. Little Huasanga, dragging the skirts of a petticoat that looked more like a shirt, the long sleeves slobbering over the fingers of her hands, ran after Yumí. She was the spy, the go-look-and-tell, the one who wrote anonymous letters with the pretended scrawl of an illiterate that were dictated by the Zabala woman and which she would circulate at night under the doors of the houses in Tierrapaulita.

It was a nameless piece of cowardice that had been proposed. A piece of cowardice and filth. Swallowing that . . . But it was the only way she could do away with the attraction of the mistress's sex, swallowing it.

She took advantage of the fact that they had left her alone, Yumí and the dwarf Huasanga, whom she watched with the eyes of a mouse in a vegetable market. When they returned, they would not find it, they would look for it in vain, she would already have it in her belly.

She was afraid. She hesitated. Like a twinkling star, she shook her thoughts, which stretched out in little beads of icy sweat across her brow. Tazol had made her pregnant through her navel. He had left her Tazolito. And Yumí had not been jealous, because the pregnancy had been through the navel. And if now she became pregnant from the pregnant mouth of a female and there was born . . . what could be born from two females?

She put her eyes out through one of the windows into the blinding glow of the sun. She had to burn her eyes with the clarity so that splinters of light would wound her pupils, and blinded by it, she went groping toward the place where it was . . . she felt around with the tips of her fingers in the emptiness of the clay container filled with water where she kept it, and she only found the frog, the frog instead of the sex of the certain Mulata.

III

The Strange Science of Curing

The sexton, Jerónimo de la Degollación, returned with the curer and this jingle: Cure-cure-cure, curer of the curate! Cure-cure-cure, curer of the curate!—a jingle which, as the priest said, was not even funny. And how funny is that little bell that accompanies the last rites?, the sexton thought without stopping his cure-cure-cure, curer of the curate! A play on words I wrote and smote the hurt of evil that you quote, open or closed, a surfeit of the magic mote, oh, man who keeps a goat in Tierrapaulita, where the sheep are goats, drive out the ghosts! A play on words that fate took note of with a coat that toasts the curate's cheeks with groats and bloats his brow! A play on words I vote that will have your curer cure the curate of his skin that better fits a shoat!

"Will you be quiet, son of Ascalon, by your name and because you slash instead of slaughtering?" the priest spit out, overcome by rage, and added, "Where is the healer?"

"Here he is," the sexton replied, humbled by Father Chimalpín's scolding. "He's the most famous in Tierrapaulita. His name is Mucunuy Quim, which means Dawn-Grown."

When the healer entered, his feet wrapped in silence, he leaned over, tasted the flavor of the ground with the ten tongues of his hands as he touched the tips of his fingers to the dust on the floor, and he arose, unable to hide his pupils—he barely had any eyelids—from the look of the priest, raising his head of dark hair, very dark, with bristles that reminded the priest of the hedgehog's quills where those spots of dry smallpox that he was wearing had had their origin. The healer said a few words in the native language, cutting the magical thread of his silence, a silence which had carried the priest far away, so far that he felt extremely tired now as he came back to his scars.

"Oh, most felonious Candanga, false beast, tricky angel, don't think that this mask of rain that has made holes in my face will cut off my voice! I will go out at night—everyone is gray in the dark—and I will cry out against your insidious shout, your tricks of an insolent teller of tales, the words of Ecclesiastes: 'Woe unto wombs that have conceived! Woe unto breasts that have been suckled!' "

And that was how it was. Now that the healer was facing him, he remembered his running about Tierrapaulita in a nocturnal fight against Candanga.

What an aroma, what a maddening aroma came from the fecund land, of pomegranate trees with opened fruit from which rubies fell, of rose-apples and their cloying smell, of banana groves guarded by flocks of fireflies of furtive life, pursued by eye-piercing mosquitoes who, when they saw those golden eyes light up and go out, would try to get inside and blind them; the fragrance, the reflection of the large Spanish dagger flowers, candlesticks of greasy wax, white, dazzling, broken against the deep blackness of the night, and the strong smell of the different chile plants, garden chile, biting gold, chocolate chile, even more biting, green chile, raisin chile, burned chile, the dark color of a rooster, *chiltepe, zambo* chile, *uluté* chile, scarlet and infernal, an odor that brings on coughing, strangling, and snorting, not only in a man but in coarse iguanas.

Oh, the Tierrapaulita nights, stirred up by the stormy shouts of: "Breeding tiiime today! Breeding tiiime!" as they commanded the deaf; nights with skies that stuffed human breasts with stars when there was no longer any room for stars in the sky and they came down on the prowl like gallows wasps until they almost smothered men and women!

"Breeding tiiime todaydayday, breeding tiiime!"

"No! No!" Father Chimalpín went shouting through the streets, ready to drop, his cassock caught up around his ankles, the points of his shoes bumping into the stones. "No! No! Sons of hell, no! Abstain! Abstain! No, sons of hell! Woe unto wombs that have conceived! Woe unto breasts that have been suckled!"

"Breeding tiiime! Breeding tiiime!" screamed the toothy

302

devil, pursued by the shadow of Father Chimalpín, a person who knew that the good is always a struggle, work, overcoming, because evil has only to exist, and that's enough, that's why there are more evil people than good ones, more devils than saints.

"No! No!" the priest kept shouting, anxious to grab the devil and give him a good cuff on the face as he felt the darkness putting out its scratching claws on all sides, because it is well known that devils help each other out, and Candanga, the half-breed devil, was being helped by Mandinga, the Negro devil, who was always on a holiday, sweaty, with a toothpick in his mouth, or a cigar, surrounded by pretty ebony females, swaying with their lewdness fore and aft, some sort of fireworks in their eyes, and tricks of the will-o'-the-wisp in their nipples and hips.

But why remember all of that, now that he was face to face with the famous healer, the master healer Dawn-Grown, Zac Mucunuy, or Mucunuy Quim, who was nothing but eyes, eyes that scarcely had lids, eyes in a lake that extended up toward his temples, toward his forehead, toward his cheeks, barely divided by the thin line of his nose, his ears widely separated and standing out, greenish in color like leaves, his lips like the mouth of a jar burned by tobacco juice, cheekbones enameled with the shine of a laugh in an absent half-moon that seemed erased from his face, as if obeying his thought.

Father Chimalpín could not take away that look of his of someone sick with scars—the hedgehog had left his face as if he had been hit with a shotgun blast of rock salt—from that pair of lakelike eyes.

Dawn-Grown, looking at him, looking at him, was getting inside of him, calming him, like a good tamer of primates in the jungle, a tamer of first-born clouds, those from the beginning of the rainy season, black and big-bellied, a tamer of orphaned rays of lightning manipulated by Juan Nojal on his mountain top, a tamer of the ticks of noise that bring blood out of the soul, a tamer of people frightened by their shadows, the leftovers that we carry with us as an expression of our occult mystery.

The priest began to be upset by that restful restlessness—what other name could one give to the indescribable storm cloud that was gaining power over his senses as he perceived things as if he were in a wooden and breakable state.

Music of the sacrificers of rabbits was invoked by the healer to attract the cacao-counters, spiders that leave a terrible eruption that rots the flesh on the skin of sleepers. Black, filthy, yellow eyes, they retreated before the healer's muddying look.

"Why did you call us if you hold us back?" complained one of the cacao-counters, not with words but with threads of a spider web, threads that had small, luminous dots.

"Why should I want to see you," drooled Dawn-Grown, as he spoke to the spiders with saliva threads, "my Atlantis virgins of funereal plush, except to ask you how it happened that widow pox rained down onto the face of Father Carmelo Chimalpín?"

"Not Carmelo," the sexton intervened, "Mateo!"

"Well, then, Mateo."

"It rained! It rained!" A cacao-counter jumped up to weave a web of small threads with little knots, thinking they were playing give-and-take.

Dawn-Grown, Mucunuy Quim, the healer, spit-spoke immediately, poking at the play of saliva that made up his words, his breathing was agitated: "It trained? Was it raining, or was someone in training?"

"Both . . ." the spider wove.

"Ah, both." The healer took some time, how difficult it was to gather enough saliva together to spin that language. "You mean that it was raining and someone was training!"

"A fine kettle! This one wasn't the only one who was trained!" A cacao-counter came upon the scene, spinning her language out with threads of black saliva. "I was trained too."

"Are you going to slander us?" a third spider put in.

"There's no need to!" salivated the new witness in black.

"A hedgehog!"

"Quiet, there was no such hedgehog!"

"It was a fossil, I know it, I know it!"

"A fossil? Gabby old fool! All it had of a fossil about it was what a centipede has when he burns with a frozen burn as he passes by. In spite of his fierce-pointed fire, thistles changed to quills, that hedgehog burned like the frozen burning plants have, and he spread out over the flesh the little pricks called slave smallpox."

The healer interrupted at once, casting the play of his cobweb threads into the air: "Slave smallpox?"

The spiders grew silent, and the healer was silent, facing the priest who was immobilized by his look, in the inner circle of his magical power. Slave smallpox, he repeated mentally to himself, not from the tack pricks of a fossil animal. What remained was to find out whether they had pierced his understanding. Whether he thought well, or whether his thought came out through the holes like liquid through a sprinkler.

He thanked the cacao-counters for their information, and he gnawed on the silence beside him that was like the sweet brains of a deer.

The small animal, wounded by the teeth of Dawn-Grown, fled, leaving behind a trail of blood or red brains, whose still warm answer, before it dried out, were these scabs or pieces of advice:

"Nine baths, nine days, cooking along with stallion thistle. Warm drinks of cassia with some sticks of cinnamon, some drops of anise, lemon, and witch honey. Dressing in red and not exposing himself to the light too much."

He thanked the deer for his advice. Nine bows of the head, the mastiff collar of his old man's ribs made a flinty sound, while the little animal, badly wounded, brains of sweet silence, went away.

But the deer came back. Erect, his head like the second hand of a watch, his eyes out of orbit, he scratched the ground with his foot, just as if he were digging a hole to plant what he was going to say:

"And if my remedies don't erase the scars, he will have to be turned to ash."

Mucunuy Quim, the healer, wrinkled his mouth and his brow.

"Turned to ash?" he ventured, doubting what he had heard.

"Yes," the deer nodded, "turned to ash by a soft fire of dry tendrils from a thorny bush, the thorniest you can find."

"How does one go about turning him to ash, precious throat?"

And it was precious, the throat of the blinking deer, twice, three times he blinked the yellow wing flaps over his black pepper pupils that were shining, protruding.

"Turning him to ash by soft fire," he explained, "is to burn him during the hot part of the morning sun, after he has been whipped with shreds from the tendrils of a thorny bush."

"And if that has no effect, if those mustard seeds don't leave his face, it could be worse, some scars are lentils, what other cure do you have for me, little delicate stone deer? Tell me, little deer combed with the cosmetic of distance, eyes of carrot water, damp nose of breezes that blow and steer northward!"

"If it were laziness of the pores . . ." the deer reflected, "but it's not . . ."

"No, it's not laziness of the pores," Dawn-Grown interrupted, Father Chimalpín was still motionless beneath his look, and Jerónimo de la Degollación, all ears, afraid that they would give the priest something that would really upset him, because he was already in bad enough shape from that "Breeding tiiime today, breeding tiiime!" that the Devil was shouting all through the interminable nights of Tierrapaula, as it was beginning to be called now that it was being modernized.

"And who knows . . . who knows whether or not it's laziness of the pores . . ." the deer took up the words again, with a nervous shaking of his patent leather lips, chasing his little ears frontward and backward, as if he were listening for some dangerous sound, "unless the bluebell of lust had nested in his heart, and backward pores were left on him from that drained carnal passion, like smallpox marks, and then the wise thing would be to use an ointment made from the blood of a calander killed in song."

When the healer recovered, the deer had already left. He had disappeared with the speed of wind and a sprinkling of musical drops went on ahead to the canopy of rain that was packing its threads tight until it formed a loom on which the breath of the wind wove a mirrorlike figure, a water quail, no larger than a dove, with a small round mirror in the middle of its head, blue back and breast, blue wings and tail, all of it like a glowing coal.

306

"Divine water quail!" Dawn-Grown hastened to greet it, his right hand over his heart, "what advice does your little round mirror give to cure Father Carmelo . . ."

"Lay off the Carmelo business," the sexton intervened, "his name is Mateo!"

". . . Mateo Chimalpín," the healer went on, "of that dew he has of smallpox scars, small as bird shot, fired at him point-blank by someone in ambush? May the Square Deity of Day be favorable to us, so that we can see the answer from your little round mirror!"

"The most likely cure," the shiny bird answered under the rain that was forming bubbles of glasslike pockmarks, "is to wash his face with water from a rock that has been exposed to the night dew for seven nights in a row."

"Is that all?" asked the healer, smiling.

"That isn't all, let me explain to you!" The quail flapped her wings, annoyed at the untrusting little smile of Mucunuy Quim. "In the bottom of the clay receptacle where the rock water will condense, you have to put a little mirror, the little mirror of my head, a reflection of the sun captured at dusk, so that in it, just as in gold, the glow of the stars will be embedded, and that glow, as he washes his face, will erase the cuts!"

The rain eased up, and when its threads thinned out, the bluish vision of the water quail had been erased.

"Male Umil, Dawn-Grown calls on you for help at this hour of movement situated in some point of the seventhousandtwohundred days of our lives! Tell us what kind of copal, white copal to perfume the gods, or black copal used to make round and bouncing balls for games, should be used to make the mask that can be placed wet on the face of this man to erase the little holes left on him by the hedgehog quills!"

The Male Umil, always invisible, could be felt approaching at the call of the healer by the steps he made that sounded like drinks drunk by the great taster of men's walking, the skin of the earth.

His voice was heard near and far away.

"It is not so easy, Dawn-Grown, it is not so easy! From white copal for burning and chewing, and from black copal for playing-balls, you must make the mask that you

307

will place on the face of the one who was pock-marked by the quills of the hedgehog, in superimposed layers, and you will begin with a black layer on the left side and a white layer on the right side, only this first layer will be of night and day, then a layer of white copal will come, which will simulate light, clarity, the sun, then a layer of black copal, made of rubber, which will simulate night, shadows, the non-road, and in successive layers you will count seven white and seven black, and you will leave them on his face until they are dry, so that they can be torn off later with one pull, and the holes will stick on them and his face will be clean!"

"We will try everything," exclaimed Mucunuy Quim with a humble voice, "but if this remedy of a soup of layers by day and night does not give results, what else do you advise, Male Umil, always invisible?"

"Ah! Ah! Ah!" the latter exclaimed. "I would advise a remedy that is the most efficient of all, but unfortunately it could not be used on this patient because he is a priest. I would advise him to go to bed with a virgin who has a rash, so that in the jiggling of love his bites would fall off, and her rash would go away in blood."

The sexton drew back in the face of such lack of respect; Father Chimalpín, poor thing, was still motionless under the eyes of the healer, not just because the person in question was invisible, but because after he had spoken, a solid notable made his appearance.

The one who had just come in was a sacrificer.

Jerónimo de la Degollación became upset and was on the point of saying that he was the only one there with the name of a slaughterer.

The new arrival was wearing a tunic made from pieces of human skin, a heart painted on his chest with blood, a brick-colored heart. On his fingers hundreds of hearts were palpitating in agony like wounded birds.

"My double," the healer said, "I know that you took your *chilate* brew, but no one better than you, one whose hands are pricked by the heart of the victim as it jumps out of the virile chest, torn out by your fingers, can give more sage advice, as astrologer and high soothsayer, as to what would

308

erase the scars of quill smallpox! Speak with your shell trumpet! Sound your emerald voice!"

"A sure thing," the sacrificer answered, "would be to mount him on the Meat-Eating Mule one dark night and let it carry him off. When he comes back, from the trotting of that mysterious animal, if he was born lucky, that is, he will have cast off all the dry little seeds on his face."

"My double, by the skin of the flayed person covering you, by all of the sacrifices that you have consummated, by all the hearts that have fluttered in your hands, you must have some other advice, because how could we mount on the Meat-Eating Mule someone who is a priest like you, someone who drinks blood in his chalice everyday, without exposing him to the possibility that the evil beast might kill him or disappear with him into the blackest part of night?"

"It would be worse to mount him on Cadejo."

"Impossible, sacrificer, impossible! He would carry him off and what could we do?"

"Only by mounting him on the mule or on Cadejo and walling up the four corners of the square of Tierrapaulita, the way they do during bullfights."

"Only that way, but no . . . The cure is getting worse than the illness."

"Or if you mounted him on Sisimite!"

"Cashtoc be with us! He'd skin him, that's true, but he'd leave him all palsied!"

"There's nothing left except the mule."

"Such ingratitude!"

"Or, it occurs to me . . . the certain Mulata is around here with a big broom made out of a dead man's hair, sweeping the house of the great sorcerers . . . take the dead man's hair away from her and mount him on that big broom of lust!"

"Cane without mane, mane from the cane, mane!" the healer hastened to say to please the Great Sacrificer with a play on words, but then, rolling his eyes in a shameless way, he added: "Mounting him on the stick of the certain Mulata's broom would not be dangerous, but the fact is that the smallpox the Father got seems to have come from lust."

309

Dawn-Grown laughed with his painted teeth, the uppers blue and the lowers red. An interminable laugh that shook cold on the back of the sexton and on the body of Father Chimalpín, paralyzed by the eyes of the healer, just like a manikin made of hemp.

"Father! . . . Father! . . ." the sexton went over to speak to him at the bidding of the healer—it was good for him to hear a familiar voice—but there was no answer.

Little by little, as Jerónimo de la Degollación called him, he recovered and told how he had gone far away to look at himself in many many mirrors, and since he had come back with drops of mirror in his eyes, he let loose large, sad tears from the edges of his great eyelids.

"Well, what does your healer say?" the cleric inquired as he woke up.

"He said up . . . the set-up . . ."

"He said up . . . the set-up . . . I'm fed up!"

Dawn-Grown intervened: "I said that we will use two kinds of cure, Father. Natural ones and occult ones, the kind that are wrapped up. We'll begin with the natural ones."

The priest tasted his dry mouth, waiting for the other one to speak.

"First a laxative . . . to erase the traces of the Fire-of-the-Beautiful-Lord."

"Bring two doses," the churchman indicated. "One for this fellow and another one for me . . ." and he was wondering what that Fire-of-the-Beautiful-Lord could be.

"But, Father, I'm not pock-marked!" the sexton exclaimed.

"For having gone to get this Indian pal of yours who's going to make me drink God knows what kind of mess!"

If that's the way it's going to be, God help me! the sexton said to himself, trembling at the thought that he would also want him mounted on the Meat-Eating Mule, if they decided on that stern measure, on Cadejo, on Sisimite, or on the certain Mulata's broomstick.

"After the laxative, we'll let three days go by, and if the shell doesn't come off, if the pock marks haven't been erased, we'll prepare a *temascal* . . ."

310

"And what's that?" the afflicted priest inquired.

"It's nothing bad, Father," Jerónimo intervened, "it's a steam bath."

"On a bed of porous stone," Mucunuy Quim, the healer, added. "Water vapor, but the bed must be of porous stone, because the cure comes with the absorption of the dry pock marks through the pores of the stones."

"And if they don't go away, if they haven't left me after those baths . . ." the priest despaired. As the hours passed, as he looked and looked into the mirror, he felt more and more unfortunate.

"Then," the voice of Mucunuy Quim, Dawn-Grown, grew hoarse, "we will proceed to the wrapping cures. We will get a star for you to eat."

"But how can I eat a star?" the priest raised his angry voice, he had already suffered enough with his strainer face to be listening to more foolishness.

"If the evil was done to you by some sorcerer who had his body dressed in star spines," the healer explained without changing his countenance because of his patient's anger, "we must counteract it with your eating one, two, three stars, you may even have to eat nine."

"This man is crazy!" the priest complained, his eyes fixed on Jerónimo de la Degollación.

"Patience, Father," the latter begged, weighing the fact that eating stars, ugly as they might be, like eating a fish raw, eyes and golden spines and all, was better than riding the Meat-Eating Mule.

"We'll close the door a little," the healer said, and as he left it ajar, he added, "the proof is in what can be seen."

And in truth, as the three of them stood there in the shadows, out of every little perforated spot like a smallpox scar on the cleric's skin, a golden light came out, greenish and yellow, bluish and reddish, as if a star were lighting his face from within, twinkling, and as it twinkled it changed the color of its glow.

"And how can I swallow it?" The priest became nauseous thinking about it, thinking about a great star stuck in his gullet, not noticing that he himself looked like a black star, a star that had gone out, with his cassock in pieces, torn, in

311

shreds, shreds that looked like arms or fingers . . . he trembled, as if the eleventhousand arms would come out of him again.

"What do you mean, how can you swallow it?" the sexton intervened. "In one gulp, Father, in one gulp"—maybe he could encourage him that way.

"In one gulp, no! In one gulp, no!" The priest drew back. "What will I do if it gets stuck in my throat, and I can't swallow it or spit it up, because I won't be able to get it out of my mouth any more . . . will I strangle? I'd rather have the scars."

"Bite it, Father!"

"But it's not easy to bite a living star!"

"And you couldn't spit it out either," intervened Mucunuy Quim, the healer, "someone who can swallow and then spit up a jagged star spits up a jaguar; the higher wizards multiply jaguars by swallowing jagged stars."

"But, Mr. Healer, what's the use of talking about supernatural cures if Father can rid himself of that mask of pock marks that the hedgehog left him with the laxative and the steam bath on a bed of porous stone?" the sexton interrupted with a questioning tone, afraid that the business of the Meat-Eating Mule would be mentioned.

"No, Jerónimo, let him talk! What kind of abomination have we fallen into, good Lord! Into what kind of a maze! Into what kind of infernal brushfires! Open that door, because I'm giving off a glow, it's a glow from hell, the glow of a worm!"

"Ah! Ah! Ah!" The healer opened his large mouth. "It's a star of glowworms that you have to eat."

"Of what? Of worms?" the cleric reacted. "A more infamous glow than that inside of me, because I'm already giving off a dead man's glow!"

"The damp glow of the worms will expel from your body the dry light which the hedgehog injected with his quills," Dawn-Grown said.

"One nail to draw another nail, Father," the sexton said like an acolyte, following the healer, who was leaving on his feet of silence after having made a short bow to the patient, who was obsessed with looking in the mirror, touching his cheeks, scratching his scars, as if they could come off with his fingernails.

"Are you going for the laxative, Mr. Healer?" Jerónimo asked.

"Yes."

"It's nice that you didn't tell the Father that business about the Meat-Eating Mule," he stuttered, blowing the intertwined intentions of his voice almost into the other's ear, "or that business of putting him to bed with a virgin who has a rash, so that she would get over her rash—sh . . . sh . . . , what a wonderful cure!—and he would get rid of his pock marks . . . and I understand that it's all a manner of speaking, but where can you find a virgin with a rash, even for a cure . . ."

"There's everything at the Cleaning Woman's."

"In Tierrapaulita?"

"Didn't you know about it?"

"No."

"That's strange, because the Cleaning Woman is famous."

"Far off?"

"Right over there. If you come with me, I'll show you."

"Just so I can know about it. Villages have their secrets, and since church people can't go into certain places . . ."

"It's over there," the healer pointed out, "that little house with a low roof, painted white."

Jerónimo did not miss a single detail of the house or of the place where it stood. Opposite a public fountain with washbasins occupied by women who were washing volcanoes of white clothes. The smell of common black soap mixed with the stench of milk and cow manure from a nearby dairy, and beyond that with the odor of burned bone from the hoofs of animals being shod in a nearby blacksmith's shop.

Mucunuy Quim said goodbye to the sexton.

"I'm going to look for the herbs, I'll be back with the laxative in a little while."

The Virgin with a Rash

Whom had the healer gone to tell? Let him take all night
giving the priest a laxative—his good candle, his good
toilet, and his folded pieces of newspaper—because he,
Jerónimo of the most absolute Slaughter, was going for a
virgin with a rash at the Cleaning Woman's. The sun had
not even gone down yet, and he was already jiggling his
knees, waiting to go out into the street. He groped at his
face as he shaved. All of the mirrors were being put to
use in Father Chimalpín's room, even the one that magnified
and made his pock marks look like craters on the moon.
Using pails of water, he took a bath beside a font, quickly,
so that he would not be discovered naked by one of the
old women who were coming by to inquire about the health
of the parish priest. He combed his hair, he lit a cigarette,
and he was even tempted to put a flower in his buttonhole.
Tierrapaula! Tierrapaula! he said to himself, and he
stretched out his arms as if all of it were going to belong to
him, where waiting for him were a virgin with a rash, the
whole town, all of its women. Tierrabendita, blessed land,
blessed art thou and blessed is thy fruit! He bit his tongue.
He had not been able to think of anything else to say. And
if Father did not get his laxative? He was almost humming
it, he felt so happy: steam baths on a bed of porous stone!
And if the baths did not rid him of the great holes the
hedgehog had given him, the cure, as they knew, was a
virgin with a rash. So that's where I'm going in Father's
place, and since it must be healthful, something good will
come to his sybaritic sexton and his reverence will be left,
as a last resort, with a ride on the Meat-Eating Mule. He
evidently needs a little ride. A ride on a female or a ride
on the mule to get rid of those scars. And I'll take the one

on the female. For myself and for his health. And the one on the mule, well, who else but the party concerned himself . . .

He almost burned his fingers and his lips. He was smoking a live coal. Two brotherhood members were squatting and waiting at the door of the parish house, motionless, like white ghosts, and when they saw him come out, they greeted him with a jump of their hats.

"Go in, if you want. I'm going on a little errand. Then Father won't be left all alone."

"Is he ill?"

"Quite ill. God's will be done, my sons, God's will be done!"

And while the sandal steps of the brotherhood members strung off into the silence and the darkness toward the inside of the cloister, Jerónimo de la Degollación started walking through the streets of Tierrapaula, the modernized name of Tierrapaulita, with the step of a conqueror who was putting on a show in the shadows of the night. When he came to a corner, he thought he glimpsed a feminine figure, a face wrapped in gauze that was smiling at him. She had come out of a blank wall. Catch up with her. Find out who she was. Could she be the virgin with a rash?

He quickened his pace, but the distance that separated them was always the same or just a little less, just enough to incite him to walk faster. He was walking faster and faster, faster and faster. He was almost running. He was running and he would have fallen into a deep gully if a curtain of cold sweat, the materialization of some weeping willows, had not stopped him.

Another woman was waiting for him. A yellow one. Large Gypsy eyes. Breasts bulging underneath her tangled hair. "As I get close to her, she'll start to go away," the sexton said to himself, but that was not how it was. He was the one who was going away, the one who could not reach her, as he saw her separated from him by the distance of his voice. As it agitated her clothes, the wind revealed vinegar-colored legs. But why could he not cover the distance that separated them with a leap? A leap, but for what reason? It would make him ridiculous. There she was, there, within reach of his hand. Something saved him when, ready for anything, he closed his eyes to leap at her. An endless howl. The howl of a very long dog, who began there on that corner and ended at the next one. It brought him back from the deception of distance his ears had given him and with the speed of a stone shot from a sling, he retreated to the place where he really was in relation to that most beautiful Gypsy, more than a woman, a yellow, luminous star. The bray of a donkey who was nursing a foal finally oriented him. He was walking among donkey pens closed in by barbed wire, and he ought to look for the street. But how could he get there without scratching his clothes on the wire, because to get back now, with his five senses intact once more, he would have to be so very careful as he risked his skin.

"No more visions . . . flesh!" he said to himself, coming out into the street, bathed in the sweat of the dew and the soap of the moon.

The public fountain with its washbasins. Nobody and, yet, in the silence of the night, the sound of pouring pails could be heard—*chipuchi . . . chipuchi*—the chattering of the washerwomen and their hissing as they panted.

"Flesh!" Jerónimo repeated to himself. "No more visions . . . flesh! . . . flesh! . . ."

He spat saliva out from around his jagged teeth. That yellowish saliva of black tobacco that wizards spit out when they are creating jaguars. He had the feeling that because of carnal sin his spine had become lengthened down to his heels, like a diabolic tail. He kicked the idea away, rebelling against his remorseful religious fear that was trying to deprive him of the total enjoyment of a woman, of rolling around like a Turk with the virgin with a rash. Oh, if he could only stop being a believer and revert to being an atheist, an unbeliever, a pagan! He rapped his knuckles on the door of the Cleaning Woman's house, a small rap that he repeated more strongly, without getting any answer. Strange, because one could sense that there were people there. He made his eye round and the size of the keyhole, thinking of the moon that was becoming round like an eye to spy through the keyhole of the sky. There were people there. Whispering could be heard. Jerónimo was yearning to find naked women. "Flesh! . . . flesh! . . . flesh! . . . ," he repeated to himself, his mouth pasty, his sweaty armpits titillating, his groin afire . . . flesh! . . . flesh!, because what was here was no longer a vision.

And what surprise did he find?

A big man kneeling beside a snake. He was deciphering enigmas. His face had hoe marks of shadows, leprous-looking splotches, black and blue marks, and a lock of hair hung over his brow.

"Will you," the Cleaning Woman was asking the snake with wide-open, lidless eyes that drifted in the painful light of the candle, "will you," the Cleaning Woman repeated, standing with a candle in her hand beside the kneeling man, "will you help Suerto Rodríguez? He begs you on his knees, with his eyes upon your eyes, precious mistress of the little stones of fate. And as he begs you, Suerto Rodriguez tells you how unhappy he is, living in the salty world of tears, where each morning the deep sea breaks from its pits against the sand, just as the sea of men does against life. He tells me that he wants to go live with you and become caretaker of your silence."

The snake twisted about under the spell cast by the voice of the Cleaning Woman, a white woman, fat, with red, stringy hair, green eyes, as if it understood her words.

"They are emeralds," she said to it, "they are emeralds, these precious things that Suerto Rodríguez brings you."

That big man there nodded with his head that they were emeralds, the flame of the candle wavered under his breath, and there was a singed smell now from the lock of hair hanging down over his brow.

"Genuine precious stones," the Cleaning Woman insisted, squatting down, moving her white face closer, her green eyes, her caramel hair, to the triangle of the snake's face, "emeralds the size of the fingernail of my little finger, and he will leave us just enough, the ones you want, the ones you need to cover up your face."

At that moment the woman perceived that they were being spied upon, it was instinctive, and Jerónimo, when he felt himself discovered, tried to slip his bulk away, but attracted, hypnotized, paralyzed by the sight of the snake, he lost time and . . . he was swallowed up by the earth, no, by the door that opened so fast he fell reeling on his face, foot over foot over foot over foot over foot and finally, from the snake, a soapy smoke, from Suerto Rodríguez, the gallop of a horse on the cobblestones of the street, from the Cleaning Woman, complaints:

"Why were you spying? Who sent you to spy? Such a dirty custom!"

"Mucunuy Quim, Dawn-Grown," Jerónimo managed to articulate.

"Ah, that fellow!"

"But not to spy."

"What for, then?"

"For a cure."

"A cure?"

"For the virgin with a rash."

"For the 'lovely'?" the Cleaning Woman said more softly. "But let me put the light on, it's better that way with sweet things," she added as she scratched a match—the flame leaped forth miraculously—and lit a candle, "it's better that way with sweet things, because light is sweet, it's honey, it's sugar, and people look sugary in the light, even if they're bitter."

"Mucunuy Quim . . ." the sexton ventured.

"A very fine healer, but I find that he has one defect: he believes in strong remedies, and he prescribes that way, the way he prescribed for me when I had rheumatism that was paralyzing one of my legs; put it in an anthill . . . I did—what else could I do—and by the great whore I dug my nails into the palms of my hands, my teeth into my lips, I pissed, and a reddish fire, like seeing the worst kind of erysipelas, came up my sick shinbone. I was cured, but afterward the druggist Santano explained to me that it was fornic acid. 'The hell with what you say and keep it away from me!' I answered that vegetarian, that worshipper of Saint Badthief, because since he knew about my business with girls whose torment did not seem so ugly to him, I thought that he was saying fornic because of fornication, but no, there really is such a thing as that fornic acid."

"And he's just prescribed a rather strong remedy, as you put it, and that's why I've come to ask you on behalf of the party involved, if it's true about the virgin with a rash."

"The party involved is you, of course, don't beat about

318

the bush. I'm an old hand at this business. A person talks about a third party when he doesn't have any confidence in himself. She's at your disposal, I have her living with me, she cleans her skin during the day, and at night she turns it over to the rash."

She came over and stroked the visitor on his back.

"I'll get her ready for you. Take your clothes off. No one can go into that child's room if he's dressed. Undressed and in the dark. I'm going to wake her up and have her get into the double bed."

"I was wise to come," the sexton calmed his remorse to himself, "because in this way, in case Father can't throw off the husks of the smallpox with the laxative and the *temascal* bath, before he mounts the Meat-Eating Mule, he can come here. A false mustache to throw the Cleaning Woman off the track, because, after all, who will know that it's he who's working in the dark with the little maiden with a rash in order to get rid of the bites of the Fire-of-the-Beautiful-Lord."

A double bed, a marriage bed? Jerónimo was filled with anguished pleasure—he, who had never married, suddenly getting into a bridal bed and finding there, all huddled up in a marvelous wedding night, a little virgin with a rash of love, an itching of welts that she would scratch up against his male body in search of relief until the rash went away with the sweat and swing of feelings, amorous surrender, that instant when the eyelids, part of the cosmic night, can wipe out reality and the unreal is born.

"Your clothes, your shoes . . . you have to take everything off—" the eager Cleaning Woman came back—"and you'd better give me your shoes, I'll take care of them, so that when you're ready to leave you can leave me an offering for having been with the 'lovely' and I'll give them back to you. It's not that I don't trust you, no, but I don't want to happen what happened to someone the other day. His shoes had disappeared. Where didn't we look for them? Where didn't we? But it was like a mystery, and he had to go away barefoot. It could only have been a ghost, because the house was all locked up. He had to go away barefoot . . . not even in his stocking feet, because if he had gone away in his socks, the neighbors peeping out from behind their blinds would have said that he was looped from drinking too much, and if he had put on a pair of my shoes, with high heels, they would have said that he was . . . one of those fellows."

"A mystery . . ." Jerónimo tried to agree, more and more anxious to be in the virgin's bed.

"A mystery that was not so mysterious, because it was cleared up later on. The guy owed Don Chon, the shoemaker on the square, for the shoes, and it seems that Don Chon had been following him everywhere and, knowing that he was here, he had slipped in and recovered his merchandise while the other one was making love. That's why—what did you say your name was?"

"Jerónimo de la Degollación."

"Lordy!" The Cleaning Woman rolled her green eyes, raising up the edge of her hand over the back of her neck like a headsman's ax.

He took off his shoes, what a cold feeling, his warm and honeyed socks sticking to the cold brick floor.

From the holy offerings, and he lost his breath, he did not like it, with the help of a hook he had extracted money for the offering, as the madam was calling what he was giving for something that should not be paid for, much less by him, who, as he suppressed his conscience of a reducer of poor boxes, had come to test the virgin with a ra . . . shshshsh . . . whether it was good or bad, recommendable at least, as a cure for Father, because that business of putting him up on the Meat-Eating Mule, never! It could not be! He was against it! It would be better for him to stay with his face all pock-marked, because a diabolical animal like that might carry him off to hell in his new cassock and with his tonsure growing out.

The Cleaning Woman disappeared with the shoes, while the sexton shivered in his skin, not knowing whether from the cold or from his carnal appetite.

"I went to do the 'lovely's' hair and put her in bed, that's why I took so long."

"Where is she?" asked Jerónimo de la Degollación, with his voice short, gasping, helping himself breathe by using his mouth, since his nose was not enough, and there he was, drinking, chewing the air, his head feeling loose, as if it

320

were hanging by his hair, falsely on his shoulders as bolder men coursed through his arms that were anxious to embrace that virginal body.

Flesh! Flesh! No more visions! No more Weeping Women! Away with Siguamonta and away with Siguanaba! Flesh! Flesh!

"Another thing I wanted to tell you—" the old woman blinked her eyelashes of smoke—"I'm going to leave you alone in the house, as if you were the master. I have to give some urgent help to a woman who is in great, great trouble. An acquaintance of mine. The certain Mulata, you must have heard of her, she's been heard of so much . . ." She disappeared momentarily under the bell of the skirt that she was slipping over her head as her house petticoat fell to her feet, at the same time as she was saying with her voice muffled by the clothes, "Yes, she's trying to get back the half of her body that they took away from her as punishment, but not her power, her witchcraft, her magic, and she's been dispossessed, with no invisible help, exposed to being eaten up by light or shadow. And all of this happened, not everything poured has its reward, as a result of her having gone through a civil wedding with the wizard Yumí, only a civil ceremony, because that fellow Yumí had already been married as God ordains to Catarina Zabala, the one that the ungrateful wretch did not hesitate to sell to the Corn-Leaf Devil. He did it for riches."

She took a dark shawl with long beards out of a chest and threw it over her shoulders. The trim looked like drizzle. And she went on:

"The ingratitude of a man! What was certain was that the Zabala woman pardoned her husband and got him back after imprisoning the Mulata in a cave. But a great earthquake came and a volcano vomited great amounts of lava, and goodbye good God—it left Yumí's lands without a single animal, without a single tree, without a single planted field, it was like looking at the curve on the shell of a black tortoise as it disappeared into the horizon. With the pushing of the earth and the shoving of the hills, the Mulata escaped from the cave, asleep like the moon, and she went around like a wandering vine, because she is a divine wanderer, until life brought her face to face with Yumí once more; according to what people say, it was during a Requiem Mass sung by a great spider with a cassock and eleventhousand arms and legs at midnight on Good Friday, a Requiem Mass that Yumí and the Mulata, already married civilly, took advantage of to get married in mourning. The dress worn by the lemon-colored Mulata bride was black, her dowry coins were black, the rings were black. Someone who has been married in the church during a living Mass, it is well known, can be married again, also in the church, during a dead Mass, a Mass for the dead."

The sexton, waiting in his underwear to possess the virgin, from whom he was separated by a few steps and the threshold of a timid door, in order to give himself airs, confided to the Cleaning Woman that he was a good friend of the "illuminated" person into whom the certain Mulata had been demonized (the Devil demonizes, he does not become incarnate) so that she could slip into the church.

"Well, my boy, I'd be very much afraid of that fellow!" the Cleaning Woman noted after sinking, removing, and sinking once more big, toothy combs into her fiery hair, and she continued speaking:

"And that was where this latest involvement began, during the Requiem Mass. The Zabala woman, a great witch, was dozing, nodding, rather, butterflying with sleep like all old people, just as every night while she waited for Yumí, when under the door, just like a small snake, she saw the tendril of a creeping plant come in, come over to her bed and whisper in her ear that her 'better half,' the magnificent sorcerer, was getting married in the style of the dead. 'Style of the dead?' the Zabala woman sat up, asking and moving, because she knew that it meant that her husband and the certain Mulata were getting married beyond life."

Degollación, growing more and more lustful because of the waiting, was jumbling his eyes, joining and separating the pupils just like a crab, the skin on his back in shivers, his mouth dry, and his ears, during empty pauses, attent to the bedroom where the virgin with the rash was waiting at that instant and for that instant—everything else, the eternal verities . . .

The Cleaning Woman was leaving and not leaving, ready

to go out now, with her shawl on, her squeaky boots, and the keys in her hand, she was leaving and not leaving, prompted to run and help the Mulata, and held back by the itch to gossip with Jerónimo about what the latter, filled with lust with the virgin in reach, not only did not care about at that moment, but who, desperation of desperations, had to listen to the old woman while he knew it all so much better because he had lived it, he, he, HE . . . who, by playing a chamber-potter, had provoked Yumí into developing into a hedgehog . . . what, what could the Cleaning Woman tell someone who could still feel the sharp needles of that prickly beast on his skin as they drove him mad with pain, while inside of him the consubstance that the Mulata had left behind (when a member is amputated it keeps on feeling . . . what it must be like when it is a whole being) was twisting with pleasure from the dome of his palate to his toenails at that most ferocious of all cohabitations, the multiple amorous possession attained by the penetration of erect spines into the passive pores of feminine skin and, if he remembered correctly, he had heard her exclaim: "This is my hour of heaven . . . my strange hour of heaven!"

"Well, as I was telling you," the Cleaning Woman went on, now taking some small steps prior to opening the door and leaving, "the Zabala woman didn't have to be told twice. From sheet to street, along with Huasanga, the sex-stealing dwarf. Mass for the dead? She didn't like the smell of it, she wondered who was playing dead. Her husband getting married? The dead woman smelled even worse. Requiem wedding? She planted herself in the church with the sex-stealing dwarf hidden under her skirts, ready to oppose the joining of two beings in a union that would have no end, because they were getting married for the rest of their deaths, and not only did she manage to prevent it but she also saw to it that the Cursing Wizards, the Yellow Wizards of Malcam, condemned the Mulata to lose half of her body in the Cave of Flints, half of her lunar body, not because of her shadowy wedding, her enigmatic nuptials with a response for the dead . . . for that there would be sentences by black judges in the resting places of death! They condemned her for something that has no pardon: for having abandoned

323

a possessed person, which is the same as abandoning her home! She had abandoned the person she had been possessing, do you understand? She had left the possessed person who had been possessing her in the very best kind of diabolical fornications . . ." (ME . . . and that's why I'm here, Degollación was on the point of shouting as if slaughtered; he was confused, cross-eyed, nauseous, unable any more to calm his well-armed and, according to him, unsurpassable virilities) "she left her possessed person halfway, going back on the pact she had made with the devil of God, the Christian devil, the foreigner, the good one, and whom she was representing in a challenge to the green devil of the Indians, incarnate in Yumí." She lowered her voice and folded her eyelids, just like sails, over the green seas of her eyes, and she added: "Just between us here, the devils were fighting over the right to destroy the Father—that new one who arrived a while ago . . . and who challenged Candanga . . .

"She went to perdition for it, what can we do," the Cleaning Woman sighed after a pause, "losing the enigma, her occult powers, the consistency of the invisible cloth. Poor Mulata! She went into decomposition. She went wormy inside, the way the sky goes wormy during an eclipse, and also, on the outside, her honey body grew scabby when she went to the aid of Yumí, who, changed into a fire hedgehog, was doing battle with a black rain spider, a loud spider with legs formed by fringes of shadow glass and jet."

And after a pause, her hand ready to open the door: "That Yumí was no stranger to witchcraft based on bristles. His first master wizards had been wild boars. He even called himself Hayumihaha. What is certain is that the Mulata, unable to do anything for Yumí as he fought with his fiery quills under the black rain that had spider eyes, a spider's body, paralyzed them with her white shadow from the moon, a fog stone that could turn to stone when she wanted it to, porous stone that could turn to marble if she wanted it to, and she has the reverse power, to turn stone or marble into fog, she had, that is, because now she has been dispossessed of her magic, and I must go help her so that they do not eat up light or shadow on her, silence or sound, those invisible things that surround us and which must be neutralized by our combining them, because otherwise they will destroy us."

And she went out muttering: "Whoever holds me, get out! Get out of my body! If he dances in front of me, I'll spit on his face! If he dances behind, I'll blow him a great wind with a blond mane! Goiter pain! Monkey mane! Woven frame and warpy lip of the sex of the 'dwarfy'! I was born face down, and when I die I'll be face up! Bat, protect me! Precious star! Mountain of stars! Let my word be a sound and true trickery! Let my word be the true deity as it faces the words of rebels and of cursers! Let the one who goes with me go before! Let the one who goes with me go behind! Go behind me, stone feather, male scorpion, bastard dart . . . me myself . . . me somebody else . . . me everybody . . . me forever!"

When the Cleaning Woman left, moon tallow skin and eyes of green bottle glass, the slam of the door made the house tremble, furniture and objects shook in the shadows that were rusty from the light of the candle, and when the sexton crossed the threshold of the bedroom where one could hear the virgin breathing as if she were scratching the rash with her respiration, he took as much time as the priest would take during the Gospel of some future Sunday to say, *"Quasi modo geniti infantes . . ."*

He jumped naked into the bed and nothing could be seen of him, like a person who has thrown himself head first into the water, until he could feel his body floating in a liquid absence of everything, turned inside out, such was his terror, with all of his organs on the outside, from his lungs and his heart to his snakelike intestines, and he on the inside, with his shining skin, aware of the love that his intestines, endless serpents, thick and thin, was making with the pockmarked snake of night that had wrapped him up. All of his inner meat market, blood, clots, humors, lungs, muscles, tendons, veins, arteries, membranes, lymph, in direct contact with the virgin with the golden rash.

"Breeding tiiime today! Breeding tiiime!" could be heard as it was shouted outside in the unmemory of the darkness.

Clutch . . . grab onto something . . . onto somebody who would not be the serpent that was pock-marked with reflections, fluid, mobile, moving in small sections of flooded fields . . . grab onto himself as he approached shoreless eternity, but how could he hold his body if it did not exist . . .

"Breeding tiiime today! Breeding tiiime!"

Go back to being himself in the midst of that ant hill of gestations that was overflowing the banks of the infinite night? Himself? How? Along the path of the snake that was lying with him (along the path of stretching out, stretching out, without knowing where he was stretching out to, giving of himself), lazy, tame, no larger than a small woman and in the waves of the carnal storm, carried away, enveloping (stretch, stretch, stretch, stretch), tumultuous, torrential (it could not be water, and it was water), foamy, foamy white fire (it could not be fire, and it was fire), downy, dark blue (it could not be the air, and it was the air) . . .

"Breeding tiiime today! Breeding tiiime!"

. . . and it was air, teeth of bubbles, devourer of moist earth, a petrified avalanche on the slopes of the hills, deep, piled up, the blindness of blind nights, the builders of cob-web-scaffolds set up to trap stars . . .

. . . the nickle-plated rash.

But how could he grab onto his body which did not exist and which felt happy at not existing . . .

fear . . . the only fear, everything that the material could become, a point, a line, a voice, a sound, a cramp. Oppose it! Oppose it before it was too late! Speed up fibers and senses and not let go, not let go of the virgin with a cold rash, with eyes of soft phosphorus and the breath of soil from which a plant with bitter flowers has been uprooted . . . not lose contact with the splashing of her liquid oceanic scales, with her lustrous skin of a world map with the unknown painted with the downiness of sleep . . . not get lost in the oily twisting of her gears as they go penetrating into the emptiness, the dumping place for one who does not come back or return (. . . who is chopping whom to pieces? . . . what a furious struggle! . . . how his thoughts were being chopped to pieces!) . . . touching reality . . . how horrible, how like a whipping . . . and how dangerous not being able to dream again about the throbbing virgin, replaced by the true serpent (the virgin's leg had no end, he was lengthening his foot to reach the instep of that little foot with the tips of his toes), yes, how dangerous not being able to feel (the snake was looking at him with the look of a naked woman) the virgin's breasts again, less hers as he kissed them (metal skin, reptile skin, he was reptile skin, slippery skin)—the woman whose breasts he kisses leaves them and goes away, goes away toward where he had been penetrating (it was obvious that he would not find her), moving his arms like a swimmer lost in the night of deep waters. It was dizzying, the snakelike darkness revolved and turned about to stop him from getting to the manikin (the virgin with a rash), made out of weightless wood and with needle marks from the needle of a woman in an interesting state who had been tied down with little dots, like scars, a talisman that was placed next to a smallpox victim so that the plague would not leave marks on his face. But . . . was it not a hallucination? . . . he was in bed with a . . . with that . . . the one that Suerto Rodríguez had been praying to on his knees . . . the same one . . . he could feel the shiver of sweat-blood . . . the taste of breath cut off in the mouth . . . paralyzed by that disgusting house reptile that ate rats, spiders, the sixth sense of the house, nightwalking, who went from the dining room to the kitchen, and from the kitchen to the bedrooms, in addition to the courtyards and roofs, with the eyes of a servant.

What did she think? What did the Cleaning Woman think a "virgin with a rash" was?

And now? What could he do, shut up in there? What could he do there, naked, shoeless, and with the door blocked by the tame reptile, courteous, bored, patient, well mannered, and, nevertheless, ready to block his way, because each time he approached, it gave a hissing grunt?

He left. Climbing on the tiles. He left under the stars and, wrapped in the sheets that he had used to get down from the roof, he fled through the streets, fearful of coming upon the Meat-Eating Mule, that furious mule that feeds on meat and walks through the streets early in the morning before the roosters crow, kicking on doors and biting those who were not complying with the command to breed.

"Breeding tiiime today! Breeding tiiime!"

"We're hard at it!"

"Breed . . . time . . . day!"

"Today and tomorrow and every day. I'm a newlywed!"

From all the doors and windows in Tierrapaulita there came male voices from husbands or lovers intent on procreation with their partners. And at the house where there was no answer, where a man and woman capable of breeding lived, the storm of kicks from the Meat-Eating Mule would not be long in coming.

But the Meat-Eating Mule was not walking that night. His legs were getting weak. The sexual decoy. A little virgin with a rash. A trick. A trick of witchcraft. The hazy moon among the greeting clouds. And how long had he been asleep? Whom did he ask, the cats? A dog howled in front of a tree. He was howling because his smell told him that the wood of that trunk would be used for a coffin. Coff-coff-coffin for whooooooo! . . . the howls grew longer, coff-coff-coffin for whooooooo! And the tree was weeping leaves. The sheet got caught between his buttocks, which he was holding tight together out of fear, the sheet that was covering his back, because he was tripping on the other one as he advanced with long steps, longer and longer, almost falling down. He did not know—who would ever know —until he got to the parish house . . . this street, and the next, and the next, and the next, he never thought that he had been so far away from the central square . . . somebody . . . some light . . . the silence . . . the watchman . . . they were wobbling . . . it was quaking . . . punishment . . . punishment . . . no . . . no . . . it was not Saint James on his horse . . . it was Father Chimalpín, mounted, riding the Meat-Eating Mule . . . where was it taking him? . . . where was it not taking him? . . . this way . . . that way . . . what that bestial animal was trying to do was throw him . . . it ran . . . it bucked . . . it lowered its head between its legs . . . it raised its legs into the air . . . it warped . . . it turned and turned and turned, just like a top or like air that comes out of a whirlwind, raising clouds of dust as it disappeared with the priest on top, his cassock hitched up, his clerical hat down around his ears, his face so pale that it looked more like a skull . . .

It Is Quaking on the Moon

. . . among fallen-down houses . . . some with two stories
. . . houses with two stories that were sitting down, left with
one story, he was advancing, he thought he was advancing,
but he was retreating instead, Jerónimo, staggering to the
rhythm of the buildings that were drawing away from each
other, drawing away from their centers of gravity, and
suddenly they would come back . . . the finest of feathers
. . . the finest of plumes, the palms . . . like dusters in the
hand of the earthquake as they brushed the walls so that
they would fall down nice and clean . . . but oh! oh! . . .
one almost lopped off his arm . . . it pulled off his sheet . . .
rip-rip-rip, as it knocked him down . . . he might as well
crawl . . . it had given them no time to escape . . . a few
were saved . . . the sleep-eaters, however, remained asleep
under the weight of their ceilings and walls . . . threads of
blood that the thirsty lime of whitewashed walls dried up at
once . . . they were centuries that were sucking blood . . .
it was quaking . . . main beams fell down and buried themselves point first among frameworks of curled-up crossbeams
that were licked by the little red tongues of the tile roofs
as they fell . . . water from the faucets giving itself a bath
. . . itself . . . bathing itself all alone as the earth swung,
sprinkling, splashing, pouring out . . . so different from the
liquid that was coming out of broken pipes and which,
for a moment, maintained its shape of a liquid snake . . .
someone held him back . . . a bloody mass that grabbed at
him before it fell . . . others came out . . . they fled . . .
the ground was dancing . . . the Meat-Eating Mule! . . . the
Meat-Eating Mule! . . . who said that? . . . he said it, standing up, he had managed to stand . . . Santano! . . . Santano!
. . . he ran over . . . dead . . . dead in his nightshirt . . . the

rats were roaming among his poisons . . . long tails . . .
little pink mouths . . . little eyes of light that peeped
through glass of yellow, blue, greenish, whitish substances
. . . beyond death, nothingness . . . nothingness, Santano,
Saint Anus, Saint Badthief in a sailor's undershirt with
black stripes underneath his nightshirt and the drugstore
on top of him . . . the oils . . . the alcohols . . . the essences
. . . the nothingness, Santano, the nothingness . . . and the
repugnant smell of syrups! . . . exact . . . the exact clocks,
so exact, had stopped at . . . it was impossible to see . . . it
was quaking . . . it was still quaking . . . that is to say, the
ruination was making the city deeper . . . penetrating it
. . . from the surface of everyday life . . . the hallway
with people, the cornices with doves, the cobbler surrounded by clusters of old shoes, the flowers from the
window sills squashed under the pieces of pots, gratings, and
the earth that had held them, upset and still wet from the
sprinkler . . . with little holes . . . from the sprinkler . . .
last night, before going to bed (forever) . . . that big girl
. . . now she is lying sunken with the bedsprings, ribs and
lungs plowed under, fresh hair, young, and the old wool of
the mattress . . . there is no inside or outside . . . there are
no houses or streets . . . everything is outside and inside
. . . everything is house and street . . . he stopped . . . he
could barely stand with the weaving of the earth . . . he
stopped to wrap himself better in the sheets that the
Cleaning Woman had put on the bridal bed . . . wedding
. . . connubial . . . epithalamium . . . fuck! . . . he drew
out some splinters of a laugh from between his incisors and
swallowed hair, which is what one swallows when one is
enraged . . . little virgin with a rash . . . what if the healer
prescribed it and the priest went . . . he would die right
there of fright . . . the evil girl became a snake . . . orient
himself . . . get there . . . get to the church soon . . . but
how could he orient himself without streets? . . . he . . .
he . . . he was up in the air . . . grab on . . . but on to what,
because everything was falling . . . there was no longer any
place to put his feet . . . there was no stable ground . . .
the ground was there and it was not . . . it was not and it
was . . . he fell to the ground . . . cold . . . nausea . . .
deafened, and not because the underground rumble was

loud . . . no . . . no . . . the proof was that he could hear the peeping of the swallows who were escaping . . . it was deafening, and it was all due to the falling of the depths into the depths . . . the wall . . . the wall opposite . . . he crawled as best he could . . . a cloud of dust, just like a big sheet . . . naked . . . no . . . no . . . he pulled on his sheet . . . two . . . no . . . one . . . well . . . you can't get into bed with the virgin dressed . . . the earth was not quaking . . . it was quaking on the moon . . . they were right, the ones who said . . . destruction on the moon that looked as close as the palm of one's hand in that immense solitude . . . quick . . . so quick that right then . . . those things were forming . . . crawling . . . what? . . . what do you mean, what? . . . crawling to get away . . . from the "lovely" who was raising her head as if searching . . . as if searching . . . he grabbed a stick . . . a stick is so immaterial in the moonlight that it seemed as if he were grasping a bunch of wet rays . . . but he did not stop, he continued on among lambs with so much light on them that they seemed to be made of silver, wild boars over six feet long who cast immense shadows, rapid deer who materialized and just as quickly disappeared . . . he was looking for the Cleaning Woman, just like a dog who has lost his master . . . he was the dog . . . he was going along, unable to get up, on his hands and feet . . . gravity . . . what an atrocious thing . . . no one knows . . . the curved dome of the church . . . he managed to see it . . . the curving . . . the clouds of dust . . . everything falling to pieces and coming up out of the structures, solid just a moment ago, those great clouds, orange, gray, opaque, without joints, hiding the trees torn up, not by the wind, by their roots, by a subterranean wind in their roots, a shaking that was boiling . . . a cold boiling . . . grasshoppers . . . hopping frogs . . . strange multiplications of the holes of blind vermin who were seeking the moon . . . he picked up what was left of the sheet, dust-covered, muddy, bloody, and along with the sheet age-old cobwebs, heavy, black with shadows and wet soot . . . cobwebs bathed in the urine of a madman can cure madness . . . a different atmosphere . . . horror . . . it was not fantasy . . . the trees with a base of tall roots that had come tumbling out

331

of the earth, wet with the sweat of someone giving birth under the moon that looked so close to all who saw it that they thought it was going to land on top of them . . . what an affliction . . . what an intimidation . . . no . . . no . . . do not let the earth lose its last moon . . . other moons had fallen to pieces just like that . . . the Meat-Eating Mule did not stop . . . what did it matter to the infernal beast that the moon was falling down . . . that the trees were growing like green shadows over their many-storied roots that went up to the sky, since it had Father Chimalpín mounted on its back . . . but the mule was not the only thing that was bucking, the whole earth was . . . hills and valleys in soapy waves were pushed against the grain by serpentine fissures that flowed along roads torn out like pieces of hairy skin, along with the breaking of bubbling water that ran to hide itself from the moon . . . "Ding, dong, ding . . . sexton, sing, where are the bells, make them ring! . . . Sexton, sing, make them ring . . . make them ring . . . where are the bells, make them ring!" . . . that was what Father was shouting to the rhythm of the jumping mule as he beat the hoofs of his hands in time to the beating of the hoofs of the mule that were going ding, dong, ding . . . which also seemed to be asking . . . "Sexton, sing . . . sexton, sing . . . the bells, the bells . . . make them ring!" . . . and he was able to hear it, because as fast as his feet would carry him, he was following the evil meat-eating beast that did not go forward as if in headlong flight, but would stop in its diabolical bucking, a flip to the right, a flip to the left, as if trying to unscrew all of its mulish tantrums, without paying much heed to the rider on its back with his cassock hitched up, his hat down over his ears, pale, unhinged, toothy, a skull, he was already dead or about to die, without saddle or blanket, stuck to the very hair of the beast by some kind of enchantment or other . . . finally, *ding, dong, ding,* he was left behind, because he ran out of breath, the sheet soaked in sweat, *ding, dong, ding,* as he now thought it was funny to be called . . . now that the bells were no longer there . . . fallen . . . sticking like leeches to a shoulder of the dome that had been disjointed from the apse . . . He raised his eyes up to the sky . . . not a cloud . . . indigo . . . completely indigo . . . not even stars . . . barely visible in

the powerful nearby light of the moon that was about to fall
and where, judging from the shaking of the earth, it was
still quaking . . . worse, if the Meat-Eating Mule carried him
off to the moon . . . one jump of that beast . . . it could
do it . . . the immense disk looked so close . . . it kept on
bucking . . . it was part of the earth that had taken it into
its head to shake off everything on top of it . . . church
. . . buildings . . . houses . . . he rolled his eyes about all of
the heights that closed him in, as if in a hole with no way
to get out, looking at Tierrapaulita, in a fervent effort to
find out where the mule was going with Father . . . eyes that
cannot see . . . he did not say it . . . he would have liked
his thought to have a tongue so that he could bite it . . .
Chimalpín, more than just his superior, was an old companion from his earliest schooldays . . . and what he had
got himself into . . . alas! . . . because he had not listened
and had made fun of that old parish priest who spoke like a
hoarse rooster when he had returned from this out-of-the-
way place telling about everything the devils had done to
him . . . what a funny little priest! . . . how old-fashioned!
. . . thinking that natural forces, earthquakes and hurricanes, were the work of the Devil . . . and talking about
giants, as if we were in the age of Enoch! . . . he said all
of that, and how funny it had been, with feigned surprise
and discreet laughter, along with looks loaded with intention
when he spoke about the coconuts that had the sex of
urinating women on them . . . and what was all that, what
was it: a children's game, the tricks of primitive devils,
compared to what had happened to them since Chimalpín
had challenged Candanga on that Good Friday . . . no, no
. . . nothing about eyes that cannot see . . . even if they
don't see, it hurts me! . . . oh, healer, you evil man! . . .
that they stripped him, that's the least . . . it's going to toss
him off a cliff . . . it would have been better if he'd been
left with the smallpox scars . . . ugly . . . yes . . . very ugly
. . . like scars of the worst kind of pox, fat, black . . . it
would be wise for him to look for some clothes . . . but
where, since the cloister was on the ground and the Cleaning
Woman's house was also on the ground . . . where he had
got undressed and where he would not return in order not
to meet the virgin with a rash . . . it would be better for him

to continue on with his dirty sheet, repulsive, unable to touch himself . . . it's going to drive him mad . . . it can drive him mad . . . of course it can drive him mad . . . the beast bucking and the earth bucking, running wild . . . and all the while the other one was talking Latin to the mule, who was turning, turning, turning around, yes, he was crazy, crazy like the fellow from Assisi with the wolf . . . and let's see, what was he proposing to it, what was he proposing . . . it ate flesh . . . flesh . . . flesh . . . a beast of flesh on which he was riding . . . yes, only madness can make a miracle possible, the beginning of a miracle . . . the madness of talking for the sake of talking, of not complaining . . . being silent . . . being mute . . . the final fascination of the successive death . . . not just the first one . . . not just the first death . . . after that first death there are other deaths . . . someone between the honey, and in this case unfaithful, funny, goes . . . something makes him stick . . . it was flesh-eating . . . flesh . . . flesh . . . intolerable . . . should (he?) destroy it? . . . destroy . . . annihilate . . . burn . . . (he?) . . . the beast . . . the flesh-eating beast . . . the one who feeds on flesh . . . without a male you, without a female I, he said, and he struck the neck with his open hand, a handsaw with horse-hair teeth, the neck of the animal, and prodigy of prodigies, it obeyed him, and he should order it to stop bucking . . . the earth and the mule . . . the mule and the earth . . . demons and animals with long and short hair become tame from being talked to . . . a strange language . . . mulish . . . uncountable wrinkles of forest shadows hung in the emptiness on the disk of the moon . . . the inverted vision, from the earth to the sky in folds of gigantic frogs, mute, titanic cyclopses . . . who was speaking to whom . . . now the mule was talking to . . . sane . . . it had become sane . . . now the one who was demanding that it buck was he . . . more than the earth and the sky that was drinking in blue, without a single cloud, with the coldness of liquid slate . . . sand banks . . . white thorns . . . landing places for lakelike stars . . . what a gigantic ant, this one . . . and that other one . . . thin working-class cathedrals in the contraband of the starry fireflies that came sailing in . . .

why wasn't it bucking . . . where was it going, so tame
. . . because it had stopped quaking on the moon . . . in
the hollow palm of that fingerless hand . . . trying, without
fingers, to grab things . . . cloud things . . . bird things
. . . dream things . . . the silence which is weightless . . .
the wind . . . the air . . . the miracle . . . the light madness
. . . where was it taking him . . . trees of lice that were
peeping out . . . it quaked, or it was the subterranean
shaking . . . the calisthenics of the earth that continued on
. . . they were not peeping lice . . . that was what they
were called, trees of peeping lice . . . but he went close and
saw . . . trees of eyes that went peep . . . peep . . . like
little chicks that were only eyes . . . eyes like eggs without
shells . . . "Peep . . . peep . . . peeping, all eyes, all lice!
. . . Peep . . . peep . . . peeping, eye, lie, lice!" . . . he would
have kept on repeating, if the mule had not taken a stumble
and made the folds in his stomach jump and left him almost in the air, as it bumped its rump on the ground . . .
but could he beat that animal with . . . because of the
meat-eating business, just one person . . . because he too
was a flesh-eating beast, except on days of abstinence . . .
very rational, but very meat-eating . . . another country?
. . . no, the same one, but in the moonlight it looked like
another world . . . rough . . . ragged . . . whipped by op-
posing winds . . . the noiseless walking of the sleep-walkers
. . . those who eat dreams become earth . . . ant hill earth
. . . and that was where he was going . . . it could not be . . .
a sign . . . a sign announcing with all its letters . . . "Child
Factory" . . . it's mine . . . it's mine . . . it's mine . . . he
repeated to himself without cease . . . ah! . . . ha! . . .
this is where the evil one has his clandestine factory for
making children! . . . he remembered all of his exorcists
. . . he would insult him . . . he would insult him . . . he can
only be conquered by being insulted . . . vituperation . . .
scoffing . . . affront . . . vile slander . . . theological insults
above all . . . that would make him beside himself, and the
Devil outside of himself loses everything and is easy prey
to grab . . . he would grab him and he could put his factory
for making children on the moon . . . with frozen tears,
such was his emotion as he wept thanks, and he would have

335

leaned over and kissed the mule, if that beast had been kissable, which, as if it did not want him to read the sign, turned quickly from right to left and suddenly stopped and did it in reverse . . . make him sick . . . that was what it was trying to do . . . but they were already inside the factory . . . the great snail . . . the great snail drew out his head with little horns . . . he seemed to be blindly seeking the moon . . . the air was like glass . . . a dream of glass . . . the air is a dream of glass . . . the smaller snails were moving with the movement of the dew . . . and others even smaller . . . and some almost invisible . . . the breaks in the earth made them move with startling slowness through the brittle silence that was being broken by their wild musical touch, percussive, syllabled . . . he could not dismount, stuck to the hair of the mule, as he tried to rise, it gave a whinny with volcanic lungs . . . kicks instead of rocks . . . dust instead of sulphureous vapors . . . although there was something of brimstone, because it had farted, farts of roasted meat, and it did not stop any more, even if the rider did not ask it, was not going to explain to it that he wanted to relieve it of his weight, it was still enough for it to hunch over little by little, as if authorizing him to get off. He did so rapidly, and he took hold of the first piece of wood at hand . . . insult him with everything an exorcist had, and if he came upon him, a whack . . . a whack and the name of Jesus . . . an underlying clarity, rosy dawn and roses, which had nothing to do with the bright moon above that was tightening its silvery glow that soaked him with luminous little points, and in an instant he felt himself a prisoner in a rose garden of miniature roses, but the roses disappeared and in the place of roses, snails stuck to his skin, and they were speaking to him . . . *turutric* . . . *turutric* . . . *turutric* . . . and the oozy things were covering him with a sticky coating . . . *turutric* . . . *turutric* . . . he began to scratch . . . those things were really smallpox . . . immense smallpox stuck to his skin . . . impossible to get them off . . . he was being skinned alive, and as soon as what seemed to be a scab fell off . . . another snail climbed on . . . *turutric* . . . *turutric* . . . *rututurotric* . . . *rututurotric* . . . we want to be born . . . we want to be born . . . he closed his eyes to hear better . . . *rututurotric* . . . *rututu-rotric* . . . we want to be born . . . we want to be born . . . we are . . . what we are . . . what we are . . . but we want to be . . . we want to be . . . and Your Worship is opposed . . . why are you opposed . . . why is he already in life and does not want to let others enter . . . why is he opposed to breeding . . . he gave a worse leap than the mule, and began to beat all around him with the piece of wood, as if he really were clubbing someone, and he was so blinded that we went over and gave a huge clout to the mule, who had a kick ready for him and was already coming over to bite him when a burst of wind held it back, twisted it, paralyzed, enough time for all the trees to become covered with snails and mollusks with long and short drool, the slaver lathered down like a beard . . . we want to be born! . . . we want to be born! . . . we are creatures of life and no one will give it to us! . . . why are they going to leave us here in the trees and on the ground and under the ground, on stones and under stones, in the water and in the sand, where there are grubs and dampness, the filth and stagnation of water? . . . how is it that there is an ingrate who is opposed? . . . we are creatures, we are not slugs or snails . . . human creatures! . . . but who will give us human shape as long as Father Chimalpín is opposed? . . . He heard no more . . . it was monstrous, trees without birds, with snails that were moving about like little eyes of children that were damp with hope . . . the rancorous mule drew back every time he approached . . . if it was not the Devil who was helping him and if it was the Devil too . . . he ought to get back to Tierrapaulita as soon as possible . . . *tutututurotric!* . . . *tutututurotric!* . . . we want to be born! . . . we want to be born! . . . as long as he lived he would not forget those things that were not voices . . . a kind of music . . . a kind of music . . . what a sweet demand, wanting to be born . . . how just . . . how divine . . . coming into life . . . he spoke again to his meat-eating companion, and it burled its wrath with a sequence of blinks, while Chimalpín got back up on its spine . . . *tuturutric!* . . . *tuturutric!* . . . he was already going far away and he could still hear the distant ticking of the stellar

337

snails, those in whom life was latent, hyaline . . . spectral
. . . without stirrups . . . without reins, he was descending,
bathed in the nickel-plated glow of the moon, his cassock
drawn up, his clerical hat over his ears, disjointed, without
the pock marks now . . . he passed and passed again his
hand over his cheeks, his forehead, his nose, his ears, his
chin, nervously using the tips of all his fingers, that was
what he had two hands for, to make sure that it was true
that the bucking of the Meat-Eating Mule had taken away
all the pricks that cursed hedgehog had given him . . .
telepathy between the rational and the irrational . . . a
communication of thought . . . the mule stopped to drink
some water in a puddle and from there, among the waves
and bubbles that the water was making as the animal was
tonguing it, snorting in the liquid, while it moved its head,
with both nostrils, he looked at himself with his face clean
of pits . . . no, the tremor did not shake him, it was two
women, a big one like a sergeant, whom Jerónimo does not
recognize at the moment, and a dirty one whom he had seen
once before . . . a familiar face . . . of course, the tumblings
. . . not the tumblings . . . the bucking of the beast was
going to drive him mad . . . but he . . . he wanted to follow
it . . . he followed it without reaching it and there he was
with his nakedness and his little sheet, shoeless, sockless, in
the open, fleeing from the danger of everything that was a
wall or a roof, his eyes crawling with dreams, dreams that
cannot be slept, awake dreams . . . it has stopped quaking
. . . they shake him . . . they tell him to stop . . . but he does
not listen to them, he stays on the ground . . . stop for
what? . . . so that the ground will buck again and he will
feel like a drunkard and have to sniff along the whitewash
of some wall . . . better to be sitting down the way he was on
the hot rubble . . . it was a nice warm life inside the houses
. . . the fallen houses still kept their warmth . . . "Hey,
Sheet!" . . . one of them is talking to him . . . "Sheet!"
. . . it was the old woman who was talking . . . she did not
recognize him . . . calling him "Sheet" . . . the Cleaning
Woman calling him that, as if she did not know his name,
Jerónimo de la Degollación, Santo Panza of the Quixote
Chimalpín . . . but what kind of a Saint Panza . . . he

had stayed behind, while the other one was going off to nowhere on the meat-eater . . . "Hey, Sheet" . . . the other woman shook him, the younger and thinner one . . . an ash-coated container ready for baking . . . And since he did not respond to that "Sheet" business, they went away . . . the stars were shining clearly down over the ruins . . . dreams were being volatilized and nothing was left . . . there in the distance . . . ears emptied out . . . in the distance . . . the Cleaning Woman talking hot and fast . . . "You haven't told me that secret, Mulata . . ." The night smelled of piles of straw wet with dew. "The secret?" that poor unfortunate doubted. It could not be the Mulata, it could not be, so young. The moon was shining more and more strongly . . . "Yes, the secret! . . ." the Cleaning Woman insisted. "I will point with my finger, and in that direction you will find a house that must be visible at this hour, the house of the great sorcerers, a very large house . . . go in without knocking and . . ." when she realized that Sheet was approaching, the Mulata lowered her voice and she barely made herself heard . . . "He's very old, he can't defend himself, he's paralyzed and he has bones of gold . . ." "Luckily it's stopped quaking . . ." Sheet observed as he came up to the two women, "but there are piles of dead people" . . . "And all of this is just as certain as a dream . . ." answered the Mulata, who could not be she, so young, but she looked so much like her, only if she were her daughter . . . her daughter? . . . but the Mulata . . . "Where did you say it was?" the Cleaning Woman interrupted . . . The Mulata raised her hand and pointed with her forefinger . . . and the Cleaning Woman disappeared . . . Sheet shrugged all over . . . behind the Cleaning Woman slid the snake that was following her like a dog . . . "Sheet" . . . he heard that the unbaked, not the baked, vessel was speaking to him (women are baked, just like vessels), but he too, under that dirty sheet without stitching, had some breaks in him, and that is why they say that an unbaked woman can always find a man with breaks in him . . . "Sheet, I know you very well . . ." "And I know you, at least I know your . . . I don't know . . . you're your daughter, you're the daughter of the one I knew . . ."

"Yes, I'm the daughter . . . I'm the daughter of the one I am . . . I'm my daughter . . . I'm my mother . . ." (Which is going to drive him mad . . . if this one who has his feet on the ground, it's true that it's bucking, is already nutty, what can my dear Father be like, riding that most abominable of beasts, the Meat-Eating Mule.) "Ah, yes, yes," Sheet answered, "you are your own daughter, you are your mother and you are your daughter . . ."

They both laughed, so as not to bite each other, they were so close again, never as before, when he had her with him, inside of him, like a poison that was sustaining him . . . No, it couldn't be she . . . impossible that she was the same one . . . "And what became of your mother?" Sheet ventured, shooing away a cloud of black flies, sticky from the moon. "Didn't you know? Coyotes tore her to pieces." "But you were left . . ." Sheet made his voice roguish, almost amorous. "But the way I was left . . . dispossessed of everything . . ." "Everybody is dispossessed of everything . . ." and Sheet turned his eyes to the ruins that had been Tierrapaulita. "Didn't you lose anything?" she asked him. "Not much . . ." "Well, I lost my magic . . . my occult powers . . . my power of enchantment . . ." "One couldn't tell . . ." Sheet insinuated . . . but she gave no sign that she knew she was the object of his veiled flirtation . . . now he has me outside, the Mulata was thinking, a Mulata of unbaked clay, but just the same as when he had me inside, because we're in the same tremor . . . They had grown silent . . . under their feet . . . they had to grab each other so as not to fall down . . . grab each other . . . embrace each other . . . and the tremor continued outside and inside . . . the earth and their bodies . . . "Let's flee . . ." she proposed . . . he trembled at the thought . . . how could he flee Tierrapaulita without knowing where the Father had gone with *his* mule . . . it was *his* mule now . . . "Let's flee . . . my sign is the moon . . . your sign" (she was addressing him familiarly now) "is water of teeth" . . . "Let's flee . . . I must live . . . they unmade me and they made me again, but what good is it for them to have made me young . . . a virgin . . ." (another snake, thought Sheet, cured of frights) "they took away from me, they did not

340

leave me a single little piece of mystery, for having come out in defense of the Square Deity, the Chief of the Four Corners, incarnate, my story is so sad, in one of the most formidable sorcerers of Tierrapaulita, Celestino Yumí, but Celestino Yumí, changed into a hedgehog, was not fighting with any devil, but against a spider of black rain . . ." "Ah, ah, ah . . ." exclaimed Sheet. "What he did not know was that Candanga, the Devil of God, the Devil of Heaven, the Christian, whom I was representing, at the same time that he was in me and I was in a possessed sexton, was hiding in the body of the spider that was the priest and who was also demonized, do you understand me, Sheet, do you understand me? . . . My role was to fight against the evil spirit lodged in the body of Yumí, who was the Infernal Christian Prince, and against the latter I fought to the utmost, he tried to ruin me with the dirty story of his small-pox, but I opposed him with the vain but historical tale of the Chamber-Potters, and there we were . . ." Sheet was far removed from what the old woman turned young was talking about, that mother of herself, desubstantiated as a child-bearer and reformed as a daughter, because he was thinking about the Meat-Eating Mule, an infuriated beast who was going about removing the marks of the smallpox from the one who would have been better off if he had remained a spider with eleventhousand legs, with the devil inside and all, because the devil inside is a guarantee, a guarantee, after all, because since he takes care of himself, he takes care of the person, and outside he is always an enemy and a threat . . . "Oh, yes . . . yes . . ." Sheet blinked and bit his lips and on his lips what he was going to depose, deny, rather, because in the mouth of this person who said that she was the daughter of the other one and that she was the same certain Mulata, except without her magic, there was trickery, slyness, left-handedness . . . first she had attacked him, changed into a hedgehog already, and then she had run into the church to fight with the tonsured spider with the black cassock and eleventhousand legs, but he kept quiet . . . "Sheet, we have to flee," she insisted, "we have to escape from here before it's too late . . . destruction on the moon and in Tierrapaulita, neither houses nor streets . . ." He

341

could not, Sheet could not, it was impossible for him, Father had gone off to hear a confession very far away, and he should be back at any moment, if he was coming back . . . he lost his voice . . . the animal that the relatives of the one who was dying had brought for him so that he could go where that person wanted to vomit up his sins was, was an evil animal . . . meat-eating, he continued with the thought . . . happy with his lie . . . with his big lie . . . "Funny!" she answered him, her lips without blood, her eyes without glow, what she could have done with the flesh of those lips, and the mirror of those eyes, if they had not deprived her of her power as intermediary between the real and the unreal . . . Sheet faltered downward as he heard her say that, while she gathered up her hair, black, but blond now from the dust . . . "Funny!" because there was nothing funny about it . . . stupid woman . . . neither in the truth nor in the lie, riding a Meat-Eating Mule because of the ingratitude of the healer, or mounted on an unbroken beast . . . the air . . . the air . . . the air is not moving . . . she said, he thought . . . everything was in suspension . . . the leaves . . . the leaves . . . not seeing the leaves moving . . . awake, because they were awake, they looked awake, like the stones, like the vegetables in the gardens, like the fruits in the orange groves, like dogs, like the cats, the big birds, the song birds, the hens, the roosters, the turkeys, the *pijijes* who were not sleeping, awake, suspended by threads of moonlight, visible, and by invisible threads of what they were expecting to happen . . . what . . . what . . . what was going to happen that had not already happened in that town of people who were gray-haired from the dust of ruins, white with dust, their noses walled up with mucus and dust, and the dry wrinkles of their lips like cracks in the dry ground . . . the heavy step of the Cleaning Woman could be heard in the distance . . . but first, long before she appeared, following the whimsical geometry of chaos and delirium of fallen-down walls and fences, the lake-green greasy snake came first, its eyes so far apart, almost fallen to the sides of its hewn head, and it lifted up its neck, as if to see if they were there, understanding like a dog, although, closer now, its movements were heavy, it was

scraping as it crawled from the weight it had on top of it
. . . a bundle of golden bones that were shining in the timid
glow of the moonlight . . . Sheet became alarmed to the
point of losing his breath, he did not like the sight of
snakes, it cut his body, and less that unfortunate there,
changed into something less without her poisonous fangs,
without her pouches of poison, changed into a whore
and a servant, the one who recalled the sight of Suerto
Rodríguez, the big kneeling man that he had seen through
the keyhole, and, worst of all, which had anointed his
face, a laughable cruelty, his adventure with the fantastic
virgin with a rash, making the small sheet he was wrapped
in heavier on him, and because of which he now had
even lost his name, they called him "Sheet," his *nom de
guerre,* no . . . his *nom de catastrophe* . . . he thought
about the sacred vessels . . . the chalices, the ciborium
. . . the monstrance . . . but right there, no matter what
it might cost, he would get them back . . . the Cleaning
Woman was capable of everything, if they were capable
. . . no . . . better not to think about Father . . . his skin
was growing cold . . . The dispossessed Mulata remained
impassive, oh how she needed her magic splendor to
celebrate properly the deboning of Yumí's golden skeleton, the meticulous crawling of the envoy who was bringing her the enchanting bone structure as a present, luminous,
that of the potent young man she had met at the fair,
next to his good friend Timoteo Teo Timoteo, riding a
fine horse, harness and saddle embossed with pieces of
silver, and the magnificent sorcerer who had married her
in a Requiem Mass for all, for all of death . . . the
Cleaning Woman did not appear . . . what could have
happened to her . . . Sheet, what could have happened to
her . . . was she crushed by some falling stone? . . . there
are so many walls standing but on the point of falling, and
they fall down and no trace of someone passing by . . .
But they had heard her coming, walking, heavily, loud . . .
it was enough to drive one mad that she had been coming
toward them . . . that she was coming . . . coming . . . and
not arriving . . . she was probably still approaching after
she was dead . . . the ears . . . wrinkled plates of vertical

balances, auditive, weighers of the silence of the depths ... such a mystery ... the mystery of those steps that were coming toward them ... The snake, stretched out under the moon, was waiting for them to remove the bundle of bones of reddish, fleshy gold ... "Sheet, why don't you take a look to see if she's coming!" ... she was using formal address again, the formal "you" is solemn and that moment was too, "along the trail of the snake, she was getting Yumí's bones ... Can't you hear her steps, Sheet? Can't you hear her steps?" ... Sheet moved his head, at least it looked affirmative to her ... "Who served as acolyte at that Mass the night I married Yumí for the rest of my death?" she asked unexpectedly when she saw Sheet standing where he was, without moving, in spite of the fact that she had asked him to see if the Cleaning Woman was coming ... the steps continued ... the steps continued ... if everybody buried in the ruins of Tierrapaulita began to walk ... if all the dead began to walk ... the earth would be full of steps ... "Move, man, you look dead!" ... and he moved and Sheet was dead, a short time back, a long time back, it did not matter, after death the first minute is already eternity ... his eyes open ... yes ... that had fooled her ... "I'm sorry!" she tried to babble ... he was damp, cold, sticky, lean, hair white from earthquake dust ... his teeth closed tight, biting the emptiness ... Without losing time, the steps went away, she untied Yumí's golden bones from on top of the snake, her back to the moon to cover the theft with her shadow, but in a luminous trickle of brightness, in storms of light, the lunar rays passed through her transparent body and lit things up as she leaned over the snake and untied the bundle ...

From among the ruins the powerful Niniloj, the mother witch, stood up. Her lament for Yumí was flowing beneath her mask of dust. He had died when the house fell in. His head had been crushed. The rest of his body, intact. But someone had quartered him, someone who doubtless had known that he had a skeleton of hard gold. And it was not like that at all. Pure legend. His bones were white, sponges of lime and other substances. Let him have a good road to travel. The whole night is nothing but eyes. What good are

they to see where he plants his feet on the other side.
Only his head crushed. The rest of his body intact. That was
how he went. The moonlight tastes like a woman's milk.
His skin, his head, and his bones, all together, I will bury
them as soon as it dawns. Day will soon be painted. It's
already time, but the sun is afraid to come out and see what
the big moon that was out last night has done. The earth
was quaking so close by that the quiet atmosphere of Tierrapaulita also began to quake and underneath the town too.
Mutilated? The church and some other buildings mutilated. The rest on the ground, the way a person falls down
with an attack. And with their dwellers inside. Few were
saved. Looking like canoes, the buildings on the hills were
sinking into the earth that was moving like water, opening
and closing in a maddened wave. His head crushed. His
body intact. Some time, some time it had to happen, Yumí,
but not like that, it was like a betrayal that way, and
worse was the impertinence of quartering your corpse that
was intact, like the one of this poor fellow knocked down
over here . . . He had no time . . . She took out a small
sheet . . . Oh, God, the dead, their look goes dry on the
altar of cloudbursts! To be dead is similar to when it begins
to rain and rain and one goes to bed watching it rain and
rain for days and nights. I'd better cross myself . . . she
did not really raise her hand, and if she raised it, it was
merely to splash her forehead with the sign of the cross, as
a rain of fine earth fell on her, thicker, thicker, stones,
clods . . . she tucked her old woman's face into the darkness of the moon covered by an enormous . . . she could
not see what . . . to close her eyes . . . and she moaned
. . . the weight . . . the weight of everything that was
falling on top of her . . . she would not be able to move
. . . where she began, her legs, her feet, her buttocks sucked
dry like old rags . . . her teats like potatoes, just a shell,
and it was beginning to pile up around her and she could
no longer remove it . . . she drew out her arms . . . it
meant something to be that way . . . to have her hands
free . . . to use them against the mass of the mountains
that were falling down on Tierrapaulita . . .

When day was painted on the sky, Father Chimalpín appeared on the mule, which was treading here and treading there and unable to decide how to come down anywhere, because nowhere could it find a path from up above to down below, a path that led to town . . .

"Breeding tiiime today! . . . Breeding tiiime! . . ." he came along the road shouting like the devil, prepared to enter Tierrapaulita shouting like that so that no more little children would be reduced to mollusks for lack of procreators, progenitors.

But where could he shout, to whom could he shout?

"Breeding tiiime! Breeding tiiime today!" for there was no longer anything because there was nothing left of Tierrapaula, as it was called by the inhabitants who liked up-to-date names, covered by mountains that had slipped down like clouds as they rubbed against the disk of the moon, so close to the earth that summer, the highest peaks of the Sierra Madre, part of the Andean chain, a slipping followed by an avalanche, not of snow, but of white light, fire of the lava family, "white fire," worse than volcanic lava, which is black fire, it consumed, it evaporated, it dissolved, what the sorcerers and soothsayers called *the thing that goes beyond us,* and what people from former times used to talk about without loosening their tongues very much, their eyes like little flies in front of the webs of their wrinkles, it was a fire so terrible that it had done in other cities what it had done to them, on a fixed date, according to what was written in the hieroglyphics of the *table of astronomies.*

A total muteness. Not only of what is communication, tongue, language, speech, song, noise . . . The silence, the silence itself was also silent between the earth and the sky, while the day painted itself along with immense feathers of fire, along which, on even more luminous grooves, furrows of little colored feathers ran as they piled up, pushed by who knows what wind, toward the place where Tierrapaulita had been and was only buried, and from which Father Chimalpín could not take away his eyes, as if from looking into the midst of that sea of tumbled mountains, from staring and staring at the same spot, his eyes were able to penetrate toward the bottom until they found it. Suddenly he touched

346

his cassock . . . he had the feeling that he had lost something . . . something that he was missing . . . he turned from one side to the other, probing . . . searching . . . and he touched himself again. He did not give it any importance. He did not give it any importance, but the Meat-Eating Mule was not there. Was that what he was looking for? He refused to confess it to himself . . . and he preferred to cross himself, but when he raised his arm, his hand was lost in the air, it did not reach his forehead, it fell apart on him, it was not there, just as the mule was not there either and had left no trace.

He left off . . . who? . . . he could not see very much and just a thin thread of noise was perforating his ear. He did not recognize them until he was in the ambulance. They did not look like stretcher-bearers, but people from another planet, by their clothes, by their movements.

Another day and still no diagnosis.

His teeth, yes, his teeth, how strange, they were growing . . . his ears too . . . and his fingers . . . and his nose . . .

Yes, it was that kind of leprosy, but . . . (he laughed beneath his sheets as the doctors left) he would not turn into an elephant . . . if he told them about the business of the spider with eleventhousand legs . . . he had pock marks without ever having had smallpox . . . that should be told to the resident physician . . . it was an antecedent . . . he called him . . . the knob for the bell was growing smaller and smaller in his growing pachyderm hand . . . the doctor listened to him . . . he was on his way to being an elephant now, but he had already been a spider . . . a spider with eleventhousand legs to do battle with the devil with eleventhousand horns who had appeared to him in the form of a fire hedgehog who pricked his face with smallpox scars . . .

Another week and still no diagnosis and more and more eaten up and with his skin thicker, floating, sailing in a tear (he caught it with his tongue as it passed close to his mouth so that it would not reach his neck, it was his, a little salt and water), sailing, floating on the far-off steps and voices, and even though he could not see very well, he was barely able to see, his hearing was getting better, and he could give

347

himself the pleasure of losing himself in the cathedrals of his eardrums, pure flowery Gothic, while the doctors were shuffling X-ray pictures and consulting test results, and he could hear the chorus of boys and girls whom he had instructed for their first communion in Tierrapaulita . . .

> *Happy am I,*
> *I want nothing at all,*
> *the blue of the sky-y-y*
> *is my home and my hall!*